Love
thy
Neighbor

Love
thy
Neighbor

A NOVEL BY
MARK GILLEO

THE
STORY PLANT

The Story Plant
The Aronica-Miller Publishing Project, LLC
P.O. Box 4331
Stamford, CT 06907

Jacket design by Barbara Aronica Buck

Print ISBN-13: 978-1-61188-034-2
E-book ISBN-13: 978-1-61188-035-9

Visit our website at www.thestoryplant.com

For information, address The Story Plant.

First Story Plant Printing: March 2012

Printed in The United States of America

Acknowledgments

I would like to take this opportunity to thank more than a few people who supported me in this endeavor. First and foremost, I would like to thank my family and friends. I don't recall a single incident when anyone told me that I was crazy (even if they were thinking it).

In addition to the moral support of family and friends, in particular my wife Ivette, I would like to thank some people who took the time to read the manuscript for this novel, in its various forms, and to provide meaningful feedback.

So for my A-team of readers I would like to thank: Jim Singleton, Fabio Assmann, Michele Gates, Claire Everett, Don Gilleo and Sue Fine. At the risk of missing some others, I would also like to thank the following people for their set of eyes: Ginny Donaldson, Debbie Ingel, Mary Weber, Jim Mockus, Michelle Couret, Ivonne Couret, Ray Rosson and Paula Willson.

Finally, I would like to thank Lou Aronica for taking a chance on me and this book.

Author's Note

(This part is true.)

In late 1999 a woman from Vienna, Virginia, a suburb ten miles from the White House as the crow flies, called the CIA. The woman, a fifty-something mother of three, phoned to report what she referred to as potential terrorists living across the street from her middle-class home. She went on to explain what she had been seeing in her otherwise quiet neighborhood: Strange men of seemingly Middle-Eastern descent using their cell phones in the yard. Meetings in the middle of the night with bumper-to-bumper curbside parking, expensive cars rubbing ends with vans and common Japanese imports. A constant flow of young men, some who seemed to stay for long periods of time without introducing themselves to anyone in the neighborhood. The construction of a six-foot wooden fence to hide the backyard from the street only made the property more suspicious.

Upon hearing a layperson's description of suspicious behavior, the CIA promptly dismissed the woman and her phone call. (Ironically, the woman lived less than a quarter of a mile from a CIA installation, though it was not CIA headquarters as was later reported.)

In the days and weeks following 9/11, the intelligence community in the U.S. began to learn the identities of the nineteen hijackers who had flown the planes into the World

Trade Towers and the Pentagon. In the process of their investigation they discovered that two of the hijackers, one on each of the planes that hit the World Trade Towers, had listed a particular house in Vienna, Virginia as a place of residence.

The FBI and various other agencies swooped in on the unassuming neighborhood and began knocking on doors. When they reached the house of a certain mother of three, she stopped them dead in their tracks. She was purported to have said, "I called the CIA two years ago to report that terrorists were living across the street and no one did anything."

The CIA claimed to have no record of a phone call.

The news networks set up cameras and began broadcasting from the residential street. ABC, NBC, FOX. The FBI followed up with further inquiries. The woman's story was later bounced around the various post 9/11 committees and intelligence hearings on Capitol Hill. (Incidentally, after 9/11, the CIA closed its multi-story facility in the neighborhood where the terrorist reportedly lived. In 2006 the empty building was finally torn down and, as of early 2011, was being replaced with another office building).

There has been much speculation about what the government should have or could have known prior to 9/11. The answer is not simple. There have been anecdotal stories of people in Florida and elsewhere who claimed to have reported similar "terrorist" type activities by suspicious people prior to 9/11. None of these stories have been proven.

What we do know is that with the exception of the flight school instructor in Minnesota who questioned the motive of a student who was interested in flying an aircraft without learning how to land, and an unheeded warning from actor James Woods who was on a plane from Boston with several of the purported terrorists while they were doing a trial run, the woman from Vienna, Virginia was the country's best chance to prevent 9/11. To date, there has been no verification of any other pre-9/11 warnings from the general public so far in advance of that fateful day in September.

For me, there is no doubt as to the validity of the claims of the woman in Vienna.

She lived in the house where I grew up.

She is my mother.

Mark Gilleo. October, 2011.
Washington DC.

Chapter 1

Present day

It's hard to remember the appropriate prayer when you're running from an angry chef waving a meat cleaver. Hadar, sweat streaking down his dark skin, his thick black hair bouncing with every stride, recalled one verse and hoped it was enough. *Allah, you have promised to help us in our time of trouble and need ...* For the fifteen year old, the need was now. As a newly discovered thief, he wished he knew a prayer for forgiveness. Between dodging a slow moving white two-door and stumbling through a small pothole in the roughly paved alley, he realized he had never learned one.

And now was not the time to stop and ask.

Hadar kept his thin arms pumping, his loose-fitting, long-sleeve shirt flapping. He went over the plan in his head and considered where it had gone wrong. He tried to ignore the obvious. Trouble had found him long before his busboy accomplice was spotted heading out the back door of the restaurant with a patron's sports coat rolled up in a dirty tablecloth.

Hadar looked back over his shoulder. The chef was still there, still charging. The obscenities had subsided, the chef's yells replaced by the steady rhythm of feet pounding the ground. Hadar heard the meat cleaver smack the side of something metal. He didn't look back to see if it was intentional. It didn't matter. Either way, the result was the same. He was scared.

As he ran, Hadar's mind flashed back to the beginning. His recruitment to the dark side had been easy. A last minute errand to the market for his mother had been his first step down the wrong road. A dark road. With the daily bread in one hand and change from the purchase in the other, a deep voice had called out to Hadar from a dust covered Mercedes as he made his way home under a setting sun. Initially, Hadar had kept walking.

Then his instincts failed him.

When the same Mercedes pulled into the alley between Hadar and his family's three-room apartment, he froze. He tightened his hand on the brown bag holding half of his family's main course, and made the decision to walk past the car as quickly as he could. These were his alleys. If anyone tried to lay a hand on him, he would vanish like a ghost.

Or so he had thought.

As Hadar passed the car, the window of the Mercedes opened. Fighting to look away, he succumbed to curiosity and glanced into the abyss of the interior. A thousand rupees grabbed his attention and held it. The wad of cash in the driver's hand was more than his father made in a week of bloody-knuckle work as a construction expert in concrete. A thousand rupees. It was a lot of money for a well-worn, middle-aged man. For a fifteen-year-old boy it was a gold ticket on the Hell Express. Hadar took the money, listened to the instructions, and thanked the Devil. There were no rules to the agreement, save one: Don't get caught.

So far, Hadar hadn't. The chef with the meat cleaver was looking to change that. Maybe change a few anatomical features while he was at it. The chef, blood and food stains on the front of his white apron, wasn't giving up. He wasn't fading. His pace was strong, steady. The chef knew the boy had expended his youthful burst. Now it was a matter of endurance, an issue of stamina.

With every step the scale tilted in the chef's favor. The man with the cleaver had been running since his stint with the other CIA. His first pair of running shoes was a twenty dollar knock-off brand from a hole-in-the-wall vendor in Manhattan's Chinatown who offered no refunds and no returns. Three months later he ran through the treads. For a chef from the mountains of Pakistan, the running path along the Hudson was one of the main attractions near the campus of the greatest chef factory in North America: The Culinary Institute of America. Jogging was the only healthy hobby the chef ever had. He could run a 5k in less time than it took to gut and butcher a lamb.

The cigarettes Hadar had started smoking with the money from his deliveries were taking their toll. Who knew the chef would follow his busboy down the alley and see him rifling through the pockets of the liberated jacket? Who knew the mad cook would take up chase? Who knew the chef could run like a Kenyan marathoner?

Thoughts came to Hadar in a flood. He stumbled again as he turned into a slightly uphill alley. *Oh, Allah! Help us to hold fast all together to your path, even in the shaky times.* He took another quick right behind the back of the furniture shop, panting his way past two elderly men who were attaching fabric to a wooden frame. The two old men looked up moments later as six-inches of stainless steel swung by in the hand of the chef.

Another day in Islamabad, another crime.

The city was a perfect dichotomy. Next to the ancient town of Rawalpindi and its crowded hectic streets, downtown Islamabad stood as a modern example of the best and worst of the Middle East and the West. In the early 1960s, realizing it wasn't strategically prudent to have the seat of government in the same proximity as the country's economic center and largest port, the president of Pakistan decided to relocate the capital from Karachi to a swath of undeveloped land in the northern region.

With a design from a Greek urban planner by the name

of Doxidas, construction on Pakistan's new capital began. The first government tenants moved in by the end of the decade and the northward surge of bureaucracy continued until the last politician completed his relocation in the early eighties.

But Doxidas, the Greek god of development, was a visionary. He knew that once you moved the government, people and additional jobs would follow. So beyond the main district of Islamabad with its glass buildings and five star hotels, Doxidas had planned for expansion. Thanks to Greek foresight, unlike many burgeoning cities, Pakistan's new capital expanded in controllable pre-planned chunks. Sector by sector downtown Islamabad merged into residential areas, tree-lined streets, and green parkland. Schools and small businesses sprouted up on secondary roads in neighborhoods where neighbors lived middle-class lives in the shadows of Western architectural influence.

These were Hadar's neighborhoods. Islamabad was Hadar's city. His father had helped build it. Hadar had explored it on foot as a youngster, trailing his father to job sites on weekends, watching concrete buildings go up wall by wall. As he got older, he exchanged his sneakers for an old bike and expanded his scope. He knew more than the roads. He knew the alleys and the footpaths, the parks and the trails into the plains where opium and marijuana grew in unmarked fields. It was hard to beat the knowledge gained from the curiosity and natural energy of a teenage boy with an itch to travel to the edges of his world, as far as his body would take him.

Perspiration dripped from Hadar, his shirt clinging to his torso as he closed in on the rendezvous point like a homing pigeon. Block by block he made his way to his personal ATM. For a second he thought about changing routes, making another lap around the neighborhood. His legs wouldn't allow it. He took one final look back and for the first time in over twenty minutes he didn't see the chef. Two more quick turns and he saw his finish line.

The man in the dark shirt standing by the long car looked

up as Hadar wheezed towards him. The man quickly shooed away two other boys near his vehicle and focused on Hadar who was staggering like something between a drunk and an out-of-shape fifteen year old who had asked too much from his body.

"Did you get one?" the tall man in a dark button-up shirt and linen pants asked nonchalantly to the gasping teenager.

"Yeah," Hadar choked out.

"Is there a problem?"

Hadar shook his head.

The man condescendingly put his hands on his knees and whispered straight into Hadar's ear. "Do we have a problem?" he repeated, almost hissing. "You're out of breath."

Hadar looked into the darkness of the man's eyes and shivered. Hadar stood, reached in his pocket, and handed-over the phone. "My money," Hadar said, still straining for air.

The man opened the phone and saw that it was working. The signal strength was good. The battery was three-quarters charged. He reached into his own pocket and fished out a thousand rupees.

"Give me the phone," the chef said, slowly coming out of his jog as he rounded the corner.

The man near the car looked at the chef. "Get lost."

The chef was armed. He had just run halfway across the city. He was not going home empty-handed. He knew that reasoning with the boy may not prove fruitful. Reasoning with an adult would be easier. He approached the man in the dark shirt and looked him in the eyes. They were both in their forties. They both had solid, natural builds. They both cut meat for a living.

"He stole the phone from my restaurant, in front of my patrons. It's the third time this year. I can't have my restaurant known as a den of thieves."

"Which restaurant?"

"The Kamran."

"You serve infidels?"

"I serve everyone," the chef answered. "Except thieves," he added.

The man in the dark shirt nodded. He looked at the phone in his hand, the last rays of the day's sun bouncing off the silver casing.

"OK," the man in the dark shirt conceded. He extended his hand with the phone in his palm and the chef swiped it in one smooth motion.

"What are you going to do with the boy?"

The man in the dark shirt looked at Hadar who was regaining his breath.

"He needs to be punished," the chef added.

"He will be."

Hadar's eyes grew wide. He pulled his hands off his hips and stood straight.

The chef looked at his prey and stepped towards Hadar for a final reprimand. He extended his hand, the small antenna from the phone protruding towards the boy. "If I see you near my restaurant again, I will cut off your hand myself." The chef didn't mean it, but hoped the boy believed he did.

"Thank you," the chef said to the man in the dark shirt. They nodded at each other, eyes locked. The chef turned slowly for his long walk back to the restaurant. He would make at least one patron happy. He would walk into the restaurant and return the phone to its rightful owner. And then he would have to throw away burnt food worth ten times the value of the phone. A good reputation doesn't come cheap.

"May Allah be with you," the man in the dark shirt said to the chef.

The chef turned to respond, only to hear the sound of his neck breaking and his favorite heavy blade hitting the ground.

Hadar froze.

The man stooped quickly and picked up the large blade by its wooden handle. He looked down the quiet narrow street as he approached Hadar with the meat cleaver. "I told you, don't get caught." Hadar looked at the knife. Traces of blood ran down the blade next to dried slivers of animal fat.

Hadar stammered. He took one step to the right and the man casually blocked his path. He tried to feign a direction change, but his rubbery legs gave him away. With his last bit of strength the fifteen year old tried to go over the hood of the car.

The man caught Hadar by the hair, turned him around in mid-air, and drove him into the wall. He repeated the motion twice and on the third impact, Hadar's skull cracked.

The man left the boy on the ground, next to a pile of rubbish from an overflowing bin behind a printing shop. He casually walked over and grabbed the phone from the dead chef's hand. "You won't be needing this," he said quietly, slipping the phone into his pocket. He dragged the body of the chef next to Hadar. The young man's lungs were taking shallow, final breaths. As Hadar gasped, the man wiped the meat cleaver on the chef's apron. "Good luck on your voyage, my friends," the man in the dark shirt said in a soothing voice with spooky sincerity.

The man took one last look down the narrow street and opened the door to his car. He started the sedan and checked the rear-view mirror. No one. He put the car into drive, looked up, and watched a metal door swing open. He kept his foot on the brake and eyed the meat cleaver lying amidst a half dozen cell phones on the seat next to him.

An elderly lady with a small shopping bag exited the back of her one-story house a few yards away. She fiddled with the latch on the gate as the car moved slowly forward, small rocks crunching under the weight of its tires. As the car turned the corner out of sight, the driver heard the first scream. He remembered a prayer for forgiveness that Hadar had wished he had known. *Allah, I seek refuge in You from any evil I have committed. I confess to Your blessings upon me, and I confess to You my sins, so forgive me. Verily none forgives sins except You.*

Chapter 2

There is crazy, and then there is crazy. Clark Hayden knew the difference, and the madness in the Immigration and Customs lines at Dulles International Airport barely registered as a blip on his crazy meter.

The middle-aged man in front of him, draped in a dark raincoat, carried on a conversation with himself, fingers in his ears to drown out a crying baby in the distance. A mother with a pitchy, nasal New York accent chased her twin two-year-old boys, grasping for them as they weaved in and out of the people in line before snagging one and reeling him in like a fish with pudgy arms. A young couple plugged into a single iPod was speaking the silent language of love through music. The boy's head bounced slightly to the beat, long strands of pink hair bobbing near the end of his nose, the volume loud enough for Clark to hear every four letter word in the song's lyrics. Behind the rocking couple, a group of Chinese nationals sat on their luggage, rattling back and forth in tonal floods.

Clark took a deep breath and exhaled. He nudged his duffle bag a few inches across the floor with the toe of his gray sneaker. The businesswoman behind him, Blackberry in hand, closed the gap in the line and jammed her rolling suitcase into his Achilles. Another deep breath. Just as the Dalai Lama recommended on the meditation CD he had bought with his last wad of yen from his three-week stint in Tokyo.

Clark pinched a tattered novel between his knees and removed his baggy gray sweatshirt with the Nike swoosh stitched on the front. He was down to a plain white t-shirt with sweaty pits, the last layer of clothes between himself and the heat of the terminal. The last layer between himself and a human with any semblance of pride.

The line in Dulles International's terminal snaked through half a football field of straight-aways and hairpin turns made from temporary barriers with nylon belts stretched between poles. The crowd behind Clark grew steadily, pushing forward from their arrival gates like dough being shoved into a funnel. At Christmas, navigating through Immigration and Customs was like making a trek to the original nativity scene. Time stood still. There was no food or water. Progress was measured one step at a time. All he needed was a camel.

Clark kicked at his bag again with his foot.

In gold letters framed against a blue background, the sign above the door just beyond Immigration read "Welcome to the USA." The customs officer on duty beyond the Immigration checkpoint nodded towards Clark from his stool without the obligatory "next in line." A narcotics dog passed within sniffing distance of his jeans, the handler in a crisp blue uniform looking for any indication of prohibited goodies. The four-legged import-enforcer briefly stuck his nose on the edge of Clark's suitcase and then moved on to its next suspect. The handler followed the dog's lead. *Amazing animal*, Clark thought. A finely tuned machine, powered by repetitious training, and Milk Bone diligence.

"Where are you coming from?" the customs officer asked with Clark's passport and paperwork in his hand.

"Japan."

"What was the purpose of your trip?"

"I was in a robotics competition."

"Robotics?"

"Yes."

"What kind of robots?"

Clark sighed quietly and opted for his elementary explanation. "We design robots to go through mazes, up flights of stairs, through a few inches of water, over balancing beams. They have to do simple tasks like moving an object from point A to point B." He looked at the customs officer, hoping the simple illustration was sufficient and there was no need to get into gyroscopic balance and infrared vision capabilities.

"Where are these robots?"

"The rest of the team is bringing them back. Well, actually the rest of the team will ship them back. They can be pretty sensitive to travel."

"How long were you gone?"

"Three weeks."

"How did you do in the competition?"

"MIT kicked our butts, but Tokyo University kicked theirs."

The customs officer looked at Clark's worn duffle bag and his single suitcase. "Do you have anything to declare?"

"A bottle of sake."

"Three weeks over the holidays and only one gift?"

"I'm on a student salary. It was either souvenirs or food. I chose the latter."

Clark was rewarded for his wit.

"Please place your bag on the counter," the customs officer responded.

Clark exhaled again, the departing rush of air sounding more like a perturbed sigh than an exercise in relaxation. The customs officer glared over his gray moustache. He dug around in Clark's black duffle bag with one hand and eyed the suitcase, threatening to open it.

Looking towards the next person in the never-ending line, the customs officer gave his automatic response without making eye contact. "You're free to go. Welcome home. Happy holidays."

Clark took his passport and pulled his bag off the long, shiny aluminum table. He walked through the final smoked-glass barrier, happy to be back in the land of forty-plus-inch waistlines.

The automatic exit doors led to a sixty degree drop in temperature from the warmth of the terminal with its teeming bodies. Clark scanned the horizon and focused on the pink sky and the last remnants of the day's sun as it dipped behind the mountains in the distance beyond Leesburg. A nipple-tightening gust of wind rippled Clark's shirt, and a pair of early twenty blondes eyed him as he scrambled to pull his sweatshirt over his dark brown wavy hair. His naturally athletic build concealed, the ladies smiled as they piled into a waiting minivan. Clark adjusted his glasses, an old pair with frames that needed updating, and grinned through the side window of the vehicle as he danced his way across two lanes of traffic. A light layer of post-snow slop concealed the lines in the access road that encircled the airport. He jumped to the curb and yanked his suitcase onto the sidewalk. With his free hand he slapped the trunk of a parked taxi. A minute later he slid into the back seat.

"Where to?"

"Arlington. Between Clarendon and Pentagon City, just off Washington Boulevard."

The cabbie nodded, eyeing the rear-view mirror.

In a half hour Clark would be home, back into the real madness. He was coming home three days early. And it was going to cost forty-five dollars to the taxi driver from Ghana to surprise everyone.

Bing Crosby caroled Clark through the closed door with his dream for a White Christmas, as good as any prediction on Old Man Winter's plan for the D.C. area. The Potomac, Chesapeake, Appalachians, and rolling farmland all converged on metropolitan Washington to make weather gumbo. The precipitation depended on the day's ingredients and how long they were in the atmospheric pot. The Nation's Capital could spit out a minus-five Christmas Eve or a sixty-degree New Years Day. One just never knew. This year the meteorologists were calling for a brutal winter, and so far the forecast was right on target.

Clark pulled the storm door and the weak hinge on the aluminum frame held for a moment before releasing its load, the metal banging into his suitcase. He pushed the interior wooden door open with his hip and the small Christmas festivities in the living room ground to a sudden halt.

Maria Hayden, dressed in green pants and a bright red sweater, heard the front door open as she was returning a ladle to a bowl of fruit punch. She looked across the room, past her holiday guests and overdone decorations, and her knees buckled. She grabbed for the edge of the counter and swiped an unattended glass of eggnog onto the floor. She composed herself as Clark smiled, pulling his suitcase into the room and shutting the door behind him. Unable to speak, tears welling in her eyes, eggnog splattered halfway up her elf pants, Maria stomped her way across the small living room floor and hugged her son until he quietly surrendered.

"Mom, you're crushing me," Clark said like a squeeze-toy running out of air.

For twenty-five years, Maria Hayden had held the record as the oldest woman to give birth in Fairfax Hospital through natural conception and delivery. Sure, there were a dozen older women on a smorgasbord of fertility meds who had given birth since, but Maria Hayden was different. She had avoided the on-ramp to menopause and was in her late-forties when her purported infertile eggs and her husband's dysfunctional sperm decided they didn't appreciate their respective titles. At forty-nine, Maria Hayden gave birth to her first and only child. Her son would be twenty-six in March, but she easily passed for his grandmother. When she was a young mother it had upset her, snide comments made from women less than half her age while they pushed their strollers through the park and wedged their kids into the grocery carts at the supermarket. Now, Maria didn't give a damn about her age. She had bigger concerns.

After a moment of smiles and tears in the middle of the annual Hayden Christmas party, Clark's mother rubbed his cheeks and ruffled his hair. She turned him around, patted his belly, and checked his weight with motherly eyes.

"My son," she finally said, first to Clark, and then to the room as if she was introducing a newborn to the world. Everyone smiled, Bing Crosby moved on to "I'll Be Home for Christmas," and the warmth of the room engulfed Clark like a comfortable blanket.

Clark made the rounds, first with relatives, a number countable on the fingers of one hand. His mother's older sister, Aunt Betty, sporting a new walker, wanted to hear all about "China" and the food. Clark smiled, his teeth exposed, his disappointment hidden, and told her the egg-rolls in Beijing were superb. Someday he would find out.

Clark's slight-of-build second cousin, Eugene, a retiring bald federal employee making a hundred grand a year doing nothing in the truest sense of the word, gave Clark a quick "Welcome back," and then vanished into the oversized cushions on the sofa. Clark shrugged his shoulders slightly, grateful for an abrupt end to the most uncomfortable annual conversation in the mid-Atlantic.

Clark approached his neighbors, a piece of ham hanging off the edge of his thick paper plate. An elderly man and a young woman with a daughter in her lap sat face-to-face in old wooden dining chairs. As Clark approached, the woman, dressed in a traditional Muslim headdress with Christmas colors, looked up through her thick black-framed glasses.

"I like your hijab," Clark said. "Green and red, very appropriate."

"Just thought I would show my festive side for my Christian neighbors. I had to make it myself."

"It's great."

Ariana looked at Clark and the dark circles under his eyes. "It's good to see you. Your mother didn't stop talking about you and your trip," Ariana said, her olive skin radiating in the light from the Christmas candle on the side table.

"Your daughter has gotten bigger."

"As has her vocabulary. She is starting to talk up a storm."

Clark bent his knees and looked the young girl in the eye. "Hi Liana."

Liana, big dark eyes resting over perfectly placed dimples, nodded once and then buried her face in her mother's chest.

Ariana smiled. "She's acting shy, but trust me, once you get her going she never stops."

"Thank you for keeping an eye on my mother, Ariana. I appreciate it."

"Don't mention it. I just stopped by to say hi, to see how she was doing."

Clark looked her in the eyes, through her thick-framed glasses. "I know it's not that easy."

"Nor is it that bad."

Clark smiled to avoid agreeing. "I don't know if you have heard or not, but I have decided to move back home. I should be able to take better care of her in a week or two."

"You're moving home?"

"I don't really have a choice. Aunt Betty is knocking on eighty and she can't drive until she gets hip replacement surgery. Her cousin Eugene is no spring chicken and lives in Annapolis. It's just easier for me to move home. I have one more class to take and a thesis to write, but I can attend the class remotely — *interactive education* they are calling it at Virginia Tech. I'll have to drive down to Blacksburg occasionally but it won't be that bad. My professors understand."

"As long as you finish school. That's the most important thing you can do right now," Ariana said.

"I'll finish. I've come too far to quit now."

"I hope so."

Clark paused for a moment, watched his mother buzz around the room, and then changed the subject. "Where's your husband?"

"Working, as usual. He said he might stop by if he gets home in time. You know how he is. He's not much for crowds."

Clark looked around at the eight people in the room. "He should be fine then. There isn't much of a crowd here."

Ariana laughed quietly and her two-year-old daughter followed suit with a muffled giggle from the depths of her mother's sweater.

"What was that? Did you say something, Liana?" Clark asked, shaking the girl's foot, her face still hidden.

Liana looked up at Clark and proudly stated. "I like airplanes."

"You do?"

"Yes, we saw them at the airport," Liana said, eyes wide.

"Did you know we have airplanes in the basement?"

The young girl smiled coyly and then turned away again.

"Leave the girl alone and have a drink," Mr. Stanley interrupted, his raspy voice cutting the air. He reached out his arthritic hand and Clark grabbed a seat, the last seed from the Hayden family tree landing in a lopsided wicker rocking chair next to his favorite neighbor.

An octogenarian with a full head of silver hair and World War II stories, Mr. Stanley had been spinning yarns since Clark was in grade school. A million-in-one shot had brought the two together; a misdirected soccer ball fired two houses away that somehow managed its way through a small bathroom window. When Clark knocked on Mr. Stanley's door offering to pay for the window and asking for his ball back, an unlikely friendship had been born.

When Clark became old enough to pull the cord on the mower and push it around the yard with a reasonable amount of predictability, he started earning twenty bucks a week during the warm season. By the time he hit high school, he had added raking leaves, cleaning gutters, and shoveling Mr. Stanley's driveway to his list of money-making duties. His pay increased over the years and when Clark turned sixteen Mr. Stanley began shoving pre-screened Playboy magazines into brown bags as supplemental income.

"How was Japan?" Mr. Stanley asked. "Were the people polite to you?"

"Very polite. Distant, but very polite."

"Don't forget what they did to our boys on Bataan. Treated them worse than rabid dogs."

"I know all about it."

"Don't forget; that's all I'm saying."

"I won't forget, but I'm also trying to look towards the future."

"You gotta keep one eye on the past and one eye on where you're going."

Clark sipped off his eggnog. His brown wavy hair was heading out of control. Two hours waiting on the tarmac at Narita and another thirteen hours in the plane had sucked a few years from his appearance. "I also want to thank you for your help looking after my mother."

"You're welcome," Mr. Stanley said, waving his hand in the air. "We all pitched in."

"You took her to the grocery store."

"I was going anyway. Have to take that Cadillac for a spin just to keep her breathing." Mr. Stanley paused and took a gulp of eggnog from his paper Christmas cup. "Your mother gets along fine, as long as she doesn't forget to take her pills."

Ariana, Mr. Stanley, and Clark fell into a moment of quiet understanding and then Clark spoke. "There is a lot of stress worrying about someone all the time."

"I understand," Mr. Stanley responded, his blue eyes alive.

"We understand," Ariana added.

"I probably shouldn't have even gone to the robotics competition. But we put a year of work into those. And the World University Robotics Competition is a good thing to have on your resume."

"We understand," Mr. Stanley said again. "You don't have to convince us. You're doing the best you can. You play with the cards you are dealt."

Ariana changed the subject. "How did you do?"

"We came in sixth. MIT and Cal Tech were the highest placed U.S. universities. Oslo University came in third. Tokyo University took the title. We made a lot of friends. We were dormed on the same floor as the team from MIT. We got to be pretty close, outside of the competition."

Mr. Stanley spoke. "Always good to make friends. Especially smart ones. You know what they say…"

Clark rolled his eyes as his neighbor and friend prepared to pontificate. "No, what do they say?"

"If you're the smartest person in your group of friends, you need to meet new people."

"There's truth to that," Ariana said.

Clark smiled and then turned his thoughts to his mother. He looked at Liana who was still clutching her mother's bosom.

Mr. Stanley broke the silence. "We're glad you made it home in one piece. And if you need any help while you are making the move back from Blacksburg, you know where to reach me."

Clark knew his mother was more effort than Mr. Stanley and Ariana were admitting, even on a good day. He had been keeping an eye on her since he was in grade school. But there were things to be thankful for. His mother still knew where the two bathrooms in the house were located. She still managed to make it down the small flight of stairs to handle the washer and dryer at the back of the garage. And on any given day she could appear completely normal to an outside observer. It was the sudden emotional swings, the nonsensical outbursts, the moments of blankness that worried Clark and scared the shit out of everyone else.

"Once I get back into the house, things should improve."

Mr. Stanley and Ariana nodded but said nothing. They knew better.

Clark watched his mother mill about the kitchen acting as normal as any seventy-four year old woman with a penchant for baking. As if to prove she had heard the conversation, Maria Hayden stepped towards the dining table with impeccable timing and presented a massive tray of baked goods, a pile of gluttony begging for a glutton. The smell of the already baked Christmas ham was immediately overpowered by cream puffs, hazelnut cookies, and a warm pecan pie.

"Good thing I didn't eat the ham," Mr. Stanley said. "You can always count on your mother and her desserts," he added, drawing air in through his nose.

Clark picked up his glass of eggnog and took a sip. There was a faint hint of booze that wasn't there a minute ago. "It has a little kick to it. Did you make the eggnog?"

"I'm appalled at the suggestion," Mr. Stanley said, smiling.

Clark distracted Mr. Stanley with a pat on the back and a look over his shoulder. With his free hand he lifted the shiny container from his neighbor's hanging jacket pocket.

"Look familiar?" Clark asked.

Mr. Stanley swiped the flask out of Clark's hand and looked around suspiciously. "Of course it does. You don't carry something in your pocket for three decades without knowing what it looks like." He twisted off the top and took a slug.

Clark smelled his eggnog and took another sip. "Probably improved the taste."

"That's the Christmas spirit."

Ariana's husband arrived with a quiet knock and Clark moved to the door. A familiar face smiled under the porch light and Clark pushed open the storm door.

"Nazim. Good to see you."

Nazim flashed a brief smile and gave Clark a disingenuous hug. His waiflike build was barely large enough to reach around Clark's shoulders. "I thought you were coming back next week."

"I was, but I decided to come home early to surprise my mother."

"How was your trip? How was the competition?"

"Great. Really great. We didn't win, but we made a good

showing for Virginia Tech."

"Good. Good. You know, there is no substitute for foreign travel to learn more about yourself and your own country."

"You're right. Please come in."

"Only for a minute."

Nazim quickly greeted Maria Hayden as Clark sat back down. Mr. Stanley gave Clark a nod in the direction of Nazim, covertly making a face of disdain.

Nazim moved towards his wife and whispered in her ear. "It's time to leave."

Ariana looked up at her husband. "Just a few more minutes. Let me finish the dessert. I don't want to be rude."

Nazim locked eyes with his wife for a second and then put his hand on his daughter's head. "How is my favorite girl this evening?" Liana looked up at her father and reached for his dark beard. Nazim grabbed his daughter and put her on his forearm.

Maria Hayden came out of the bedroom with her digital camera flashing. She took one of Nazim and Liana, father holding his daughter like a prized possession. She snapped a picture of Clark and Mr. Stanley sitting shoulder-to-shoulder.

"Let's have a group picture," Maria said. "Everyone stand in front of the Christmas tree in the corner."

The people in the room took little steps across the tiny living room, dancing around the coffee table, finding their place in front of the artificial tree with tacky reflective pink tinsel.

"Smile," Maria said.

Maria took the picture. "Now I want to be in one," she said.

Ariana stepped forward and changed places with her. She looked through the viewfinder and took a step back. With everyone in focus, Ariana pushed the button and heard the fake shutter sound of the digital camera impersonating its manual predecessor. Ariana shared the picture with Maria and put the digital camera on the table. "We have to get going. Thank you for inviting us."

"Thank you Ariana. Thank you for everything."

"You're welcome."

Maria Hayden pulled her neighbor toward the corner of the room. "Can I ask a question?"

"Sure."

"Can you see my hair?"

"Sure I can," Ariana answered. "It looks wonderful this evening."

"No, I mean, I feel it growing out of my scalp," she answered in a rising voice. As eyes turned towards her, she scratched at her head and repeated herself several times, her voice reaching a crescendo that overpowered the Christmas CD. And just as suddenly as her voice had risen, it dropped to a whisper before she added, "I hope no one notices."

"No, Maria, you look fine," Ariana answered, smiling to the room and taking Maria by the elbow. "Now, let's see if we can get you your medicine before I leave."

Clark watched as his mother performed her ever-frequent ritual of a mental meltdown. The Christmas party was officially over.

There is crazy, and then there is crazy.

Chapter 3

Ariana turned on the nightlight and closed the door to her daughter's room. She walked down the carpeted hall towards the light stretching out from the plastic chandelier over the dining room table. Her husband's chair was empty and she quietly called out his name. No response. As Ariana turned the corner to the kitchen and reached for the knob on the cabinet over the counter, eight hundred pages of advertising crashed into her rib cage, sucking the wind from her lungs. As his wife doubled over, Nazim raised the thick Yellow Book with both hands and hit her on her back, driving her body to the floor.

"Don't you ever disobey me in front of others again."

Ariana coughed. There was no blood. This time. She tried to speak but her lips only quivered. Her thick-framed glasses rested on the floor, out of reach. Her brain fought to make sense of what happened, what had set her husband off. It could have been anything. But every curse had its blessing, and for Ariana the blessing was the fact that Nazim didn't hit her in front of Liana. A blessing that the child didn't see her mother being punched. The reason was simple. Nazim was afraid of his daughter. Afraid of what she could say now that she could speak.

The curse was that Ariana never knew when she had crossed the line. She never knew when the next blow was coming. She merely had to wait until they were alone to learn her fate for past indiscretions.

Ariana gasped slowly for air. She didn't cry. The pain she felt in her side wasn't bad enough to give her husband the satisfaction.

"When I say it is time to leave, it is time to leave. There is no room for negotiation in this marriage."

Ariana panted as her mind flashed back to the Christmas party. She immediately realized her faux pas. "I didn't want to be rude to Maria. She spent days making dessert. She is old. Do we not respect our elders anymore?"

Nazim pushed his wife onto the floor with his knee, a reaction Ariana fully expected. "You are my wife. This is about you and me. Our neighbor has nothing to do with it." Nazim looked down at Ariana sprawled on the linoleum and spit on her with more mock than saliva.

"Maria is my friend."

"Well, her son is coming home and she doesn't need you."

Nazim dropped the Yellow Book on the counter with a thud and went to the basement. Ariana gathered herself, pushing her body onto all fours and then pulling herself up by the front of the oven. She looked at the Yellow Book and her blood boiled. It was like getting hit by a cinderblock with soft edges. When it hit flush, it left very little bruising. As her husband intended. For a man of slight build, Nazim could generate power when a beating was needed.

Ariana took inventory of herself, one hand propping herself up on the counter. She had been beaten worse. Far worse. By other men before she met her husband. Her eyes moved beyond the Yellow Pages and settled on the knife set on the counter, the shiny German steel resting in its wooden block holder. She grabbed the fillet knife, caressed the blade with her eyes, and then pushed the thought from her mind.

Her husband called her from the basement and she snapped out of her momentary daze. "Coming," she answered, putting the knife back in its designated slot in the wood. She knew what was coming next. It was always the same. A physical assault followed by a sexual one. She reached up her skirt and removed her panties. There was no sense in having another pair ripped, even if robbing Nazim of the joy would cost her a punch or two.

Christmas, *the season of giving*, she thought as she made her way down the stairs into the chilly basement.

Maria Hayden took a shower in the main bathroom on the first floor. The aqua-green porcelain of the tub and toilet were leftovers from the fifties that easily gave the bathroom the title of ugliest room in the house. Maybe the ugliest room on the block. The bathroom was wedged between the front door and a small room that had once been Clark's bedroom. His room was now a sewing vestibule. A piece of furniture his mother referred to as a hobby table combined with a chair and a bookcase to occupy most of the floor space. Oil paintings of flowers and mountain scenery now hung on the wall where Redskins posters and a Sports Illustrated Swimsuit Calendar once held prime real estate.

Clark was sitting at the dining table near the entrance to the kitchen when he realized his mother was taking a shower in the old bathroom. He cocked his head to the side and closed his eyes for a moment. He got up from the table and walked into his mother's bedroom, past the large post bed, and clicked the light on the master bathroom switch. It was exactly as he thought. Exactly as he had feared.

The master bathroom had been a labor of love. His father, with the help of two fellow blue-collared acquaintances, had worked on the addition for nearly a year. The bathroom and the new walk-in closet protruding from the back of the house were two exceptions to the original rectangular shape of the house. And Charles Hayden had died a month after laying the last tile.

Clark looked around at the new fixtures and the unused tub with whirlpool jets. A tear welled up in his eye, but didn't fall, the salty fluid refusing to break the edge of his eyelid.

A tube of toothpaste was on the sink and Clark picked it up. The tube was hard, almost petrified. There were remnants of stubble in his father's razor on the sink top under the mirror. His father's eyeglasses were on the small towel shelf, his deodorant lying on its side in the medicine cabinet. Clark wanted to cry, to enjoy a full-fledged wheezing tear-feast, but didn't. It was a promise he had made to his father to be strong. It was a battle he had fought daily for over a year before conquering his emotions.

He thought about putting the glasses, the deodorant, and the razor back under the sink where he had put them a dozen times before. *What the hell?* he thought, *it's Christmas.* He turned out the lights and returned to the living room.

The cordless phone on the nightstand rang twice before the sleeping hand reached over and knocked it from its perch. Nazim mumbled. Ariana answered with equal gibberish. The phone continued to ring. Beneath the edge of the dust skirt on the queen mattress, the black phone with the digital display rang one last time before the searching hand found its mark.

"Hello," the still sleeping voice said.

"Assalamu alaikum," rang an unforgettable voice from the past.

"Wa alaikum assalam," the now waking voice said on automatic pilot. Arabic was neither participant's mother tongue, but it was the language of Islam, and that was enough.

"It is time."

The mattress shook as the dark form of a body shot into the upright position on the bed.

"How many?"

"Four."

"When?"

"Be ready. Assalamu alaikum wa rahmatullahi wa barakatuh."
The phone went dead.

A minute of silence passed in the darkness. The mattress
shook again and Nazim stood and walked to the bathroom to
relieve himself.

"Do you need anything?" Ariana asked dutifully. It was
the last offer she would ever make to her husband.

"No," he answered as the bathroom door shut. Five
minutes later Nazim was asleep.

Ariana went to the kitchen and quietly opened the pantry
door. She stood on the small stepping stool and rummaged
through the top shelf, gently pushing aside jars of flour, sugar,
and wheat germ. Her husband hadn't cooked or cleaned in
his life, certainly not in their lives together. She knew the only
place to hide something was right under his nose, in a place
he would never scratch.

The small glass jar with the airtight seal read "cleaner" on
the side, written with magic marker on a strip of masking tape.

Ariana returned to the bedroom and sat on the bed with
her back to her husband. She slipped on a pair of green rubber
gloves from the kitchen and listened to her husband fall into
his rhythmic snore. She watched him sleep and waited for his
mouth to droop open, waiting for the snoring that had kept
her awake year after year. Then, in minute doses, she sprinkled
in her magic potion. She waited, repeated the task, and waited
again. It wouldn't be long.

Nazim woke gasping. He reached for his wife and grasped at
the empty comforter. He turned the switch on the light next
to the bed, but the cord was unplugged. His throat burned.
His eyes watered. He strained for oxygen.

"Help," he said, sucking in air as he staggered out of bed.

Ariana turned on a small light on the dresser. She was

sitting in a plain wooden chair in a t-shirt and pink cotton panties. Smiling. "There is no help."

Nazim grabbed at his throat.

"What have you done?"

"It was done long ago. Long before we met. You were merely a pawn," she said without emotion.

Ariana watched as Nazim fought for air, for the strength to summon rage. "You bitch!" he gurgled. He grabbed the clock radio and threw it at Ariana. His wife ducked as the black plastic box smashed into the wall.

Ariana stood and stepped towards him. Nazim staggered forward and reached out with both hands, his death rage focused on his wife's neck. He never got close. Ariana hit her husband in the nose with the palm of her hand and felt the bone crush. Nazim's head snapped back and Ariana hit him in the solar plexus with a reverse punch polished by years of training. Nazim's lungs emptied and he began making a deflating noise. He stooped over and Ariana slapped both of her husband's ears with cupped hands, bursting one of his eardrums. Now in total control, control she had fought to exercise for far too long, Ariana snapped her hips and drove a back kick into Nazim's neck. As her husband wheezed, she finished him off with a front kick to the crotch.

By the time Nazim's hands reached his groin, he was dead.

Chapter 4

The chill from the top of the closed toilet lid gave Ariana goosebumps as she looked down on her husband's slim body in the bathtub. Her ex-husband, she thought to herself with satisfaction. Nazim had been dead ten hours and rigor mortis had already set in around the jaws and in the torso. His eyes were closed and his body seemed to take on the color of the off-white bathroom tiles like a chameleon blending into its surroundings. Gravity played its law-of-physics card and blood pooled on Nazim's backside, the lowest part of his body. His arms were folded over his chest. A faint purple bruise surrounded his Adam's apple. His nose was obviously broken, the bone jagging left, the nostrils laced with traces of dried blood.

But it was a clean death. As clean as she could make it and still keep it up close and personal. She had wiped her husband's face with wet tissues dipped in bleach and removed most of the blood while it was still fresh. The tissues went down the toilet. She wiped two additional drops of blood from the warped hardwood floors in the bedroom and flushed the incriminating evidence. She knew that there would be traces of blood on the micro-level, but she didn't care. A few drops of blood in any home could be explained by a bloody nose, a cut on the finger, shaving with shaky hands. Besides, by the time the authorities started looking for her, it would be too late.

The only real crime scene was the body. As clean as the bedroom was, if the police arrived for reasons she could not imagine, she would have some explaining to do. She checked her watch. The body would be gone soon enough. Long before the temperature in the corpse began to rise again from decomposition. Long before the smell from rotting flesh alerted the neighbors.

She wished she had more time. If she had, she would take care of the body where it was. The flesh, bones, and hair were no match for a bath of hydrochloric acid. But getting her hands on a few gallons of lethal acid on Christmas Day was going to take more imagination than just believing in Santa Claus. Time was a gruesome luxury she didn't have.

She thought about the phone call she had received. She began to wonder long ago if contact with her would ever be made. The first few years of her assignment had passed slowly. Then came 9/11, concealed excitement, and more years of silence. She began to think she had been forgotten forever. But, as she found, it is hard to rest quietly when you are trained to kill and have an I.Q. of 170.

In the hours since her husband's death, Ariana's natural state of heightened awareness had switched into overdrive. There were going to be lies to tell. Lies bigger than the one she had been living. After all, she was a housewife and a mother. These were truths. She was also a killer. Her personal tale up until now had only required her to omit one part of the story. From this moment on, each lie would have the potential power to bring her down, to end her service to a higher power. She reminded herself to keep it all straight. One discovered lie and one suspicious person could start a bloodbath.

"Mom," Liana called out from the other side of the door.

"Just a minute."

"I need to go potty."

"Use the one in the hall. I'll be there in a minute."

Ariana pulled the shower curtain closed. Her daughter's

voice reminded her that she had a bigger decision to make than what to do with her husband's body.

Clark stomped his heel into his boot, tied the laces, and stepped outside onto the porch. A thin layer of ice covered the cracked concrete slab and Clark grabbed the iced-over railing as he found his balance. "Christ," he said, settling himself and checking the content of his jacket pocket.

The branches on a pair of dogwoods in the front yard drooped from the weight of their shimmering coat. Clark maneuvered down the small flight of stairs with his Vibram-soled Timberlands and shuffled his feet on the uneven walk that led to the small driveway. He stopped at his mother's car and listened to the silence of the middle-class neighborhood on Christmas morning.

He looked up the street, the sun reflecting off the ice-covered cars stuffed into driveways barely long enough to accommodate two vehicles parked end-to-end. The original middle-class neighborhood had been comprised of classic tract housing built in the fifties. Square box homes with nearly identical floor-plans produced from cookie-cutter molds. At the peak of the post World War II expansion, one-story ramblers with unfinished basements had stretched for a mile in any direction. Clark's parents had lived on Dorchester Lane long enough to remember when the original sod was laid.

Clark looked down the street from his mother's slice of paradise. He could see the changes. The last ten years had seen an explosion in the geometry of the residences. Everyone with money, and half those without, began slapping up additions with such fervor that anyone with a hammer could open a booming home improvement business. The neighborhood began to shift from architectural boredom to eclectic hell. Bathrooms jutted from the front of houses. Garages, most now stuffed with the collected crap of life, were constructed as close to a neighbor's property line as regulations would allow. Bay windows opened next to homebuilt greenhouses, next to two-story decks. Carports and master suites melted together. The neighborhood looked as if a drunken Lego team had won a competition to ruin the original blue-collar, tract-housing charm.

Gone were the kids who used to play in the streets. Classic games like team hide-and-seek and murder-the-man-with-the-ball had been relinquished to the trash heap of neighborhood activities. If Dorchester Lane and its neighboring houses were harboring a secret stash of children, they were hiding in the basements, plugged into their video games.

At the incline at the end of the driveway, Clark pushed forward with his right foot and let gravity carry him to the edge of the street. He slipped and slid his way past his neighbor on the right and turned towards a slightly uphill battle on a sloping icy driveway.

The thermometer in the window faced outward and Clark squinted from beneath the hood on his blue jacket. The red line bumped the bottom of the twenty-six degree mark. With his bare knuckle, Clark knocked on the window of the side door at the top of a small metal staircase. Icicles hung from the gutter above, the points of the inverted spikes threatening downward.

Arthritic feet hobbled to the door after the third set of knocks. The curtain in the small window moved and an eye peered out from the crack. Mr. Stanley fumbled for the small lock on the storm door and yanked the handle.

"Good morning, Clark."

"Good morning."

"Did you come to spread sand and salt on the driveway?"

Clark's eyebrows jumped. "Actually, no. But if you need me to, I will."

"Not necessary. I was just testing you. There's a kid a few blocks over who usually stops by when it snows. Charges forty bucks to shovel."

"Not bad cash."

"Inflation since the last time you worked for me."

"Nothing gets cheaper."

Mr. Stanley shivered and hustled Clark inside. Clark pushed the door closed behind him and the blitz of senior citizen scent assaulted his nose. Clark took a deep breath. It was just like tearing a Band-Aid off a hairy arm. Some things you have to do quickly.

Mr. Stanley's was a combination old folk's home and bachelor pad. Every molecule was frozen in motion, each electron covered in its own layer of dust. The air was warm, the lack of movement stifling. The smell was between musty and old, sweet and sour. It wasn't anything a year with the windows open wouldn't cure.

"Here's something I picked up for you in Tokyo," Clark said, pulling a small bottle from his jacket pocket. "I meant to give it to you last night, but things kind of ended suddenly."

Mr. Stanley looked at the bottle and held it at arm's length to read the label. Particles of sparkling bits moved about in the liquid at the bottom of the bottle. Mr. Stanley turned and held the small glass container to the light.

"What is it?"

"It's Japanese sake," Clark said, waiting to deliver the punch-line. "It has flakes of pure gold in it."

"Gold?"

"Pure gold."

"Why in the hell would I want to drink gold?"

A damn good question, Clark thought. A question he had been wondering since he bought it. Clark appealed to Mr. Stanley's more practical nature. "Just think of it as something extra to go with the alcohol."

"Seems like a perfectly good waste of gold to me."

"I guess. But the Japanese aren't the first to consume it. Different civilizations have been eating it for years. As a metal, gold is somewhat unique. It is biologically benign. Passes right through the digestive system without any adverse effects."

"You know your metals."

"My father's hobby."

"Do you want to try it out?" Mr. Stanley asked, mocking as if he twisted the cap.

"It's eleven o'clock Christmas morning."

"But it's Christmas night somewhere. What else do you have to do?"

"I'll take a rain-check."

"All right, but I can't guarantee there will be any left by the time you make up your mind. Except for the gold flakes in my daily constitution."

"I'll risk it."

"How's preparation for the big move?"

"I haven't even been home for twenty-four hours. There are some things to do. First I need to see what is going on down at 'the hole.' Blacksburg is a four hour drive and all my roommates are either still in Japan or back visiting their families."

"The hole?"

"That's what some of my roommates' girlfriends have been calling the house we live in."

"I see."

"With my roommates there's no guarantee that the house is even still there. But the rent is paid through January, so I will be moving back in over the next couple of weeks. Whatever fits in the back of the Civic. One load at a time."

"Son, you know you probably don't have to move back home. Your mother should be fine, if you wanted stay in Blacksburg for a few more months."

"I probably would if Aunt Betty hadn't broken her hip. My mom is not getting any better. Or younger. It is time. I see her slipping."

"Ahh. We're all slipping a little, and someday, even you will start to slip."

Clark forced a smile and nodded towards the sake bottle. "Merry Christmas, Mr. Stanley."

"Merry Christmas, son," Mr. Stanley responded, feeling as if he had crossed some unspeakable boundary. He changed the subject. "Could you help me with something?"

"Of course."

Clark followed Mr. Stanley to a small bedroom down the hall that had long ago been converted to a study. There were piles of books in the corner. Enough paper was scattered around the room to take out an acre of timber. Crossword puzzles covered the desk. A magnifying glass rested on yesterday's edition of The New York Times. A high-watt sunlamp was clamped to the edge of a bookcase behind a leather chair. A painting rested on an easel in the corner, the portrait of a woman almost complete.

"Who is the woman?" Clark asked.

"It's my wife when she was young."

"I don't think I've ever seen a picture of her at that age."

"Certainly not an oil portrait. There is only one in existence as far as I know, and you are looking at it."

"Nice."

Mr. Stanley pulled a box from the top of the small bookcase under the window.

"Can you help me change the ceiling light in the hall? I broke the cover over a month ago."

"How did you do that?"

"I was cleaning and put the end of the broom right through it. Forty years that thing has been up there. Took me forever to find a replacement. Most of them are made of plastic these days."

Clark pulled the light cover from the small cardboard box. "No one's coming by to help you around the house?"

"I don't need any help."

"What about your nephew?"

"He stops by once in a while, but hell, he is more helpless than I am. Fifty years old and he can barely take care of himself."

"You could have asked Nazim."

"I don't trust that guy. Never did."

"What's not to like? He's quiet, helpful, and keeps his property clean. I mean, we got people parking their cars on cinderblocks in this neighborhood, in case you haven't noticed. This guy actually plants grass in his yard every year."

"The neighborhood is not what it used to be."

"Yeah, but I don't think a neighbor would turn you down if you asked for help."

"I don't want that guy in my house."

Clark shrugged his shoulders then removed a pile of books from the seat of a wooden chair and dragged it into the hallway. He removed the remnants of the previous light shade, carefully catching the few inches of glass near the screw in the center. He put the new cover in place and tightened the screw.

"What are your plans for the day?" he said, stepping off the chair.

"Going to my brother's in McLean."

"That's good. Family is good."

"Family is good. The in-laws that come with that family can be hell."

"I wouldn't know."

"You want something to drink?"

Clark didn't, but tried to be polite. "Water would be great."

"Water? Hell. You will join me in a coffee."

"Then a coffee would be great."

Clark followed Mr. Stanley as he walked backed through the house to the kitchen. Clark turned at the dining nook and looked at the backyard. Old trees and rusted chain-link fences marked the territory of his neighbors' properties. Mr. Stanley's old metal shed leaned to the right, remnants of the last snow following the slant in the roof.

"I see the neighbor finished his construction."

"Coleman's Castle?" Mr. Stanley asked from the kitchen.

"Is that what they're calling it?"

"No, that's what I'm calling it."

"Well, it's one hell of an addition."

"They're calling those McMansions."

"I know," Clark said.

"Everyone on the street has some kind of addition, but Mr. Coleman's house takes the cake. Two and a half stories, including the loft. A nice big chimney with huge glass windows. It looks like an addition from Better Homes and Gardens. Something you would see in a ski chalet. Except his neighbors in the back are the only ones who get to enjoy the view. And the only thing Coleman gets to look at is the ass-side of our property. From the front of his street, the house still looks like a rambler. A one-story rambler with a big penis sticking up out of the back. The damn thing looks ridiculous."

"He has the right to build on his house."

Mr. Stanley continued his rant. "In fifteen years there will be no middle-class neighborhoods left within a hundred miles of D.C. It's going to be either a million dollar mansion or a flop house where you chase the roaches away long enough to fall asleep. You know, two blocks away four houses were just bought and bulldozed for the lot. Some software CEO. The real estate market may have crashed, but not for the rich."

"People don't have to sell."

Mr. Stanley chose not to hear Clark.

"Rich people are funny. Even the rich like to claim they are middle class. Families with three kids, five cars, seven cell phones and ten televisions. Ask any of them and they will tell you they are middle-class." Mr. Stanley paused to see if Clark was listening, then continued. "I'll tell you right now, if you can't see in at least one of your neighbor's windows, or can't hear your neighbor giving the goods to his wife through the walls, you are not middle-class. If you own two homes, and I don't care if one of them is a shack in the mountains, you are not middle-class. Middle-class neighborhoods are defined street by street and block by block. People who live month-to-month and have to save to rent a house for a week at the beach for their summer vacation."

"What about the preacher at your church? Rumor has been for years that he has a second house."

"That man is going to hell. You can't be a man of the cloth, claim the souls of your parishioners to save, preach against the seven deadly sins, and have a beach house. It just doesn't work that way. If you have enough money to help yourself to a beach house, you have enough money to help those in need. Bastard."

"I don't know about calling a man of the cloth 'a bastard.'"

"Excuse me. I meant stingy, greedy, *reverend* bastard."

Clark tried to end the bitching that old men seem to perfect over the course of their lives. He looked at the small bird that landed on a bird feeder in the middle of the yard. A sea of seeds were scattered on the ground under the feeder.

"Been bird watching?"

"I have a pair of big blue jays visiting the yard that I haven't seen before. They are just remarkable."

"Shouldn't they have migrated?"

Mr. Stanley looked genuinely offended. "Smart ass."

Clark looked up at Mr. Coleman in the distance as the neighbor entered the tower of his castle and sat down. A few seconds later Coleman tipped a bag of junk food upward and the orange foil of the bag covered his face.

Clark stared out the back window as Mr. Stanley delivered the coffee. They reminisced about the neighborhood and the time Clark hit a yellow jacket nest buried in the back yard with the lawn mower. Twenty-two stings and a trip to the emergency room in a Cadillac going ninety.

They heard a car door shut and both men looked across Nazim and Ariana's back yard. Ariana was standing at the end of the driveway. A large box lay on the ground next to the car.

"Aren't you going to go help your neighbor?" Mr. Stanley asked.

"Do I have a choice?"

"You could have some of that gold sake and leave the heavy work to her husband."

"I gotta get going anyway." Clark pulled the zipper on his jacket to just below his chin.

Mr. Stanley didn't want his guest to leave. "How is everything else?" he asked, touching the coffee cup adorned with a Christmas tree to his lips.

"Well, I will be twenty-six soon and I'm spending my

winter break moving back into the basement of the house where I grew up. Granted this is a small improvement over last year when I was still reeling over my dad. I have spent the last six months taking a double load of classes so I can get out of school as fast as I can to start working, which according to everyone I know, I will probably hate. And, oh, I found a stack of letters in the kitchen from the IRS, who is threatening to sue my mother unless she can explain discrepancies in my father's tax returns for the last five years." Clark thought about mentioning his mother's mental capacity, but that was like flogging a horse that was never going to find its feet. "Things really couldn't be much worse," he added.

"Things can always get worse."

"Good morning," Clark called out making his way down his third slippery driveway of the morning. "Can I help you with that?"

Ariana's eyes opened wide and she stole a glance over her shoulder. Her heart raced and her blood ran fast through panic-stricken arteries and veins. One end of the box was on the rear-seat and she was pushing the other end with both hands. Two smaller boxes were on the ground near the trunk of the car.

Clark approached smiling. "I was visiting Mr. Stanley and saw you with the boxes from the window," Clark continued as he balanced on the icy ground with his arms.

Ariana pushed the large box across the back seat of the car and shut the door with authority. As she turned to greet Clark she flashed her best housewife grin. Small beads of sweat formed under her eyes, beneath her thick black-framed glasses.

"Good morning, Clark. Merry Christmas."

"Happy holidays," Clark answered.

"How is your mother doing?"

"Fine, fine. Thank you for your help last night."

"Don't mention it."

Clark looked into the car at the large box. Ariana smiled again.

"Can I give you a hand?"

Ariana paused for a moment. "Sure. Thanks. There are only two boxes left."

Clark walked to the back of the car and Ariana opened the trunk. He bent at the knees and grappled with the bottom corner of the box.

"Where's Nazim?" he asked through a half-grunt, putting the bottom of the box on the edge of the trunk.

"He took Liana for a walk. He said the cold was invigorating," Ariana shook her head as if her husband were alive and crazy.

"I hope Liana is wearing ice skates."

Ariana watched as Clark picked up the second box and the bottom sagged.

"Just put it anywhere." She held her breath and hoped the obvious questions would remain in oblivion.

"What's in the boxes?" Clark asked innocently as the last box thudded into place in the trunk.

"Old stuff I have been meaning to get rid of."

Clark nodded. "I have a bit of that to take care of myself," Clark said.

"I thought today would be a quiet day. A good day to get some end-of-the-year cleaning accomplished. And with my husband out of the house, I can throw away a few things. Or at least put them in the car."

"It's a good day to be inside if you ask me."

"Unless you want to be alone outside."

Clark cocked his head to the side and a hint of perplexity showed on his face. Ariana ignored the reaction and noticed Clark wasn't wearing gloves.

"Well, next time you should make Nazim carry the heavy stuff. Those boxes are pretty hefty."

"I'll tell him you said so."

As Clark walked away, Ariana's eyes pierced his backside. Helpful neighbors could be a bitch.

Chapter 5

The beat up black Volkswagen Golf turned around at the north end of Dorchester Lane and made the trip down the street in the opposite direction. They watched the houses pass by in descending number order and slowly pulled up to the curb in front of number 202.

Karim, Syed, and Abu looked at each other. Their dark black eyes exuded a seriousness that sent shivers down the spines of everyone they encountered, most recently the young girl behind the counter of the gas station mini-mart near Culpepper, Virginia.

Syed, his head touching the fabric on the ceiling of the car, looked at the number scribbled on the torn corner of white paper. "That's it," he said to the two other men. He folded the Northern Virginia street map and shoved it into the small pocket on the lower half of the door.

Karim killed the lights and turned off the engine. All three men looked around at their surroundings and tried to get their bearings. "Who goes?" Karim asked, his hands still on the wheel. His unshaven face hid the gauntness in his cheeks, the physical effects of weeks on the road easier to hide than the psychological ones.

No one moved. Karim spoke again. "Either someone volunteers, or we all go." Thirty hours after meeting in a truck stop outside of Houston, trust was earned slowly. Suspicion, even of one another, was their shared lifeline. "Then we all go," Karim added with a very slight accent. Syed and Abu nodded in silent agreement.

Karim looked around. "Let me pull the car on the other side of the street and away from the front of these two houses. I would prefer to be out of sight and heading in the right direction if we have to leave suddenly."

The neighborhood was quiet. The clock on the dash read 2:13. Give or take an hour, they were on schedule. It was easier said than done when every step was revealed by a distant master on intermittent communication according to an unknown timetable.

Syed opened the passenger door and unfolded his six-foot-three frame from the small German compact. Abu, the smallest of the three, pushed open the back door and a loud screech rang out into the night. All three men ducked as if the sound were gunfire, as if stooping would save their lives. "Quiet," Karim said, the white of his eyes visible in the darkness.

"If we had a better car…" Abu answered

"The car is fine," Karim answered, usurping the role of leader. "Let's go."

Syed led the way across the yard and the three men turned their back to a stiff wind. Flakes of snow whipped by in streaks of white. They knocked lightly on the door, waited, and knocked harder. "Where are they?" Syed asked, towering over Abu and Karim.

"What makes you think it is a 'them?'" Karim asked. "We have no idea who is on the other side of that door."

Abu, his cheek scarred, checked the handle of the ten-inch knife in the small of his back.

Maria Hayden's eyes had opened with the screeching car door. She slept light. Always had. The side-effects of the myriad medications she took daily had stolen a decade of shut-eye from her life. A faint knock on the door forced her to sit up in bed. The second knock led her to slip on her bathrobe and walk in short strides to the front door. She watched through the stretched tunnel-view of the peephole as the hand of a dark-skinned man reached towards her door and knocked again. Her heart skipped a beat. She let go of the edge of her robe and leaned closer to the peephole. She placed her palms on the wood panels of the door and switched to her right eye. The fourth knock was even louder and Maria jumped slightly, her right hand hitting the chain on the unlatched chain lock over the deadbolt.

The subtle but unmistakable sound of metal hitting the door brought the unknown standoff to a pause. Karim glanced up at Syed's face then shifted his stare to Abu. The group froze. After seconds that passed like hours, Karim broke the silence.

"Assalamu alaikum. We have traveled a great distance and pray for your hospitality."

Abu shook his head.

Karim repeated the standard Arabic greeting followed by the specific words he had memorized long ago.

Syed spoke to his two accomplices. "Something is not right. Let's go."

Abu quickly agreed with the taller Syed. "He's right; let's go." Karim took one look at the Hayden's front door and the numbers 202 that ran down vertically. Without speaking he nodded and flicked his head towards the car. Maria Hayden watched as the three men vanished beyond the vision of her peephole. Hands shaking, she took one more look outside the edge of the living room window and saw nothing but darkness. She walked back into her bedroom and opened the phone book to the listings in the blue pages.

The three men waited in the darkness of the black car to see if the neighborhood had noticed them. A porch light three houses away was the only company for the increasing wind and heavier flakes of snow. Karim started the car as Syed checked the scrap piece of paper with the house number on it. Abu cursed from the backseat. "Let's get out of here."

Karim hit the headlights and Syed yelled.

Standing in front of the car in a winter jacket and black hijab, Ariana stared at the three men with an expressionless face.

"What the hell?" Karim asked as Ariana approached the side of the car. She knocked on the driver's side window which Karim rolled down with the manual handle.

"I believe you have the wrong house."

Karim and Abu looked at Syed who sheepishly consulted the number on the paper for the tenth time. "It's the house number I was told."

Ariana stared through him. "I'm going to give you instructions and you are to follow them exactly. There is a Giant supermarket about a mile from here off Curtis Trail Boulevard. It is open twenty-four hours a day. It's not too far from 395 and there are always other cars. Park in the side lot, away from the main road. Go into the store and get some bread, milk, and whatever else you want to eat. I will meet you in the side parking lot when you get out of the store. Be ready to get whatever you need from the car. You will be leaving it there."

"Why milk and bread?" Karim asked.

"Because I need milk and bread," Ariana answered.

"How do we know we can trust you?" Abu piped in from the back seat.

"Because I haven't killed you already," Ariana answered.

The three men in the car paused momentarily. Karim nodded and put the car into first gear. Ariana watched as the black VW drove out of the neighborhood. She went into her house, grabbed a black cylindrical item from under the sink and headed for her car.

Maria Hayden picked the beige phone off the stand on the bedside table. Hands shaking, she unfurled the curly wire that ran between the handset and the base of the phone. She pinched the receiver between her ear and shoulder and carefully punched the numbers as she read them from the phone book. She listened to three rings before a woman's voice answered from the other end.

"Central Intelligence Agency."

"Hi," Maria said nervously. "My name is Maria Hayden and I would like to report some terrorists."

The soothing voice on the other end of the phone showed no emotion. "Yes. What is your location?"

"Arlington, Virginia."

"And where are the terrorists?"

"They were at my front door."

"What were they doing?"

"They were knocking."

"Can you describe them for me?"

"Three Middle Eastern men. One was tall. One was shorter. The other had a beard."

"When did this occur?"

"About five minutes ago."

"Where are they now?"

"They disappeared?"

"Disappeared?"

"Yes."

"Ms. Hayden?"

"Yes."

"How do you know they were terrorists?"

"What else would they be?"

"Of course," the woman replied from the three person call center staffed in an unnamed building in downtown McLean not far from Langley. "Could I get your address and phone number, please?"

"Sure," Maria answered. She gave the information slowly, carefully spelling out her address in full and repeating her phone number twice.

"Ms. Hayden, if you see these men again I suggest that you call 911. They can respond much faster than we can."

"911?"

"Yes, ma'am, the general police emergency number."

"But you are the CIA; it's your job to catch terrorists."

The voice sighed ever so perceptibly. "Yes, Ms. Hayden. I will pass your information along."

"I see," Maria Hayden replied, not sure if the conversation was over.

The woman with the soothing voice let Maria know it was. "Have a good night, Ms. Hayden."

"Good night," she answered into the dead line.

Ariana parked next to the black VW and looked around. The side parking lot of the Giant supermarket ran to the back of the building and sat in a small gully that could be tricky to navigate in the snow. Ariana stepped from her beige Toyota Camry and made one lap around the VW, taking inventory. She walked away from her car and as she turned the corner to the large brick structure she hit the auto-lock button on her keychain. Her car alarm chirped as she headed for the store entrance.

Karim, Syed, and Abu were in the frozen food section, throwing a combination of vegetables, cheese pizzas, and organic complete meals into their cart.

"I can't believe our contact is a woman," Abu said with distain. "They are soft." In the light of the frozen food aisle, the pock-mock scar on the right side of his face was obvious, almost gruesome. The flesh had a texture that was neither human nor reptilian, but somewhere in between. "And I don't like being threatened by a woman."

Karim spoke. "We don't know anything yet. She might just be an intermediary. Her sex doesn't matter. Only her conviction concerns me. Nothing else."

"I assure you that I am not soft," Ariana said.

Syed and Abu jumped and let the door to the freezer slam shut. "Shit," Syed said, adding some intelligence to the conversation. "That is the second time you have snuck up on us."

"I know," Ariana said. "I am unimpressed."

Karim looked at Ariana, their eyes locking. He slowly redirected his eyes downward and she felt his eyes cover her body from her hijab to her toes.

"There are supposed to be four of you," Ariana said.

"As you can see, there are only three," Abu said.

"Did we lose one?" she asked.

"I was told to pick up two," Karim answered.

"Who told you?"

"A voice on the phone."

"How did they reach you?"

"I went to an Internet café and checked a pre-arranged email account. In that account there was a draft message. A message that had never been sent so it couldn't be monitored. I followed the instructions in the draft email. I bought a pay-by-the-minute cell phone at a 7-11, and saved the number in a different draft folder in another pre-arranged email account. Then I waited for a call. They told me where I could pick up a car. I got the car and met these two at a truck-stop outside of Houston."

"How did you two know where to go?"

"We were told before we crossed the border."

"Crossed the border? Together?"

"No," Abu answered. "We met in Houston."

"So there are only three."

"Yes," Abu answered.

"Meet me outside at your car in five minutes," Ariana said over her shoulder as she walked away.

The three men rounded the corner, each with a brown bag in their arms.

"Put the food in the trunk of my car," Ariana said, motioning towards the Toyota. "Open the back of your car and get your stuff."

"What do we do with the car?"

"I said we are going to leave it." She reached into her pocket and shoved the electric screwdriver into the screw on the license plate. The screwdriver buzzed for a few seconds, went silent, and then buzzed again. Karim took three worn backpacks from the back of the VW and threw them in the Toyota. Ariana removed the single license plate and threw it in the trunk of her car with the three backpacks and groceries.

"Get in," she said.

"Do you think it is a good idea to leave the car here?" Abu asked.

"I think it is a better idea than parking what is likely a stolen car in my driveway."

Karim smiled as he got in the passenger seat.

"Now what?" Abu said.

"Now we wait. I was told to receive four people and there are only three of you."

Chapter 6

Beautiful trouble arrived in a burgundy four-door Ford 500 wearing a business suit, glasses, and carrying a handful of legal accordion folders. Clark heard the car door slam and he picked up his pace. He shoved the old Hoover in the hall closet and pulled the sliding metal doors shut. He walked past the open bathroom door and saw his mother applying the finishing touches to her lipstick in front of the mirror.

"Are you ready, Mom?" Clark asked.

"Finished," she answered, turning off the light.

Clark made one pass around the dining table and took a last glance at the stack of files. He looked at the set of mechanical pencils resting next to the calculator and decided they were too geeky for his own good. Studious was good, geeky was not. He swiped the pencils off the table and threw them in the small drawer in the corner cabinet. He plucked a pen off the kitchen counter and threw it on the table as he headed for the front door.

The word "geek" bounced around in Clark's head as he eyed the studious-looking IRS auditor with silky auburn hair coming up the front stairs. *Well, this may not be so bad after all*, he thought.

Clark took quick steps to the door in anticipation of a closer look at his guest. His first sight was an eyeful of an official Department of Treasury IRS Auditor badge extended into his face.

"Lisa Prescott. IRS auditor."

Clark smiled. Just like in the movies.

"Hi. I'm Clark Hayden, please come in. I hope you didn't have too much trouble finding the place."

"The neighborhood is a little counter-intuitive. I called you from the gas station on Route 110 and it still took twenty minutes to get here."

"Yes, these old neighborhoods can be tricky."

"The dead ends don't help."

"We like to call them cul de sacs," Clark said. "Dead end is passé. We're shooting for something more yuppie. Change the clientele in the neighborhood."

IRS Auditor Prescott looked over at the dining area table and nodded almost imperceptibly. "Is that where I should go?" she asked.

Clark cleared his mind of lust and snapped to attention. "Yes. May I take your coat?"

Lisa removed her outer layer. Clark tried not to stare. She couldn't have been much older than he was. Maybe she had a year on him, certainly no more than two. Clark took her coat, looked around, and put it on the arm of the sofa.

Lisa found a dining room chair and sat down, her bust concealed behind her oversized brown folders. Clark noticed a cup of coffee on the table that he hadn't seen the IRS auditor bring in. He read the wording on the side of the cup aloud.

"Jammin' Java."

"Yes."

"I like that place. It's hard to find a good coffee shop that plays live music."

"It is the only one that I know of," Lisa answered. "But what I really like is open mic night."

"You sing?"

"No, but I go sometimes to listen. There's more than just singing."

Maria Hayden came from the kitchen and introduced herself. She followed with further niceties. "I put the kettle on. Can I interest you in a cup of tea?"

"I have a little coffee left, but some tea would be nice," Lisa answered with a beautiful smile underneath her button nose.

If Clark had stopped to listen, he would have heard the proverbial gloves hitting the floor as the minx in front of him sharpened her bureaucratic claws.

Clark positioned himself in the chair directly across from Auditor Prescott. "Can I call you Lisa?"

"No you may not."

"How should I address you?"

"Ms. Prescott."

"You can call me Clark."

"Fine, Clark it is. As you may know, I'm investigating your mother and father for tax discrepancies over the last two tax years. As I mentioned over the phone, they filed a joint 1040, so even though your father is deceased, and please accept my apologies, your mother is still responsible for the information presented on those forms. Her signature is there. She benefited from any misrepresented tax information that would have enriched your father's financial standing. I think it is safe to say that these infractions are, what I would consider, severe."

"What does 'severe' mean?"

"Generally I classify severe as any infraction that could result in jail time."

Clark looked over at his mother in the kitchen and then back at Auditor Prescott. In a quiet voice he spoke with conviction. "My mother is seventy-five years old and she has diminished mental capacity. It would never happen. No one in their right mind would put her in jail."

"Never say never, Mr. Hayden."

"Clark."

"Clark," Prescott repeated. "Do you have power of attorney

over your mother's affairs? Without it, I am not authorized to speak with you."

"No, I don't. My aunt does. My mother will answer your questions and I will sit next to her."

"Fine. But I will not be directing any questions towards you. If you choose to obtain a Power of Attorney, I will need a copy for my files."

There was something about being reprimanded by someone his own age that made the whole exchange more insulting than it was. Clark didn't know what to make of the IRS auditor. Her eyes showed kindness and warmth. Her tongue was as sharp as a razor. Auditor Prescott ran some hair behind her left ear. "Can we get started?"

"When my mother finds her seat."

Small manila folders poured from the auditor's larger accordion style one. Prescott stacked the folders into piles under a system that only she understood. When she finished arranging her papers in accordance with her thoughts, she began.

"So, Ms. Hayden. Do you understand why I am here?"

"Yes. You think I'm cheating on my taxes."

"Well, not necessarily you, and not necessarily in the present. But there are several discrepancies that we have found in looking at your taxes for the last two years."

"I see," Maria responded sarcastically.

"We have reason to believe that either you or your husband has failed to claim substantial income on your returns for the last two tax years."

"Says who?" Maria Hayden answered.

"Says the IRS."

Auditor Prescott pulled out several pieces of paper. "These are deposits made into two different bank accounts over the last two tax return years. You can see that they were endorsed by your husband."

Maria looked at the signature and nodded. Clark pulled out a previous year of his parents' tax returns to compare the signatures. He too nodded slowly.

"One of the accounts was in the now-defunct Riggs Bank. Most of the deposits were cash."

Clark interrupted. "Lisa, can I ask a question?"

"Ms. Prescott."

"Yes, Ms. Prescott. May I?"

"Please."

"How did you get this information?"

Lisa Prescott looked at Maria and answered the question. "Ms. Hayden, you were identified as a subject for audit at random. The initial audit is run by an IRS auditor. A criminal investigator is assigned if one is needed."

"I see," Maria said again.

"The IRS has many avenues for identifying and pursuing tax evaders. We have the $10,000 limit on wire transfers and certain other financial transactions, and we allow for anonymous sources to provide information on tax evaders. Audits are still the largest revenue generators."

"I'm sorry, but did you just say that you allow anonymous sources to turn in other citizens?" Clark asked.

"Yes."

"Who would do this?"

"An anonymous source means that we don't know whom."

"How the hell does that work? Anyone can just turn in another person as an anonymous source?"

"Absolutely. There is a service center in California that only handles anonymous submissions."

"I would like the address," Clark said.

"Why?"

"I need to report 435 members of Congress and 100 Senators."

Lisa Prescott smiled involuntarily, her cute face framed by wisps of auburn hair.

Gotcha, Clark thought. Not even an IRS nutcracker was immune to well-timed wit and charm.

"The address is public information. I can provide it, or you can look it up," Lisa said, shuffling to a new stack of paper. The dimples on her cheeks strained to remain hidden. She stole a glance over the frame of her glasses as Clark put his hand on his mother's arm. "Of course, there needs to be first-hand familiarity with the situation in order for an anonymous submission to have merit. It is not a witch hunt."

"I understand" Clark said. "So, from what you have said, my father was stashing away money and not paying the taxes on it."

"I cannot answer that question to you, Clark. Your mother needs to ask it."

Clark put his hand on his mother's shoulder and whispered into her ear. Maria Hayden repeated the question closely enough to get the point across.

Auditor Prescott responded. "It appears that way. It is not a difficult formula. Add up the deposits, look at the tax forms and the declared wages, and see the difference. These deposits exceeded your parents' income, as stated on their tax returns."

"I see," Clark said, stealing another glance at his mother to see if she understood.

The interrogation and banter went on until lunch. In the process, Clark learned a valuable lesson that all Americans figure out sooner or later: if the government wants to fuck you, it is only a matter of when and what position they prefer. KY is optional and applied purely at the government's discretion.

The conversation dragged on through two pots of tea, twice as many bathroom breaks, years of tax forms, stock holdings, pension plans, IRAs, major purchases, and the deed on the house. Clark kept up with the numbers and the total was anything but impressive. His parents were blue-collar. Even with the accounts and deposits in question, they spent their whole lives just getting by. A lifetime of labor under scrutiny for some twenty thousand dollars of mystery money.

Clark spoke. "I would like to take a crack at summarizing our meeting here today. My parents have lived, God rest my father's soul, for a combined hundred and forty years, and the IRS is interested in twenty-two thousand dollars that appears, as you put it, to have come out of nowhere?"

"You summed it up for your mother nicely. That is correct."

"So you say."

"So the paperwork says. Numbers don't lie."

"Numbers lie all the time. Don't you read the newspapers? You can have multiple conclusions from the same statistical study."

"I don't believe everything that I read."

"You said it," Clark proclaimed. "Neither do I."

"Well, today is just a preliminary meeting. I will give you a week to get your ducks in a row and to examine the discrepancies we discussed. Perhaps there is a reasonable explanation that neither of us is yet aware of. But these deposits are no mistake. Whether they can be explained is another matter altogether."

Clark ignored the last statement. "So we get to meet again?"

"I think it's safe to say."

Clark walked Ms. Prescott to her car against her protest. He waited until she hit the alarm on the American sedan and then opened the driver's door. Lisa Prescott smiled and walked past Clark to the back door. She placed her folders in the rear seat and turned towards Clark who was still standing at attention like a chauffer driver.

"Thank you," she said, offering the first genuine kindness of the day.

"I knew there was real person in there trying to escape."

"My job doesn't allow me to be a real person."

"Maybe not, but I sized you up before you hit the front steps."

Lisa Prescott stopped and looked Clark in the eyes. "Assuming you're right, and that there is a real person trying to escape, what gave me away?"

"You were singing to yourself as you walked up the sidewalk. A real bitch would have stopped singing in the car." Clark paused for a second. "Sorry, I probably should have chosen another word."

"Consider us even."

"Would it be inappropriate for me to ask you out?"

"Yes. It's against regulations."

"Not mine."

"I'm prohibited from personal relationships with those under my investigational jurisdiction."

"Investigational jurisdiction? Try to say that five times really fast. You must have a team of lawyers over there in the Treasury Department thinking up terms."

"We have a few."

"Well, technically you are investigating my parents, not me. I'm just an intermediary."

"You will likely obtain Power of Attorney."

"A mere technicality."

Lisa Prescott sighed, smiled and bit her lip. "I'll see you again in a week."

Clark walked through the small hall that ran from the kitchen to the back of the garage. The concrete floor in the narrow passage was as cold as the frozen earth outside. His breath billowed out a white mist that stretched forward a foot before dissipating. He wiped his sneakers on the small green plastic mat and stepped into the laundry room his father had built with the attached garage shortly after Clark was born.

Clark flicked the light switch and stepped from the laundry room into a garage that had never housed a car. Light trickled in through two small windows on the outer wall and through a set of glass panes on the roll-up door. A smell hung in the air that Clark associated as a mix of burnt metal and oil. It was the smell of a machine shop, and not all the Lysol at a Costco could change that.

Clark walked around the shop in the presence of his father's image, a ghost still standing at the machines, intermittently breaking to look over blueprints at the small work table. Clark pulled the cover off the lathe and let it fall to the concrete floor. The lathe was a six-foot beauty, a machine designed to spin a piece of metal or wood horizontally at rapid speeds while applying a cutting blade to the side of the object, resulting in the production of spheres and cylinders.

Clark ran his hand over the cutting control, just as he had when he and his father had crafted a handmade Louisville slugger replica in junior high school. Clark turned the knob on the control and the geared wheel moved effortlessly. His father called the grease he applied to the gears "Toyota slick" and he ordered the lubricant directly from the manufacturer. It lasted forever, his father had said, and Clark was starting to believe him. Clark reminded himself to run the machines and check the de-humidifier in the corner that emptied into the yard through a hole in the wall of the garage.

Clark moved to the stand-alone milling machine with the Computer Numeric Control pad. The semi-automated CNC pad could guide a drill bit into a solid object, accurate to within a thousandth of an inch. A fraction of a human hair. More than precise enough to drill the wheel holes on a winning pinewood derby car in Boy Scouts.

The machines were part of his father, as much as the old wool jacket and matching gray hat that he wore six months out of the year. Clark had tried to get his mother to sell the machines and there was no shortage of interested buyers. Many of his father's friends had inquired about the machines in the months after the funeral. His mother refused to discuss it. And Clark knew that if his mother was still keeping an old tube of toothpaste in the bathroom, she sure as hell wasn't ready to let go of something that symbolized her husband for fifty years. Maybe the trouble with the IRS would change her mind. The machines could settle some of the current bill to Uncle Sam. Cover some prescriptions, too.

Clark shuffled slowly through a set of standing toolboxes and shelves. He passed a huge stack of metal stored on the shelves in the corner, scraps of leftovers that included prototypes, car parts, and other bits and pieces whose origins were a secret Clark's father had taken to the grave. An old drill-press divided the unused precious metal. Aluminum was the metal of his father's profession, but all machinists worth their salt had a stash of the good stuff. Titanium. Magnesium. Inconel. Clark ran his hands over the shelves of unused metal—cubby holes of tubes, squares, cylinders, and rings. There wasn't a shape on Earth his old man couldn't reproduce. And there were a thousand pieces no longer on this Earth that his father had made with sweat and his machines.

Clark caressed the handle on the band saw and snapped out of his daze. He stepped past the small desk against the wall and opened the dented metal filing cabinet in the corner. He pulled out stacks of folders from the top drawer and flipped through the tabs. Blueprints, orders, invoices, copies of checks. Clark grabbed the folder labeled "invoices and billing," took another adoring look around the room, and hit the lights on the way out the door.

Clark leafed through the financial papers from his father's filing cabinet as his mother finished the dishes. She wiped her hands on the towel on the counter, put her apron on a hook in the wall, and disappeared into the bedroom. She reappeared with the family photo album and found her seat next to Clark on the sofa.

"Do you remember this?" she asked showing a photo of an elementary school-aged Clark at a petting zoo trying to run from a goat with an appetite for his sweatshirt.

"How could I forget? I still hate goats."

"Your father saved you."

"Yeah, Dad gave the goat a knock on the head it probably still remembers."

"That animal was possessed, I tell you," his mother said, making a sign of the cross.

Tears ran down Maria's cheeks as she flipped the black pages of the thick book, photos from a lifetime of events pinned to paper with triangular corner holders. She had just finished her second Christmas without her husband of fifty years. Her second Christmas as a widow. Clark offered his shoulder to cry on. For himself, he was done crying. He looked at a picture of his father dressed in a suit and then pried the photo album from his mom's fingers and put it on the table.

Chapter 7

Ariana looked out the kitchen window at the back end of the white seventeen foot moving truck. The words Piedmont Delivery were written in burgundy letters that arched across the side of the vehicle. The reverse lights were on and an intermittent beep blared with force that belied the size of the truck.

Ariana stuck her head around the corner of the kitchen. Her three guests were sitting in the living room. Karim and Syed were examining a map of the D.C. area spread across the coffee table. Abu was sitting on the floor, trying to make his way through a copy of USA Today. They were studying the enemy. Three hundred million potential targets, not including the 1.8 million Muslims in the US population.

"Everyone in the basement," Ariana said.

Karim looked up from his hunched over position. "What is it?"

"No questions. Get in the basement. All of you."

Abu slammed the paper shut with a rustle. Karim looked at the short-fused member of the group. "Let's go. And bring your paper with you. You need the reading practice."

"I don't need to read to know how to kill."

Ariana walked up behind the seated Abu and put a finger in the small crevice between the bottom of his ear lobe and his jaw. She pushed his head into her knee and let the agony of the pressure point rush through his neck. Abu squirmed in pain. Ariana loosened her grip slightly and spoke. "No, you don't need to read to know how to kill, but you need to know how to read to avoid getting us killed before we complete our task."

Abu reached up with his hand and tried to swat away Ariana's grasp. As he did, Ariana stepped back and Abu rolled back from his seated position onto the carpet.

Syed and Karim smiled slightly and stood. Abu rubbed the side of his neck and gathered himself, searching for the dignity he had just lost.

The basement door shut and Ariana reached for her jacket as the footsteps of her guests faded down the stairs. Her black hijab in place, she pulled on her coat and hustled out the door.

In the truck, James Beach flicked off the radio and slammed down the pedal-mounted emergency brake. He grabbed the single key from the ignition, pushed the heavy door open, and lowered himself to the ground in one large step. His tattered Baltimore Orioles jacket looked absolutely new compared to the state of his faded, threadbare jeans. James reached for a small folder of paperwork wedged behind the driver's seat and shut the door.

Ariana, trace remains of adrenaline still in her blood from the confrontation with Abu, rounded the corner of the van with a smile.

"Can I help you?" she asked the man with the disheveled brown hair and piercing blue eyes. "I'm not expecting any deliveries." Ariana measured the delivery man quickly. Six-foot one, one-hundred and ninety pounds, athletic. In need of a change of clothes and a shower.

James stepped forward with the folder in his hand and Ariana noticed the poorly done tattoo on his right wrist protruding just below the end of the sleeve.

"I'm here to be received," James said as if he had uttered something profound.

Ariana stepped back, creating room between herself and the deliveryman. "I'm sorry?"

"I'm here to be received."

Ariana stared into the man's eyes. James Beach stared back.

"I'm going to ask you a very important question. Are you sure that you have the right address and the right message?"

The cold stare from Ariana gave James goosebumps. He opened his folder and read from the script. "Assalamu alaikum. I have traveled a great distance and pray for your hospitality."

"Then I shall receive you," she said.

James stuck out his hand and Ariana looked at it without moving.

"Why the truck?"

"What?"

"Why the truck? This neighborhood has eyes. Small yards. Curious minds. You should have at least disabled the reverse alarm."

"I only had an address. I didn't know what kind of neighborhood it was."

"What's in the truck?"

James Beach smiled. "You're going to love it."

James dug in his jeans for the brass key to the large Master Lock hanging on the back of the truck. He turned the key and pulled down on the square block that housed both ends of the u-shaped steel bar. With another smile, James pushed the rolling door up. Stacks of large brown burlap sacks about the size of garbage bags filled the back of the van halfway to the ceiling. Ariana pushed on the side of a sack to feel the texture. The bag gave way slightly. She ran her hand down the outside of the bag and felt a twinge of excitement.

"Is that what I think it is?"

"Yes."

"How much is in there?"

"Four thousand pounds, give or take."

Ariana quickly did a calculation in her head that only a handful of people on Earth would know how to do, and even fewer who would relish in it. The results of her calculation would make the average person lose their lunch, or at the very least, their appetite for dinner.

"You want to see?" James Beach asked, slowly reaching for the buck knife from his back pocket. Ariana shifted her stance slightly preparing for a possible attack. James Beach noticed the attention gained by his movement and removed his hand from his pocket, empty.

"Lock the door on the truck and follow me inside," Ariana said. James Beach headed for the door as Ariana looked up the street under the midday sun and wondered how many eyes were on her.

James Beach sat on the old cot in the basement with Syed on his left and Karim on his right. Abu sat backwards on an old dining room chair, his legs spread to each side. Ariana pulled the curtains in the small windows that were high on the wall, level with the ground outside.

"He's American; we can't trust him," Abu started.

"I agree," Syed added, stroking his chin.

Karim remained silent and watched as Ariana unfolded a large map and put it on the floor.

James spoke in his defense. "I'm American but I am also a Muslim."

"It's not the same," Abu added.

"Why not?"

"Because you do not share a thousand years of spilled blood at the hands of the infidels. You *are* an infidel."

"Do I need to have relatives who have died in the name of Islam? I thought our faith was measured by faith. Faith and action. What else is there?"

"Pure blood. You are American, right down to your blue eyes."

James opened his mouth to respond and Ariana intervened. "Enough," Ariana repeated. "We don't have time for this. I will deal with it later. There may be reasons that an American was sent. For one, his name would not raise suspicion if, for example, he were the driver of a truck that was pulled over."

"What's the name on your driver's license?" Abu asked.

"James Beach. But I have also taken the name Mohammed Al-Jabar."

"Enough," Ariana repeated. "We have a more urgent problem. I need to take care of the truck outside."

"I can drive it," James offered.

Ariana thought. "You will wait here with everyone else. I will be gone a few hours. If anything happens to me, I may need to call." She pointed at Karim. "Only you answer the phone."

"Why him?" Abu asked.

"Because his voice is similar to my husband's."

She turned her attention back to James who spoke. "I have a pre-paid phone. It is clean."

Ariana's mind was on the cargo in the back of the truck. "No. From this moment on, every step we take needs to be erased. There are no retreats. No going back. No duplication of activities. If we use a computer, the computer gets destroyed before we move to the next phase. If we use a cell phone, it gets destroyed. I will get us all new phones this afternoon. It will take me a few hours. Once I have the phones, I will give them to you when the time is right. I also need everyone's clothes size. Shirts, pants, shoes. Head, feet, waist, inseam, chest. Everything. But first, I need to get that truck out of the driveway. That is a delivery truck. Every minute it sits in the driveway it draws more suspicion. Every minute it spends in the driveway without someone delivering something is another second that I have to cover with a lie. Delivery trucks generally deliver and leave. I'm a Muslim woman and the delivery man is a good-looking American. People could start talking. Even if they are joking, it may help them remember an important detail later."

The knock on the kitchen door made everyone jump. "Shit," Ariana said. "No one move. I'll be right back." Ariana ran up the stairs and peeked out the window.

The dark blue government-issued hat bounced around the small window in the door. "Is that you, Mel?" Ariana asked.

"Yes," he said stretching the word into two syllables. "I have a package for you," Mel the postman said from under the brim of his USPS winter hat.

"Just leave it on the porch,"

"I need a signature."

Ariana opened the door and offered her arm for the signature. Mel handed her a pen and Ariana scribbled her name in the small blank on the green receipt. "You having something delivered?" Mel asked motioning towards the truck in the driveway.

Ariana looked quickly at the name on the side of the truck and the wheels in her mind spun. Piedmont Delivery. "Yes, my husband ordered a handmade dresser from an arts and crafts place near Front Royal."

"Super, super. New furniture is always nice."

"Yes, it's quite a piece. Thanks for the package, Mel."

"Thank you. Have a great day."

Ariana looked at the package and watched as her mailman walked down the driveway next to the truck. She cringed as Mel Edgewood studied the name on the side of the van before he cut across the corner of the yard to Mr. Stanley's.

Chapter 8

Allan Coleman's thick belly sat on the edge of his desk, resting just in front of the keyboard. His body strained to breathe, bands of fatty tissue pushing his stretch pants to their limits. Unhealthy bulges of cellulite rode up his chest, a deep fold of flesh drawing the boundary between the top of his stomach and flabby man-boobs. Oversized buttocks oozed from the sides of the chair under the armrests, his fat ankles squeezed into a pair of white sneakers.

The newly built office in Coleman's Castle was a roadmap to obesity. An empty bag of Frito Twisters protruded from the trash can supported by a box from the dozen Krispy Kreme doughnuts he had eaten earlier in the day. A thirty-two ounce plastic cup rested on the corner of a small table, away from his computer and the spaghetti of wires that ran along the floor in every direction. His nails were chewed short and dandruff dripped off his shoulder, rolling down his arm in the direction of his elbow.

By most accounts, Allan Coleman was wasting his life. His cholesterol level was over 300. His blood pressure was a monumental 220 over 160. His doctor told him to lose weight. Allan ate to compensate for the stress of the doctor's orders. Gastric bypass was suggested. Allan refused. He believed he had an exercise routine. Every thirty minutes he walked to the small refrigerator on the far side of his office and retrieved a Coke Classic. With the completion of the two-story addition and the onset of winter, he augmented his usual workout by going down one flight of stairs, opening the side door, taking two steps, and retrieving another log to put on the fire. It was as much exercise as he cared to do.

The oversized ergonomic chair was little compensation for the natural stress his frame endured by carrying an extra average-sized human on his skeleton. Allan Coleman rolled his neck, cracked his knuckles, and quickly pounded out an email to a team of programmers and help-desk gurus halfway around the world. Allan was a work-induced shut-in. He couldn't even recall the year of his last date, unless he counted Little Debbie — the vixen of desserts who held a strategic, immediate gratification advantage over the second most important woman in his life — Betty Crocker.

"Ping," the speaker on his computer screamed with another message. He was living in a high-tech world where email wasn't fast enough. The homegrown instant messaging system forced on its employees by his company was the bane of Allan Coleman's existence. Thirty seconds to reply was the standard. It didn't matter if you were in midstream of urinary relief or performing the Heimlich on a lunch guest. Any longer than thirty seconds and his phone would start ringing. Allan didn't live on Eastern Standard Time. He was on telecommuter time. And his conversation of the night was identifying a software bug with a pack of Indian programmers in Mumbai.

But what Allan didn't qualify for in the superficial world of size two dresses and six-pack abdomens, he made up for in knowledge of ones and zeros. They were the building blocks of digital life, the binary DNA of every computer system and piece of software in the world. As the head of level five technical support for the graveyard shift, working for the last American computer maker, Allan got the tough cases. The unsolvable electronic mysteries that his underlings in India couldn't handle.

Allan's eyebrows jumped at the rumble in his own stomach and he reached to the right and grabbed his black wireless headset. As his intestines churned, he fumbled to hang the upper portion of the device over his ear. He adjusted the mic so that it was a comfortable distance from his mouth, close enough so he could be heard, far enough away so that he could cover it with his free hand and so that it wouldn't impede food consumption. He turned off the speaker function on the expensive phone, stood, and adjusted the angle of his flat-screen monitor. He was now free to move about the cabin. He wasted no time in running straight up the aisle.

The third wave of pain hit as he was turning to face the still open door and pulling on the elastic of his pants. The exodus began before his butt hit the seat. He fumbled for the mute button on his hand-free device and tried to concentrate on the conversation as unearthly sounds resonated around the new bathroom. His computer pinged twice and he tried to look through his now tearing eyes at the flat screen across the room. There were two beeps on the line and Allan let them ring unanswered. He had bigger problems.

Twenty minutes later, still in the seated position on the throne, Allan stammered through a few clarifying points, trying to control his bowels for a moment of silence.

With shaking legs, he stood and flushed the evidence of severe internal bleeding into the sewer system and on its way to the Chesapeake Bay watershed. He exited the bathroom weakly, sweat dripping, trying to catch up with the conversation, giving orders to colleagues who were looking out their window in Mumbai at one of the largest metropolises on the planet. Allan looked out the back of his castle at the single light in the kitchen window of his neighbor's house.

"You don't have time to get the flu," Allan said to himself as a case of chills ran down the skin on the back of his neck. He walked slowly to the corner and reached for another log to throw into the large stone hearth on the far side of the room. He pushed the log into the fire with a poker and returned across the floor to his computer and a new set of "pings."

Allan tried to open the attachment on an incoming email. His vision blurred and he mis-clicked three times before he found his target and the Excel spreadsheet opened. He continued to fumble with the mouse, his first inclination that something was wrong, something beyond the leftover Chinese take-out he had eaten as a late night snack. A man like Allan, someone who had spent ten years with a mouse attached to his finger, eighteen hours a day, didn't make a habit of mis-clicking. The pointer finger on his right hand was the only part of his body that was Olympic-athlete caliber. He noticed his head beginning to throb and his throat was sore. Eighty-hour workweeks were catching up with him.

By three in the morning, Allan had lost his appetite. He made two additional trips to the bathroom and was now feeling pain in his kidneys on both sides of his back. He went to the medicine cabinet in the bathroom for another dose of Advil and stared at what looked like traces of blood on his lips. He opened his mouth and pulled on his cheeks, worried by the bleeding gum lines. He rinsed his mouth with water and swallowed the ibuprofen-based pain killer. He washed it down with twelve fresh ounces of Coke.

Allan vomited bile to begin his last call of the night. By the time he wedged himself back into his seat he had lost most of the feeling in his arms. He struggled for the prescription bottle he kept at the back of his cluttered desk. He ripped the top off the brown plastic bottle and pills spilled over his desk and keyboard. He scooped up two and put them under his tongue. He leaned his head back in his chair and waited for the magic to work. The pain was everywhere, his back, his head, his kidneys. His heart felt as tight as a marathoner's calf. He tried to breathe, tried to imagine relaxing on a beach.

His computer screamed "ping, ping, ping" as the big man's head crashed into his keyboard and his chair rolled back.

Sitting in the dark, Ariana watched her neighbor from between the blinds in her bedroom. She was sitting in the same spot she had sat the first time she saw her neighbor watching her, his eyes focused on the back end of a high-powered pair of binoculars. Unfortunately for her neighbor, he had caught her practicing her martial arts. She had thought about calling the police, but didn't want to be on record with any law enforcement agency. She knew there would be a time for paybacks.

She marked the time in her head and waited to see if Allan Coleman would reappear in the window. Twenty minutes later, with the lights still on in the room and no sign of the King of Coleman's Castle, Ariana let a small smile escape her lips.

Chapter 9

Ariana placed a piece of duct tape over the drain in the sink, just as she had done to the drain in the shower. Another thick layer of duct tape was crossed in an X over the toilet seat. The handle on the toilet was covered with additional straps of the adhesive-backed, all-purpose material. Finished, she looked around at her handiwork. She caught a glimpse of herself in the mirror and she liked what she saw. Her eyes were calculating, working. She felt alive.

At the foot of the stairs to the basement, Ariana turned on the lights and clapped her hands several times. Her guests were on the floor, sleeping as much as the rest of the neighborhood in the hours before dawn. Karim stirred first, squinting through one eye before forcing the second open.

"Turn off the lights," Abu said, his head under a pillow. James Beach rolled over on his side, still in his sleeping bag in the corner.

Ariana clapped again. "Everyone wake up. Now!"

The room stirred with a sudden sense of urgency. Syed was the first on his feet, standing almost at attention in a loose-fitting pair of boxer shorts. The white t-shirt he had on was too short for his torso and his midsection showed.

"Pack up everything you brought with you. Everything.

Leave nothing behind. When we walk out of this basement, we will not return."

Fifteen minutes later, the room was spotless. Each member of the group had their backpacks and a sleeping bag in hand. The rest of the room was sterile. A sofa and two old dining chairs were pushed against the wall. A small table sat in front of the sofa.

Satisfied, Ariana said, "Get everything and bring it upstairs. James you go up the stairs first. Then Abu, then Syed, and then Karim. I want you to walk in single file towards the bathroom in the hall and stop at the door."

"What is this?" Abu asked.

"Shut-up and do it," Karim said. "For once, try not to think that you know everything."

The four men got in line and Ariana stood behind them. "Let's go," she said, and the formation moved up the stairs.

In the hall, James stopped at the bathroom door as instructed. His backpack was on his right shoulder, his sleeping bag under his left arm. Behind him were Abu, Syed, and Karim. The four men and their belongings filled the narrow hall. Ariana walked past the men and stopped on the other side of the bathroom door. She turned around and continued the routine she had devised earlier in the day.

"Place your belongings on the ground in front of you and remain standing."

Four backpacks thudded quietly as they hit the carpeted hall. In turn, Ariana picked the bags off the floor and dragged them down the hall into her bedroom. Next she carried the sleeping bags from in front of her guests. The four men remained, clothed only in their sleepwear, standing in the hallway. James' blue eyes grew wide.

She opened the bathroom door and looked at the only American. "Get in and strip down. Naked. Leave your clothes on the floor. The door will remain open. You will take a thirty second shower, long enough to thoroughly wet your hair. You will then turn off the water, get out of the shower, and I will give you new clothes to wear. All the drains are sealed, as is the toilet."

"Is this necessary?" James asked. "What does this prove?"

"Yes, it is necessary. It may not prove anything, but you are still going to do exactly as I say."

"What if I refuse?"

"Then I'll kill you."

"You can't kill all four of us."

Ariana took one step towards James. She reached up and put her finger at the base of his throat before pushing downward and hooking the inside of his sternum. Immediately both of James' hands shot towards his neck. "I didn't say I would kill all four. I said I would kill you." She pushed her finger deeper into James' body cavity and he gasped. Then she let him go and took two steps back. "Besides, the four of you can't do anything without me."

James stepped into the bathroom and undressed. Ariana waited until he was in the shower with the water running before collecting his clothes and throwing them down the hall towards the bedroom.

When the water stopped, Ariana handed him his new set of clothes through the still-open door. When James was dressed, Ariana nodded and he stepped from the bathroom. "Sit down to my left," Ariana said.

In turn, all four men went through the sanitation process. When they were finished, all were dressed in jeans and other American clothes typical for a winter night.

The four moved to the living room in silence as Ariana continued to execute her plan.

"We are leaving tonight. This is going to be the routine. Everyone will leave with the clothes on their backs. Nothing else. Everything you brought with you is gone."

"What about our passports?" Karim asked.

"They are gone. I may be able to get us driver's licenses for IDs if we need it. That depends on time. Right now you need to understand that everything you brought with you into this home will stay in this home. No exceptions. Our success will be determined by our deaths, and we will not need these items."

"Where are we going?" Abu asked.

"I'll be taking you to our new location. We need to hurry. We need to finish before the sun comes up. Given our time constraints, your travel accommodations may not be first class."

It was before six in the morning when Ariana helped Karim into the trunk of her Toyota Camry, against a protesting Abu.

"Both of us won't fit."

"Both of you have to fit."

"Why?"

"Because it's going to be light in an hour. The neighborhood is going to come to life and I don't have enough time to take you individually." She paused for a moment, pushed on Karim's back and said, "Think thin."

Karim climbed into the trunk, his legs laying over Abu's. He moved the sleeping bag that their heads were resting on and tried to get settled.

"You fit better than Syed did," Ariana said.

"Well, he got to ride by himself."

"We are out of time. I can't take you one-by-one."

"Can't you just blindfold us?"

"And drive the two of you around the nation's capital? Two blindfolded Arabs?"

"I can go without the blindfold," Karim offered.

"The others traveled in the trunk. You two will also travel in the trunk."

Karim continued to protest and Ariana reached into her pocket and pulled out a black rectangular device the size of a cell phone. Karim started to speak but his voice was cut short by 80,000 volts of electricity. As Karim's body arched and twitched, Abu tried to climb over his incapacitated traveling partner. Ariana quickly redirected the stun gun to Abu's exposed neck and he joined Karim in uncontrollable thrashing.

"Watch your head and arms," she said as she shut the trunk

quietly. She took one look around the dark neighborhood and wondered if she would need to come back.

Ariana crossed the train tracks on Georgia Avenue and entered into a non-residential area highlighted by a dozen businesses bordering on bankruptcy. She turned left down an alley just inside the D.C. city limits near Takoma and snaked behind two old brick buildings. She rounded the corner near a lot with crushed cars stacked ten feet in the air, the rolls of razor-wire on the fence costing as much as the junk it protected.

At the end of a small road the lot widened into an open patch of asphalt and mud, a mixture of blacktop and exposed ground. She pulled the Camry over near the last warehouse on the well-hidden block. Unpainted cinderblocks with a brick façade supported a two-story metal roof. The building stretched forty yards across. On the left was a single bay door with two lone windows six feet off the ground and completely blacked-out from the inside with plastic trash bags and tape. In the middle of the warehouse stood two huge bay rollup doors, each large enough to park an oversized tow truck. The large windowless doors took up most of the front of the warehouse. Near the right hand side of the warehouse Ariana slipped her key into another solid metal, windowless door and disappeared as the spring-loaded hinge pulled the door closed behind her with a resounding thud. She took one look around the warehouse and checked on the Piedmont Delivery truck in the otherwise empty floor. She hit a green button on a hanging control panel and the door on the left chugged upward. She went back to her car and drove the vehicle into the car bay.

When the large bay door shut, she exited the car and walked to the rear of the vehicle.

"Rise and shine," she said, opening the trunk.

Karim nearly leaped from his confines, pulling himself out by the edge of the trunk.

"What the fuck was with the stun gun?" Karim asked, the veins in his neck and forehead pulsating. Abu joined in the verbal assault and tried to exit the trunk but his legs were asleep, the blood trying to find its way back into his lower extremities.

"The stun gun was a necessary evil. You'll both live."

"You touch me again and that is more than I will be able to say for you," Abu said, still in the trunk.

Ariana pulled out the stun gun and a blue electric current danced between the delivery prongs. "I'm the only one in the position to make threats," Ariana added, cooling Abu's temperament.

Karim helped Abu up by the armpits and both men looked around at the warehouse.

"Where are we?" Abu asked.

"Home," Ariana answered.

A small seam of light escaped from beneath a door on the far side of the concrete expanse. Karim followed Ariana toward the light as Abu limped slowly behind them. They approached the door and Ariana knocked once before opening it.

Chapter 10

Officer Jim Singleton pulled himself out of his police car and walked up the driveway. He hated house calls. He had, in fact, ignored the first inquiry from a worried out-of-state relative who had tried to reach the resident in question. The man's employer called next, concerned that its star employee was incapacitated. When Officer Singleton got a third call from the man's brother, the fifteen-year veteran decided he would personally stop by the house in question on his way to lunch. Not because it was his duty, but because it was near his favorite gyro restaurant.

Walking up the three steps of the front porch, Officer Singleton, crumbs from breakfast still in his brown beard, knocked on the glass in the upper-half of the white storm door. "Arlington County Police, can you come to the door please?"

He waited for a moment and looked at the neighbors on both sides of Coleman's Castle. He knocked again. "Arlington County Police Department, I would like to have a word with you."

Officer Singleton's memory served up a fresh reminder of the time he kicked in a front door after being called to a house for domestic abuse. As the door smashed open, Officer Singleton had pulled his gun on a local doctor delivering a doggie-style, free medical exam to one of his office assistants. Knocking three times became the standard for all future house calls.

Singleton walked to the side door of the house at the end of the driveway. He knocked once more, and reached for the knob. The door swung open.

Singleton identified himself three more times from the new stainless steel kitchen. He listened intently for any sound as sunlight shined through the bay window on his dark blue uniform. The house echoed with an eerie silence. Five years pushing papers hadn't dulled his senses. He knew there was a body on the premises. The only thing left was to find it.

Out of respect for the dead, Officer Singleton announced himself as he entered every room. He scanned the original three-bedroom, one-bath layout, and stood at the top of the stairs to the basement. He looked up at the skylight over the new foyer in the back of the house, and walked up the staircase which opened into an office with a view of the neighborhood. Officer Singleton enjoyed the view just long enough for his brain to register the large body on the floor in front of the desk.

"Good God," he said, stooping to find a pulse on Allan Coleman's neck. At thirty-six hours after death, the victim was cold. Not in-the-refrigerator cold, but certainly chicken-on-the-counter cool. Officer Singleton wrestled Allan onto his back and looked into the grimace of pain still frozen on his face. His eyes were almost bulging, his mouth open in a painful, stretched grin. The officer looked around the room. He grabbed the tri-fold leather wallet off the desk and checked the driver's license. Allan R. Coleman. Singleton looked at the face of the deceased and compared it to the picture. The DMV-issued photo was far more appealing than the one now on the victim's face. He checked the contents of the wallet and pulled out three hundred and forty dollars. So much for a robbery.

He put the wallet on the desk and saw the white pills. His mind switched into detective gear and he noticed several more pills lodged between the keys of the keyboard. He grabbed one with his fingers and brought it to his nose. He scanned the work area, checked the floor, and found the prescription bottle on the other side of the victim's head. Nitroglycerin.

Officer Singleton called dispatch and reported that he had found the body of the individual reported missing earlier in the day. He took one look at the obese man, set the bottle on the table, and walked downstairs to wait. Case closed.

Clark heard the ring and searched for his cell phone under a pile of papers on the dining area table. He answered on its fifth ring.

"I thought I saw your car in the driveway," the voice said.

"Yeah, just arrived with another load of stuff."

"Got a few minutes?"

"What's up?"

"Grab something warm. I'll meet you out front."

Clark did as he was asked. Two minutes later he was standing at the foot of Mr. Stanley's driveway. The World War II veteran was ambling down the drive in a huge dark parka with a white furry fringe around the hood. Clark looked at his neighbor and realized just how far down the scale of importance fashion was for a man in his mid-eighties.

"Where are we going?"

"Around the corner. It's time to be nosey neighbors."

Clark walked with Mr. Stanley through the small blacktopped path that ran through county land between his house and the Krause residence on the far side of the dead end.

"You know, I remember when this park was nothing but woods. The trees were the only buffer between the W&OD railroad and the housing development."

"How long ago was that?"

"Most of the rail traffic was before even my day, but I think the last train passed through in, oh, must have been 1968 or so."

"Well, at least we don't have train whistles screaming through the neighborhood. I'll take a bike path anytime," Clark said, referring to the recreational area that now extended along the former tracks, stretching from D.C. to Leesburg, forty miles west.

Clark added, "I haven't been in this park in years."

"It hasn't changed much, except for the paths. Once they laid down blacktop, they opened the park to dog walkers and strollers."

"That might be better than the former clientele. When I was a kid, we used to find all kinds of stuff back here. Beer cans, condoms, underwear."

"I'm not sure that's any better than dog shit."

"Maybe, but some of those condoms we found were used."

"You can't prove any of them were mine," Mr. Stanley said, straight-faced.

Clark laughed loud enough for it to echo in the leafless trees. "Well, it was good to be a kid. We used to catch crayfish, play war, splash in the creek."

"Nothing like getting wet and dirty as only boys can do with God-given material."

"For a while, and then one day we found ourselves older, dumber, and more adventurous. I am not sure whose idea it was, but one day we decided it would be more fun to build a swing to *go over* the creek than it was to trounce through it. I learned an important lesson that day."

Mr. Stanley pulled the left side of his parka back away from his ear so that he could hear Clark as he talked. "Which was?"

"If you are going to build a rope swing, don't use a garden hose. Particularly if your friend is Jimmy Shultz who weighed a hundred and fifty pounds in the sixth grade. Hoses stretch more than you think. Not only was that the day I learned about the elasticity of a stolen garden house, but it was also the day that I learned the expression 'to get racked.'"

"Sounds like Jimmy Shultz learned the real lesson."

"I guess you are right about that."

"You know, you were probably the last generation to play outdoors. Nowadays, between video games and child molesters, kids don't play outside."

They approached an intersection of paths and Mr. Stanley

took a right. A minute later they were on the street behind Dorchester Lane. An ambulance with flashing lights was parked in front of Allan Coleman's house. Before Clark asked, Mr. Stanley answered.

"I saw the flashing lights out the back window. Figured it was my duty to at least come and see what was going on."

"Your duty?"

"My duty as a good neighbor."

"I thought it was nosey neighbor."

"Call it what you want."

"I just did."

Clark had yet to win an argument with Mr. Stanley. The reason was simple. The cagey neighbor didn't fight fair. Whenever the tide in the debate turned against him, Mr. Stanley quit talking. Sometimes he blamed it on his aging ears. Most of the time he simply acted as if the conversation was over; and if one-half of a two-person conversation deemed it over, it was.

Coleman's neighbors from the next street over huddled near the corner of the dead man's property line where a chain-link fence met a small wooden post. A middle-aged woman wearing only a sweater hugged her teenage children for warmth, support, or both.

Clark talked with Mr. Stanley as they strolled up the sidewalk, still fifty yards away from the scene. "I think the show is over."

"Why do you say that?"

"No one seems to be in a hurry. The EMT driver is sitting behind the wheel, talking on the radio. The cop on the front porch is more concerned with his nicotine intake than with what's going on in the house."

As if on cue, Officer Jim Singleton cupped his hand over the end of his cigarette trying to light it against the wind.

Clark stepped toward another middle-aged mother, appropriately dressed in a black down jacket. "What happened?"

"Looks like Mr. Coleman had a heart attack," the woman's son said. His eyes were glued to the side door of the house.

His mother hushed him and put her fingers over her lips.

"How long has he been dead?"

"The cops won't say," the boy answered through teeth with braces.

The mother rolled her eyes and looked down at her son. "It appears that Mr. Coleman died in the last day or so. Natural causes. He obviously wasn't the most health-conscious individual."

Everyone's suspicion was confirmed with the arrival of the long black car that opened from the rear.

"This is going to be interesting," Clark whispered to Mr. Stanley. "This guy was huge."

Mr. Stanley flicked his head and Clark followed. "Good afternoon, officer. My name is John Stanley. Former Marine Captain. What's the story?"

"Retired Marine?"

"Yes sir. Retired with enough shrapnel in my ass and legs to set off the detectors at the airport."

Clark looked at Mr. Stanley and bit the inside of his cheeks.

"Did you know Mr. Coleman?"

"He was my neighbor. We exchanged greetings from time-to-time."

"Well, Captain, Mr. Coleman passed away sometime in the last two days, most likely from natural causes."

"Who called you?"

"His brother and his employer."

Officer Singleton was summoned from inside the house. "If you would excuse me."

Inside the house, it took four people to get Allan Coleman into the extra-large body bag and six to get him onto the stretcher. With the joints of the stretcher protesting, the six adult men struggled to maneuver Coleman's three hundred and seventy-eight pounds of deadweight down the stairs.

Inside Coleman's office, no one seemed to notice the stack of voyeur-themed porn on the floor in the corner under a recent *Time* magazine, or the high-powered binoculars that rested on the windowsill overlooking the neighborhood.

Chapter 11

The natural light from the outside was tracking across the ceiling in the morning sun, waking the cavernous room from its gray darkness. The new rays of indirect sunlight struggled to push through the windows near the top of the wall into the garage turned warehouse.

Abu and Syed were busy cleaning, their arms tired, their fingers wrinkled from the damp towels they had used to wipe most of the surfaces of the warehouse, as far up as they could reach. Karim was on his hands and knees with a scrub brush, working to remove hardened bird droppings that dotted the floor near the base of a main support beam. Ariana walked by and looked up at the ventilation hood above. She put it on the list of things to secure.

James drew the short straw and got the bathrooms, of which there were two. The American Muslim was at work on the small bathroom near what would become the group's sleeping quarters. The single sink and toilet were covered in mildew from months of non-use. The shower stall was a science experiment-in-progress, a green fungus growing out from the grout lines to reach half-way across each tile.

Next to the crude bathroom facility was another heavy steel door. Ariana opened the door and the hinges squeaked. A wave of must greeted her. She checked the floor for water and touched the wall. It was cold and moist. She looked up at the window twelve feet above. The confining walls and the lone trace of light above sent Ariana back in time. She shut her eyes and saw the steel door shut behind her. She felt the club come down on her head and the boot hit her in the ribs. She shivered, and opened her eyes, thankful she had avoided the memory of her final lesson in her training years before. Thankful for unconsciousness as she lost the last remains of her innocence.

Mentally back in the room, she walked off the dimensions between the walls. When she was finished she smiled, the specifics of the warehouse, down to the cubic-foot space, were as she memorized. But for some reason the room she was in now felt smaller, tighter. With her soldiers in mind, she imagined the configuration of the barracks. She stepped out of the room for a moment and tried to pinpoint the direction of Mecca with as much accuracy as she could. The far right corner, she thought to herself. She smiled. With bunk beds, she could have received twice as many men.

Satisfied, Ariana made her way across the warehouse, glancing at her Toyota Camry and the Piedmont Delivery van that occupied the garage turned warehouse floor. She put her key in the lock, entered the small office in the corner and shut the door behind her. She flicked the lone light switch on the wall near the door and the ten-by-ten foot room received its first light in three months. The glass walls of the office looked out onto the floor of the warehouse. Two sets of metal filing cabinets stood in the corner side-by-side. A lamp and a black phone sat on the desk in the middle of the room. The outdated calendar on the wall depicted a large-busted woman with a handheld drill bending over the side of a motorcycle. It was hard to tell if it was an advertisement for the motorcycle, the tool, or for silicone implants.

Ariana noted what she needed to have a business up and running. Paper, pens, a computer, folders. Her eyes looked around the room, envisioning a fully functioning office. Or at least a room that would give the appearance of one. She picked up the landline phone and the dial tone greeted her ear. She put the phone back on its cradle and checked the desk drawers. They were locked, just as she had left them.

She opened the office door, looked around at the warehouse and her human resources. Then she curved her thumb and middle fingers to make a ring, pushed them to her lips, and let out a whistle that froze the room.

"Everyone stop what you are doing."

Karim stood from his battle with the dried bird crap on the floor. Abu and Syed dropped their rags. James emerged from the bathroom on the back left.

"I wanted everyone to gather so we can go over some ground rules."

"I hope it doesn't include a weekly cleaning list," Syed said, rubbing his left triceps.

"It does. But hopefully we won't be here too long," Ariana paused for a moment, waiting for James to get closer to the office door, and then continued. "Welcome to our home away from home. As you can probably tell by the hydraulic lifts in the floor and the other interior design features, this warehouse was once an automotive garage. It has a long-term lease, paid through an untraceable party, and it is as safe a haven as we are going to find. There are no neighbors, but we are in an urban area. You will have to take my word for this. If I catch anyone stepping outside the confines of these walls, I will kill them."

She didn't wait for a reaction.

"I chose this location for a variety of reasons, so if anyone has any complaints, look no further for a target for your ire. I have been here off and on for the last year or so. Checking on the place, making sure the electricity and water still function. I also cleaned from time to time, believe it or not."

"There are six rooms in total. We have the main warehouse floor, where we are standing. There are two bays with twenty-foot doors. Large enough for any operation we may need. Behind me is the office. It has a working landline phone that none of us will use. I will make some acquisitions for the office in an attempt to modernize the atmosphere. But by and large the office is to maintain appearances only. None of you will go into the office unless accompanied by me."

Abu and Syed rolled their eyes.

"To your left, my right, there are three doors on the wall. As you have discovered, the room at the back of the warehouse is a bathroom. There is a shower stall, a toilet and a single sink. I expect everyone to keep this room clean. As well as yourselves. I cannot have my men smelling like they haven't bathed in a month. It would draw unneeded attention when the time comes to execute our plan.

"The door next to the bathroom is your sleeping quarters. There is a window. I have affixed a mihrab on the wall so that you will know which direction to pray. I will also get a space-heater, some beds, and other items so that you will feel comfortable. There should be no personal effects from anyone outside of the sleeping quarters. I will be sleeping in the office.

"The oversized third door on the left side is locked and is to remained locked. Its contents are of no consequence to any of you. Ditto goes for the truck. The door is locked and I have the only key."

Done with the left side of the warehouse and the office, Ariana walked towards a set of double doors on the right side of the former automotive floor.

Ariana explained as she went through the motions. "Beyond these double doors is a smaller room that was owned and operated by a printing company." The doors swung open and the men stepped forward to look down the length of the room. "There is a door at the front of the shop, but it has been sealed shut. It cannot be opened by normal means. Don't waste your time trying. There is a bathroom in the back, also with its own shower. I had these double doors installed when the lease for the property was executed."

"Why do these places have showers?" Syed asked.

"Hygiene and safety precautions. A lot of facilities that

work with chemicals have showers for emergencies. Which probably explains the print shop. In any case, we have two bathrooms at our disposal. For now, we only use one."

Syed shrugged as if the answer were sufficient.

Abu interjected the obvious. "But if we have two…"

"We use one," Ariana said without negotiation. "Any questions so far?"

The men fumed and said nothing.

"Good. Until we are operational, when I am out of the warehouse, I expect all of you to remain in the sleeping quarters. Consider it home. If you must use the bathroom, please do so one at a time, and be brief. Also, feel free to use the bathroom for wadu. We will all need our faith. And keep the talking to a minimum. Discuss the weather. Nothing personal. Nothing revealing."

The men looked at each other suspiciously.

"Understood?" Ariana asked.

The men nodded.

"Ok. Let's not lose sight of why we are here. I will also speak with each of you individually. Later this evening I will be running some errands and picking up a few things. If there is something that you absolutely must have, let me know and I will consider it. Now, get back to work."

The group grumbled as it broke and returned towards their work. Ariana stepped forward and grabbed Karim by the arm. "Not you. We need to have a word." Karim followed Ariana into the office and Abu and Syed paused long enough to peek back over their shoulders.

"Please have a seat," Ariana said as she shut the door to the office.

Karim did as he was told and forced his backside onto an uncomfortable wooden chair.

Ariana sat down and opened her purse. She slowly slid a pre-paid cell phone across the desk in the direction of Karim. "If anything happens while I am out, you will be responsible for calling me."

"Of course," Karim answered. He looked over his shoulder at the warehouse and could feel Abu and Syed's eyes straining to see through the open Venetians as they resumed wiping the walls. Ariana shook her head slightly, and Karim understood her warning to be careful.

"Unless you have to contact me, I want you to keep that phone powered off and out of sight."

Karim looked at the phone and opened the cover. "Untraceable?"

"Completely. Especially if we use them only once."

"Are you sure?"

"Positive. I've tested them from time to time. Not only are they untraceable, but if you call someone, the display shows only 'incoming call.' The laws are changing quickly though. In another year it will be impossible to get a pre-paid phone. If you plan on using a legitimate ID anyway."

"How are the other preparations?"

"Fine. I still have things to do, and will need some time to make some meaningful purchases."

"You look worried."

"There is a small complication."

"How small?"

"I'm concerned that someone will start to notice a family has gone missing. I need to call a neighbor."

"That's not a good idea."

Ariana thought for a moment before concluding. "We have no choice."

Karim noticed the use of the word "we" and he smiled.

Ariana continued. "A family doesn't just get up and leave their house unattended. Neighbors will start to worry. People will start to ask questions and get suspicious. Someone will call the police."

"I see your point."

"And with a child missing, well, you are talking about fodder for national news."

Karim rubbed his beard and stared out the window of

the office. "Sounds like you could have been better prepared."

"I had no warning. My family was one part of the equation that was fluid."

"I understand. Make the call to your neighbor, but be brief, Ariana. We have come too far. We have waited too long."

Ariana nodded, though it was not in deference. "If the others ask what we were talking about, tell them we were discussing special skills you have or training you have received. I will ask each of them in turn so that no one is overly suspicious. Once I am done with their debriefing, I will need to run out for supplies."

Karim got up from his chair and slipped the cell phone into his pocket. As he headed for the door, Ariana added, "Tell James to hurry up with the bathroom and tell Abu he is next for his debriefing."

Ariana hung the CVS bag on the hook on the wall. The narrow bathroom with the single shower stall was designed for mechanics to clean up after work. If the walls could speak they would attest to having never seen what was unfolding before their grout-laden eyes. She dug through two hundred dollars worth of self-improvement and then loosely separated them into different piles on the freshly cleaned floor.

She placed a bag of clothes on the top of the closed toilet lid. She removed the outer layer of her black headscarf, revealing most of her cheeks, her ears, and the side of her neck. She pulled the inner tube of her hijab from the back of her head and her dark brown hair fell to her shoulders and radiated in the light from the bulb above the sink.

Her bushy eyebrows were the first to go. It was the one thing she couldn't change with Nazim as her husband. Clothes could be changed. Hair could be curled. Glasses could be removed. But semi-permanent change was something she couldn't allow herself until now.

She plucked her eyebrows, one hair at a time. The first pluck made her eyes water. As she continued, the small pricks of pain became therapeutic. When she was done plucking the meat of the brows, she shaved the edges with an eyebrow razor. She splashed water on her face and admired the high arching brows that had taken the place of her previous untamed, near uni-brow, pair.

Next she picked up a box with a high-priced fashion model on the side. She opened the tab on the box and pulled out a plastic cap and tied it over her hair, the strings on the cap tying under her chin. With the same pair of tweezers she had used to assault her brows, she spent half an hour pulling strands of her hair through the holes in the tight-fitting shower-cap like covering. When she finished, she read the instructions on the back of the box for a second time. She pulled out a small bag, prepared the concoction as prescribed, and pasted a mix with the consistency of honey onto the strands of hair she had pulled to the outside of the rubber cap.

Forty minutes later, Ariana admired herself in the mirror.

Her knee-length skirt was the most revealing thing she had worn outside of the bedroom in decades, before she knew better. Her low-cut black sweater with the swooping neckline showed off a very perky set of C-cup proportions, the strap of a new black bra peeking over the edge of her shoulder. Her make-up had been a labor of love. It had taken a few tries to get the combination just right: eyeliner, eye shadow, blush, and red lipstick. Too much make-up and she would look like a hooker. Too little, and it would defeat her efforts to look like anything but a conservative Muslim woman. She jettisoned her glasses for her contacts. She put a cubic zirconia on her neck and the sparkling diamond look-alike fell nicely between her breasts. Just another attention grabber to get the male population staring at her cleavage. Clairol Auburn dye #7 had flavored her hair just enough. She was no longer a Middle Eastern housewife. She was an Americanized woman of unknown ethnic background.

And she was a knockout.

Chapter 12

FBI Agent Chris Rosson was sitting in a small room with a glass wall. A new hire to the Bureau fidgeted slightly in his chair across the table.

Agent Rosson's perfectly combed gray hair told the new recruit nothing about his age. The agent's first gray had appeared at the widow's peak on the left side of his head at the age of fifteen. He plucked it out after the novelty had worn off, but another gray, joined by a battalion of identical invaders, soon took its place. In high school, his friends would pull them out in algebra class, during recess, in detention. All to no avail. By the time he was twenty, Agent Rosson had more grays than his grandfather. His Aunt Millie told him that he wasn't the first. There was a great uncle in Atlanta who was gray and dead by his mid-twenties. At fifty-two, Rosson had at least avoided the latter.

The new hire was a recent graduate of the Academy and, in the Bureau's expanding effort to match skills and interest with position, the wet-behind-the-ears bureaucrat was making the rounds and asking questions to personnel from different sections. As the new recruit fired off various inquiries from the FBI-approved hiring manual list, Agent Rosson thought about interrogations, his mind transforming the clear glass interior wall into a two-way mirror.

"What was the most interesting case you ever worked on?"

There were few things Agent Rosson did better than reminisce about the good old days in the Bank Robbery Division. "The Cowboy Bandit."

"The Cowboy Bandit?" the new hire with tightly cropped dark-blonde hair repeated.

"That's right. The Cowboy Bandit. This guy robbed dozens of banks, year after year, in full view of the camera, and we never even got close."

"He was never caught?"

"Never caught, but later identified," Agent Rosson clarified, taking a sip of coffee from the white Styrofoam cup on the table. His jacket was back in his cubicle; his shirt wrinkled, obviously the second day it had been worn since its last trip to the dry cleaners. Single, he wasn't opposed to wearing his shirts for three or four days, if the weather was right and the pits didn't get too sweaty. He had ironed his own shirts once and vowed never to do it again. Not when the Korean dry cleaners down the street was charging eighty-nine cents a pop.

"I'm not sure I follow."

"The Cowboy Bandit left a notarized letter for the good people of the Bureau in his will documents."

The young new hire, a conservative white kid in a suit that had been on a store rack the day before, looked surprised. "How many criminals inform the Bureau of their deeds after they die?"

"It happens. But this was the only time I was personally involved in a case that did."

Agent Rosson sized up the new agent. "Sure would make it easier for us to solve the crimes if everyone took that approach."

"Yes, sir. I guess it would."

"You don't have to call me 'sir.'"

"Yes, sir."

Agent Rosson shut his eyes briefly and shook his head. Then he continued. "The interesting part was that the Cowboy Bandit was actually a woman. She dressed like a man, wore a fake beard, big sunglasses, even looked like she had a chew of tobacco in her cheek, though she never spit. Not that it would have mattered. This was long before DNA testing was used for law enforcement purposes."

"No one ever theorized that she might be a woman?"

"You would have thought. But then again, she would have been the *Cowgirl* Bandit. All I know is I spent a thousand hours watching bank security films. Looked at hundreds of still shots. Saw her from the front, the side, the back. She was good. She missed her calling as a male impersonator in Vegas. Probably could have made as much money as she stole."

"How much did she get away with?"

"Forty-one banks in eleven years. I think the total take was just under $600,000."

"That comes out to about sixty grand a year."

"Give or take. All the banks were in Texas. Started in San Antonio, moved to Dallas, went back down to Austin, and then hit sporadically all over from El Paso to Houston."

"They mentioned in the Academy that half of all bank robberies go unsolved."

"True. The number was even higher in the eighties. I think the success rate peaked at a seventy four percent in 1989. Hell, there were times back in the day when I thought about robbing them myself."

"Why so high?"

"Lots of reasons. At the top of the list was the similarity between the M.O. of most bank robbers and customer behavior. The average bank robber writes, or has something written on a piece of paper, approaches the teller, and waits for the teller to process the transaction. Every customer in a bank does essentially the same thing. There is no suspicious behavior. Bank employees are told not to resist and to hand over the money. So for all intent and purposes, the transactions look normal. Banks are also typically located in high traffic areas. No one wants a bank in the middle of nowhere because a bank needs to be where the customers are. Banks are in the parking lots of shopping centers, on major roads, in the center of town. They are transient in nature. The average bank customer parks his car in the parking lot, walks in, does a transaction, and is gone in two minutes. Ditto for the average bank robber. The guys who get caught are usually the ones who go in with guns blazing."

"What about the silent alarms and dye packs. The academy says they're standard in all banks."

"The silent alarms are good, if you can get to them unnoticed. They are usually located far under the counter, or in a drawer, or under a cover, so the teller doesn't trip them accidentally. You can't have them right under the lip of the counter or too close to the teller's feet. Banks did for a while, and the cops were forever chasing false alarms from tellers with big feet and fat thighs. If a bank robber lets the teller know that he is watching for any movement towards the silent alarm, the teller usually won't hit the button until the robber is out the door."

"And the dye packs?"

"Even a bad thief can spot one pretty easily. They feel different. If you hold a stack of bills with and without a dye pack, you would be hard pressed to find anyone over the age of eight who couldn't tell the difference."

"So why did you give up on bank robbery? Why the Anti-Terrorism Task Force?"

"The Executive Director for Counterterrorism came into the room during a monthly Bank Robbery Division briefing and asked if anyone was interested in two of the FBI's newer divisions: Anti-Terrorism and Cybercrime. There was a lot of talk about refocusing the FBI towards bigger and badder criminals. Me and a couple of buddies raised our hands."

"That was it?"

"That was it. Rubbing a magic lantern and having a genie pop out wouldn't have been any faster."

"And the training?"

"We had a few classes on the structure of terrorist organizations, sources of funding, myths about religious fanatics. The simple truth is that we are in new territory. There are no rules and sure as hell no rulebook."

"What do you do, day-to-day?"

"Read the news, follow leads, most of which are dead ends, write reports. Enter data into the tracking database."

"Sounds exciting," the young man said taking a sip of water.

"There is nothing glamorous about the day-to-day operations of the Bureau. The busts are great, but there is a lot of legwork needed to get the bust. Unless you get lucky."

"How many times have you been lucky?"

"A dozen, though to be fair I should probably subtract two from my lucky count. One for each of my ex-wives."

The young man looked at the clock on the wall. "Time is up."

Agent Rosson looked at his watch, an old clunker that went through batteries like a moth in a closet of wool sweaters. "If you have any follow-up questions on the Bureau, let me know."

"Thank you, I will. I have two more sessions today and need to put in for my preference by the end of the week."

"Don't get your hopes up. There is still a good chance the Bureau will ignore your preference."

"I'll keep that in mind."

"Good luck to you," Agent Rosson said standing. He threw his empty cup towards the trash can in the corner and it bounced off the rim onto the floor.

"No, good luck to you," the new hire said as he watched the cup find the floor.

Chris Rosson, thirty-year FBI agent and three years from mandatory retirement, banged his computer mouse on his cluttered desk and tried to steer the cursor towards his email inbox.

The first email in his inbox was a notification that his request for a new computer had finally been processed. It had only been nine months since the current dinosaur on his desk had frozen for the first time, a small snafu which forced him to spend two days with a geeky kid from technical support with questionable hygiene. Per the email, Agent Rosson was now on the computer waiting list, a mere two months from new hardware. In the meantime, he practiced hard love with his six-year-old Compaq.

"Piece of shit," he said loud enough for the occupants in neighboring cubes to hear.

"The List" came via email every Monday. One hundred and eleven was the magic number for the week. One hundred and eleven calls and letters made to the CIA and passed forward to the FBI.

Every Monday morning the Director of the Joint Terrorism Task Force, the JTTF, received the email and perused it with his morning coffee. This morning was no different. Between a call to his wife and a visit to the barber in the basement, the Director sent the email to his chief bureaucrat underling who divvied the leads and sent it on. All the leads from the CIA were handled locally by members of the FBI's JTTF. The Director was adamant about the leads not going to field offices. He wanted the responsibility for that little list to remain in the building. After a career in the Federal Bureaucratic Institute, he knew it was hard to tear an agent a new ass long-distance. And if something on the list were overlooked or mishandled, there would be a long list of asses in jeopardy.

Chris Rosson was on the rotation for "The List," the only moniker for the CIA email that wasn't too offensive to utter in public. For the last four months, Rosson had averaged fifteen leads a month. Not a large number, but still enough work to be an inconvenience when added to his usual duties.

But the list was more than just leads. The FBI had thousands of leads of their own. Tens of thousands. And with the current number of Anti-Terrorist agents in flux between a hundred and a hundred and fifty, the ever-growing list of leads would always exceed manpower.

Not that the Bureau wasn't trying. It had hired hundreds of analysts since 9/11. They were packed into office buildings around the Beltway from Tysons to Clarendon to Pentagon City to Bethesda. Young men and women with no knowledge of the world but with college degrees and computer skills hired by defense contractors with innocuous names like Enteon, Pitre, MACI. Companies that produced nothing but paperwork.

These college grads worked nine-to-five prioritizing leads according to a matrix that an old man with a security clearance and no intelligence background had created in a room full of equally under qualified nodding heads. Leads were initially filtered by concrete intelligence parameters such as suspicious name, suspicious location, backgrounds related to the Middle East. For a college grad from Indiana, everyone one except Larry Bird fit the bill. On more than one occasion, usually during happy hour, Agent Rosson had publicly claimed, "If the U.S. avoids another 9/11 in my lifetime, it will be just dumb luck."

So far the luck was holding out.

Rosson clicked on the email and opened the attached Excel spreadsheet. He looked for his name and saw the four new leads he had this week. Two from New York, one from Boston, and one from Detroit. He printed out the three-page document and perused the rest of the list for kicks. All the information would have to be entered into the FBI tracking database, each with a case number and an assigned agent.

On the third page he stopped on the last entry. The street name seemingly popped out from the page. He checked the name of the agent assigned to the lead and then looked over at the stack of files in the corner tall enough for a full-grown, armed-to-the-teeth terrorist to hide in. *What the hell,* he thought. He bound from his desk and followed the maze of blue and gray fabric walls to the far side of the floor to a row of cubes with a semi-obstructed view of Pennsylvania Ave.

"Good morning, Agent Taylor," Rosson said with a smile. The middle-aged agent with wire-framed glasses looked up.

"Agent Rosson. What can I do for you?"

"I saw you on the list from the Agency."

"The shit list stops for no man."

Rosson nodded. The headache he had woken with was finally subsiding. "I wanted to know if you'd be interested in swapping a lead with me."

Agent Taylor laughed from his seat in an impeccably organized cube. Pens and pencils were lined up next to perfectly stacked legal papers. "Swapping a lead? What, do you have something in Miami?"

Agent Rosson smiled, his gray hair almost shining in the reflection from the light directly overhead. "No. I have the less desirable but still promising areas of Boston, Detroit, and New York."

"Christ, Rosson. It's winter. If one of those leads pans out I might have to head north. We are in the middle of one of the coldest seasons in memory, in case you haven't noticed." Agent Taylor knew he had a fish on the line, but he wasn't sure if he wanted to catch it or not. "Which of my leads are you interested in?"

"The one in Virginia."

"Hell, no," Taylor responded. "Hell, no. That lead is almost on my way home. Besides, the director plays by the book. He takes that list very seriously. You do the investigation for the leads assigned to you. I'm responsible for that lead and for entering it into the task force tracking system. That system generates a report that goes to the director."

"Well, actually, there is a provision that would allow me to request the lead from the director."

"The 'special knowledge' provision? Unless this lead has something to do with a terrorist robbing a bank, I doubt you would have a chance."

"I do have special knowledge that could assist with this lead."

"What's that?"

"The house on the list is on Dorchester Lane. I sort of know the neighborhood. I grew up a few blocks away."

Agent Taylor looked up at Rosson from his seat and peered intently through his glasses.

"No swapping, but if you want it that badly, I'll give it to you."

"OK."

"I'm not finished," Agent Taylor said, pushing his glasses up his nose. "If I agree, you have to get permission and fill out the paperwork for both of us. Then you have to do the data entry. And I want to be copied on any related correspondence."

"Fine," Agent Rosson said.

"Besides, it's probably nothing. Most of the leads from the Agency are good American citizens who have watched too many movies and think that the local cab driver they had that morning was planning an attack."

"Just the same, thanks."

"No, thank you."

Agent Rosson walked away dreading the exception report he would have to file just to make one phone call to Maria Hayden.

Chapter 13

The smell from an open bag of Taco Bell chalupas hung in the air around the small table in the back of the store. Boxes of hiking boots, winter hats, and gloves lined the far side of the room, inventory that had arrived in time for the latest snowfall but which the crunchy granola generation staff had yet to put in order. A set of surveillance monitors rested on a shelf above the water fountain near the hall that led to the emergency door at the back of the massive outdoor adventure store.

Rick Peterson, his long blonde hair pulled into a ponytail, looked up at the monitor that relayed an image of the retail floor near the camping equipment. Without taking his eyes off the monitor he guided his backside onto an empty metal chair. "You owe me three bucks," he said to his coworker, Bruce, a college graduate with a peach fuzz goatee and no plans for the future other than to see the world. At minimum wage it would take him a decade.

"You still owe me five from last week."

"Then I owe you two. Unless you want to pay me the three you owe me for today, and I can pay you back eight next time."

"I will take my chances with you owing me two."

"You don't trust me?"

"Should I?"

"If you want to eat," Rick said, pushing the bag of fast food towards him on the table.

"Then I guess some trust is in order."

Rick pulled out a chalupa and slid it across the worn black table.

"What do we have here?" Rick said, his ponytail draped on his shoulder.

Bruce turned his head towards the surveillance camera. "She's wearing a winter coat. You can't even see her ass."

"Oh, I can see her ass. I have x-ray vision for asses and perky tits."

"What's the wager?"

"Ten bucks says I can get her to take off her jacket. Another ten says she has an ass you would grab, and tits you wouldn't know what to do with."

Bruce took another bite of his chalupa, hot sauce squirting out onto the corner of his mouth. His eyes were fixated on the screen. "Looks like I won't need to bet you. She's taking off her jacket."

On the monitor, Ariana peeled back her winter coat. Her push-up bra settled half of the bet that wasn't made.

"Nice tits."

"Perfect."

Unaware of the surveillance camera, Ariana put her jacket in the crook of her arm and bent over to look at lanterns on the lower shelf.

"And a great ass too."

"It'll do."

"It'll do? Dude, you're not someone who can be too picky. You would do crusty Sarah in woman's shoes, and she hasn't gotten any since you were born."

"I don't like women with dust on them."

"Fifty bucks says I can get this girl's phone number."

"You can't even pay for the dollar lunch menu at Taco Bell."

"Twenty."

"Done. But I want some collateral."

"I'll show you collateral," Rick said grabbing his crotch.

He brushed crumbs from his shirt and took a long slug from the straw in his pink lemonade. He paused for a moment, gargled with the drink in his mouth, and left the back room to enter the floor of the store.

He beelined it for the camping gear, zooming past a rack of NorthFace fleeces and Gortex outerwear guaranteed to keep you warm and dry in a blizzard at thirty below zero. Ariana was standing at the end of the aisle, a small stove in her hand.

"Can I help you?" Rick asked, his eyes devouring the woman he saw as prey and a ticket to a quick twenty bucks.

"No, thanks. I'm just looking," Ariana said, glancing slightly down the aisle before turning her attention back to the display of stoves.

"Going camping?" Rick asked, unfazed.

"Maybe," Ariana answered without looking over. "And I don't need any help."

Rick heard the hint and chose to ignore it. "Well, choosing the right stove can be tricky, depending on what kind of camping you want to do. Some of these work better at a higher altitude. And of course weight has a lot to do with your decision. You don't want to carry more weight than you have to."

"I see. Thank you for your time."

"Where are you going camping? I have been hiking all over the U.S. Been to Everest base camp. Climbed Machu Pichu last spring. If you take the original Inca trail it is a real test of endurance."

Ariana moved to the next stove.

"You don't want that one. It's more expensive than the others, but the canisters hold less gas."

"Thank you."

In the back room, Bruce watched as his coworker tried desperately to make a connection with the woman on the screen. The twenty bucks would be a small subsidy for his weekend beer bill.

On the floor, Ariana had reached the point where not answering the salesman's questions could be seen as something to be remembered for.

"Which do you recommend?" Ariana asked, thawing without getting too warm. "There are so many to choose from," she added, still giving the store clerk as much of a profile view as she could.

"Where're you going?"

"I'm going camping in Havasupai, Arizona."

"I love Havasupai. The waterfalls are just awesome. Have you been?"

"No, I've never been. But I've always wanted to go to the Grand Canyon."

"Well Havasu is not really the Grand Canyon. I mean, it is better than the real Grand Canyon, but not the same Grand Canyon you see in travel brochures and in movies. Havasupai is on the west end of the Canyon. You have to hike ten miles and go through an Indian reservation. It is an oasis in the middle of the canyon really."

"I've seen pictures."

"Where are you from?" Rick asked.

Ariana didn't answer the question and smiled instead.

"I noticed a very slight accent. Maybe Pakistani. I have always been good with languages and accents. One of those gifts that I am not sure what to do with."

Ariana turned the attention back to a stand-alone gas burner. "How about this one?"

"That one is pretty good. Easy to use, easy to travel with. Replacement canisters are easy to find. It doesn't have the largest flame base, but if you are looking for something light, that's a solid choice."

Ariana ran through her mental checklist of things to buy while considering whether to break the salesman's neck in the middle of the camping supply section. With a foot sweep and directed downward momentum, she could make it look like an accident. Except for the cameras. And her need for supplies.

Rick plowed forward. "So you didn't tell me. Was I right? Are you from Pakistan?"

Are you kidding me with this guy? Ariana thought. She

hadn't had anyone comment on her accent in five years. Her fluency was native and she had studied long and hard not to have an accent. "Something like that," Ariana said.

"I knew it. We should have made a bet."

"What kind of bet?" Ariana said, now facing Rick. Her eyes twinkled with an energy that Rick felt in his Royal Robbin hiking pants.

"Dinner."

"Then I guess you would have owed me dinner."

Rick was too keyed up on testosterone to realize he was facing a thousand potential ways to die, and none of them involved whips, chains, or bed sheets.

Ariana pulled the packed Camry into the parking bay on the right next to the Piedmont delivery truck. The four men emerged from the sleeping quarters when the driver's side door shut.

"Help me unpack the car," Ariana said, holding a paper bag full of spray paint and another bag with painting supplies. She was slightly irritated and the four men noted the change in her usual cool demeanor. Maybe it was the tight skirt and sweater. A change in appearance can alter one's attitude.

"What did we get?" Karim asked.

"I bought cots to sleep on. Sleeping bags. Backpacks. Duffle bags. I bought two camping stoves, some pots to cook in, some pack-and-go plates and silverware. I have enough food in the trunk to feed five people for a month. I got identical watches for everyone. We will have to synchronize the time on the watches down to the second. I also picked up some office supplies and two space heaters."

"And in the bags? Karim asked, motioning towards Ariana's arms.

"Spray paint for my car. Time to go from beige to blue. It doesn't have to be pretty, just a different color. We also need to paint over the side of the delivery truck. White."

Abu went to the car to remove the food. Syed and Karim helped unload the backseat. James pulled the foldable cots off the floor of the backseat.

"Put the food in the corner. That will be our kitchen," Ariana directed as she walked towards the office. "It's near the bathroom and we won't have to drag our dishes across the warehouse to wash them."

As the men took trips to unload the food and equipment into the designated areas, Karim approached the office door. "Did you run into trouble? You look perturbed."

"Nothing I couldn't handle. But I need to limit my visits to the outside world. There's too much potential for trouble."

"What else do we need?"

"There are a few things that I need to have delivered, but I have to purchase them in person."

"Regulated items?"

"You'll know when they arrive."

Chapter 14

Maria Hayden moved between the dining area and kitchen, her hands never empty. She was busy answering questions and, more importantly to her, playing the role of host for her only guest. The buzz of the alarm clock at five-thirty in the morning had done nothing to quell her enthusiasm. She saw the alarm as the starter's pistol to a day in the kitchen, a race to prove her cooking prowess on an unfamiliar stomach. A mixer with rapidly drying dough remnants on its blades rested on the counter next to an old cookie jar with a cracked lid. A rolling pin covered in flour protruded from the single basin sink. A glass jar of sugar was open, its red cap pushed to the back of the stove. And if a half-dozen desserts weren't enough to keep her occupied, she had started a batch of her top secret, garlic-laden spaghetti sauce.

Maria finished sprinkling a heavy dose of confectioners sugar on a cake fresh from the pan and brushed her hands on her apron. She rounded the corner from the kitchen and filled Agent Rosson's cup with another tank of dark brew.

"Cream?"

"Yes, please," Agent Rosson answered for the third time in as many cups. He was being served, and served well, but he had already noted in his notebook the mental lapse with the repeated question about cream in his coffee.

Maria reached for the milk on the table and poured it into her guest's mug.

"Do you mind if I ask you a few more questions?" Agent Rosson asked.

"No, not at all," Maria said. "Have I mentioned how wonderful your hair is? It is so thick. Thick and fabulously white."

"No, you hadn't mentioned it Ms. Hayden. Thank you for the compliment. A full head of gray hair has few admirers."

"You look like Sean Connery."

Agent Rosson wasn't sure about the actor having either gray hair, or a full head of it, but kept the speculation to himself. He hadn't made much progress in the hour he had been sitting there. Maria Hayden was the master of redirect. Not knowing if it was intentional or not, Agent Rosson plowed forward by going back to the beginning one more time.

"When did you see the three men in question?"

"Oh, there is no question about it, I saw three men."

Agent Rosson grinned. "And when was this?"

"A few weeks ago. A weeknight. Maybe a Tuesday."

"And could you describe them?"

"I thought I did. They were Middle Eastern. Dark skin, dark eyes. One was tall."

"And you saw them through the peephole?"

"Yes, I only saw them through the peephole."

"Then what happened?"

"They knocked on the door and I watched them for a minute. Then they said something about hospitality and disappeared."

"Disappeared?"

"Vanished into the night," she answered with drama.

"I see."

"Would you like another muffin?"

"No, thank you."

"Do you have any other ethnic neighbors?"

"Sure, sure. There is a German couple up the street and a

Korean family that bought two houses next to each other on the next block. And then there is Nazim and Ariana, across the street, 203 Dorchester.

"Nazim and Ariana?"

"Yes. They live next door to Mr. Stanley. Nicest couple you have ever met."

"Are you sure it wasn't Nazim and—what did you say—Ariana? Are you sure it wasn't them at your door?"

"Positive. I said it was three people, didn't I?"

"Yes, you did." Agent Rosson paused for a bite of a scone and another sip of coffee.

"Do you mind if I use the bathroom?"

"Please. It is the first door on the right," Maria said, pointing to the opposite side of the living room.

Agent Rosson waited for his bladder to drain, something that took longer with each passing year, and shook his friend before flushing. He washed his hands and moved closer to the mirror to check the nick on his chin from an aggressive, pre-caffeine swipe of his razor earlier in the morning. As he stuck out his chin, his elbow hit the mirror, and the spring-release medicine cabinet door opened. Agent Rosson moved his left hand from the shaving injury and peaked behind the mirror into the medicine cabinet.

The entire middle shelf was lined with dark brown prescription bottles. Agent Rosson turned the first bottle on the left and read the label. Xanax. He looked around the closed bathroom and felt a twinge of guilt that he easily pushed passed. He moved his thick fingers to the next bottle and repeated the motion across the bottles on the bottom shelf, facing each prescription outward so he could read them. Xanax, Valium, Prozac, Asendine. Lithium Carbonate. Flaunxol. All of them made out to Maria Hayden.

"Someone is on serious medication," he whispered.

He slowly shut the door to the medicine cabinet and found himself staring back in the mirror. *What?* he said to himself. *It was an accident.*

And he almost believed it.

The sound of the front door opening startled him, and he looked around the bathroom as if he were a criminal trying to clean the crime scene of evidence. He heard a male voice through the closed bathroom door and took one last look around.

Clark jumped a little as Agent Rosson stepped from the bathroom. Clark looked at his mother in the kitchen and then back at Agent Rosson, not sure what to make of the situation.

"Clark, we have a lunch guest," a voice wafted from the kitchen.

"I can see that," Clark answered. He turned toward Agent Rosson and introduced himself. "Hi, I'm Clark Hayden."

Agent Rosson stepped forward. "Agent Rosson, Special Agent, FBI."

"FBI?"

"That's correct."

"Well, that's not what I expected."

Agent Rosson smiled. "Understandable."

"You know the IRS was here earlier in the week."

"I guess you're lucky."

"How's that?"

"Most people always want to know when the government is going to do something for them, put all their tax money to good use. I guess you and your mother are getting the velvet glove treatment. Home visits by two government agencies in the same week."

"I think I'd refer to it as the lubricated latex glove treatment."

Agent Rosson shrugged his shoulders almost imperceptibly. "Well, I'm here following up on a phone call from your mother regarding a threat to Homeland Security."

Clark looked at his mother who was placing cookies on a plate, and then motioned towards the dining area table. Agent Rosson nodded in response, following Clark across the rectangular room.

"Did your mother mention that she called the CIA?"

Clark looked over his shoulder and shook his head. "No she

didn't. She did mention something about strange men at the door a few weeks ago. I assume that's what we're talking about."

Agent Rosson opened his notebook. "I should preface this conversation by saying that any information divulged here is highly confidential."

"Understood."

Clark could smell the coffee in the air. He wanted his mom to stay in the kitchen and called to her, "Mom, would you mind making some tea?"

Maria Hayden wiped her hands on her apron as she stuck her head around the corner. "Is black tea, ok?"

"Sure."

Agent Rosson watched the interaction between the mother and son. "Did you see the people whom your mother called about?"

"No, I wasn't home, but I'm staying in the basement and you can't hear anything from down there anyway."

Agent Rosson wrote in his notebook. "Well, several weeks ago your mother called the CIA to report suspicious terrorist activity in the neighborhood. This information was passed onto the FBI, and I was assigned to investigate."

Clark dropped his voice and eyed the doorway to the kitchen before dropping his voice. "Sometimes it's hard to see, but my mother has diminished mental capacity. I think you may be wasting your time."

"Just the same, there are questions I need to ask."

Clark unzipped his blue ski jacket. "Fire away."

"Did you see the men your mother claims were knocking on the door?"

"Again, no."

"Have you seen anything suspicious in the neighborhood? Anything out of the ordinary?"

"One of our neighbors passed away earlier in the week."

"How did he die?"

"Heart attack, I think. He was a pretty large individual."

"When did this happen?"

"The other day. Monday maybe. Well, the ambulance

and police found him on Monday. I'm not sure when he actually passed."

"Where did the deceased live?"

"On the next street over."

"And what did you say his name was?"

"I didn't. His name was Allan Coleman. At least, that's what he was known as. I never really met him. I said 'hi' over the fence a few times and ran into him at the store once. The man loved Ho-Hos, judging by the contents of his grocery cart."

Agent Rosson scribbled.

"Have you seen any—as your mother put it—strange Middle Eastern men in the neighborhood?"

"No. We have Pakistani neighbors across the street."

"What do you know about them?"

"The husband is kind of distant. Doesn't talk much. The wife is very kind. She helps out my mother quite a bit. They have a daughter named Liana. She is two or so."

"What do you know about the husband?"

"He works in a garage or gas station as a mechanic. Somewhere in P.G. County I think. Like I said, he doesn't talk too much."

"Ever see guests at your neighbors? Relatives?"

"No, now that you mention it. I think I met the husband's brother once a few years ago. I don't remember his name."

"Nothing else that comes to mind?"

"Not really. I mean, they are a pretty typical family. They take care of their property. They don't make much noise. The wife helps out in the neighborhood. Between you and me, they are as likely terrorists as my mother is."

Agent Rosson looked at the table full of goodies and smiled. "Well, I certainly don't think your mother is associated with Al-Qaeda, unless she is their official dessert maker."

"Un-official dessert maker."

Agent Rosson laughed a little, the notch in his belt tighter than he remembered it being, even over the holidays. For twenty five years, he had taken great pleasure in telling people he had the same waist measurement that he did in college. Then he hit fifty and he had to alter his ego-line. Another hour with Maria Hayden and he would be at the tailor, getting seams expanded.

"Let me leave you my card. If you see anything suspicious, please don't hesitate to give me a call. We can never be too careful these days."

Clark reached out and took the card from Agent Rosson's hand. "I will, but trust me, my neighbors aren't terrorists."

Maria Hayden popped her head around the corner. "I can make us lunch if you would like?"

"I already ate," Clark responded.

"I'm stuffed. I couldn't eat another thing," Agent Rosson answered.

"Ok, but I insist you take a walnut muffin for the road. They are one of my specialties."

Clark nodded and Agent Rosson took the hint.

"I'm sure they are."

"I will put them in a bag for you."

Agent Rosson smiled. Just like mom.

"Do you think you will be able to find them?" Maria asked as Agent Rosson packed his notebook into a small leather briefcase and stood to put on his coat.

"Who?"

"The terrorists."

"Oh, I'm sure there is nothing to worry about, Ms. Hayden. Thank you for your time and for the food."

"Come back by anytime."

Clark watched from the window until Agent Rosson reached the government-issue black sedan parked on the street. He unlocked the door with his remote keyless entry keychain and placed the muffins on the passenger seat. He checked the number from his notes and looked at the house across the street.

Number 203. He called into the office to check his voicemail and clicked the phone shut without returning any calls. *You might as well check it out while you are here,* he thought.

Rosson knocked on the front door with authority and waited. He looked at the door, with its shiny brass knocker and eyed the small mail slot midway up the door. He flipped the slot subconsciously with his left hand and knocked again. He waited an additional minute before walking in front of the house on the uneven sidewalk until he reached the driveway. He turned left and ascended the short staircase to the side door of the kitchen.

He peered over the curtain on the lower glass pane and peeked into the home. The kitchen was clean. The dining area spotless. He had an obstructed view of the living room and a long look down the dark hallway. He knocked again though his intuition had already answered the obvious: no one was home.

Agent Rosson spent the afternoon going through files accessed through the FBI's central database, the Terrorist Screening Center (TSC). Most of his efforts were focused on Nazim, then Ariana, and when his information didn't yield anything suspicious, he turned his attention to the personal background of Maria Hayden.

After thirty minutes of reading Maria Hayden's run-ins with the law, one of which included walking down the shoulder of the beltway in her bra, Agent Rosson decided he had read enough. He opened the Ziplock bag and pulled out one of Maria Hayden's self-proclaimed specialty walnut muffins. *At least she can cook,* he thought as he put the muffin on a napkin and went to the breakroom to pull a chilled Diet Coke out of a slowly dying community refrigerator. Back at his desk, he shoved a quarter of the muffin into his mouth and chewed. As his saliva glands worked to moisten the dense bread, his taste buds came to life, emitting a silent alarm for something in his mouth that shouldn't be there. Hacking the remains of the walnut muffin onto his napkin, Rosson recognized the taste. Maria Hayden, walnut muffin expert, had put cloves of garlic into the dough. "Crazy old bird," Rosson said aloud. He slugged half of his Diet Coke without stopping and pulled up the form report for an "unreliable source" on the CIA generated lead list.

Chapter 15

Clark looked at the incoming call message on the phone and prepared to berate the solicitor with the unknown number for calling a phone on the "do not call" list.

"Hayden residence."

"Hello, Clark?"

"Speaking."

"It's Ariana."

Clark checked the number on the phone again.

"Hi Ariana. How are you?"

"Fine. Fine. I have some news. We had a family emergency and had to return home rather suddenly."

"Home, home?"

"Yes, we flew out the other day in a bit of a hurry and have been on the road for the last seventy-two hours."

"I hope it's nothing serious."

"Well, my father has been in poor health for a while. It wasn't entirely unexpected."

"I hope he pulls through."

Ariana paused, considering how far she wanted to take the lie. "Right now, it doesn't look good."

"Sorry to hear that."

"Thank you. I had a favor to ask. I was wondering if you could keep an eye on the house for a few weeks?"

"Of course. What do you need me to do?"

"Just keep an eye on the place. Water the plants. I have canceled the paper and am canceling the mail tomorrow."

"Does my mother have a key to your house?"

"No, but there is one on the side porch in the storage room. It's on the top of the doorframe on the inside of the door. At least it should be."

"I think I can find it."

"If it's easier, you can take the plants to your house. There are three of them that need water. One in the living area, one in Liana's bedroom, and one in the master bedroom."

"How often do you water them?"

"Once a week during the winter. I left the thermostat at 65, so they should be ok for now. Maybe you could water them in a few days."

"Not a problem. Anything else?"

"No, that should be all."

"Do you have a number where I can reach you?"

Ariana paused. "Not at the moment. I'll have to call you back. We're staying at my aunts. She doesn't have a phone."

"Where are you calling from? Maybe I can take down that number."

Ariana's mind raced for second before she calmed it. *Be careful, she reminded herself. Every lie has repercussions.*

"I'm calling from the hospital. One of the doctors is an old family friend."

"You want to give me that number? Just in case."

"I'll have to call you back, Clark. Someone in a white jacket needs to use the phone."

Clark stopped his premature search for paper and pen. "Ok. I'll take care of the plants and keep an eye on things."

"Thanks. I'll be in touch."

• • •

Ariana hung up the phone and threw it to Karim who was sitting in the chair on the other side of the desk.

"Destroy it," she said, expressionless.

"Do you think that was a good idea?"

"I told you I had no choice."

"You could have asked another neighbor."

"I could have, but that would have been suspicious. I've spent a lot of time with his mother." She paused, her mind drifting before coming back. "It was necessary."

"Then why do you look worried?"

"He asked for a number where I could be reached."

Karim's dark eyes flickered with a hint of danger. "What do you know about this kid?"

"He isn't a kid. He is very adult. Grew up with older parents. Spent most of his life taking care of his mother. He is very bright."

"Maybe too bright."

Ariana looked around the small office. "Don't worry about this neighbor. I have him covered."

"And if he turns into a problem?"

"Then I'll take care of it."

"Killing another neighbor is not prudent."

Ariana looked over with a quizzical glance as if to indicate Karim was being preposterous. "I'll kill them all if I have to."

Chapter 16

Clark set the table for a quiet lunch. A working lunch — working on getting the IRS off his mother's back while working on getting into the IRS auditor's pants. He hoped the dress shirt he was wearing would help on both fronts, but if he could only conquer one of two missions, he knew which one it would be. You can only go so long without getting laid. Eventually you just lower your standards until someone fits the bill, get your shag in, and then raise the bar right back where it was. If the IRS hottie blew him off, he would be dropping the bar more than a few inches.

His mother was in her bedroom, ironing clothes that she hadn't worn since her husband's death. Clark listened to her sing to herself as she ironed, the song out of tune and the words a little jumbled. But it was his mother, and her voice, bad singing and all, had a pleasant psychological effect on him.

The sound of the car door shutting made his heart skip a beat and he checked himself in the mirror on the wall on his way to the door. It was time to shine, to dust off the old Hayden charm that he and his father were famous for when the need arose.

Clark flung the door open with a smile, and a wrinkled skin IRS auditor on the other side of the storm door flashed her tobacco stained teeth. Excitement ran from Clark's face as he opened the door.

"Good afternoon Mr. Hayden. My name is Patricia Moody. I am the IRS auditor taking over the case for Auditor Prescott."

Clark didn't hear another word for the next hour until the replacement agent was safely back in her car, the cloud of tobacco stench that followed her finally removed from the living room.

The comic stepped onto the small stage to a smattering of polite applause. His face turned slightly red, the color accented by the lighting system that focused its rays towards the stage and those bold enough to step on it. A hand-me-down suit from his older brother hung loosely off the comic's shoulders, the sleeves a tad too long, the pants a little baggy in the waist. Something he could grow into. A dab of hair gel was perfectly sculpted in the front of his black wavy hair. There was no pretense in the comic; he resembled what he was—a teenager in a borrowed suit. In his left hand was a small notebook, crib notes for the crib he was in. It was his first crack at stand-up and the sparse crowd was hoping for something better than the one-man-band-without-an-instrument performance they had just suffered through. The fact that the performer was tone-deaf didn't help with the audience who was typically forgiving in nature.

Clark walked in off the sidewalk and swiped at the droplets of rain on his gray wool overcoat. He approached the cashier and ordered a hot black tea, something to take the chill off. The male cashier with the pierced eyebrow and red hair handed him his change and said, "It's open mic night in the back. Free of charge. Take a look if you like. We are booked through the first hour, but after that we still have openings."

"I don't sing or dance."

The cashier leaned forward. "Neither do most of the people coming on stage."

"Maybe next time," Clark said, grabbing his cup and a cardboard insulation sleeve with Jammin' Java printed on the front.

The young man on stage was hitting the microphone with the palm of his hand, expertly exemplifying the surefire way humans have devised to jumpstart sensitive electronic equipment.

Clark worked his way from the well lit service counter in the front of the shop to the darker back area where a few rows of folding chairs were haphazardly lined up facing the stage. The tables on the edge of the room were occupied and Clark found a seat in the back row of chairs as the young comedian in the borrowed suit moved past his introduction into his routine.

"I would like to start with a joke that is short but sweet. A man comes into the bedroom with a sheep under his arm. He wakes his wife and says, 'Honey, this is the pig I have been sleeping with.'"

"His wife opens her eyes and says 'That's not a pig.'"

"The husband quickly replies, 'I wasn't talking to you.'"

The crowd snickered. Clark laughed out loud. He looked around the room, and the light emanating from an open notebook computer illuminated a face he recognized. The comic launched into a series of infidelity jokes, and Clark approached the small table and the woman who had her nose in her notebook computer.

"I missed you today."

The young lady with the auburn hair and button nose looked up and said, "Clark Hayden."

"Auditor Prescott. Or may I call you Lisa?"

"No, you may not," she answered smiling.

"Your replacement told me you had moved on to bigger and better things."

"I got a job as an IRS special agent. Criminal investigator. I put in for the position over a year ago."

"Criminal investigator? Do you get to carry a gun with that title?"

"Government issue."

Clark stumbled. "You're kidding."

"Not at all. But I haven't been trained yet. Range practice starts next week."

"Then I guess it's safe to sit down."

"This week," Lisa said, far more friendly than she had been in his mother's house, grilling Clark and his mother over mystery money.

"Are you working?"

"Not really work. I had a few things to finish up and didn't feel like sitting at home."

"So you came to open mic night?"

"Sure, why not? I told you I love this place. But I'm guessing you remembered this and that's why you're here."

Clark blushed a little. "You left me little choice when you pulled the ol' switcharoo with Ms. Moody."

"Mrs. Moody."

"She's married? That's hard to believe."

"Be nice."

"How can you work in here?"

"It is pretty quiet, really. Despite the fact you have people reading poetry, telling jokes, playing the guitar, usually acoustic."

"There's a piano on stage."

"Who doesn't like a piano? Besides there are usually some characters in the crowd. Someone interesting to talk to."

"Do I qualify as interesting?"

"The evening is young. We'll see."

The comic on stage started on a long joke that kept Clark and Lisa at rapt attention. "A man comes home early from work and busts through the door of his condo expecting to find his wife having an affair. The man goes room-to-room looking for his wife's lover and finds nothing. He stops in the kitchen, looks out on the balcony, and sees a pair of hands holding on to the railing. Infuriated, he goes onto the balcony and smashes the fingers of the hanging man with his fists. After a few seconds, the man hanging on the rail falls ten stories and lands in some bushes. The husband looks down and sees the man has survived. Still in a rage, the husband goes into the kitchen and pushes the oversized fridge across the floor and through the balcony railing. The refrigerator falls ten stories and lands on the man in the bushes, killing him instantly.

"A few seconds later the dead man is standing before the Pearly Gates with St. Peter. There is another man in line and St. Peter is checking the list in his Godly notebook. St. Peter says, 'Well, unfortunately, we only have room in heaven for one more soul today. So what I am going to do is have both of you tell me how you died, and the one who died with the most unusual story gets in. The other guy has to wait in purgatory until tomorrow, and let me tell you, purgatory isn't that nice.'

"The two recently departed looked at St. Peter and then at each other. Each man shrugs his shoulder in agreement and St. Peter nods towards the first man.

"The man who appeared first began. 'Well this afternoon I was out on the balcony of my eleventh floor condo washing the windows of the sliding glass door. I tripped over a potted plant, lost my balance and fell over the railing. Amazingly I caught myself on the rail of the balcony below me. Being a good Christian,' the man said with a wink, 'I thanked God for saving me. The next thing I know the neighbor from the floor below me comes out onto his balcony and starts smashing my hands. I try to hold on, but eventually I fall ten stories and hit the ground. Amazingly, I live, and once again I thank the Lord for saving my life.'

"St. Peter has stopped writing in his notebook and is staring at the man in disbelief.

"'So I am lying in the bushes and I look up and I see a refrigerator coming over the balcony. The next thing I know, here I am.'

"St. Peter looks at the man in amazement. 'That is one hell of a story. I think that's going to be hard to beat.' He turns toward the second man in line and says, 'Let's hear what you got.'

"The other man clears his throat and looks at St. Peter.

'Imagine this … you're naked and hiding in a refrigerator…'"

Clark and Lisa looked at each other and she laughed first. "Interesting material for a high school kid," she said.

The sophomoric comic went on for another five minutes and walked off the stage to a standing ovation. Clark turned towards Lisa. "You interested in grabbing something to eat?"

"I have to get going."

"Where do you live?"

"Pentagon City. Arlington Ridge Road."

"If you don't mind going over the bridge, I know just the place."

Lisa thought about the offer. "No discussing your parents' case."

"Come on, you aren't working on my parents' case any longer. You're out of reasons."

"Maybe I don't like you," she said, revealing her dimples.

Clark smiled as he stood. "We both know that's not true."

Chapter 17

Clark and Lisa walked into Zed's Ethiopian restaurant in Georgetown twenty-five minutes later. Traffic was at a standstill on the bridge over Rock Creek Parkway and brake lights stretched the five blocks towards the Key Bridge.

Two groups formed a semi-circle around the unmanned podium near the entrance to the restaurant. Clark looked at the photos on the wall while everyone else waited for a waitress to appear. The prominent picture on display near the door was then Governor George W. Bush with his chimpanzee smile standing next the Ambassador of Ethiopia.

"Who is he?" Lisa asked, pointing at another picture.

"That's Sugar Ray Leonard, former boxing champ and local sport product. He grew up in Maryland somewhere." In the photo the boxer had his arms up in a defensive stance with the owner of the restaurant, the picture taken on the sidewalk just outside the glass door from where Clark was standing.

A smattering of pictures of famous politicians and TV personalities ringed the small waiting vestibule. A group picture of an unidentified sports team was on the wall near the first step of the stairway that led to the private dining room on the second floor. Clint Eastwood, Mike Tyson, Rudolph Guiliani. Zed had a following. The food was good, the atmosphere unique, and everything on the menu was under twenty bucks.

The groups in front of Clark were seated, and when the hostess returned Clark spoke, "A table for two, please."

Long fingers wrapped around a gold-colored pen and checked a table off the map of the restaurant. "This way, please," the hostess said, her dark Ethiopian features contrasting with her traditional headdress.

Clark and Lisa followed the hostess through the crowded restaurant to a table next to the window overlooking the action at the convergence of M Street and Pennsylvania Avenue.

"Your waiter will be right with you."

"No hurry. Thank you."

Moments later, the waiter appeared as promised and set two menus on the table along with a set of napkins, sans silverware.

Clark opened the two-page menu and eyed Lisa. She was wearing a button-up white sweater, the mid-region attracting the attention of Clark's eyes, if only for a moment.

"I'm glad I was able to see you again," Clark said.

Lisa looked around the restaurant. "Thank you for the invitation to dinner."

"Thank you for accepting the invitation."

"Thank you for agreeing to my ground rules. There will be no discussing the case."

"I think that is enough thanking each other for one evening." *Unless I get really lucky*, Clark thought. *Then I might throw in a prayer to boot.*

Zed's chicken and beef sampler with chicken Doro Watt, beef Kaev, and Alich came on one large plate. "Enjoy," the waiter said as he left.

"Where are the forks?"

"It's Ethiopian. We eat it with our fingers."

Lisa's eyes widened slightly, her eyebrows jumping momentarily.

"Never eaten beef with your hands before?" Clark asked.

"Why would you say that?"

"You flinched a little."

"Flinched."

"Yeah, flinched. You flinched a little when I said we eat with our fingers."

"I don't think I'm much of a flincher."

Clark let it go, and ripped a piece off of the small spongy bread that served as an eating utensil. "You have to use the bread to scoop up the food."

Lisa watched as Clark wrestled with a sauce-covered piece of chicken before popping it into his mouth. Lisa pulled up the sleeve on her white sweater and cornered a piece of beef near the edge of the plate.

After the meal, Lisa leaned back in her chair. "Taking someone to an Ethiopian restaurant on the first date is a make or break strategy."

"Why do you say that?"

"Well, you're eating with your hands, which can turn some people off right away. Then you are eating off the same plate, not exactly the most hygienic thought. Then there is the fact that not many people even know what Ethiopian food is. It conjures up images of a desert country ... eating rice and whatever.

"I figured, why waste time to see what you are made of. If you can handle this as a first date, you must be pretty adaptable."

"Adaptable? Is this what you are looking for in a woman?"

"It's right up there with cute and smart."

Lisa laughed and Clark knew things were going places. Maybe not tonight, maybe not to her place, but in his mind the launch sequence had begun. All he needed was patience, the right coordinates, and a nod from Mission Control.

The walk along the frozen C&O Canal was brief. Another small rain shower forced them into Teaism for some warmth. They worked their way to the back of the restaurant, Clark gently steering Lisa with one hand on her waist. They sat down in a dark corner on large wooden tree stumps that had been converted into chairs.

After several minutes of perusing the tea list, Lisa spoke. "So tell me, what kind of man was your father?"

"I thought we weren't discussing the case?"

"I wasn't asking for the case."

"I guess we have been working this backwards. First you find out about my parents' finances, then you meet mom, and now we are on a date. Not exactly the normal progression of things."

Lisa listened and her blues eyes sparkled under the low hanging lamp over the hand-crafted table.

"My father was a good man. He didn't always know what to do with me, but he was a good man."

"Were you trouble?"

"My father was in his fifties when I was born. He'd spent most of his adult life believing a physician who had told him that he would never have children. I came along and kind of ruined his retirement plans."

"You weren't close?"

"No, we were close. It was just different. You can't play ball in the backyard with your father when he starts pushing seventy."

"No, I guess not."

"But we learned to have a relationship in other ways. You know, the first time I understood what my father did for a living, I saw him in a different light. I was thirteen and my father proudly sat me down on the sofa in the living room in front of the TV. On the screen was a picture of the Space Shuttle orbiting the Earth with its payload doors wide open. I listened as my father explained the sequence of events and when the satellite separated from the fuel module, my dad jumped to the television and pointed, 'There. That big circular piece right there was made in our very garage.'"

"Not many people could say that."

"That's what he said. Until then I had never thought much about what my father did. I had never really understood all those hours he spent in the garage with blueprints and metal and wires. And those huge machines. For me, the garage was just a room in the house I went to when I needed a screwdriver or a hammer. But after that, I started paying attention. Satellites became a common thread of a lot of conversations."

"Satellites? Not your everyday conversation."

"My father knew everything there was to know about satellites and model airplanes. The former was his job, the latter was his hobby. Quite a combination, really, and not one that many kids are interested in. Still, those conversations about satellites kept us close through the spring and summer when the Redskins weren't playing."

"So, what do you know?" Lisa asked, moving her body forward a little as if she were going to hear a secret.

"About satellites?"

"That's the topic."

"I know more than I should. Satellites fly around on different orbital paths and at different altitudes depending on what the satellite is designed for. Equatorial satellites fly between a hundred and a thousand miles up. Stationary satellites, by comparison, are positioned over twenty thousand miles above Earth. A lot of satellites used by TV stations are in stationary orbit, just sitting up there beaming back info for a growing couch potato population. The first communication satellite in stationary orbit was used to broadcast the 1964 Olympic Games from Japan."

"I did not know that."

"A good Jeopardy question."

"I guess so."

"The Space Shuttle flies at an altitude of about two hundred miles above Earth. At that altitude the shuttle acts like a satellite, from a law-of-physics perspective. It travels around the Earth at over 17,000 mph. At that speed, the astronauts on board experience a sunrise or sunset every hour. The International Space Station also flies at an altitude of two hundred miles, which makes sense given that the Space Shuttle services the space station."

"I've seen that on TV."

Clark smiled. "Spy satellites, often referred to as spysats, and military satellites fly considerably higher, in the range between 600 to 1,200 miles."

"What kind of satellites did your father build?"

"Some were for commercial purposes. TV satellites, weather satellites, communication satellites. But the good stories were the military satellites. Satellites that could read something the size of a license plate at night from 600 miles up. Satellites that could spot underground geological phenomena. Underground nuclear tests, for example … And then there was the Divinity Satellite."

"What did that one do?"

"The Divinity Satellite was so secret that it was built in a hundred different locations and pulled together through five sub-assembly plants. The final assembly took place on a military base, under the watchful eye of B-2 bombers and a fully armed tank unit."

"So what did it do?"

"According to my father, the Divinity Satellite was built for one purpose only — to communicate with God. He said there was no other explanation."

Lisa laughed and Clark's heart melted just a little.

"Even now, I look up at the sky sometimes and think about the pieces of metal my father made which are circling the planet hundreds of miles in the air. It's hard to see satellites here in the D.C. area because there is too much light pollution, but if you get out in the country, away from the lights, you can actually see satellites zipping across the sky at night. They look like tiny, fast-moving stars."

"Fascinating."

"What else did your father make?"

"All kinds of stuff. Armor piercing plates for intelligence vehicles. Made to order suitcases to hold communications equipment."

Lisa looked curiously at Clark. "Don't take this the wrong way, but why was your father making this type of stuff in his garage?"

"Are we talking about the IRS investigation?"

"No. I'm just curious. I know, according to IRS records, your father ran a business out of his home."

"That's correct," Clark answered. "Hayden, Ltd. After he officially retired, he continued to work from his shop in the garage. He usually worked on jobs that had been subcontracted from larger companies. He knew a lot of people and they kept him busy. The defense contractor industry is a tight-knit group. Most of the big defense contractors have offices around the beltway, in Maryland, in Virginia. They reside in large nondescript buildings that cast shadows on the cars stuck in traffic on 495. My dad worked at E-Systems for years, on Route 50 near Fairfax Hospital. His company, and others, would get work for huge contracts, tens of thousands of man-hours. In order to meet the deadline for these projects, the defense contractors sub-contracted out portions of the jobs to smaller companies. In turn, these smaller companies sub-contracted out portions of their work to others. If you are good at what you do, and are a trusted individual in the community, which my father was, you could always find work. And that is how spy satellites, or portions of them, ended up being built in my garage."

"Pretty amazing."

"Don't get me wrong, my father spent his career bouncing around between big-name defense contractors in the area, which, love them or hate them, are legitimate companies. But given his line of work, and the machines he had in the garage, he was in a profession where he could take his work home with him. Though it wasn't until after he retired that he opened his own business, for supplemental income."

"I'm starting to get a picture of a man who worked very hard."

Clark nodded and looked away in reminiscence. "My dad had another good story he used to like to tell. One day, when he was still working at that place over there on Route 50, a big truck pulled up to the loading dock at the end of the day. A guy in dress pants and a nice shirt got out from behind the wheel of a truck."

"A truck driver in dress pants?"

"Exactly. So this guy walks to the back of the vehicle as

my father approached from the shop area. As the door opened my father started to scratch his head. In the back of the truck, stacked floor to ceiling, were dozens of school desks."

"School desks?"

"Wooden school desks."

"And…?"

"The well-dressed driver starts waving around a work order that he has and claims he needs immediate help. My dad starts calling upstairs to see if the order is legitimate and after a few calls, and some ass-chewing, they start unloading the desks. When they finish unloading the contents, the driver goes into the cab of the truck and pulls out a blueprint. Everyone gathers around and the man explains that he wants the wooden desks turned into rungs to be used in rope ladders."

"Why?"

"As my dad explained it, this guy was not into questions and answers. My dad, who was pretty quick to assess things, surmised that the ladders were for some covert CIA mission and that the desks were being used because they were untraceable sources of wood. So if one of these rope ladders got left behind, in whatever mission they were part of, the material couldn't be traced back to its source. Or at least, someone would have a hell of a time trying to connect a wooden rung on a rope ladder with an old school desk bought from public school surplus."

"Makes you wonder what the government is up to…"

"You work for them."

"But I'm one of the good guys."

"So was my father."

"Anything else I need to know about you?"

"I'm the control man for Virginia Tech's Robotics Team."

"The control man?"

"The driver. The guy with the remote control."

"Because your father flew model airplanes?"

"You were paying attention. My father tried to instill his love of model airplanes on me, but it didn't stick. But I had a gift for the controls."

"I wouldn't mind trying to fly a plane."

"Well, when you start flying model airplanes, you have to have a buddy system."

"What's that?"

"It's like driving school. If you go to driving school the instructor has a brake and a gas pedal on his side of the car, just in case. Well, when you are flying a remote control airplane that can cost up to a thousand dollars, generally the guy who bought or built the plane doesn't want some novice pilot crashing it on its maiden voyage. So they set up a buddy system. Two remote controls running on the same frequency. One of the remote controls has a switch that allows the controller of the experienced pilot to override the controller of the novice pilot. When I was young I used to fly occasionally and my father was always standing next to me with his own controller, ready to take over if I lost control of the airplane. My controller was this God-awful bright red color with a bright red flag on the end of the antenna announcing to the world to pay attention. It was the equivalent of driving a car with a 'student driver' sign plastered across the back of the vehicle. Standing out there on the radio control pitch with that bright red controller and matching antenna flag. It was embarrassing for a kid."

"Did you ever crash?"

"I almost crashed a few times, but my old man saved me."

"So you didn't like flying airplanes, but you like driving robots?"

"It's a lot easier to drive a robot. You are only dealing with two dimensions."

"What else do I need to know about you?"

Clark stumbled a little before continuing. "There's something else you may find either extremely interesting or extremely boring."

"How can I refuse a segue like that?"

"In high school I set the national record for memorizing Pi. I memorized Pi to the 1,679th decimal place."

"Good God. Why?"

"No reason really. I have a gift for remembering numbers."

"I would say so."

The new couple took turns sipping their tea and the waitress delivered the bill.

Clark pulled out his wallet as Lisa dug into her purse. She scribbled on the back of a "buy nine, get the tenth drink free" punch card from Jammin' Java. "Here is my home number, though I guess, according to what you say, you might not need me to write it down."

"Are you saying there is another date in our future?"

"There could be," Lisa answered coyly.

Clark looked at the card. "This is great. Either way, I get a free latte with only two more drinks at full price."

Chapter 18

Diplomatic immunity is great if you can get it. Travis Keyes had it and flaunted it. He parked his BMW in tow-away zones, had turned drinking and driving into a hobby, and had received more than one citation for taking a shortcut over the sidewalk when the traffic was at a standstill. But that was in Dhaka, where the sidewalks and roads melted together during the raining season into puddles that could swallow both a car and its occupants.

Pakistan was a little different. There were more rules that needed to be "officially" followed. The rules never changed, just the adherence to them. For Travis Keyes, Pakistan was far more advanced than Bangladesh. More advanced meant better perks. Better housing, better food, better amenities. But better perks also meant less freedom to break the rules. Sure, diplomatic immunity still gave him carte blanche to break all the rules he wanted, but more people noticed. More people complained. It wasn't good diplomacy.

The latest perk Travis had discovered was a firm-bodied office assistant in the Commercial Foreign Service Department. The dalliance had started in the embassy with a friendly glance, which escalated into an even friendlier office blowjob, and culminated with a downright personal, take-her-from-behind on the thirty-foot conference room table used to sign low-level treaties. Tonight was going to be different. Maybe something as mundane as the missionary on his own bed followed by a good night's sleep. He had two hours to decide.

Travis Keyes clicked the remote control and the BBC reporter came to life. His top-floor apartment with meager views was in the secured compound on the wealthy side of the city. Like everything else in his life, his TV was the best money could buy. Pumped in by satellite, his large screen flat panel was capable of pulling in two hundred and ninety-seven channels. Everything from the Discovery Network to Japanese game-shows where contestant ran through obstacle courses designed to temporarily incapacitate the participants at every wrong step. His TV provided a twenty-four hour a day, non-stop, crap-o-rama fest. The exceptions to the rule were his lifeline to the real world: BBC and CNN. He needed the coverage that both channels provided, live news fixes that never stopped running, never went off the air—an endless supply of real-world morphine, the one drug that most foreign service officers needed after a long day of dealing with the local population.

Travis, his smoothly combed dark hair still in perfect position, loosened his red tie and took off the jacket to his navy blue suit. He went to the kitchen and opened the refrigerator. The lone remaining Bass Ale stared at him from the sparsely populated shelf.

The expatriate life was good if you could get over the little things. The big things were part of the package—a different country, a different language, a different culture. They were the givens that expatriates knew were part of the job. There was no more sense in complaining about them than for a felon to argue about the bars on his cell.

It was the little things that made the difference. A real Sunday paper with the morning coffee. Not having to wake up at four in the morning to watch the Superbowl. The ability to get a pizza that wasn't slathered in mayonnaise, or sprinkled with fish or corn or crickets or whatever the local delicacy was.

The best way to cope was to focus on what you could get rather than what you couldn't. And Uncle Sam with his 300 million tax-paying supporters gave well. While the pizzas may have been crap, the free housing, the tax breaks, and the all expenses paid lifestyle meant that Travis Keyes would return to the U.S. with a quarter million dollars in the bank. Uncle Sugar was sweet, indeed.

Travis' butt found the sofa, and a small squeak escaped from the leather-on-leather friction between the seat and back cushions. He looked up at a news story of a wayward dolphin swimming up the mouth of the Thames and flipped through the day's short stack of mail. Travis paused at the last envelope and the wheel in his mind began to turn. He shoved his finger under the tab and ran it the length of the envelope, pulling out the bill with the subtle enthusiasm of a detective on the hunt.

He quickly scanned the list of calls. Six to his mother, one to his brother, one to his financial planner, and one to his old college roommate to place a bet on the Lions in their first playoff appearance in years. He looked at the last two calls. "I'll be damned."

He took a sip of his only surviving beer and reached for the phone on the table. He glanced at the clock on the wall and calculated the overseas time as quickly as it took him to hit the first numbers on the phone.

The phone on the other end rang and Travis Keyes waited for someone to pick up. When the message machine system answered, he paused, thought about leaving a nasty message full of implications, and hung up instead. Diplomacy was his profession.

Five minutes and half a bottle of beer later he said, "Fuck it." He called the same number back, this time leaving a detailed message with his name, number, and why he was calling. Then he called the other number on the bill.

Chapter 19

Clark opened the door to the outside storage closet at the top of the short staircase that led to the side door. Every house on the street with a side kitchen entrance had the small storage space, a convenient architectural idea that disappeared from tract housing blueprints by the time Flower Power was in full swing. Clark pushed the handle of a snow shovel to the side and put one foot inside the closet, reaching up with his right hand. He ran his fingers along the top of the inside of the doorframe and found what he was looking for near the left corner.

He fumbled with the key and a moment later he was inside his neighbor's house. The house was warm and Clark unzipped his jacket but kept it on. He announced his presence to the empty home and listened to the complete silence return his call. You can never be too polite.

Clark made his way through the kitchen and checked the gas on the stove. It was something he had learned to do at an early age, the product of growing up with a "forgetful" mother in the house. He found a red plastic watering can on the floor of the pantry in the kitchen and turned on the spigot to let the cold water run for a minute. Watching the water made Clark thirsty and he ducked his head under and took a gulp. It was an old habit, one that he had picked up from his father, a man whose hands were often too dirty, greasy, and grimy to touch the cabinets and get a glass. Clark was the only person he knew who still drank water from the tap, glass or not. People bitching about the price of gas seemed to forget that they were paying twice that amount for bottled water. Four billion people on the planet would kill for the quality of U.S. water. Except for Americans.

Clark swallowed the chilly water and put his finger in the stream from the spigot to check the temperature. He was convinced that room temperature water was better for plants, though the last biology class he had taken was in the 10th grade and he had barely passed.

He strolled through the living area and eyed a potted plant on the floor, the sunlight from the window tickling the upper leaves. Clark poured water into the plant and the dry soil effortlessly soaked up the elixir of life. He headed down the hall with the watering can in his hand, the spout dripping slightly.

Liana's room was painted pink with matching frills on the bedcover. Stuffed animals clung to one another, threatening to tumble and fall from a chair in the corner. The plant in Liana's bedroom was smaller but just as thirsty as its larger sibling in the living room.

Clark moved down the hall towards the master bedroom and cautiously pushed open the door to a room he had never seen, much less entered.

The dark wooden bed was made to perfection, its white comforter almost taut. Clark hit the lights and located the plant in the corner near the window. He walked across the hardwood floors, their beams creaking as they absorbed his weight.

Clark slowly directed the stream of water into the pot and jumped as the phone next to the bed came to life. Water spilled on the hardwood and Clark set the watering can on the floor and went into the small master bath in search of a towel. The phone rang four times before the answering machine turned on, the recorded stern voice of Nazim echoing across the room. "You have reached the Shinwari residence. We are unable to take your call at the moment. If you leave a message we will get back to you as soon as we are able." The English message was followed by a briefer one in Urdu.

Clark stood near the phone for a moment staring at the black digital message machine with its lone blinking red light. When the message machine cut-off, Clark stood in eerie silence. He turned his attention back towards the plastic watering can and finished what he came to do. As he shut the door behind him, he silenced the little devil sitting on his shoulder telling him to "go ahead, listen to the message one more time."

The devil seemed to forget that Clark didn't need to.

Karim was sitting in a leather-backed chair in the corner office of the warehouse watching the local news on a small color TV while reading a stack of newspapers that Ariana had picked up during her morning errands, which was primarily a surveillance drive around the neighborhood. She made one lap around the warehouse on foot, and then drove through the maze-like industrial park she and her four-man team now called home. She drove slowly to Georgia Avenue, the main thoroughfare of traffic, and then came back to the warehouse from a small one-way entrance near a shady neighborhood on the other side of the industrial park. She kept documents in a folder on the front seat of her car, papers that showed the company she worked for and their address in the industrial complex, in the unlikely event that she was questioned by anyone with a badge on their uniform. But the south side of Takoma on the D.C. side of the line wasn't harboring any gold mines or diamond deposits. Rabid dogs and barbed wire were the security systems of choice.

But Ariana also knew that a warehouse with secure doors and high windows, while undeniably effective at keeping the outside world out, was equally effective at keeping the inside world in. It was a basic tenant of defense, extolled in *The Art of War*, and tried and tested in a thousand skirmishes since. As many military groups learned in the jungles of Vietnam, and the family of the deceased learned in state-side funerals, the rule was clear: defend your bunker, but not so well as to cut-off your own escape route.

The door to the office was cracked when Ariana opened her laptop and punched the keys for her password. Connected to the Internet with a wireless broadband card she had stolen from a temporarily unoccupied laptop at the local coffee shop, she logged on to her Logitech Live 8i Home Security System.

Karim watched over the edge of the newspaper. When the screen opened, Karim asked. "You have a camera set-up?"

Ariana sat in blue jeans, sneakers and a black knit sweater. Her breasts were outlined nicely and Karim's eyes dipped as Ariana answered smugly. "Yes. A motion-activated system. There are three cameras. One in the basement, one in the living room, and one in my bedroom."

"Expensive system?"

"Not at all. Most of the computer peripheral companies these days have some sort of web-camera security system. A lot of them are marketed as baby-sitter cameras. People are suspicious these days. They want to know if their children are being treated right and that they aren't in Molester Day Care. There have also been a few cases of shaken-infant syndrome that have gotten a conviction based purely on evidence from a baby-sitter camera."

"Sad statement for society."

Ariana bit her tongue and chose not to rant. She had seen the best and worst of both societies in the U.S. and at home. "Anyhow, I made a few upgrades to an off-the-shelf system. The camera in the basement is imbedded in a fully functional smoke detector on the ceiling. The one in the living room is incorporated into a picture frame. The one in the bedroom is in the new clock radio on the bedside table."

"How much did the upgrades costs?"

"What do you care? I have access to money."

"As do I."

Ariana stared at Karim, measuring the comment. She answered. "I bought the three hidden camera devices at a little shop called *Spies Are Us* in Georgetown, just off Wisconsin Avenue, not far from the Soviet Embassy."

"An appropriate location for a spy paraphernalia shop."

"Quite. Makes you wonder."

"Paid cash?"

"Of course. And I looked good. Told them I was giving them as a gift for my husband. Told the store clerk that we were voyeurs, of sorts."

"I hope you're kidding."

"About which? Being a voyeur or telling the clerk that is what I wanted the camera for?"

"Either."

"I just went in, asked a few questions and walked out. I was wearing a hat, muffler, and sunglasses, and I was the most underdressed person there. That shop is not interested in what people are doing with the equipment they sell."

"The shop may not be interested in what you are doing, but there could be people who are interested in who's going into that store. Private detectives, the police."

Ariana chimed in sarcastically. "You're right. The police may even be interested in brothers who want to spy on their sisters. Office workers who want to catch employees stealing the coffee money. The college student who wants to video his roommate cheating with his girlfriend. Real national security stuff."

Karim stopped talking for a moment, sulking. "All I'm saying is that you could have used another shop. I mean, a spy paraphernalia shop down the street from the Russian Embassy?"

"I heard you the first time," Ariana said squinting as she stared at the computer screen.

"How often are you checking this?" Karim asked.

"The cameras have a wireless feed to a laptop I left in the attic which transmits through the wireless router in the house, which I left on. The cameras are all 0.5 Lux, which means they work pretty well at night and indoors. They all shoot monochrome video with autofocus." Ariana paused to see if Karim was still listening. "So, if any of the cameras in the house detect motion, it starts recording for as long as there is sustained movement in the field of sight. The camera turns off after sixty seconds of non-motion. The laptop has over 750 gig of memory, so the camera can record for eight hours, on all three camera feeds, in low res. But if someone is in the house for that long, we will have problems."

"No alarm?"

"Not exactly. If motion is detected in the house, the camera switches to record mode and the computer sends me an email. Of course, I can always log into the system and view the rooms under security at any time. But in this case, the computer is sending me a text message to one of the pre-paid cell phones I bought."

"What did the message say?"

"Possible intrusion … 10:37."

"What set it off?"

Ariana turned the computer screen a little.

Karim pulled the chair to the end of the desk. He inhaled Ariana's scent and she caught him. "Knock it off. This is business."

Karim took his second tongue-lashing of the hour, this one more playful than the last.

Ariana spoke as she watched the taped video feed on the computer. "It's my neighbor."

"The boy from across the street?"

"He's not a boy."

"The young man from across the street?"

Ariana rolled her eyes.

Both watched as Clark entered the living room with a red plastic watering can.

"He's watering the plants. Just like I asked him to."

"Let's hope that is all he's doing."

Ariana looked around the rest of the house from the view in the camera. There was some mail on the floor near the front door and Clark stooped to pick it up and put it on the table in the small foyer area.

"Nice neighbor," Karim said. "Very considerate."

Ariana watched the screen, expressionless. The view on the computer blinked once, and then re-opened with Clark entering the bedroom.

"Nothing unusual."

"No. Not yet."

The video showed Clark turning on the lights. Small mistake, Ariana thought. *I should have left the blinds fully open.* It was a minor detail, but something she committed to memory.

"He's watering the plant," Karim said, taking his turn at giving the dialogue. "Stop right there."

"We'll go back when we finish."

"Something startled him. He's going into the bathroom."

Clark came back into view of the camera.

"He is staring to his left."

"The phone," Ariana said. "The phone must have rung."

They both watched as Clark approached the phone and fumbled around the black edges of the device.

"He must be looking for the volume." *Mistake number two,* Ariana said to herself. On the screen Clark stood next to the phone with the digital voice recorder. Then he stepped away, finished watering the plant, and left the room.

"How long ago was this?"

"The security system sends out an email once triggered. It took me a couple of minutes to log on." Ariana fumbled with the mouse for a minute. In the lower right hand corner of the screen, the time and date appeared. "It happened six minutes ago."

"We need to hear what's on that message," Karim said, his dark eyes suddenly darker, more brooding.

Ariana had already pulled out a new pre-paid cell phone card and was calling her home number. She punched the code for the answering machine, clicked the speakerphone button on the top of the phone, and held her breath.

"When they finished listening to the call, she played the

message again. She grabbed a pencil and scratched a note in shorthand on the notepad on the desk.

"Fuck, fuck, fuck," Karim said before adding a few mother-tongue swear accessories that included a unnamed person's father and a goat.

Ariana sat back in her chair, and pursed her lips.

"What do we do now?"

"Right now we do nothing. He has nothing. He heard a phone call from someone in Pakistan. I'm in Pakistan, as far as he knows. The message is now deleted."

"You should have disabled the home phone."

"I couldn't. I need to be reachable. Eventually, the phone will get cut-off when no one pays the bill. But until then, people need to be able to call the house and leave messages for myself or my husband."

Karim took a deep breath. "I, too, have people who need to reach me," Karim said.

"Who?"

"Contacts."

Ariana looked at Karim with her dark eyes. "What have you done?"

Karim's head dipped slightly. "I made a call."

"When?"

"From your house in the neighborhood. The day you drove the moving truck here. The day James arrived with the truck."

"Why? Did I not make it clear that we are following my program? I am in charge. I told you to answer the phone if it rang. I did not tell you to use the phone."

"It was necessary... I was suspicious. Besides, I knew we would be leaving that location."

Ariana sighed. "I can only keep up with my own lies. I cannot keep up with yours."

"Without me, you would be nowhere."

"Is that what you think?"

"That is what I know."

"You don't know everything. You think I was sitting on

my hands playing housewife in suburbia waiting for you?"

"Weren't you?"

Ariana paused. "I have made plans of my own. You may think you know me, but that was a long time ago. A different time and a different place. I'm not the same girl you 'rescued,' as you once put it."

"It was a long time ago, but you have not changed."

"Change cannot be measured from the outside. Real change can only come from within."

"Perhaps," Karim conceded. "I still need to use a phone."

Ariana opened the desk drawer and pulled out a pre-paid Nokia. She threw it overhand across the desk and Karim snatched it out of the air. She slid a pre-paid calling card across the desk like a Vegas dealer and Karim stopped it with his shoe as it reached the edge.

"You use it here and now, in front of me."

"Suspicious?"

"I wasn't until now."

Chapter 20

The door to the sleeping quarters pushed outward into the dark warehouse floor. The shadow of the office lurked in the distance, lights off, blinds pulled. The outline of a man in sweatpants and t-shirt pulled the door shut and took three slow, but natural, strides towards the bathroom entrance. An arm reached into the small bathroom and quietly flipped the light switch. The light fixture over the sink illuminated the surroundings briefly before the closing door left only a sliver of white in the crack between the door and the cold concrete floor below.

The man waited. He could feel his heartbeat. The silence was thick and heavy, his ears searching for signs of movement. A low rumble from a passing truck teased the limit of his hearing, the vehicle in the distance, well beyond the confines of the warehouse.

He gave himself five minutes to complete the task. It was a reasonable period of time for a middle-of-the-night bowel movement. Any longer and he risked someone waking up and noticing he was gone. He would have preferred a daytime reconnoiter, but with three men keeping an eye on each other, and natural suspicion running high, the opportunity was not making its way to the surface.

Moving faster than he had before, he moved down the far wall of the warehouse. He passed the door to the sleeping quarters and could hear one of his bunkmates still snoring heavily through the door. A few paces later and his hand felt the outline of another door. The oversized steel door had an additional latch attached to the wall and secured with a padlock.

He paused, looked across the warehouse floor. The truck in the parking bay blocked his view to the office, just as he had noticed the previous day. Calming his breath, he pulled a small stiff wire from the pocket of his t-shirt. He ran his fingers across the front of the door and felt for the lock. His fingers danced over the metal. His mind went into work mode. *A shrouded padlock with dual ball locking. Most likely a five-pin cylinder.* He took another deliberate breath and inserted the wire.

Two minutes to go before the alarm clock in his head went off.

He went through the first cylinder of the lock like a Ginsu knife through a beer can on a late-night infomercial. The second and third pin fell with only the slightest adjustment. The final two pins protested briefly but succumbed to the deft touch honed by years of practice, some legal, some not. He glanced over at the warehouse floor and pulled down on the body of the lock with his free hand. Only a small click escaped into the cavernous void of the warehouse.

Moving faster, he removed the lock from the latch that kept the oversized door sealed, looping the u-shaped bar through the hole without metal touching metal.

He reached for the latch, and pulled gently. He picked the lock on the knob in less than ten seconds. He paused and turned the knob on the door on the left with the precision of a criminal dueling with a combination lock on a bank vault. He felt the tension in the knob and reversed direction slowly, releasing the knob when it reached its original position.

Something was not right.

He took the wire he had used to pick the locks and straightened it in his hand to its fullest length. He ran the stiff wire in the crack around the outside of the door, beginning on the lower right and working up and to the left. He ran it across the top of the door and then down. Halfway down the door, adjacent to the knob, his wire caught resistance. He pulled the wire from the crack and reinserted it near the floor and worked upwards. The same resistance met him just below the lock. *A security system*, he thought. *Very clever and very untrusting.*

With less than thirty seconds remaining on his internal clock, he closed the latch, replaced the lock, and pushed the U bar into its locking mechanism with an audible click. With ten seconds remaining his hand opened the bathroom door and quickly turned off the light. By the time the countdown hit zero, he was back in the sleeping quarters fluffing his pillow.

Chapter 21

Mr. Stanley had the routine of an old man. Compared to other demographics, the old-man routine varied less and, when it was forced to change, there were complaints, dentures in or not. Mr. Stanley got up every morning at six sharp wearing matching pajama tops and bottoms, usually plaid, though he had nothing against stripes. This morning his black and green plaid outfit almost matched the slippers he kept in perfect line at the end of the bed. Lining up his shoes was a habit from the military. He had learned early that searching in the dark for your boots when the air raid siren screamed was not very martial. On nights when the bombs never ceased, he had slept with his boots on.

Mr. Stanley stood with creaky knees, the shrapnel wounds to the muscles in his legs concealed by his pajama pants, and walked around the wooden bed frame to retrieve his glasses from the lone bed stand on Mrs. Stanley's side. He had given his wife, God rest her soul, that side of the bed on their wedding night. It was the first of many marital concessions. Even in passing, Mrs. Stanley kept her side of the mattress. For fifty-six years of marriage, and the five years since, that side of the bed wasn't his.

Mr. Stanley's old-man routine continued in the bathroom. With slippers on his feet and his eyeglasses on the edge of the washbasin, he splashed water on the face, followed by a two-step shuffle to the john for some standing relief. It didn't matter if he got up twice in the middle of the night or not. Three times wasn't out of the question. The wisdom that came with being in your mid-eighties was priceless. The body that came with being eighty-plus needed improving.

Finished in the bathroom, he exchanged his slippers for a pair of slip-on insulated duck shoes, and read the thermometer on the outside of the window. He grabbed his coat off the white peg in the wall and wrapped it around his body, still in his PJs. He let both sides of his jacket flap, unfastened. With a lack of fashion sense forgiven to old men, Mr. Stanley walked out the door to get the paper at the end of the driveway. The crazy old man in pajamas and army boots out to get his paper at the crack of dawn. Except that he wasn't crazy, and they weren't army boots. But who wants to be picky?

Mr. Stanley poured a morning dash of booze directly into his coffee from a half-liter bottle of the aptly known Brinley Gold Coffee Rum. "So your mother called the FBI?"

"No, she called the CIA."

"You said FBI."

"She called the CIA, but the guy who came to our house was FBI. The CIA focuses on affairs outside the borders of the United States," Clark said with conviction.

"Thanks for the update."

"I guess you already knew that."

"Son, I did intelligence before there was a CIA. I never told you about the German Bridge, did I?"

"I'm not sure."

"Well, that's a 'no.' No one ever forgets the German Bridge."

Clark sat down and ran his fingers through his wavy hair.

"I was stationed in France for eighteen months during World War II."

"This much I know. You've mentioned French women a few thousand times in the past."

"Well, as much as I love French women, there are none in this story."

"Then I definitely haven't heard it."

Mr. Stanley, still in his pajamas, raised one eyebrow. "As I was saying, I was in my early twenties, stationed in France. Paris had already been liberated, for lack of a better word, but we were driving, or following, depending on who you asked, the remains of the happy Hitler clan back to their homeland. Our unit was isolated, as was the enemy, and we were running low on supplies and holed up for a few days awaiting orders. It was the middle of summer and it was hot. We were tired and we were sure as hell the Germans were tired. Anyway, we were in the Marne River valley, a beautiful stretch of land with a fabulous river running right down the middle of it. The banks of the river were steep with erosion; the water was about fifty or sixty yards across, and maybe twenty feet deep in the middle. After a few days we get some supplies and get our orders to move out and find the German unit we were trailing. But by the time we were armed, fed, and ready to go, the Germans had disappeared. A major who I didn't particularly care for pulled me and a buddy of mine out of our cots in the wee hours of the morning and told us to get ready for a counter-intelligence operation."

"Counter-intelligence?"

"That's what he called it. I remember looking at the man and thinking how tired he appeared. Tired from lack of sleep, tired from being bombed, tired from getting shot at."

"All good reasons to be tired." Clark took a sip of his coffee, already drawn into the story which he estimated as only half-true.

"So me and this other private—Mike Fearson from Prescott, Arizona—we go off tramping into the woods at night in search of the Germans who had slipped out of the valley somehow."

"That sounds dangerous."

"You're damn right it was dangerous. We had pistols, flashlights, a couple of outdated maps, and enough food for about a day in the wilderness. But we were also young, and when you are young, well, sometimes the dangerous things don't seem that dangerous. So, anyhow, Mike and I spent a few nights wandering through this valley. We would come back to our unit during the day, but every night the major ordered us back out. We spotted a few bridges, or rather what was left of them, but nothing that would get the unit across the river. We had already sunk one truck and were working on sinking a half-track, in one of the shallowest areas we could find."

"How hard is it to find a unit of Germans in tanks trapped in a valley?"

"Well, the group we were after wasn't much bigger than ours. War attrition. Probably a patchwork unit trying to get the hell out of Dodge. At any rate, we assumed the Krauts were armed and dangerous, which means you kind of have to sneak up on them a bit."

"What happened?"

"After a couple of days, Mike and I were out around eight or nine in the evening, just as the sky was getting dark. We had probably covered five or six miles, one-way. Each day we went out, we ventured a bit farther than the day before. Anyhow, there was a little dirt road next to a narrow part of the river. Mike and I were kneeling down, taking a slug from our canteens, and we look out over the river and there is a man walking on water."

"Walking on the water?"

"You heard me correctly."

"Are you going to tell me you met Jesus?"

Mr. Stanley shook his head. "No, but we watched this guy walk back and forth. He did a little fishing, standing there, on the water, in the middle of this river."

"Mike and I approached as quietly as we could and scared the shit out of this guy who immediately went into a tirade in French."

"Could you understand him?"

"Seeing that he wasn't a sexy little femme, my French vernacular was useless. The French man scooted across the top of the water until he got to the shore, grabbed his tackle and stormed off, probably pissed because we scared the fish, though he was the one doing all the yelling."

"Mike and I walked down to the water. The river was gorgeous. The type of place you'd want to retire. The water was deep, with even deeper pools, near a large bend where the river took a left. Good fishing water. Mike walked down the edge of the steep embankment and I noticed some track marks, and they weren't from vehicles off any of Uncle Sam's production lines. Mike was about thirty yards away and he sees something that I can't. Next thing you know he jumps out over the river and lands, water up to his calves. I was about to yell, 'I'll be damned,' but Mike Fearson looked at his feet and finished my thought. He said with a smile. 'An underwater bridge. I guess we know how those Germans got out of the valley.'"

Clark looked mildly confused. "So the Germans built a bridge under the surface of the water?"

"That's right. Brilliant, actually. The next day we followed the river down, crossed over, and went after our friends. By the time we reached them, another unit from the South had taken care of the dirty work."

"What's the moral of the story?"

Mr. Stanley paused. "Not everything is as it appears."

"That's true. But how do you tell when things are indeed exactly as they appear?"

"Are we talking about your mother?"

"Yeah. What if she did actually see terrorists in the neighborhood?"

"You sound like you wish it were true."

"Maybe a little. It can't be easy having people tell you that you're crazy for thirty some years. It would be nice, in an odd way, if she were right."

"I think I'd rather have her be right about something else."

Mr. Stanley paused. "But, I don't know what she saw. It could have been Nazim, but I guess you know how I feel about him. The question is what do you think about what your mother claims to have seen? No one knows her better than you."

"I don't know. She claimed to have seen the Easter Bunny one year when I was eight."

"The Easter Bunny?"

"Yeah, the Easter Bunny. Have I neglected to tell you the Easter Bunny story?"

"I'm not sure."

"Well, that is a 'no.' No one forgets the Easter Bunny story."

"I guess I need to hear the Easter Bunny story then."

Clark started. "I was eight years old and it was early Easter morning. My mom had always taken the time to put together Easter baskets for my father and me, and she hid them somewhere in the house. Well, on this particular night, in the revelry of the evening, I assume my mother had forgotten to take her medication. A recurring holiday theme, I guess."

Mr. Stanley nodded.

"At some point during the wee hours of the morning my mother starts screaming, waking my father and me. We come rushing out of our rooms and my mother is in the living room, pointing into the coat rack, swearing that she just saw the Easter Bunny disappear into its hole behind my dad's favorite coat."

Mr. Stanley looked at Clark, who slowly smiled and then broke into a laugh.

Mr. Stanley spoke first. "So we have a story about the Easter Bunny and a story about a French guy walking on water."

"Jesus could have been French."

"Doubtful. What did the FBI guy say?"

"He said he would check into things."

"Well, see what he says."

"What do you think?"

"Probably nothing," Mr. Stanley responded.

Clark took a sip from his glass. "You think this country will ever forget 9/11?"

Mr. Stanley took another drink from his hi-octane, morning concoction. "I can sum up 9/11 pretty simply. On that morning, nineteen hijackers got on four planes, armed with ninety-eight cent box-cutters. Less than twenty dollars worth of weapons. With those twenty-dollars in box-cutters, they killed almost three thousand people and destroyed two buildings worth billions of dollars, and damaged another. And what was the reaction?" Mr. Stanley waited for a second and continued. "Don't answer. I'll tell you. The reaction was two wars and the creation of the largest department in the history of the U.S. government."

"The DHS," Clark answered.

"That's right. The Department of Homeland Security. 150,000 employees, another 150,000 contractors, and a budget of several hundred billion dollars over the last few years. Unfortunately, DHS has no chance of being effective."

"You aren't instilling me with confidence."

"Well, let me start with the problem that was never fixed. The weak link in that attack, from a pure tactical level, was the security screening process at the airport, and more specifically the personnel at the security screening. Let me ask you, how much faith do you have in a high school graduate to catch a determined, well-planned terrorist?"

"None."

"You're damn right. None."

"Maybe, but overtaking a plane and flying it into a pre-determined building is much harder now. The doors are hardened and secured. There are air marshals. The pilots will go into evasive maneuvers and anything not strapped down in the cabin is in for one hell of a ride."

"I imagine that's true. But a terrorist could still use a private plane packed with explosives or something even more sinister. A melt-your-face-off type of chemical. And if the crazies out there are still interested in taking down a plane, the next thing we are going to see is a terrorist with a bomb up his ass. He is going to make Wile E. Coyote proud."

Clark gave a nervous chuckle and Mr. Stanley continued.

"I have spent most of my life in D.C. I have a lot of friends and a lot of relatives who work for the government, both local and federal. I will tell you one thing for certain. The government is really only good at one thing: creating unnecessary work and not having the right people to do the work that matters."

"Now you're scaring me."

"You don't think it's true? I'll tell you what. Pick a government agency. Any of them. Go down to the front of that building on a work day and watch the people who go in. Look at them and give an honest assessment if you want these people to save your life. Ask yourself if you think these people are capable. I will bet my Cadillac that nine out of the ten people you see will not instill you with enough confidence to bet your lunch money, much less your life. We are talking about people who are incapable of getting out of the building if there were a fire. And then you take these people and add bureaucracy. Any American who thinks we are safer after 9/11 is in a state of delusion and denial."

"You're saying we are sitting ducks."

"Yes I am. We have borders to the north and south that you can walk across, and somehow, the government thinks that it is un-American to secure these borders with fencing. And if that is not their argument, then they say it is too expensive. Hell, we spent more on the military in Iraq in a month than it would cost to build a fence on both of our land borders. That is one month. Now that would be money well-spent. And someone needs to explain to me how Saddam Hussein and the search for invisible weapons of mass destruction had anything to do with 9/11. Sure Iraq has turned into a hornet's nest, but that was after the fact and because of what we did. We have sullied the good name of the U.S., created the most unstable country in modern times, and pissed off just about everyone in the world."

"And you think retribution is coming."

"Oh, it's coming. And there is nothing we can do to stop it."

Clark looked sullen. "That's about all the depressing thoughts I can digest for the day."

"Wait till you get older. They get more depressing."

"Well," Clark said, standing. "With that, I'm off." He made his way to the door with Mr. Stanley in his wake. The newspaper was on the table and Clark stopped and pointed. "Are you done with that?"

"Except for the crossword."

"Would you mind if I took the rest? Someone in the neighborhood keeps stealing ours from the curb on Wednesdays."

"The coupons are in the Wednesday paper."

"Then there's one cheap bastard in our neighborhood. A paper only costs fifty cents for home delivery."

"And it isn't even worth reading."

"Thanks."

"You're welcome. And listen, if you want to know what is going on in the neighborhood, there is one person who knows more than even I."

"Mel," Clark answered as he turned the knob.

Ariana got up before her soldiers. It was the sign of a good general. A superb military leader. Or so she had once read. It was also the result of a naturally small bladder and a personality that had migrated from generally untrusting to mob-informant suspicious.

She pulled the blinds on the office and slipped on her running pants and a sweatshirt. There were some things the Americans had perfected and comfortable clothes were at the top of the list. She folded her cot, and pushed it between the filing cabinet and the wall. She rolled up her sleeping bag and put it under the small table in the corner, out of the way.

The warehouse was cold and her breath lingered. She made her way to the community bathroom and the chill of the toilet seat took her breath away. Finished, she proceeded through her surveillance checklist as she had every morning since establishing her new residence with her adopted kin. She poked her head out the front door of the warehouse and admired the rusted fence ambiance of her neighborhood. She opened the unlocked double doors on the far side of the warehouse, and walked the length of the room that had been a former printing shop.

She walked to the back of the truck in the parking bay and eyed the large padlock on the roll-down door. Needlessly, she reached for the padlock and tugged firmly. From behind the truck she looked at the oversized door to the one room she had given strict orders not to enter. *Her room.* Her personal plan for martyrdom, though it would be a voyage through the tunnel of light she wouldn't take alone.

The rubber on the bottom of her running shoes kissed off the freezing concrete as she approached her room. She pulled on the lock, and it held firm in the latch. She smiled at the prospects of her plan. Her smile faded before she took another step.

At her feet was a piece of wire about eight inches long, its thickness near that of a paperclip. She reached down, bending at the knees as women do, and picked up the wire. She examined both ends in the sparing light of the warehouse and took the wire to the bathroom for closer examination. Under the 60-watt bulb over the old sink, she squinted at the scratches on one end of the wire, the abrasion riding out over an inch from the end. She turned away from the light and placed the wire against the width of the door. The end of the scratches matched the distance perfectly.

Ariana folded the wire with her hands until it was small enough to easily put into her pocket.

Rules were meant to be broken, she understood. *Just not her rules.*

Chapter 22

A gentle dawn mist hung in the air over the parking lot as the group of a dozen men in dark blue uniforms gathered around the back door of the white van. With the trepidation of a snake charmer's audience, the semi-circle of blue-collar workers stepped back as the rear door of the van flew open. One-hundred-plus pounds of salivating Rhodesian Ridgeback barking at eye level had that effect.

The handler of the dog yelled, not without the intended theatrics, "Easy, Raspberry, easy." The mention of the dog's name pushed the beast and its barking into a higher gear. Rob Crowe, Raspberry's owner, pulled mightily on the thick chain that tightened around his dog's neck. The dog's barking turned to a stifled wheeze as the chain dug into his thin fur and choked off the canine's air.

"Stand back. We're coming out."

The dozen men, with one exception, moved back another generous step. Rob Crowe, wearing a wrinkled uniform and adorned with greasy black hair, let Raspberry out the back of the van and jumped to the pavement. A few of the men, emboldened by the thick chain, taunted the dog from a distance. "Here, doggie, doggie. Cute little Raspberry."

Rob Crowe gave the dog two more feet of leash and Raspberry lunged forward. The crowd silenced.

"OK, are we ready?" Rob asked, his tattooed forearm wrapping around the leash.

Mel Edgewood, the man under the spotlight, spoke to the audience. "Let's move the dog between the two trailers so we don't have a mishap."

No one disagreed.

Mel, short and powerful, walked between the two unused eighteen wheeler trailers and strolled to the back of the makeshift alley. The dilapidated chain-link fence at the far end of the enclosure marked the edge of government property. The blacktop was wet from the morning dew and Mel wiped his boots on the side wheel of the immobilized tractor trailer.

Rob Crowe, Raspberry tugging his arm as if he understood the implications of a good show, followed Mel around the corner and stopped ten feet away. The dozen colleagues formed a semi-circle safely behind Raspberry and his handler.

Ten and twenty dollar bills quickly changed hands. Most of the money was on the canine. Terry Porter, a senior member of the group who had long since walked his last postal route, took all bets. He knew what the others didn't. The smart money was always on the champion. The young guys were rooting for a thrashing. The old guy with gray hair and a beard knew a champ when his saw one. Betting against Mel was like betting against Ali in his prime.

"Here are the rules," Mel Edgewood spoke with his back against the fence. The trailers on each side put him at the end of the alley with nowhere to run. "I go thirty seconds with Raspberry here. If the dog rips my uniform or draws blood, I lose. The only thing I am allowed to use in this challenge is this bag, and any other appendages that I was born with and feel worthy of risking."

Mel bounced the thick leather mail-carrier bag on his shoulder. "I almost forgot," he added, reaching into the leather bag. He pulled out a plastic grocery bag and held it in the air.

"A little incentive for my competition." He removed a huge slab of meat and stepped towards Raspberry. The dog went wild and Rob pulled back on the reigns as Raspberry went up on his hind legs. "Hold him, Rob," Mel said. "Hold him."

Mel stepped forward and let Raspberry get a good whiff of the bloody meat. Not wanting to tease the dog beyond showmanship, Mel walked back to his position and tossed the meat on the ground near the fence behind him. "And if the dog makes it to the steak, I lose."

"Let me know when you are ready," Rob said.

"Give me a sec to get set."

Mel's infatuation with his Postal Service leather carrier bag hadn't been love at first site. He still remembered feeling the weight of the empty bag for the first time, nearly thirty-five years ago. "It's heavy," he had responded to the supervisor who was in charge of on-the-job training during the end of the peace generation heyday.

"You're carrying the U.S. mail, son," the trainer had screamed. "That mail is the lifeblood of this country. What do you want to do, carry it in a paper sack?"

Mel's appreciation for the bag didn't come until his first on-the-job dog attack. With leather an eighth of an inch thick, the bag was multi-purpose. When used as a shield, battering ram, or football sledge, the thick bag took the fight out of most dogs. Even the big nasty ones tended to give up after a well-placed smash to the snout, which was usually followed by a backward somersault and a canine whimper. For someone who had never been athletic, Mel was a natural at "smacking the livestock," as they called it in unofficial postal vernacular.

His technique was perfect, though there were few people analyzing postal dog defense in comparison to, say, a baseball swing. But if smacking the livestock did become a sport, Mel would be the Mickey Mantle of the leather bags. He kept his technique simple. He sunk his weight on his powerful short frame, lowered his center of gravity to canine level, and tightened the bag to his arm. From there, it was a matter of physics. Over the years, Mel had tamed every roughneck dog on his beat. And it earned him his position as the guest speaker at impromptu seminars on how to treat man's best friend when they got unruly. The first time he showed his colleagues how to handle a beast, the monster had been a golden retriever who had nipped a neighbor's son when he tried to touch its dish during dinner. But as time passed and the "training seminars" continued, the dogs got bigger and meaner. He was sure a few had been rabid. Not only did the dogs get larger, but so did the ante and the payoffs. For Mel, Raspberry was merely next on the list.

The crowd got restless as Mel did a set of deep knee bends. "Come on, Mel," an overweight coworker yelled over the still-barking dog. "Raspberry needs to eat."

Mel winked at the crowd and then nodded at Rob. "Let him go anytime you're ready, Rob. Somebody start the clock when he does."

"I will count down from three," the man with the wad of cash in his hands said.

As Rob fumbled with the leash, Mel stared Raspberry in the eyes.

"Come on, Raspberry. Come and get it."

The huge dog, free from its leash, lunged forward and leapt at Mel. The career postal employee sprang forward to meet the dog, the leather bag pounding into Raspberry's sharp pearly whites. The dog spun around and landed on its paws. Raspberry snapped over his shoulder as he turned back around and Mel met the beast with a low crouch. The dog tried to bite the bag, failing to sink its teeth into the taut leather wall that Mel held tightly. Raspberry went high again, snapping inches from Mel's face. The veteran postman held his position. The dog spun and Mel countered. Raspberry nipped at Mel's boots, and Mel kicked the dog while smashing the bag into the canine with his thigh. The crowd went wild. Bets were doubled down. Raspberry was flinging saliva in all directions.

With ten seconds left, Mel encouraged his adversary. "Come on, puppy. Come and get some meat." The dog responded with another charge and Mel battered him back. As the crowd counted down, Mel gave Raspberry a lesson in postal dog law, successfully pinning the dog against the wheel of the trailer with the bag and all his strength.

"Time's up. Come get your dog, Rob." Raspberry's owner came over and attached the leash as Mel kept the beast trapped. Mel backed away with the bag between him and the dog, and Rob wrapped the chain around his arm several times.

"Go get your meat," Mel said to Raspberry, stepping to the side and pointing to the steak. The dog moved slowly past, as if he understood the fight was over and he had lost, and set his teeth into the thick piece of red meat.

Mel walked up to the gang of men and collected the hundred bucks he had put on himself. It was just the start of the day.

"Now get to work, everyone," Mel yelled as he put the cash into his pocket. "I haven't been late on deliveries in ten years and I'm not going to start today," he added with pride.

The large leather bag with the thick strap tugged on Mel's shoulder. He slammed the sliding door on the truck closed and bounced the bag once with his whole body to balance the weight. He was thankful the holiday season was over. The cards, gifts, and packages of the "season of giving" added another twenty pounds to his average load. Twenty pounds. Not a lot of weight until you humped it five miles, up stairs, down driveways, around fences. For the soon-to-retire U.S. postman with a half million miles logged on two pairs of boots a year, Christmas was the season of joy and Advil.

Ten years was a long time to do anything, twenty was an eternity, and thirty years at the Postal Service earned you a gold watch made in China and a free medical check-up from the neck up. Mel Edgewood had been dragging his heavy leather bag for forty-two years. At sixty-three, he was an old-timer. By his age most of the carriers had been put out to pasture; stuck pushing a knee-high pile of mail towards the first-stage sorting machine, sitting at a table in a windowless room trying to read addresses off shredded pieces of mail.

Not Mel.

As he told his wife, his boss, and the young waitress at the diner where he got his morning coffee—the day he couldn't walk his route was the day he would quit.

That day was approaching. Either God would take him, or his route would.

Clark met Mel at the door. "Right on time as usual."

"I don't like to be late."

"I don't think I've ever seen you late, though 'late' is relative."

"I tried to make it to the same house within a five or ten minute window. Barring any mechanical difficulties, of course."

"Of course."

Mel dug into his leather bag, put some envelopes in a folded magazine, and handed them to Clark.

"You moved back in already?"

Clark looked at his postman suspiciously.

"Where did you hear that?"

"Oh, I have ears."

Clark considered the statement and shrugged his shoulders involuntarily. "I guess you do."

"There's no guessing involved. I'm a mail carrier for the United States Postal Service. Believe it or not, we have our fingers on the pulse on American society. Do you know any other organization that touches virtually every American, every day of the week?"

"I never thought about it," Clark said, other questions churning in his mind.

"Did you know that the mail carriers for the Postal Service are credited with saving more lives every year than firefighters? We know when people are home, when they are away. We know when an elderly woman who lives alone hasn't picked up her mail. We make calls to the police, save people from burning buildings, perform CPR…"

"The eyes and ears of the neighborhood."

"Among other things. Like delivering the mail. For less than fifty cents you can have a piece of paper picked up from your house and delivered to your grandmother's house three thousand miles away. Three thousand miles for less than fifty cents. If there's a better bargain out there, tell me what it is."

Clark suppressed the urge to tell Mel that you can do the same thing, for free, via email and it takes less than a second. Instead, he took the inquisitive approach. "Can I ask you a question or two?"

"Shoot."

"What do you know about Nazim and Ariana across the street?"

"Nice couple. His last name is Shinwari and hers is Amin. You know it always struck me as kind of strange that they didn't have the same last name."

"Because they are Muslim?"

"Exactly. To the average non-Muslim, the religion seems, shall we say, a bit sexist. With all those veils and all. You would think that the man would want the woman to take his name."

"Maybe, maybe not. In Korea the women keep their maiden names and the children also adopt it. Every culture is different."

"And I'm not claiming to be a religious or cultural expert. Just telling you what I see."

"What else?"

"They get mail from overseas occasionally, usually from Pakistan. They are pretty quiet. Keep to themselves. They have one daughter, and I don't think I ever saw them with a visitor."

"That's true. I think I saw Nazim's brother once, but I am not sure."

"Some people like to keep to themselves. No crime in that. Hell, it would probably make the world a better place if a lot more people minded their own business."

"I know a few people who fall into that category."

"Everyone does."

"Out of curiosity, did they put a stop on their mail?"

Mel Edgewood raised his eyebrow a little and smiled wryly. "I can't give that information out. It could tell a potential thief that no one is home."

"Do I look like a potential thief?"

Both men smiled and Clark continued with his line of questioning. "So you never saw anything that struck you as unusual?"

"Not really. But, hey, I'm not a peeping Tom either. I guess the husband is a mechanic and occasionally they get an odd mail-order catalogue."

"Like what?"

"I'm not sure I should be telling you. Mail is sacred," Mel answered quietly, looking around as he did.

Clark wasn't sure if he was joking or not so he played it safe. "Mel, how long I have known you?"

"Fifteen years, more or less."

"You can trust me."

Mel looked at Clark who smiled back. "Well, a couple of years ago I remember thinking that maybe Nazim was into farming."

"Farming?"

"I remember delivering a few catalogues from John Deere and another one from Eggers. Big equipment catalogues. Not the kind of machines you would push around the back yard. Large-scale farming operations. I think it stood out in my mind for a couple of reasons. First off, they are Muslim and I don't see many Muslim farmers here in the US. Secondly, they live in this neighborhood and sure as hell don't have a back forty that I'm aware of. And, for whatever reason, they don't receive much advertising mail. Maybe they don't use junk-mail triggers like credit cards."

"I think we know they aren't farmers. Hell, I'm not even sure that Nazim knows how to fix cars and he's a mechanic."

"What do *you* think about him?" Mel asked.

"Real quiet. I get the impression that he's a man who doesn't like to be told what to do."

"Short-tempered?"

"Don't know exactly what it is about him. You ever been near someone who you knew just wasn't right, but couldn't put your finger on it?"

"Half of my coworkers."

"I don't know if I should laugh or not."

"Go ahead. I do." Mel straightened his winter postal hat and bounced the bag on his shoulder. "What are you looking for, Clark?"

Clark explained the visit from the FBI and the call to the CIA. Mel listened staidly.

"Not sure what to tell you, there. You could always dig around a little on your own. Hell, you could be a hero."

"I don't want to be a hero. I just don't want to be the guy standing around after the city has been leveled saying, 'I wish I would have checked those neighbors out more carefully.'"

"No, you wouldn't be very popular. But then again, snooping on your neighbors, particularly helpful ones, well that's not easy either. Leaves you feeling a little dirty. The kind of dirt that water and soap doesn't wash off. You know, after 9/11 there was an idea bouncing around the bureaucracy on the other side of the Potomac about having postal mail carriers serve as spies on the general public."

"You're kidding."

"Not at all. The plan was nixed before it made the approval rounds but the effect was essentially the same. If we see something fishy on our routes we call the police and the postal inspection service."

"Should I feel better?"

"You would if you saw me with a 120-pound Rhodesian Ridgeback."

Chapter 23

The folding cots were pushed against the outside wall of the small room, snuggled into the four corners, leaving an open clover leaf shape in the middle of the floor. The green canvas on the cots was stretched tautly over their foldable wooden frames. The fabric was faded from its original shade of olive green, the hinges slightly rusted, the wood darkened with age. The stamp on the left leg of the frame was still legible, the black ink designed to endure rain and snow and incoming mortar rounds. Syed thought the U.S. Army surplus cots were appropriately ironic. Abu did not. He had spent the afternoon scraping away the reminder that he was sleeping in an infidel's bed. When he finished carving, he swiped at the floor, pushing the splinters across the room. James Beach watched as his roommate turned over on his back.

"Hey, Abu."

"What?"

"How about keeping this place clean? There are four of us in this room."

Abu began cutting his nails with the same six-inch knife he had used to carve his cot.

"You need to worry about yourself. Abu will worry about Abu," he said without looking up.

James stood from his cot and turned up the small space heater. Syed, feet hanging off the end of his cot, snored quietly along the far wall, farthest away from the door. With his boot, James pushed the wood splinters on the floor towards the bottom of Abu's bed.

Knife in his hand, Abu watched James. "You need to be careful, American."

"You keep calling me American. I keep telling you that I am both an American and I am a Muslim. A Muslim just like you. I pray five times a day, just like you. I fast during Ramadan, just like you. I embrace Allah and his one true messenger, Mohammed, just like you. I obey the pillars: Shahadah, Salah, Zakah, Sawm, Hajj. And I am willing to die for my cause, just like you."

Abu was unmoved. "We shall see if you are willing to die or not."

"Every committed Muslim has to answer that question for himself."

"But you were born a Christian, no?"

"I was born a Christian, raised agnostic, and saved by Islam."

"Christians are weak in faith. It is our duty to show this to the world."

"Enough," Karim said, pulling the pillow off his face. "You two are driving me crazy. Abu, pick up the wood shavings on the floor."

"I don't have to listen to you."

The light from the small window high on the wall shone downward and hit Abu flush in the cheek. Karim looked at the scar on Abu's face. "Just clean it up. This is my room too."

James Beach looked up at the metal roof and the four cinderblock walls. Beyond the small single window and the light bulb over the door, there was nothing. He got a case of the chills as the confining images of the room ran through his mind like a film through a broken projector. He shook his head to clear the haunting cobwebs of his past.

Karim sat up in bed. "You feeling all right?"

"Fine, just a case of the chills. It's damp in here."

"We have a roof over our head, a heater in the corner, and people to talk to. It could be worse."

"Yes, it could be worse," James agreed. Karim looked hard at the American. There was a certain understanding that they had both been to the same place. Not the same location, but through the same trials of the soul. Karim spoke, "I'm going to wash in the bathroom, wadu for the afternoon salah. When I get back, someone else can go. Ariana says only one person out of the room at a time."

"Why do you get to go first?" Abu asked.

"Because I spoke first," Karim answered. He stood, reached into the new duffle bag under his bed, and pulled out a plain white towel. As the door shut, Abu spoke to James.

"So, what's in the truck, infidel?"

"Fuck you, Abu."

"Come on. You say we are in this together. Share with your Muslim brother."

"I was told not to say."

"By whom? Ariana? She is a Muslim woman. She is incapable of running an operation consisting of four Muslim men, even if one of them is American."

"I wouldn't be so sure."

"Ok, don't tell me what is in the truck. Tell me how many it can kill. Or do you not want to think that way, American?"

James' eyes penetrated Abu's, hatred stirring in the American's baby blues. "I'm not a scientist, I can't answer that question." James paused and ran both hands through his brown hair. His head dipped and then he continued, "I was told, if used correctly, the death toll could be over ten thousand."

Abu perked up. Syed magically sat up in his cot, his snoring cut off in mid-stream.

"Ten thousand?"

"What is it?"

"Something perfectly legal and perfectly deadly."

The conversation paused. All three men were now sitting

on their cots, their feet on the floor in the communal area in the middle of the room.

"Ten thousand. More than three 9/11s," Syed said to himself in wonderment.

The three men looked at each other and smiled sinister grins, flashes of dimples and teeth pleased with the possibility of mass death. Each relished the moment for a minute, the individualistic bickering replaced by the brotherhood of a common goal.

"So Syed, how long have you been here?" James asked.

"We're not supposed to talk about our lives."

"I told you what was in the truck."

"Technically, you didn't tell us what was in the truck," Abu chimed.

Syed thought about the question and then answered. "I have been here a few weeks. But I first came to the U.S. as a high school exchange student."

"No kidding?"

"Yes. I spent my junior year in high school in Michigan."

"And this time?"

"Different name, different identity, different purpose."

"How did you get here?"

"The long way. I flew from Karachi to Dubai and then took a flight from Dubai to Bangkok."

"Why Bangkok?"

"Because that is where I was told to go. I got picked up at the airport by a guy on a tuk-tuk, one of those motorcycle-taxi things with four seats. He drove me to Khao Sahn road, the main backpacker area of town, and we stopped in the back of a small shop where a guy took my picture. I followed my guide out the back door of the shop, through some back alleys to a small hotel a block off Khao Sahn road. I waited there for three days, staying inside most of the time, just venturing out for food in the evening. Three days later someone knocked on my door and handed me a new American passport with my photo in it and a train ticket to Malaysia."

"How much did the passport cost?" James asked.

"I don't know, I didn't pay. From Bangkok I went south to Surat Thani, changed trains, and then made my way over the border into Kota Baharu, Malaysia. The east side of Malaysia is very beautiful and very Muslim. Beautiful mosques near beautiful beaches."

"We have allies in Malaysia," Abu added.

Syed ignored him.

"From Kota Baharu I took a series of buses to southern Malaysia and caught a boat to Jakarta. Then I got on a cargo freighter."

"What kind of cargo?" the American asked.

"Everything, from what I was told. I mean, the cargo is in cargo holds, in containers, so you can't really see anything. The ship flew under a Chinese flag, and one of the shipmates told me that they were carrying counterfeit cigarettes, among other things."

"Cigarettes?"

"Fakes. The Chinese are making them by the billions and selling them around the world. Some of them right back to the U.S."

"They told you this?" Abu asked.

"It took three weeks to get from Indonesia to Guatemala. That is a long time for people to talk."

"That it is," James said. "Look at us. We have been cooped up for a few days and already we are talking."

Syed nodded and continued. "We landed in Puerto Quetzal, on the Pacific Coast of Guatemala. I put $300 cash in my passport at the immigration office, my new passport was stamped, and I walked right in. Three hundred dollars lighter, of course."

"What passport did you use to get into Malaysia and Indonesia?" Abu asked, showing he was paying attention.

"I used my real passport in Malaysia and Jakarta. They are Muslim countries. There is no suspicion."

"From Guatemala, how did you get here?"

"I took a chicken bus through the middle of Guatemala. They have these old buses that are converted U.S. public school buses. Some of them even have the school system's name still painted on the side. Mine was from Pulaski County. They were the exact same type of buses I used to ride to school when I was an exchange student, except for the chickens and the smell of piss. In Guatemala I stayed in a town called Flores for one night. Went to see the Mayan ruins and the pyramids in the jungle for the day, you know, the ones where they filmed scenes from the second Star Wars movie."

"I don't remember that part of the movie," James replied.

"Well, if you want to see it, go to Tikal. Closest town is Flores. It even has an airport. Nothing in Tikal but jungle, howler monkeys, and pyramids."

"You're an idiot. You shouldn't have stopped to sightsee," Abu grunted.

"I like Star Wars. Besides, this was the jungle. No police around for fifty miles. And I was waiting for someone to contact me."

"Let him finish," James said. "Why Guatemala?"

"It's lawless and the little law they have is completely and undeniably corrupt. And Guatemala is a well-worn path of drug smugglers. The South American drug cartels have built dozens of small landing strips in the jungle Peten region of northern Guatemala. They land their planes, unload the cocaine, and then destroy the planes right there in the jungle. It is cheaper than trying to fly them back. The cocaine is loaded onto trucks and SUVs and driven near the border. The groups break-up and cross the border on foot. Then they meet another set of vehicles on the other side of the border and the drugs travel north through Mexico to the U.S."

"Bullshit," Abu said, with a strong accent.

"I paid five thousand dollars and followed the drug smugglers through the jungle into Mexico. I spent two days in Chetumal, waiting for my next ride, and then we picked up a dozen people in Saltillo, Mexico. From there a mini-bus bus drove us near the U.S. border and let us out. We crossed the Rio Grande twelve miles west of Eagle Pass Texas about a month ago."

"You crossed the Rio Grande? Why not just use your American passport?"

"Probably could have, but why? I don't plan on leaving this country alive, so there is no reason for me to announce my arrival."

"Was it as easy to get in as they say?"

"Where I crossed the Rio Grande, the river was a foot deep. There were planks of boards balanced on cinderblocks, a bridge of sorts, but you could have just as easily driven an SUV through the water. I followed the boards and didn't even have to get my feet wet."

"No fence?" Abu asked.

"No. There were some posts where a barb-wire fence used to stand, and there were some signs on the posts announcing the U.S. border, no unauthorized entry. But we were running so fast at that point you could barely read the signs." Syed paused then continued. "I walked to the border town of Selig and stayed in a hotel for a few days. Showed them my American passport and got a room no problem. Took a Grayhound to Houston and waited."

"How about you, Abu?"

Karim walked in the door with a wet towel draped over his shoulder. Syed, Abu and James looked up with guilty faces.

"What were you discussing?" he asked.

"World travel," James said.

"Ariana warned us not to talk. It could compromise the mission. If one of us gets caught, the less we know, the safer we will all be."

"We are fine," Syed said, standing to stretch his lanky frame.

"You're fine? Let's see how fine you are after the CIA has run a car battery through your testicles. Let me see how fine you are when you have been awake for ninety-six hours, hanging by your arms, tied to a pole. Tell me how fine you are after you have spilled your guts and emptied your head and disclosed every minute detail."

"The Americans don't torture."

"No, the Americans hire other countries to torture. Do

you think your balls will know the difference between a U.S. battery and an Egyptian one?"

Syed looked down at his groin. Abu looked away. James smirked. "Good then, we all agree. Everyone keep your mouths shut about yourselves. I don't want to know anything about any of you."

Darkness fell as Ariana entered the warehouse. She walked to the dormitory, as she called the one-room hotel for her team, and stuck her head in.

The red streaks in her hair were not as noticeable as the push-up bra and her black skirt.

She knocked on the door and pushed her way in. "I have guys delivering some things, so sit tight."

"We have been sitting tight for six hours," Syed said. "Just a few more minutes."

The sound of wenches and hydraulics reverberated around the warehouse. A deep male voice with a hillbilly twang interjected with the occasional command. *Left, right, back.* The sound of heavy machinery moving heavy machinery lasted for an hour.

When the machines quieted, Ariana heard the man in the blue overalls call her with his Southern accent.

With her best ass-shake and her push-up bra pushing for all it was worth, she made her way to the open door on the eighteen-foot truck. The man with the blue overalls and a moustache that grew thick past the corners of his mouth was standing on the hydraulic lift.

Ariana smiled at him with her bright red lipstick. She flipped her hair with her hand and ran a few strands behind her ear. She leaned forward a little as the delivery guy looked down her shirt at her cleavage.

"Are you sure that is where you need these machines? They weigh a few thousand pounds a piece, so unless you have a forklift and some hydraulic lifters, you can't just push them across the floor."

"They won't need to be moved," Ariana replied as bubbly as possible.

"There is more room here in the main floor space," the man in the overalls said looking around.

"My boss was pretty clear. He wants them in the side room," Ariana said, smiling like the clueless secretary she was playing in her role for the day.

The man in the overalls smiled back, looking down at the perky set that Ariana showed with pride. "I need you to sign the papers for the machines. Security reasons. Post-9/11 regulations. Everything is falling under federal scrutiny these days. Even heavy machinery."

"I understand."

"If you have any problems, call the office at the bottom of your copy."

"Do you have a card?" Ariana asked.

"I have a generic company card," the man in the overalls answered. "But I can put my cell phone number on it, if you want."

"That would be great. You have been very helpful," Ariana said, licking her lips slightly.

"Your boss is a lucky man," the delivery worker said, his foot now on the hydraulic lift.

Luckier than you, Ariana thought. *You'll be dead by the end of the week.*

Chapter 24

The metal table in the corner of the warehouse was the only designated movable piece of community property. The sleeping quarters of the four men was communal, but the gray lines of private property were there if you looked for them. Invisible trip wires that each man knew existed and by which each man controlled their explosives. Syed and Karim got along well. Abu had only respect for himself. James, perhaps from growing up in America, had the most thorough understanding of the meaning of private property.

When Ariana called the four men to the table just after evening prayer, the cell members looked concerned. Since their arrival in cinderblock paradise, their daily routine had been the same. Up for prayer, breakfast, prayer, waiting, lunch, prayer, prayer, dinner, more waiting and more prayer. The newspaper that Ariana brought into the warehouse was passed around feverishly every morning. After she read the front page, the local news, and the obituaries, each man grabbed a section of the paper, and then swapped what they had with the first person finished reading another section. There was a single Koran on the knee-high corner table in the sleeping quarters, and when the newspaper had been visually consumed they took turns reciting their favorite passages.

But what the men had really learned to practice was fighting boredom. The truck that had delivered equipment into the warehouse was a much needed break from the monotony. It was almost as if Santa had slid down the chimney and sprinkled anti-boredom dust.

Ariana walked out of the far room where the machines were installed an hour before and shut the door behind her. She stopped in the office and picked up a medium-sized cardboard moving box that she had kept from her shopping excursion to REI.

Still dressed as a Western woman with Western morals, she walked towards the men sitting at the table. She didn't sway, she didn't swing. The professional flirtation she had exhibited with the gentleman who had delivered the machinery was now replaced with the professionalism of running a sleeper cell that was in the midst of an awakening.

"Is everyone comfortable?" she asked, still fifteen feet away. Her voice echoed off the wall. Her face was stern, in thought, but still present in the moment.

"What was delivered?" Abu asked. "Something that will help us do our jobs, I hope."

"Yes, something that will help some of us do our jobs."

"It's about time."

"Patience. Patience. We'll have one attempt to do this correctly, and if we fail, then we'll leave this world with unfinished business."

"Sitting in our rooms all day is unfinished business."

Karim interrupted Abu. "Hear her out. We're gathered for a reason."

All eyes turned back to Ariana as she looked down at the box in her hands. She placed the box on the table and caressed the back of the open chair in front of her but didn't sit down.

"I want to lay down some operational rules. Just so there is no misunderstanding. I have spoken with all of you individually. I have assessed your skills. Skills are the only thing that matter from this point forward. We will use first names, and first names only. We will not divulge any personal information to one another. It's not prudent. And could, in fact, be detrimental to our cause."

Karim nodded to indicate to the others that he knew best. James Beach flashed annoyance. Abu managed to bite his tongue.

"I'll now share the information you need to know, starting with Abu, who has shown he's eager to actually *do* something."

Heads turned towards Abu who looked as if he were going to growl.

"Abu is a bomb maker. Specializes in improvised explosive devices. Has experience in household weaponry which, for the rest of you, means making bombs out of typical household goods and cleaners."

Ariana opened the top of the box and pulled out several small plastic containers with twist-on lids. Each was about the size of a large shot glass. Different color liquids sloshed around in the containers as she set them on the table.

Abu's eyes lit up with a mix of trepidation and excitement.

Ariana paused when there were five containers on the table. "Here are five liquids. They are slightly different in color as you can see. Slightly different viscosity. All of the containers are unmarked."

Abu smiled. The three other men looked at the containers on the table as if they had front row seats at the start of a magic show.

Ariana then reached back into the box and began placing five identical containers, each filled with powder, on the table.

Abu nodded as if he knew what was coming.

"Five different powders, five different containers," Ariana added for the audience. The atmosphere was becoming giddy. Then Ariana removed a small glass jar with a twist lid. She placed the glass in the middle of the table between the line of liquid containers and the line of powders.

"Abu here has one minute to create a bomb from the ingredients on the table."

"Do I get to open the tops first? It may take a minute just to get the lids off."

"The tops are not screwed tightly."

"And if I don't make it?"

"You know the answer," Ariana said, her eyes once again in that dark, soulless realm. "Time starts now."

Abu's hands moved with speed and precision. One-by-one, he grabbed each plastic container with one hand, and twisted the top with the other. All the lids unscrewed as easily as promised.

"Forty-five seconds," Ariana said, still standing.

Abu passed each powder container under his nose, pausing slightly between the second and third. He dipped his finger into number four, and put the remnants on his finger to his tongue. He selected two from the five containers and put them to the side.

"Thirty seconds."

Abu stood from his seat and grabbed two of the liquid-filled containers, which were harder to handle than the powder. The liquid in the one in his left hand flirted with the top edge of the container. He smelled the two in his hands, and then dipped his nose to the table to smell the others without having to pick them up. He eyed the liquid with the bluish hue, and lifted the glass to his lips. "Food coloring in water," he said shaking his finger as if to condemn the offending cheat. He drank the liquid in one gulp, just for show, and reached for the glass jar on the middle of the table.

"Fifteen seconds," Ariana said. Karim slid his chair back from the table ever so slightly.

Abu took one last smell of the two powder containers he had set to the side and emptied them into the jar. He took the container with a liquid that moved with the consistency of olive oil and added it to the jar with the two powders. As the liquid hit the powders, the mixture started to fizz. Abu quickly sealed the lid. From his seat, he rolled the jar forcefully across the floor. When the jar met the edge of the wall forty feet away, Abu raised his hand and began a countdown with his fingers. When he reached one, he put his head in his hands. Everyone at the table followed suit as the jar exploded, shards of glass tinkling off the side of the parked truck some ten feet away.

"Very nice," Ariana said.

"What was that?" James asked.

"An old chemistry trick," Ariana said without elaborating. "With a few twists thrown in."

The three men looked at Abu. A short fuse with a deadly talent. A dangerous combination.

"Abu, clean up and sweep the floor when we are done."

As Ariana continued, Abu put the lids back on the remaining benign liquids and powders. "Syed here is trained in conventional weaponry. Handguns, rifles. Highly accurate to eight hundred yards with the proper equipment."

"A thousand yards, with no wind," Syed added.

"Make that a thousand yards with no wind," Ariana clarified. Ariana pulled a knife from the box and put it on the table. She nodded at Syed. Syed picked up the knife and weighed it in his hands. "What do you want me to hit?"

"The door frame to the office."

"It's twenty yards. At that distance I would use a gun."

"It is twenty three yards. Can you do it? That's the question."

"How many times do you want the knife to rotate?" Syed asked, perturbed at the test.

"Your choice," Ariana answered.

Without standing Syed pulled his lanky arm back over his shoulder and flung the knife forward. The razor sharp blade rotated four times in the air and stuck into the door frame of the office. "That should be about five feet off the ground. A neck shot to a man of average height."

"Why the neck?" James asked.

"A knife could bounce off a human skull. I would prefer to kill, not wound."

Ariana nodded and moved on. She reached back into the box and put a large padlock onto the table. "Next is James. A man of multiple talents. Son of a locksmith. An electrician by trade. A pickpocket by habit. A pugilist by nature."

James smiled at his description.

Ariana walked behind James and he stared straight ahead with his blue eyes.

She put a hand on each of his shoulders and looked down at his hair. "You have ten seconds to pick the lock."

James pulled his hands from beneath the table. Pinched between his forefinger and his thumbs was a paperclip. He unbent the clip and slipped the end of the wire into the lock. By the time Ariana reached three, the locking mechanism released and the U-bar clicked open.

"Where did you get the paperclip?" Abu asked skeptically.

"He pulled it off the lid of the box," Ariana answered.

"Very deft. And quite insightful. Nice anticipation of a problem to come."

"You gave it away when you tested Syed and Abu. I knew something was coming."

"What about him?" Abu asked, nodding towards Karim. All four men had perked up. The impromptu talent show had them rapt at attention. Severe isolation and boredom are easily tamed by the slightest stimulation, as any child without siblings and with a backyard and a magnifying glass can attest to.

Ariana pulled a piece of paper from her purse and put it on the desk in front of Karim. "Karim here is a little more cerebral. A little more creative. Consider him the Michelangelo of our group."

Ariana dropped a ball-point pen on the table next to the plain sheet of white paper. "A hundred dollar bill, please."

Karim's left hand plotted the outline of a hundred dollar bill with a near perfect rectangle. In under a minute the bill was complete with a Ben Franklin, slightly off center to the left, just as in the real bill. The room was silent as Karim sped through the five places on the bill where the denomination was written on the front. *The United States of America* came next, and then the serial number in the upper left-hand corner. The Secretary of Treasury's signature came next, a perfect forgery that even the Secretary would have had to look at twice. The Federal Reserve seal followed and then Karim went to work on the intricate outer frame of the bill. At the five minute mark,

Ariana spoke. "That's enough. I think we all get the picture."

James looked at Karim and the drawing of the bill. "That's fucking incredible. All from memory."

"I've had practice."

"No shit," James replied.

Ariana stood proudly over the table and then walked to her seat. "Are there any questions?"

James answered. "If we aren't supposed to discuss ourselves, why the show-and-tell?"

"As I said, it was necessary to know that we all bring different skills to the table. Our mission will depend on trusting one another. Trusting that each person has both the skills and the fortitude to perform under pressure. I think I have answered, or rather, I think you have answered the question as to whether the person next to you has the skills necessary for this team."

"What about the fortitude?" Abu asked.

"A very good question. Indeed, that is why we are here."

Ariana reached into the box again and pulled out a bag of small, slightly oval, asymmetrical objects with a chocolate-swirl appearance.

"We're going to play a game now. The objects you see here contain one of the deadliest poisons know to man."

James swallowed hard once. Syed started to perspire. Abu shifted in his chair. Karim quickly counted what he could see in the bag. Fifteen.

Ariana's eyes made their way around the table. "Everyone here is going to eat three. In turn, we are going to consume this whole bag. Decide among you who will choose mine and I will go first."

"I'll choose it," James said eagerly.

"Why you?" Abu retorted.

"Because I have no allegiance to her, as you have said many times."

"Let her close her eyes and choose it herself," Syed said diplomatically.

All men nodded. Syed reached for the bag and Ariana shut her eyes. Syed rotated the bag once in the air and the three other men nodded again in silent approval. Syed guided Ariana's hand to the top of the open bag. "The bag is under your hand. Take one when you are ready."

Ariana reached into the bag deliberately and grabbed the first object she touched. She put the object, with its detailed, chocolate swirl-like design in her mouth and opened her eyes. Looking around the table she swallowed without changing her facial expression.

Ariana opened her mouth to show it was empty, swishing her tongue around as the men inspected from their respective positions around the table. "The secret," she said, "is not to chew. If you don't chew, I can almost guarantee that you will live." She paused for affect. "If not, well, there are no guarantees." Then she added, "Who's next?"

Abu shrugged his shoulders. "I'll go next." He put his hand in the bag without taking his eyes off Ariana. He pulled an object from the top of the small pile that had gathered in the corner of the plastic bag, put it in his mouth, and followed with an immediate swallow. "No problem."

The atmosphere went from fear to aplomb. James was not to be outdone. Without asking, he reached for the bag, plucked one, and threw it in the air. He opened his mouth, moved his head to the left, and caught the object in the back of his throat, where it disappeared.

"Almost as smooth as opening the lock," Syed said.

"Almost," James answered with a smile.

Syed and Karim followed suit and then the rotation began again with Ariana. Two minutes later the bag was empty.

"Does that answer the faith question once and for all?" Ariana asked, her eyes focusing on Abu.

"As long as we all wake up in the morning," James replied.

Chapter 25

The street light peeking through the crack in the curtains hit Clark in the eyes. Outside the window, young Asian males raced their souped-up, high-pitched Hondas with blue neon lights past the Pentagon on Route 395. Fidgeting for the second night in a row, Clark's mind begged for sleep. Lisa was snoring lightly, her head facing away from him. Her auburn hair crept over the pillow, tickling his face, pushing sleep further away. With insomnia winning again, Clark stood from the bed. Lisa rolled over once and staked her claim to the real estate down the middle of the queen mattress. The red digital clock on the night stand displayed 2:33.

Clark looked out the window over the far end of Pentagon City Mall towards the Capitol in the distance beyond the Pentagon. The roads around the Pentagon curved and swerved wildly, the result of post-9/11 paranoia and the government's attempt to keep traffic farther from U.S. military headquarters. The fact that it was a plane that hit the Pentagon, and not a truck, was irrelevant. Clark watched as a high-octane rice-rocket zoomed by, followed by flashing lights seconds later. As the mix of lights disappeared down the onramp for the GW Parkway, Clark walked down the carpeted hall to the kitchen for water.

Glass in hand, he strolled into the small den on the far side of the living room. Folders were neatly stacked on the floor. The shadow of a floor lamp seemed to grow from the corner behind a leather club chair. Clark opened the laptop on the desk, pressed his thumb on the power button, and sat down in the proper posture-inducing Aero Chair. With the melodic Microsoft boot-up music fading into the background of another motor racing outside the apartment, Clark searched the computer's desktop for the Internet Explorer icon, his eyes running over names of unfamiliar applications that he had seen Lisa use. He fought the urge to poke around, and checked his personal Yahoo email account before mindlessly surfing the web. Ten minutes later, with his little devil sitting on his shoulder egging him on, Clark succumbed to the Satan of Snoop.

He opened several applications, clicked a few icons with his mouse, and closed them without making headway. When he hit the icon for the IRS' Master File Database Access, the screen opened with a soft red hue, and a pop up window demanded a password. Beneath the password, in bold font, was a warning: Unauthorized access to this application can result in prosecution by the Department of Treasury.

Clark opened the small drawer in the middle of the desk, as he had seen Lisa do countless times, and looked at the Post-It notes that were stuck to the cover of a green plastic folder. IRS criminal investigator Lisa Prescott, like the rest of the world, needed a lesson in security. She may have carried a gun but she left her passwords written down without a lock.

Clark read the Post-It notes and tried the first password on the list. On his third attempt, the screen turned from soft red to light green. He looked across the living room of the condo towards the darkness of the hall and considered what he had done. *Screw prosecution*, he thought. He was more worried about a serious breach of trust between him and the sleeping beauty in the bedroom he was falling in love with. He also knew there was something he needed to check. Just so he could sleep at night, if he could put the light coming through the curtains and the street racers outside out of his mind.

The Master File Database Access (MFDA) for the IRS is the largest single non-commercial database in the world and the second largest overall after Wal-Mart's inventory database. Clark was sitting on the front porch to the house of personal tax data and the door was wide open. He poked around the menus on the first page and read through the dozen search criteria from which to choose. Last Name, Social Security Number, Address, Date of Birth. He punched in his mother's address, and a list of supporting data filled the screen. He was sure Lisa had spent a few hours perusing the same screens he was now viewing for the first time. Somehow, the thought of his parents being investigated made his breach of trust feel righteous. If one looks hard enough for justification, one will find it.

He paused and listened for noise from the bedroom, but the sound of another police siren outside echoed off the walls of the den turned office. He hit the button for a new search and the computer returned to the previous screen. With trepidation and guilt overridden by the still-present devil on his shoulder, he changed the house address on the previous screen by one number.

Nazim Shinwari and Ariana Amin. Married in 1999. Property records showed that the house was also bought in 1999 with a current outstanding mortgage just north of $235,000. All tax forms were complete and filed on time. The couple had never been audited. *Of course not*, Clark thought. *The IRS is too busy auditing dead Americans.* Liana was listed as the couple's only dependent.

Clark went back to the opening page and searched by name. He ran a query for Nazim Shinwari as an individual and found a glut of information. He was a U.S. citizen, naturalized in 1992 in Detroit. His occupation as a car mechanic seemed genuine, as did the salary Clark imagined would go with the position. Born in Pakistan in 1969. Started paying taxes in 1990 in Dearborn, Michigan. No relatives listed.

Clark plugged the name Ariana Amin into the name field and left the address and other fields blank. An hour glass appeared on the screen and a few seconds later the computer listed nine different individuals with the same name throughout the U.S. All those were listed under their current addresses. His neighbor was the only one in the Washington area. Her records indicated that she hadn't paid taxes prior to her joint return with Nazim after they were married. Her social security number was issued in 1996. As Clark read the next field his eyes bugged. No known relatives. Clark's mind raced back to his conversation with Ariana.

"What are you doing up?" Lisa asked from down the hall.

Startled, Clark almost fell from the chair.

Lisa, wearing only a long t-shirt, was rubbing her eyes as she walked past the entrance to the kitchen.

Clark's face lit up in fear and he fumbled to log out of the application. "Just checking email. I couldn't sleep," he mumbled as his index finger speed-tapped the button on the mouse.

Lisa got closer and Clark realized the computer would not shut down in time. He jammed his finger on the power-off switch, and as Lisa's hand hit Clark's shoulder the computer went dark. "I'm finished."

"Good. Come back to bed. Keep me warm."

Clark's racing heart from his breach of trust episode combined forces with the sudden increase in bloodflow to his manhood, and he sprang from his chair. "Now there's an offer I can't refuse."

As Clark followed the well-shaped legs of his new girlfriend, the functioning portion of his brain was still at the computer. *Maybe my mother isn't so crazy after all.*

Chapter 26

The steady pulse of an AK-47 emptying its magazine pierced the air over the bustling swarm of people negotiating prices. In any other market a high-powered semi-automatic, even a perfect replica, would have sent patrons to the floor scurrying on their hands and knees. Children would have their ears covered, their bodies draped by protective mothers. But in the Sakhakot market, where twenty people a year are killed by raining bullets, no one even flinched as the AK-47 spent its load. The buyers and sellers knew that the risk of lethal projectiles was part of the trade.

Al-Zahim, hands tough as leather with steel-like calluses, wiped down a .357 magnum as he waited for his potential client to empty the full magazine into the air. When the gunfire stopped, Al-Zahim spoke. "I will throw in a case of ammunition for free."

"Ammunition is hardly worth carrying back home."

"What good is a gun without ammunition?"

"I can get ammunition anywhere."

"Not real ammunition with an official Russian Army stamp."

The patron, dressed in a traditional salwar kameez, ignored the statement. "How much for the gun?"

"Thirty."

"That's too much. The guy on the corner is selling two for forty," the customer said, gesturing towards a storefront in the distance.

"Maybe he would. But do you want a gun, or do you want a near-perfect piece of machinery? I have been in this shop for over thirty years. I make weapons that are precise replicas. Some say they are better than the real thing. Built by hand with identical material and then blessed by Allah." Al-Zahim, the art of the sale perfected over the decades, paused for effect. "But I think you already know this."

The customer stared down the sight of the weapon while pointing it across the crowd at a man selling grenades for a shoulder-launching RPG.

"You have a reputation," the patron responded, pointing the gun into Al-Zahim's store.

Al-Zahim gently pushed the barrel of the gun towards the ground. "No, I have a good reputation."

"How much for two?"

"Sixty."

"One for thirty and two for sixty?"

"That's correct."

"Forget it."

Al-Zahim leaned forward and pulled the assault rifle from the grip of the customer. "If you change your mind, you know where to find me. If you don't see me, I'll be in the back working."

The customer huffed once and walked to the next storefront.

"Did you lose a customer?" a voice called from the workshop in the back of the store.

"He'll be back," Al-Zahim answered. He grabbed a towel off the back of his chair and wiped the ever-present dust off his wares. More gunfire exploded from a .50 caliber machine gun and the trees on a hill on the far side of the market danced, leaves and branches falling to the Earth.

Al-Zahim pushed aside the small canvas curtain and entered the back of the store. His brother was working on another AK-47. A piece of metal that would become the gun's barrel was pinched firmly in a vise as Al-Zahim's younger brother lovingly filed the metal to perfection. The back of the store was hot. The air was stale. Al-Zahim's brother, in his fifties but no longer counting the years, sweated profusely. His shirt stuck to his back, his hair dripping with perspiration.

A young boy appeared at the back of the shop near the heated foundry where metal was forged, hammered, and re-forged. His sandaled feet shifted on the dirt path that ran behind the strip of shops. His clothes were sweaty but otherwise clean, his face serious.

"Are you Al-Zahim?" the boy asked.

"I am."

"I have a letter for you."

"Who are you?

"I was told not to say."

"How old are you?"

"Nine."

"Would you like something to drink?"

"No. I was told to give you this letter and return as quickly as I can."

The boy held out his hand. Pinched between his grubby fingers was a folded piece of paper. Al-Zahim exchanged glances with his brother and stepped forward to retrieve the note. The boy extended his hand, let go of the letter, and vanished.

Al-Zahim picked his glasses off the workbench and slipped them over his ears. He opened the letter and caressed his graying beard as his eyes darted from letter to letter, word to word. When he reached the end, he started over at the beginning. Halfway through his second pass, a tear ran down his cheek and his hands started to shake.

His brother stood from his short stool and put his hand on Al-Zahim's shoulder. "What is it, brother?"

"My daughter is going to be a martyr," he said. "Allah Akbar."

His brother read the note and smiled.

"That is wonderful news."

"Now everyone will see that my decision was the right one."

"I never doubted you."

"My wife did."

"It's too bad she did not live long enough to see your success."

"It is time to celebrate," Al-Zahim said, tears of joy still on his face. He reached into a wooden box similar to a foot locker and pulled out two grenades. He threw one to his brother and pulled the pin on the one in his left hand. They both exited the rear of the shop and lobbed the grenades into the bed of a small stream that ran twenty yards from the back of the shops. The Earth shook and mud rained down in large thick drips as the brothers embraced. Celebration, Sakhakot style.

Chapter 27

The small communal metal table with an unknown history in the corner of the warehouse was well-worn. Two of its folding legs were dented, bent in some past mishap and then straightened for further use. The matching chairs were equally abused, the thin padding torn from its moorings, the caps on the end of the legs long since missing in action.

Abu was stirring the pot for dinner. The night's menu included three ten-ounce servings of freeze-dried chicken and rice, heated on a camping stove. Each man was consuming the daily recommended allowance of calories, per Ariana's direction, supplemented with multi-vitamins. Syed, the lankiest of the group, had even managed to gain a few pounds. Like the others, his caloric intake was not offset by any exercise. Sleeping, eating, praying, and waiting were not on the back of any diet shake as prescribed ways to lose weight.

The freeze-dried food, rehydrated with water from the small sink in the group bathroom, was nutritional. With the daily vitamins, the men were as well-fed as the climbers at Everest Base Camp who were downing matching diets in temperatures near zero.

The three other men sat down at the table as Abu filled the bowls and passed them around. Ariana wedged herself into the corner between James and Karim, her back to the wall, a view of the floor.

Abu spoke for the group. "When are we going to get started with the machines that were delivered?"

"You will know soon enough," Ariana answered stoically.

"Blowing things up is easy. I only need a few items."

"You are naïve, Abu. You think I have you here to blow something up? I wouldn't need you for that."

Karim tried to keep the peace. "Abu, just shut up and eat."

"She keeps telling us about a plan, but I haven't seen anything yet."

"Look around you, Abu. Search for what you can't see on the surface. Why do you think we are living like this?"

Abu's eyes darted around the warehouse and he shrugged his shoulders.

Ariana spoke. "Have you heard the expression to 'leave a footprint'?"

"Yes," Abu answered. Syed and Karim looked around the table but said nothing.

Ariana spoke forcefully but calmly. "We are eating freeze-dried food to prevent generating trash. We are minimizing our baths to conserve water. We are using camping lanterns when possible to conserve electricity, though we will have to use quite a bit of electricity in the coming days. But by then, it should be too late."

"That's not a plan."

"It is survival," Ariana retorted, almost hissing. "We are not leaving a footprint, we are conserving our resources. We are minimizing our existence. I don't want anyone to get suspicious about a warehouse in the middle of a run-down neighborhood. This is our bastion of safety. We don't need someone becoming curious about spiking electricity, a blown transistor, lights, the garbage men wondering where the trash is coming from."

James shoved a spoonful of chicken and rice into his mouth and spoke before he swallowed. "I don't think the CIA has the interest or ability to monitor some warehouse somewhere for spikes in electricity. And I certainly don't think that the garbage men would give a few bags of trash another thought."

"Who are you to say for sure? After 9/11 there was a plan by the CIA to work with the electric companies to flag any commercial address for spikes in power usage beyond what was historically used."

"Urban myth," James said again, chewing with his mouth open and smacking his lips slightly. "I was an electrician. There are too many addresses, too many possibilities."

Abu's mind went back to the truck. "If the truck is not full of explosives, what is it? VX Gas? Chlorine? Fertilizer?" As Abu chewed his food, the scar on his cheek danced with animation.

"If I show you what's in the truck, you'll tell me what happened to your face," Ariana said.

Everyone at the table stopped eating except for Ariana who scooped a mouthful of food with her spoon.

"What does my face have to do with it?"

"I'm curious. I know you like to talk about your past," she added.

Syed, James and Abu all looked at Karim. "I didn't tell her anything about you guys having conversations," he said.

"Deal," Abu said. "I tell you what happened to my face if you tell me what's in the truck."

Ariana grabbed a packet of salt, and tore it open. She poured it into her hand like a magician, the salt disappearing into a closed fist. "Imagine something that could fit into the palm of my hand and kill a thousand people. Something with no smell and no taste. More importantly, something with no antidote. No remedy. The victim is faced not only with death, but gets to live with their impending doom without hope. That is real terror."

Karim and Syed put their spoons on the table and were riveted to Ariana.

"That's definitely worse than getting killed in an explosion," James said, joining the conversation.

Karim glanced at James who wiped his lips with a napkin. James pulled the white napkin away from his face and the paper smeared with a streak of crimson. He swiped the napkin across his lips again and Karim interrupted Ariana's speech. He pointed at James. "Your nose is bleeding."

James tipped his head back and placed the napkin against his nostrils.

Ariana continued. "So the afflicted will wait for their organs to shut down, one by one."

James Beach's shoulders started to shake and his head lurched forward. A raspy attempt at a word filled his throat. He raised his head and Abu jumped from his chair. Blood was dripping from the American's nose and mouth, oozing down his jaw line.

"Do something," Syed said, rising from his chair as well.

Ariana stood and got behind James as his body began to tremble. She wrapped on arm around his neck and lowered him to the ground.

"We need to get a doctor," Abu said. "Something's wrong with him."

"No one can help him," Ariana said, dragging James away from the table and dropping him on the cold cement floor.

Syed turned pale and he looked down at his half-eaten bowl of chicken and rice. "What have you done?"

"He could not be trusted," Ariana answered as James legs kicked haphazardly. His body went into a bone-wrenching spasm and then relaxed. Blood trickled from his nose onto the floor. Ariana asked for another napkin and then wiped the blood from the limp man's face.

"Is he dead?" Syed asked.

"He will be," Ariana said calmly. "But not just yet," she added with a smile. She placed James' head on the concrete floor, and found her seat at the table. Karim looked over at Ariana expressionless. Ariana looked up at Abu and Syed who were still out of their seats, frozen in place, staring down at their fallen brother-in-arms.

She picked up her spoon and motioned towards the two standing men.

"Sit down. Eat. You're going to need your strength."

Chapter 28

With few exceptions—spies, informants, and undercover agents topping the short list—nothing is more suspicious than someone guilty trying to act inconspicuously. Clark's knowledge of covert operations was limited to information gleaned from a trip to the spy museum, a few Ian Fleming novels, and watching the Jason Bourne movies. His choice of a bright orange Virginia Tech sweatshirt with a hood that dangled out the back of his blue winter coat was not going to go unnoticed by anyone with even marginal vision.

His fingers found his neighbor's key more easily on his second visit to the storage closet near the side door, and the key slipped into the lock like an old patron slips into his neighborhood bar.

The air inside the house was cooler than on his last visit and he immediately noticed the lack of heat. Compared to the balmy temperatures his mother kept at Chez Hayden across the street, Ariana's was frigid.

He started his mission in the kitchen with the small cabinets near the pantry. The top drawer was the junk drawer and it burgeoned with the usual collection of crap: scissors, unused postage stamps, a stash of colored rubber bands. Clark shut the junk drawer and looked at the front of the refrigerator. A monthly calendar for January, printed on a plain piece of office paper, was attached to the refrigerator door with a translucent suction cup. The calendar was blank. Not a notation on any day. January was void of a single doctor's appointment, birthday, or anniversary. Quite an achievement, Clark thought. The blue and white magnet on the left side of the door caught Clark's attention. He removed the magnet, read its message, and slipped it into the pocket of his jeans.

The small filing cabinet in the corner of the dining area was locked and Clark faced his first real decision. *How far are you willing to go?* He bent over at the waist and examined the lock eye-to-eye, the hood on his sweatshirt flopping down as his head dipped past horizontal. He rattled the handle on the top drawer and then ran his hands along the back of the filing cabinet. His fingers located two nails where the pressboard back of the cabinet met the hardwood edge of the frame. *I could just pop the back off,* Clark thought. *Pop the back off, take a peak at some papers, and put it right back on. No one would ever know. The lock would remain locked and maybe, just maybe, I could get some sleep.*

Clark picked up the stack of mail on the floor near the foyer. The mail slot in the front door was still slightly open, the metal hinge pinching the corner of a Capitol One credit card offer. Clark felt a small stream of air coming through the mail slot and wondered about his botanical friends in the living room and down the hall. He would check on them, and the thermostat, just as soon as he was finished with a more important task.

Clark put the inner dialogue he was having about the filing cabinet on the back burner and headed down the hall. He passed the open door to Liana's room and stepped into Ariana and Nazim's bedroom. He paused briefly to look at the two photos on the dresser, one a leather framed photograph of Nazim in a tux. The second photo was Nazim holding his toddler daughter. The husband looked relaxed, happy. Clark's eyes darted around the room and his mind registered the lack of Ariana photographs.

Whatever guilt Clark had about snooping around his neighbor's house ballooned when he opened the top dresser drawer and a silk pair of pink panties stared up at him. When you cross the line, you cross the line, and sometimes once the line is crossed it's just easier to plow forward than it is to step back.

Clark put his hand on the panties and pushed them to the side. He dug around through the underwear and assortment of socks like a squirrel looking for a nut he buried in October but couldn't remember where when the hunger struck in February.

The second drawer was t-shirts and jeans and the bottom drawer was a collection of dark dress socks and boxer shorts that seemed too small for a full-grown male to wear. *God, Nazim was skinny*, Clark thought.

The search through undergarments turned up nothing useful other than insight into Ariana's color and fabric preferences. Clark wasn't sure what he was looking for, but the locked filing cabinet in the living room was beckoning.

He had been in his neighbor's basement once, when Nazim had taken him downstairs to show him his recently purchased thirteen-drawer standing tool chest, replete with a 540-piece mechanics toolset.

Clark clicked on the light in the small shop near the bottom of the stairs. He pulled the top drawer to the tool chest and shuffled through a set of metric wrenches before moving to the second drawer. The tools seemed untouched, the stainless steel gleaming in the light from above. For a mechanic who had dropped three thousand dollars on a righteous toolset with a matching cabinet, everything looked suspiciously unused.

Clark rifled through the drawers, moving from one to another in search of the most basic tool in the collection. As Clark grabbed the flat head screwdriver with the red and white handle from the third drawer, the force of the explosion from the far end of the basement sent him chest first into the standing tool chest, his head hitting a shelf above. He staggered back from the initial impact, falling to one knee. He tried to take a breath and gasped. Blood trickled from a cut above his eyebrow, blocking the vision in his left eye. Clark shook his head as smoke filled the basement. In the clearing fog, his mind issued its first all-points bulletin. *Explosion. Smoke. Fire. Shit.*

Clark found his balance as he stood and felt his way around the corner to the edge of the staircase. The Smokey the Bear training he had received in elementary school had concluded with rule number five: *Stop, Drop, and Roll.* The rule for an explosion in the basement was obvious. *Get the hell out.*

As the first stage of panic set in, Clark felt his way around the corner to the stairs. Blood in one eye, smoke in the other, he pulled his cell phone and his thumb punched 911. He reached the kitchen, opened the door to the pantry and took a frantic glance around for a fire extinguisher. The smoke billowing from the basement intensified and Clark felt the heat from the growing flames on the floor below.

Through the vision in one eye, Clark moved to the side door on the kitchen he had entered through. He turned the knob and pulled. It didn't budge. He turned the lock, twisted the dead bolt and tried again. Nothing. He sent his elbow through the small window, reached down for the knob from the outside and cursed as his twisting fingers again met resistance.

His heart pounding, Clark peeled off his outer coat and held it to his face. The smoke turned a thicker black and Clark took three large strides for the dining area. He knocked over Liana's high chair, pushed Ariana and Nazim's dining room table towards the chest high window on the back of the house, and climbed onto the artificial wood veneer of the table. His first kick broke the window. The second kick sent the window frame and the screen to the ground eight feet below. Clark crouched on the table, his head touching the plastic chandelier, and moved to edge of the window frame, one foot on the table, one foot towards safety. A second explosion sent Clark through the window opening in the direction of Coleman's Castle.

Chapter 29

The first fire truck arrived as the plastic from the siding burned black, adding to the thicker, whiter smoke that poured from the seams of the house. A hole in the middle of the roof danced with larger flames, the massive gap giving the impression that a volcano in the living room had blown its top. Flames licked the vinyl siding near the blown out windows of the main floor.

Clark stood on the curb, his aching body wrapped in his coat, stained with blood from the cut above his eye. He nodded as the last team of firemen dismounted from their vehicle in full fire-brigade gear.

Still dazed, ears ringing, Clark crunched across the frozen yard, past the ambulance and towards the nearest firefighter. He tapped the man firmly on the shoulder with an open hand. The fire-resistant jacket felt heavy and rough to the touch. The firefighter turned, identified Clark as a neighbor, and yelled "Get back."

The voice was firm. Professional. Female.

Clark nodded to show that he had heard the command, and then leaned forward and yelled. "I just want you to know that no one is in the house. They are out of the country."

The firewoman looked Clark up and down, nodded and

pointed to a patch of grass in Clark's neighbor's yard. "Over there," she said before going in search of the onsite commander.

Hoses were unfurled from the truck, and the clapper valve on the hydrant on the far side of the street was removed. Within a minute, water was surging through the hose, disappearing into steam as it went through the hole where the intact roof had been. Clark watched with guilt as a three-man unit axed through the side door of Nazim's and Ariana's. The shingles over the side porch curled from the heat. Looking at the flames leaping from the hole in the roof, Clark's eyes then moved next door. One adventurous flame to a single tree and the fire would be within spitting distant of his favorite neighbor's house.

Moving behind the impromptu fire-line established by the female firefighter, Clark made his way the thirty yards to Mr. Stanley's house and then jumped up the stairs to his neighbor's front porch.

Mr. Stanley answered on the first knock, completely dressed.

"There's a fire next door."

Mr. Stanley looked at Clark admiring the slightly singed side of his coat, the blood, and the dull shocked expression on his face. "Were you helping put it out?"

When the fire was extinguished there were two additional holes in the roof and 20,000 gallons of water in the basement. The crowd around the house, behind the fire scene tape, had grown to over 50. Over the din of activity, Clark spent the next ten minutes talking to the fire chief in his official red-colored Suburban.

"The neighbors are out of town?" the fire chief asked for the third time.

"Yes. They are in Pakistan. The wife asked me to water her plants and keep my eye on things."

"And you were in the house when you heard an explosion."

"I was in the basement when the first explosion hit." Clark gestured to the cut over his eye. "I hit my head on a shelf.

By the time I made it upstairs to call 911, the fire was out of control. I tried to get out the door, couldn't get it unlocked and was on my way out the back window when the second, larger explosion hit and helped me on my way."

"Were you smoking?"

"No, sir."

"Where were the plants you were watering?"

"There are plants in the living room and bedrooms."

"And the basement."

"I'm sorry?"

"You said you were watering plants, and that you were in the basement."

Clark lied. "I was checking to see if there were any plants in the basement."

The fire chief eyed Clark and pondered the scenario. "You sure you weren't in there smoking dope and things got out of control?"

"No, sir. No dope, no lighters, no matches."

The fire chief nodded. "You want to go to the hospital and get that cut checked out?"

"The paramedics gave me the once over. A butterfly bandage was enough. I'm good. A little shaken up. For a minute I didn't think I would get out of the house. I'm not sure how the doors got locked. I didn't touch the deadbolt."

"Panic does strange things to people. Did you know that ninety percent of the people who drown in car accidents involving water drown because they forget to unbuckle their seatbelts? Panic."

"Well I panicked."

There was another pause. "Until I determine the cause of the fire I'm putting you in my report as someone who was watching the house, who was present during the explosion, and who called 911."

"That's fine." Clark paused. "I was watching their house."

The Fire Chief looked over at the house through the window of the vehicle and tried to break the tension. "And technically the plants have been watered."

"I guess," Clark smirked.

"Do you know how to reach your neighbors?"

"I don't, but I'll see if I can find someone who does."

"Give me a call at the station if you find anything."

"I will."

"And don't be too hard on yourself. We get a lot of fires this time of year. It was probably Christmas decorations that caught fire and hit a gas can or something else people shouldn't store in their house."

"Probably not." Clark answered. "They didn't celebrate Christmas."

"In that case, I can scratch it off the list of probable causes."

Clark got out of the Fire Chief's car and made his way across the wet street, weaving between the spectators and fire equipment. No one noticed Ariana's re-painted Camry parked four houses up with its lights off. Dressed in jeans and a sweatshirt, Ariana frowned. *Lucky bastard.*

Chapter 30

Scott Caldwell was tired. In the seat of his pickup sat his brownbag lunch and his crumpled work overalls. He yawned as he took the ramp for exit seven to Central Avenue. For seventeen years he had worked in the most inhospitable urban sprawl the D.C. area had to offer. His mechanic shop was located on a stretch of Central Avenue that was anything but central when it came to a business location. Next door was an empty lot, just beyond that a Chinese restaurant with bars on the windows that did a brisk business selling forty ounce beers with an orange chicken special for $4.99. Next door, on the other side, a used car lot offered its wares guaranteeing credit to anyone with a job. Across the street was the financial district, a run-down stretch of roadside shops with signs in the windows offering check-cashing services.

Scott pulled his truck into the manager's spot, an unmarked parking space near the side door of his shop. He stepped from his red pickup and grabbed his lunch and work clothes from the seat next to him. It was 8:57 in the morning when his key went into the first lock. He turned on the lights and looked around the office to confirm that none of his neighbors had managed their way through the three deadbolts or barred windows. He opened the front office door and made sure the Help Wanted sign was still visible to the outside world from the other side of the Venetian blinds.

In the double bay of his shop sat two cars. The first was a 91 Toyota Corolla with over 300,000 miles on the odometer. He was working on installing a new starter, new o-rings, and a new gasket to a car that otherwise had one tire in the junkyard. The owner of the car was a man in his seventies, and Scott Caldwell didn't have the heart to tell him it would be cheaper to buy another car. So he was doing the work at cost.

In the other bay was Scott's personal obsession, a 76 Camaro he had bought from a man outside of Gaithersburg. It was a work-in-progress and at his current rate of reconditioning it would be road-ready by the following spring. Fall at the latest.

Standing in the first bay, next to the Camry, Scott slid out of his jeans and into his work overalls. He turned on the radio on the workbench near the back of the shop and switched the coffeemaker on with enough water for six cups. Just enough caffeine to get him through lunch.

The phone in the office rang and he picked up the extra handset, which had long since stopped ringing, off the charger on the workbench.

"Caldwell's Garage and Body Shop. Scott speaking."

"Good morning," the voice said before stalling momentarily.

"Good morning," Scott answered, waiting to hear the symptoms, and often the associated saga, of a car in need of service.

"Good morning," Clark said again. "My name is Clark Hayden and I wanted to ask you a few questions."

"Shoot," Scott said, expecting to sharpen his pencil and give an estimate on repairs for a car problem as seen through a non-mechanical mind.

"I live in Arlington, Virginia, and I am trying to locate a neighbor of mine. His name is Nazim Shinwari. I got a call from his wife last week and she said they had returned to Pakistan to attend to family matters. She asked me to look after her house, which I did. Unfortunately, there was a fire at their residence last night and I don't have a contact number for them."

"Are you some kind of bill collector?" Scott asked.

Clark ducked the unexpected accusation. "No, not at all. You can look me up in the phone book. The Hayden residence is right across the street from Nazim's. Or you could call the fire department. Check the news this morning."

"When did you say his wife called you?"

"Week before last."

"Did she mention Nazim?"

"She said they had returned to Pakistan. Why?"

"Well, Clark. It was Clark, correct?"

"Clark Hayden."

"Well, Clark. I also got a call from Ariana about the same time. She also told me that they had returned to Pakistan to attend family business."

Clark became hopeful. Finally, someone with the same story. Someone who knew how to contact Ariana and get the simple explanation that had thus far been elusive. "Did you get a number for Nazim?"

"Nazim is dead. His wife informed me he died in a car accident on a road an hour outside of Karachi. Apparently it was a bad accident. Hit head-on by a passing truck. There wasn't much left."

Clark felt a nauseating pain in his gut. "And when did you say she called?"

Scott looked up at the calendar over the workbench. He checked the schedule for Nazim, and noted where he had crossed out Nazim's name and replaced it with his only other employee. "Exactly twelve days ago. Monday morning."

Clark thought for a minute and put the days into order. "Son of a bitch," he said aloud.

"Pretty much how I felt."

Chapter 31

The cars poured from the mosque parking lot, blocking traffic on the thirty-five mph main thoroughfare. The police officer on traffic duty stood on the yellow lines, his reflective vest shining in the afternoon sun. His face was covered with a partial ski mask, his nose exposed and frozen, clouds of warm breath engulfing his face with each exhalation. His left hand was extended as he stopped traffic with his palm and a stern look he had practiced to perfection at the academy. The officer's hand waved the religious faithful onto the main road, giving right of way to the spiritually righteous over the average rush-for-a-latte driver.

Five cars back from the traffic cop, Clark sat in his Honda, the rear-end of a large SUV blocking both his view and the sun. It took another ten minutes before Clark pulled into a spot near the front of the mosque. He removed the blue and white magnet from his pocket and matched the name from the magnet to that on the front of the mosque. He was in the right place.

Clark approached the front stairs nervously. He gingerly stepped into the foyer of the mosque and silently took off his shoes. A young man, dressed in a traditional salwar kameez, a Pakistani pants and shirt combination, appeared from behind a wooden door to the left of the large foyer. The pajama-like pants with tapered legs ruffled slightly as the young man approached.

"May I help you?"

Clark put the age of the young man between late teens and early twenties. The overgrown peach fuzz near his wispy sideburns was only one indicator. "Yes. I'm here to visit Imam Alamoudi."

"May I have your name?"

"Clark Hayden. I called yesterday."

"Let me see if the imam is available."

Before Clark could extend his hand in greeting, the young man turned and walked across the open floor of the mosque. Clark stood in his gray wool socks with orange toes and watched as the young man disappeared through another door on the far end of the prayer hall.

The foyer was decorated with mosaic tiles. There were several plaques with Arabic carved into the rich wood display. The building was quiet, an amazing accomplishment given that fifteen minutes ago there were two hundred religious faithful praying in unison.

Clark could feel Imam Alamoudi's presence when he entered the prayer hall. It was not a mystic spiritual force or an overdeveloped Middle Eastern chi that he felt. It was the vibration in the floor from three hundred pounds of flesh wrapped tightly in another salwar kameez.

Imam Alamoudi had an unkempt beard and hair that dropped midway between his ear and shoulder. There was a hint of a receding hairline, though given the Imam's height it was hard to determine the degree of follicle retreat.

The imam approached, gave Clark a once-over from head-to-toe, and extended his hand.

"Welcome to Al-Noor Masjid."

"Thank you for seeing me."

"What can I do for you?"

"I'm a neighbor of Nazim Shinwari and his wife Ariana."

"Of course, of course. They are wonderful people."

"Yes they are. My mother has been ill and Ariana has been helping out a great deal."

"That is what neighbors do. More importantly, that is what Muslims do. It is one of our tenets."

"In the interest of bettering neighborly relations, I wanted to learn a little more about Islam and, if possible, take a tour of your mosque."

The imam gave Clark a judgmental pat-down with his eyes. The imam started to speak, paused briefly, and then nodded. "Please come in."

Imam Alamoudi began his tour near the entrance to the prayer hall. "The English word 'mosque' derives from its Arabic equivalent, masjid, which literally means 'place of prostration.' Hence the name Al-Noor Masjid meaning the 'Al-Noor Mosque.'"

"What does Al-Noor mean?"

"The light," the imam answered, his gaze heavy. "Before we start, are there any rules governing what I should or shouldn't do?" Clark asked. "I don't want to offend anyone."

"The rules for the mosque are simple. In general, men and women should dress conservatively, usually covering both the arms and the legs."

"Easy when the weather is like this," Clark said.

The imam looked at Clark humorlessly, indicating that the only visitor in the building was not being as serious as he should have been.

"Sorry," Clark said. "Anything else?"

"Shoes are left at the entrance to the prayer area. This is done so that the rugs are not soiled. Women may be asked to cover their hair when visiting a mosque and some mosques will loan scarves to visitors, or those who otherwise need them."

The imam motioned towards an open doorway to the right of the foyer. "There is also a washroom for the followers to perform wadu, also known as ablution. Washrooms for wadu can range from sinks to elaborate rooms with built-in floor drains and faucets. In some form or another, they are found in every mosque. Cleanliness is vital to prayer."

"In Christianity the expression is 'Cleanliness is next to Godliness.'"

"Yes. It's the same principle, but Muslims actually practice it. Muslims wash their hands, faces, and feet before prayer as a way to purify and prepare themselves to stand before God. Five times a day."

Clark took the insult for his religion and moved forward. "It's quite beautiful inside."

"Thank you. The main function of the mosque is to provide a place where Muslims can perform their obligatory five daily prayers. It also serves as the vestibule to hold prayers on Fridays, the Muslim day of communal prayer. There are also two main Muslim holidays called Eids, which loosely translate as 'festivals.' The first festival is Eid ul-Fitr, which is the festival to celebrate the end of the holy month Ramadan. The second one is Eid ul-Adha, which celebrates Ibrahim's willingness to sacrifice his son."

"We have Abraham in Christianity too."

"I am aware," the imam said, irritated. He stroked his beard as if to consider whether to continue the tour.

"Is a mosque considered holy?" Clark asked.

"It is a dedicated place of prayer, but there is nothing sacred about the building. There is no altar, or its equivalent, in a mosque. A Muslim may pray on any clean surface. I'm quite sure you have seen Muslims on TV praying outside, in public."

"Yes, I have. On television," Clark confirmed.

The imam continued. "There are several distinct features of a mosque. The first is the musalla, or prayer hall. Every mosque is designed with the orientation of Mecca in mind. As you know, Muslims pray facing the direction of Mecca. In North America, this means that most Muslims face northeast. Prayer halls are open spaces which help to accommodate as many worshippers as possible. As you can see, there are no seats and no pews. During prayer, worshippers sit on the floor in lines. They may also stand and bow in unison."

"Do the men and women pray together?"

"A good question. Men and women form separate lines when they stand in prayers. Some mosques will have a separate area entirely for women. Our mosque has a single musalla, so women and men pray together, but separately."

A door closed in the distance and the imam looked across the prayer hall in the direction of the noise. "All mosques also have some sort of mihrab, or niche marker, on the wall that indicates the precise direction of Mecca. The mihrab is usually decorative and is often adorned with Arabic calligraphy. It is usually curved to echo the voice of the prayer leader back to the worshippers, as even the imam must face Mecca when praying, thus leaving his backside facing the congregation. Many mosques also have a minbar, or pulpit, to the right of the mihrab. During the Friday prayer service, the imam delivers a sermon from the minbar."

"Perhaps I could attend a Friday prayer service."

"You would be welcome. If you do, there are some expressions you may hear, traditional Islamic greetings. Perhaps you have heard 'assalamu alaikum?'"

"Yes. It means 'peace be with you.' And the response is 'wa alaikum assalam…' 'and with you be peace.'"

Clark heard the imam's stomach growl, and the large man in the robe-like attire rubbed his belly gently. "I haven't had lunch."

"Me either. Once in a while it's good to remind ourselves what it is like to be hungry," Clark added, feeling more religious.

"Fasting is an important part of Islam. One of the five pillars of our religion," Imam Alamoudi said proudly, though there was no indication of a recent adherence to reduced food consumption.

"Most mosques also have a minaret, a tower used to issue the call to prayer, or adhan. In North America, the minaret is largely decorative. But in Muslim countries it is a vital part of the mosque. In Muslim countries, the mosque is usually centrally located in the middle of town, and most people walk to their daily prayers. Here in America, most people drive from a farther distance. As such, the minaret and adhan are largely symbolic here in the U.S."

Clark looked at the floor-to-ceiling bookcase on the wall and the imam answered the quizzical look on his guest's face. "Most mosques have a collection of books; sometimes they have a library. These books usually include works on theology, Islamic philosophy, law, and the followings of the Prophet Muhammad. There are always copies of the Koran available as well. Would you like a complimentary copy?"

"Yes, that would be great," Clark answered honestly. So far, he was impressed with what he saw. He had to admit that Islam and the Al-Noor Masjid were running circles around the modern Catholic Church when it came to religious depth. *Pray fives times a day, everyday?* Not unless you were a nun, or a priest, or just knocked up your girlfriend, Clark thought.

"Other common features found in the mosque are schedules displaying the times of the five daily prayers and large rugs or carpets covering the musalla floor."

"I see that there's a school here, as well."

"Yes. While a mosque's primary function is that of a place of worship, it can also serve as school, a day care center, and a community center. Some mosques offer Koranic instruction, as well as Arabic classes. It's not that different from a Catholic Church with a school."

"Or a Jewish community center associated with a synagogue," Clark added.

The imam grunted his response, "Perhaps."

The tour continued for another five minutes, concluding back near the foyer where it started. The same young man who had met Clark at the door had returned and was now standing next to the imam.

"This is Farooq, he is one of my understudies. His name means 'he who distinguishes truth from falsehood.'"

"Great name," Clark said.

Clark and Farooq shook hands, something that the understudy wasn't interested in at their first meeting in the foyer.

Farooq then turned his back towards Clark and whispered upwards into the imam's ear.

"Is there anything else I can answer for you today?" Imam Alamoudi asked as Clark removed his shoes from their place on a large shelf used as a shoe rack.

It was time for Clark to get to the real question. "I was wondering if you would know how to reach Nazim or Ariana? I understand that they have gone home to attend family business, and they asked me to watch over their house. I don't have a contact name or number to reach them and, unfortunately, there was a fire at their residence the day before yesterday."

Imam Alamoudi felt the ambush but remained stoic. Without another word to Clark he looked at Farooq. "See if you can help this young man in his request."

"Yes, Imam," Farooq answered as Clark slipped on his shoes and zipped up his jacket.

Chapter 32

FBI Agent Chris Rosson was hot on the trail of his latest suspect. The evidence was straightforward. The perp had started with small assaults and minor infractions. Invasion of private property, trespassing, and loitering—judging by the turds left on the floor underneath his desk.

When Agent Rosson opened his bag of Cheetos and found not only had the air already escaped through a hole in the bottom, but that the contents of the bag had been pilfered, he called in the experts. Thanks to Rosson, there were now a dozen rat traps scattered around the fifth floor of FBI headquarters. The maintenance crew referred to them as "mice enticers," as if the distinction between rat and mouse meant anything when the vermin are scurrying over your shoes, comfortably planted from nine to five at the most advanced investigative entity on Earth.

The Director of the Joint Terrorism Task Force, Eric Nerf, had also spent the majority of his career in the pursuit of rats, usually those on the next rung of the bureaucratic ladder. It had been fifteen years since he last donned a bulletproof vest and a rain jacket with his employer's name emblazoned on the back. His shirts were pressed. His tie collection managed to keep up with the latest fashion, following the trends from thin to thick, from bland to colorful. His slicked-back black hair was gelled and dyed to perfection. As a bureaucrat he had exchanged his gun for a pen, to use his sense of investigation for general suspicion of those who worked for him as much as real criminals.

His forays onto the floor where his staff toiled were limited to the far aisle of cubes, those that stood between his corner office and the elevators. So when the Director appeared at Agent Rosson's cube and cast a shadow on the agent's workstation, Rosson's heart took a couple of un-syncopated beats.

"Rosson. I need a word with you."

"Yes, sir," Rosson answered to the back of his superior's suit as Eric Nerf turned the corner and walked towards the meeting rooms on the other side of the floor. The Director may have made a rare trip into his employee's lair but he wasn't going to demean himself by having a conversation in a cube. That just wasn't done by someone of his stature, of his rank, of his mindset. He was an office guy. He met in offices or conference rooms and he discussed matters with others who had offices. There was nothing for him in the world of cubes. He had briefly been there and had no plans on going back. As a government employee, his rise through the organization was totally independent of his ability to manage people or relate to them on their level. He was the man in charge and, as such, his subordinates were to follow orders. And orders came just as easily through email. Unless the Director was passing along a good ass-chewing, as happened to be the case.

"Shut the door behind you," the Director said as Rosson entered the room. The room was small and windowless. It had no electrical outlets, no carpet, and gray paint on the walls. Agent Rosson took a seat at the end of the table and the Director put his butt on the corner of the metal table.

"What's going on, sir?"

"Rosson, have you been working the list of leads we get from the CIA? That less than popular list of calls and letters that the general public sends to the CIA contact address and call center."

"Yes, sir. I have been working my portion of the list for the last five months or so. My rotation is supposed to end next month."

"Any progress?"

"Progress?"

"Anything that has struck a chord of plausibility with you? Any leads that made you think, 'maybe I got something here?'"

"No sir. Had a jewelry store in the Bronx that we checked out for being a potential Halawa broker. But that was in October. I have been keeping the system up to date with those leads. You can check on my comments and progress."

"I don't need to. I have always looked at that list as a dog-and-pony show. It's a feel-good list, though I am well aware of the less-than-feel-good names the agents have for it. The list is a pacifier for the general public and a get out of jail free card for our friends at the CIA."

"I'm sorry, sir?"

"The CIA, by virtue of this list, is able to send us every crackpot inquiry that comes to them from unsolicited domestic sources."

"I get the feeling you are about to tell me that I have missed something."

Eric Nerf puckered his lips and made a sucking sound with his mouth like a fish gasping for breath. "I just got off the phone with the Deputy Director of Clandestine Services at the CIA. It seems there was information on the CIA list that has since been deemed 'of interest to national security.'"

Rosson ran his hand through his prematurely gray hair. A man with great perception in most situations, he was nervous because he didn't know if he was going to get patted on the back or lose part of his derrière.

"Do you remember a house here in the D.C. area on the list?"

"Sure, it was a few weeks ago. In Arlington. I switched with Agent Taylor because I knew the neighborhood. The address sort of jumped out at me. I lived nearby when I was in junior high school. Moved before my freshman year."

"Did you visit the house?"

"Affirmative. I stopped by and spoke with the woman who made the call."

"And…"

"It was a dead-end. The woman was on at least half a dozen different medications for psychosis. Meds for schizophrenia, depression, bi-polar disorder."

"How did you obtain this information?"

Agent Rosson didn't blink. "Her medicine cabinet was open when I went to use the john. Though I didn't mention the medication in my notes for that report."

"Why not?"

"Just because she has the medicine, doesn't necessarily mean that she is using it. Besides, someone could misinterpret that information as being obtained illegally."

The Director nodded and picked at his teeth with his fingernail. "Was there anything unusual about her claim?"

"Nothing more unusual than the average call that comes through that channel. The woman claims she saw three Middle Eastern-looking men at her door in the middle of the night. She only saw them through the peephole. She said they muttered something about hospitality through the door before they disappeared."

"Disappeared?"

"I believe the phrase she used was 'vanished into the night.'"

"So you didn't buy her story?"

"Well, her son showed up as I was about to leave and I spoke with him. He seemed to have his act together. A grad student at Virginia Tech. I asked him if he had seen anything unusual and he said no, but that they did have Pakistani neighbors—a family of three—husband, wife, and daughter. He said they were a typical family. I asked a few more questions and took a peek at the house across the street where the Pakistani neighbors lived. No one was home, but there was nothing out of the ordinary. The son admitted that his mother had some obvious issues. I closed the report as an unreliable source."

"I see."

Agent Rosson considered sharing his culinary interlude with the garlic muffin but decided against it. "Where is this conversation going, sir?"

The Director of the FBI Joint Terrorism Task Force cleared his throat. "The information I am about to share is highly confidential and is not to go outside this room."

"I will leave it here."

"The CIA hit on a match for the address across the street from one Maria Hayden. It appears that a clandestine agent for the CIA has infiltrated a potential sleeper cell and has taken up residence at the same address from the list we received from the CIA. This intelligence asset represents six years of work including, as I was told, imprisonment of the agent as part of his cover."

"You're kidding."

"I don't kid. The Deputy Director made it very clear that there is to be no action taken toward this address or anyone coming or going from the residence. It was, as he put it, a matter of national security. Any attempt to investigate this address or apprehend anyone at this address will be dealt with harshly."

"Meaning?"

"Meaning you have twenty eight months until retirement at eighty percent of your salary. So don't fuck it up."

"Not a problem sir. I closed the FBI's end of the investigation the day after visiting the location."

"That's good. That's good. I'm relieved," Director Nerf said with concern. "But I am going to need you to amend your report."

"Amend?"

"Re-post."

"Exactly what am I re-posting?"

"Go back in to the system and change the reason for closing the account. Amend the 'previous unreliable source' notation with 'closed at the direction of the Central Intelligence Agency.'"

Rosson was processing the information in his head. "You want it backdated?"

"Can you do that?"

"I can change the date that I closed the report. The date that I altered the report — the date I accessed the report — that I cannot change. So if someone is looking at the report, they will not be able to see what was written before but they will be able to see the date that something was modified."

"Do it."

Rosson was quiet for a second and then asked. "Why is the CIA running the domestic list through their databases? I mean, correct me if I am wrong, but the FBI has jurisdiction over domestic terrorism. If the CIA is using the list, why bother sending it to us?"

"Deniability. If they miss something, they blame it on us, claim that the information was the FBI's jurisdiction. If they catch something and we don't, they can point their finger at us for not catching it. And if something big, something important were to slip past our filters, we will be the ones to blame. The heads will roll right here in this office. Right here on this floor."

"So much for working with one another."

"You never believed that interagency cooperation bullshit, did you? Shame, shame. You think decades of institutionalized hatred and mistrust for one another is going to disappear because the President and Congress tells it to? You can see how that worked with the civil rights movement."

"A little different, but I see your point."

"You know, there is a saying in Washington that there is only one thing worse than another 9/11," the Director said.

"What's that?"

"Being blamed for it."

Chapter 33

The wind howled along the waterfront in Georgetown. The curvy two-section five-story building that ran parallel to the Potomac housed a conglomeration of restaurants, law firms, and condos that cost well into seven figures. A fountain dissected the open air between the building sections and during the heydays of summer the seats around the pools of water were filled with young people holding hands and slobbering over their favorite ice cream. When the weather was nice, the restaurants facing the river opened their patios to throngs of young professionals who flocked to the deck chairs and tables like seagulls to a spilled order of French fries. The captains of expensive boats pulled up to the docks, luring the beautiful people from their tables for a trip to Roosevelt Island and whatever else they could talk or impress their subjects into doing. Downhill from the main drag on M Street, with its bars and boutiques, the waterfront offered a view of the Key Bridge to the right and the Kennedy Center to the left. It was an address for the kings, and those who wanted to imagine they were royalty for the afternoon.

With the wind whipping down the Potomac in mid-winter form, the action on the Waterfront was muted. The occasional brave jogger could be seen running down the large concrete path, their breath visible to the restaurant patrons who were warm and cozy behind the glass windows.

When a female Georgetown medical resident with a sensitive nose jogged downwind past the docks, she paused in motion. Legs still pumping in her high-tech thermal pants, her torso covered in a vest with her school's name, she removed her earphone jacks and inhaled. With that, the woman with dark hair and dark features stopped running in place.

Following her nose, she walked over to the retaining wall that kept the water of the Potomac, when it flooded, away from the expensive real estate. The jogger looked down at the empty boat dock. She first saw what looked like a leg protruding from the dock at water level. She moved several steps upstream for a better look. Peering over the edge, she calmly reached into her pocket, pulled out a thin cell phone, and called 911.

The dead body was stuck near the corner post of the dock, the back of the victim wedged under the planked walkway. With spring still months away, and the Potomac alternating consistency between ice water and a Slurpee, the body could have gone unnoticed for another month. Except for the smell. Nature's way of pointing the living to the dead.

The ambulance and police converged on the scene, lights flashing, sirens off. News traveled quickly. A couple of lawyers from a law firm on the fourth floor grabbed their coats and headed for the elevator. Where there was death, there was fault, and where there was fault, there was money to be made.

A small crowd braved the cold and stood on the retaining wall from a distance, watching the police pull the fully clothed body from the frigid water. When the coroner flipped the corpse on its back, a gagging sound mixed with the sound of a woman crying. The body's face was white, the mouth open.

Detective Earl Wallace, career officer with the D.C. Metropolitan Police Department, cornered the jogger who was perturbed that her run had been interrupted. He sucked in his gut a little as he made his way to the witness and introduced himself. Early fifties, black, and graying, Detective Wallace still maintained a boyish face. His knees and diet, however, protested the mere thought of an exercise routine.

"How did you find the body?"

"I smelled it," the jogger answered. The wires to her headphones now resting over each shoulder. Her red running cap was in her left hand.

"How do you know what a dead body smells like?"

"I'm a resident at Georgetown hospital. We have dead bodies from time to time. But I also did a pathology rotation in the morgue to see if I could stomach it."

"How did that go?"

"I survived. Made it through med school."

"Most of the bodies in med school are preserved."

"Yes, I know," the jogger answered, stretching her legs.

The coroner came over and whispered into the detective's ear. The detective nodded in response. The coroner zipped the black bag closed, its contents out of sight.

"Let me get your name and contact information and then you are free to go."

The jogger did deep knee bends as she gave the detective her personal information, and then jogged off in the direction of Georgetown University.

It took the medical examiner less than an hour to pinpoint drowning as the cause of death.

Detective Wallace, resident expert on dead bodies from the D.C. Robbery and Homicide unit, walked into the small office area of the morgue and hit the buzzer near the desk to let the medical examiner know that someone was waiting.

The medical examiner hit his foot on a lever that opened the door to the examination room and popped his head through the opening. He was wearing an apron smeared with human muck, streaks of undistinguishable, unmentionable bits, combined with the more discernable blood and dirt. Two dabs of powerful mentholated ointment stretched from the underside of the medical examiner's long curved nose. The medical examiner immediately recognized the officer.

"Detective Wallace. Please come in. Good to see you again."

"It's never good to see me. I only come when someone is dead. But thanks just the same."

"Like the Grim Reaper," the doctor said, returning to the table with the drowned body. The metal table was wet and water ran into the built-in drainage channels in the corners. The body was on its back, naked and fully exposed.

"What can you tell me?"

"White, male."

"Obviously," Detective Wallace said, looking down at the man's groin.

"I always start with the obvious," the doctor said with a smile. "White, male, in his mid-thirties. Cause of death, drowning, as indicated by foam in the airways and nostrils. Though that could change."

"What? The foam or the cause of death?"

The medical examiner looked over the frame of his glasses at the detective.

Wallace smiled and walked around towards the head of the deceased. "When we fished him out, he had a wallet, but there was no I.D. No driver's license. The wallet still had sixty bucks in it."

The doctor nodded. "Makes sense. Probably wasn't a robbery. I can't find any sign of foul play. No GSW, no stab wounds. No cuts. In a majority of drowning cases we find ancillary injuries. A lot of drowning victims have contusions on their head. They hit their noggin on the side of the boat, on a rock, whatever. Of course, many drowning victims also have post-mortem injuries from bumping into things in the water. This guy on the table has a few, but nothing of real consequence. There is always a danger of misdiagnosing ante-mortem and post-mortem injuries with drowning victims. Drowning victims always float face down. Given the weight of the head and the face-down position, some post-mortem injuries can bleed. But I don't think that is the case with this guy."

"He was found wedged under a dock."

"That shouldn't make a difference. The current probably carried him there and his clothes got stuck on something protruding from the dock structure. There was nothing to indicate otherwise."

"So no post-mortem means..."

"He probably didn't go too far."

"So it's not a body that came through Great Falls."

"Absolutely not. It fell somewhere east of Chain Bridge. There are too many rocks farther upstream. The body may have not traveled far at all."

"Anything else?"

"There was some residual blood in his mouth and sinus cavity that I haven't found a cause for yet. He has some scars on his knuckles. Battered hands. Looks like he was a man who wasn't afraid to mix it up. Maybe a boxer, maybe a barroom brawler. Also has a tattoo on his arm," the doctor said, pointing with the sharp end of the scalpel.

"Stating the obvious, again?" Wallace asked.

"I guess I am," the doctor answered, standing up from his hunched position.

Wallace looked at the clothes and shoes resting in the metal pan on the tile floor near the table. He picked up a pair of jeans and water dripped from them. "His dress seems normal for winter in this area. Jeans, worn hiking boots, an old winter coat."

"Yes, nothing unusual there. But it doesn't tell me how he got into the river. Hard to explain with the cold weather we have been having. Not many people are out there taking walks by the banks. Not even too many people up near the canal."

"And the fish aren't biting."

"That's true. Which is good for me. Drowning victims look better in the winter when the fish haven't been picking at them."

"What about toxicology?"

"We did a prelim, but didn't find anything. The full results should be done in a few days. I will check for the usual suspects."

"What do you think?"

"I know he drowned. His lungs were soggy; his stomach was full of Potomac water. Could have been unconscious when he drowned, but I don't know that for sure yet. But then, I guess figuring out the circumstances under which he drowned is your job."

"I guess it is."

"Can you give me an approximate time of death?"

"I'm having one of the assistants research the water temperature for the last couple of weeks. I should have a guess for you in a few hours."

"Off the top of your head?"

"Don't hold me to it, but I would say two, three days max. I think we saw fifty degrees over the weekend for a minute or two, so somewhere in that timeframe. I mean, it has been cold and there has been a fair amount of ice on the river already."

"Maybe that was the intention. Maybe someone dumped this guy in the river hoping it would freeze completely and that it would be another month before he popped to the surface."

"Possible. Sinister, but possible."

"Can I get some fingerprints and dentals? I still need to I.D. this guy."

"Already did. The prints and dental x-rays are on the counter," the doctor said, gesturing to the small work area in the corner. "The prints are a little messy, but thanks to freezing water, you might be able to get something from them."

"Thank you, doctor."

"Oh, I have one more thing..."

"What's that?"

"His natural hair color is blonde. The brown is just a dye."

Wallace walked into the station and handed the prints to his occasional partner, Detective Nguyen, a second generation

Vietnamese-American. He was impeccably dressed in a light brown suit, shoes shined. His hair was short and he had a goatee, both attributes an intentional effort to look serious and older. "Could you run these through the database and see if anything comes up."

"Still in a tiff with forensics?"

"Not that it's any of your business."

Detective Nguyen, still a baby by police-tenure standards, looked at the set of prints. "Not exactly clean."

"You wouldn't be either if you spent a few days in the Potomac."

"Are these from the guy who ruined lunch down at the Waterfront?"

"Same guy. White, male, in his thirties. Tattoo. Died from drowning. Could be accidental or homicidal. We are waiting for toxicology."

"Good thing that body didn't come floating up there during the summer. All those tourists and visitors. Someone would have lost their lunch."

"A small victory for us, a poor consolation for the victim," Wallace said. He nodded towards the envelope he had just handed to Nguyen. "How long to run those through the database?"

"A day. But if it's a priority, I can get it pushed through."

"A day is fine. Someone will probably call in to I.D. the guy anyway before the prints are run. The M.E. thought the guy had been dead for a few days at the most. He doesn't look homeless. Someone will be looking for him."

Two hours later Nguyen appeared at Detective Wallace's desk. Nguyen's part-time partner was on what he called REM patrol, something he was known to do after lunch. "Sergeant?"

Wallace opened his eyes. "Yes."

"I got a hit on the prints."

Nguyen led Wallace to the far side of the precinct, through a maze of wooden chairs and ringing phones, and down a flight of stairs to the basement. Detective Nguyen pushed open the door to a glass room and a wall of new sounds rushed forward to greet them. Wallace followed Nguyen to the far corner. "I ran the prints myself and got a hit from the National Prison System database."

"Who is he?"

"His name is James Beach. Convicted felon. Did four years in Petersburg, Virginia. Long rap sheet. Most recently did time for drug charges and kidnapping. They caught him outside Bristol, Virginia with a trunk full of meth and a fifteen-year-old girl."

"A boy scout."

"Has served time for assault with a deadly weapon and auto theft. Had a couple of DUIs."

"Make that a choir boy."

"For the last eighteen months, he has been quiet. No arrest. No infractions. Meets with his parole officer in Richmond every month. I have a call into his P.O., and am waiting to hear back."

"Let me know what you find out."

"What are you going to do?"

"Call Petersburg. See if there is anything else we need to know about him."

Chapter 34

Ariana peeked her head inside the warehouse before fully committing herself to the doorway. It was a habit she forgot she still possessed. She remembered the first time she had caught a rifle butt to the head for inattentiveness to her surroundings. Or rather, she remembered the headache and welt that persisted for a week after impact. It had been a non-lethal blow, from a teacher, but it made its point. When you are in operational mode, don't let your guard down. Even at home.

She stepped inside, and moved towards the large green button on the hanging controller pad near the door. Her eyes roamed the limited horizon as she raised the roll-up door on the far parking bay. She pulled her car inside and shut the door behind her.

As she walked away from her Toyota towards the office, Karim exited the community bathroom.

"Bathroom break?"

"Don't worry, we are following protocol. As you can see, everyone is still in the room."

Ariana walked over to the sleeping quarters' door and opened it. "I need to speak with Karim for a moment. We can start on lunch after prayer."

Syed and Abu looked up at Ariana from their seat on their cots. On the floor was a pile of playing cards. "Fine," Abu answered. "In another fifteen minutes, everything Syed owns will be mine."

"Lucky you," Ariana answered. "From here I can see all his worldly possessions."

Syed tried to smirk but it came out as a scowl.

"Just a few minutes."

In the office, Ariana shut the door and removed her coat. She had left before dawn, without make-up, wearing jeans and a button down sweater. Her nipples stiffened to the cold in the room and Karim noticed immediately.

"The package has been delivered," she said, drawing the blinds on the windows in the office.

"Your neighbor?"

"With any luck both the young man and his mother."

"Did anyone see you?"

"No. I was careful."

"How long?"

"A day or two. If it works."

"You don't sound confident."

"It was not a perfect product. That will require a little more time."

Karim sat in the chair and Ariana moved behind him, drawing a finger across his neck.

Karim felt her touch and his body responded below the waist.

"Killing the boy and his mother is a risk. Maybe an unneeded one. It will draw attention to us. To you. We are in no immediate danger from your neighbor. He knows nothing. A little nosey perhaps."

"I assure you that he'll be less trouble dead than he is alive."

"Perhaps."

"Besides it was necessary," Ariana said. She moved slowly behind him and he tried to turn to track her. She gently pushed his head so it was staring forward. "And exhilarating," she added slowly.

"The thrill of the hunt? Isn't the thrill better when the prey knows he is being hunted?"

"Not always. Killing can be enough of a thrill regardless of the prey." Ariana moved to the front of Karim and her sweater was open, her firm breasts straining from beneath a black bra.

"How long has it been?" Ariana asked.

Karim tried to count the years in his head, but his attention was elsewhere. "Too long. A lifetime ago."

Karim stood from his chair and Ariana met him in the distance between them. He leaned to kiss her and she turned her head. His lips redirected towards her neck and she let out a quiet moan.

A minute later Ariana's jeans were on the floor, her legs supported over Karim's elbows. She scratched at his exposed chest as her hips raised to meet his thrusts. She pushed him back as she felt him nearing the point of no return, and guided him to the chair. Straddling him, his face in her bosom, she pulled his hair as she took control.

The Wood Artisans cabinet and furniture workshop was down the street from historic downtown Manassas, thirty miles from D.C. The train station that had once been a stopover on the way westward, now served commuters heading east into Washington on the Virginia Rail Express. The VRE ran trains during rush hour, taking some of the burden off of eastbound I-66, a road at such overcapacity that an inline skater with a missing wheel could keep up with the pace of traffic.

The Wood Artisans sat two blocks from the station, past the brick storefronts and the Starbucks, on the other side of the tracks. The warehouse stretched for a New York City block, which was the rough equivalent of three Manassas blocks. The front half of the warehouse was a showroom, offering custom made furniture ranging from bedroom ensembles to dining room sets that cost more than a compact car. Behind the decorated wall of the showroom was a cavernous workshop where a dozen carpenters practiced their trade in a dying industry.

Ivan Kozlowski was a fourth generation carpenter.

Seated at a long workbench on the back wall of the warehouse, Ivan grabbed the newspaper which was still wrapped in the plastic bag that protected it from the elements until the neighborhood residents found the energy to fetch them from the end of their driveways. The era of the paperboy was dead. And with his death was the end of doorstep delivery. Papers were now thrown from moving vehicles driven by middle-aged immigrants or retirees. But curbside delivery did have its advantages.

Ivan pulled the newspaper from the plastic bag and an imperceptible puff of white escaped from the paper as it hit the workbench, mixing with a thin layer of wood dust that covered everything in the warehouse. Ivan ripped open a small bag of sugar and poured it into his coffee. He pulled his daily dose of donuts from the nondescript white bag and placed them on a napkin. He swiped at the front page of the paper and the dust on the photo of the President on the front page. He wiped his hand across the workbench one more time before grabbing the paper and shaking it, just to the left of his gourmet breakfast.

As he did every Wednesday, Ivan spent the fifteen minutes before work going through the mid-week advertisements in The Post. The fifty cents he saved by stealing his neighbor's paper would cost him his life.

Chapter 35

Clark's blue Honda Civic turned left at the pair of oak trees off the two-lane country road. He passed through the open gate and admired the crest of the mountains in the distance as the car crept up the long driveway. He pushed the open map next to him into the back seat and read the number scribbled on a piece of paper lying in the passenger seat. He checked the address on the house one last time. After a tank of gas, two pit-stops, two maps, and three different sets of directions from the locals, Clark had reached his destination.

He zipped his jacket and stepped from the driver's side. He stretched his back as he walked towards the white country house and up the stairs to the large front porch. The screen door was hanging cockeyed, the upper hinge holding onto the wooden frame with more authority than the lower one. A set of weathered rocking chairs sat empty, angled towards one another, a small table pinched between them.

Clark knocked on the frame of the precariously hanging screen door and waited before knocking again. A stiff wind blew through his denim jeans and Clark cursed, thankful that he wasn't living in the mountains of southwest Virginia, at least for the winter. The Blue Ridge Mountains in the summer were great for hiking and fishing. Spring brought wildflowers into full bloom. Autumn was simply breathtaking. But winter, with the trees barren and the ground frozen, was not his favorite time of year.

After knocking twice on the door, Clark peered into the living room window from the front porch. He took a few paces down the porch, the planks of wood creaking, and peeked into the dining room. He knocked on the window and announced his presence one more time. Another cutting breeze was the only response.

He walked back towards the front door, flipped the lid on the mailbox attached to the house, and peaked into the empty metal container. He looked at the leaves and twigs strewn about the porch and on the green welcome mat at the foot of the door. In his unprofessional detective opinion, no one was home, nor had they been for a while.

He began to wonder if the call he had made to a Foreign Service Officer in Pakistan, a man who felt passionately about his recently stolen cell phone, was just an additional scene in the *Candid Camera* episode that was rapidly becoming Clark's winter vacation.

He had called Pakistan over the weekend, out of morbid curiosity. Curiosity stirred up from a mentally deficient woman in her seventies. A woman whom he happened to love more than anyone in the world.

The man in Pakistan had given him a second number made from the same missing cell phone. Clark took the number to Switchboard.com, a website that matches addresses and phone numbers, and vice versa. When the second number from the stolen phone matched with an address, and that address was in Virginia, Clark knew he would be in his car first thing in the morning.

In hindsight, Clark would have preferred to sleep in and read the Post with a cup of Joe.

Clark took one lap around the yard and the eerie stillness of the old frame farmhouse made Clark nervous. The yard was deserted, the summer grass long since dead. Brown patches of weeds dotted the edge of the yard where it blended into the first layer of pasture. He announced himself as he made his way around the house, not sure of what he would say if someone actually answered. Clark thought about his explanation and then considered that it's not every day someone drives to a farmhouse to ask about a cell phone call made from a stolen phone in Pakistan. Clark mumbled something to himself that sounded like a self introduction and then caught himself. "What the hell are you doing?" he asked aloud.

Five minutes later Clark walked back towards his car, the empty house yielding no warm bodies, no greetings, no coffee, no clues. Clark's hands were chilled by the air. As he unzipped the pocket to his blue winter jacket his keys fell to the ground. A breeze blew over his back as he reached for the keys in the gravel driveway.

A pile of odd-looking stones caught Clark's attention and he grabbed one along with his keys. He brought the stone to eye-level. It felt light. The shape was asymmetrical. Clark looked down at the pile near the left front fender of his car. Then he raised his glance back at the empty yard and beyond the house.

He returned his focus to the ground, his eyes dancing across the small objects that littered the end of the driveway and continued into the yard. He shuffled his feet in measured steps, following the trail for a few yards in front of his car before bending over again and retrieving two more objects. As he ran his hand across the ground, he noticed a dozen more of the curious objects resting in the indented strips of matted dead grass where a vehicle had been driven. The sound of a slamming door in the distance broke his concentration and Clark stood from his crouch. He was getting spooked. He waited for a moment, took another lap around the house, and decided he had seen enough.

Chapter 36

The Nelson County Sheriff's office was wedged between the Lovingston General Store and the Lovingston Post Office in a row of old townhouses turned storefronts. Combined with a single-pump gas station across the street and the sawdust-floor watering hole half a block down, the handful of buildings hovering around a sidewalk statue of General Lee made up bustling downtown Lovingston and served the ten thousand habitants of the rural Virginia county. Charlottesville was down the road, twenty minutes away by Nelson County time, the standard answer for how long it took to get anywhere in the sprawling jurisdiction. If it was more than twenty minutes away, it was a safe bet the person giving directions had never been there.

Sheriff Laskey leaned back in his old wooden desk chair and the spring supports squeaked as they absorbed his weight. The sound of the chair was part of the office, as much as the old black phone with the authentic bell ringer, the dark wood bookcases on the walls, and the Mayberry-like jail cell in the back room that held the occasional drunk for a few hours until they sobered up. Real legal perpetrators were sent down the road to a larger facility in Charlottesville. Incarceration at the sheriff's jail didn't include a meal plan and the law just wouldn't permit long-term guests with empty stomachs.

Sheriff Mike Laskey worked ten minutes from the house where he had been born on a worn kitchen table his grandfather had built from trees on the Laskey family property. His father held his mother's hand as the local veterinarian tended to the business-end of the delivery and, on a sweltering summer day in 1947, Michael J. Laskey joined the world of the living with a wail. The umbilical cord was cut with a butcher's knife sterilized in a pot of boiling water, and young Laskey was three months old before he saw his first doctor. It was an aversion to medicine he never got over. Not even when gangrene set in on the middle toe of his left foot after a failed dancing lesson with a cow.

The main valley of Nelson County started south of Charlottesville and ran like retreating Confederate soldiers until the mountains pinched in on three sides. Sheriff Laskey had seen his county change over the years. Charlottesville, in Albemarle County, was wealthy. The city and its surrounding areas were pollinated with old money that spread generation to generation. Families with prestigious sounding names and the genealogical pedigree to prove them, bought up prime rolling acreage for horse farms and wineries. In the last two decades the good ol' boys who ruled the roost in Charlottesville had spread their golden wings and started swooping down on Nelson County.

It started with Wintergreen, a resort for weekend getaways, as if families living in a mansion with a pool and horses needed a place to relax and unwind. With a spa, golf courses, and ski runs, Wintergreen, smack dab in the middle of Nelson County, was a haven for the wealthy and a nightmare for a two-man sheriff office. Rich kids with too much money raced their convertible graduation presents along the winding roads, occasionally wrapping the finest German engineering around hundred-year-old tree trunks. Teenagers high on the designer drug-of-the-year ran across the golf course at night screaming, some of them believing they could fly and flapping their arms as if they were ready to prove their point. Swinger parties were known to occur, the participants some of Charlottesville's finest citizens who frolicked naked in scenes from Caligula, all in view of their neighbors through soaring glass windows.

The rest of Nelson County was a different story. Where the encroaching neighbors to the north rode their horses around their vineyards, most Nelson County residents took great pride in cultivating vintage cars in their yards. Dilapidated vehicles without engines, tires, and doors grew easily in some of the most fertile land in the mid-Atlantic.

The landscape was different in old Nelson County and so was the sheriff's clientele. The wife who cold-cocked her husband with a frying pan for cheating. The five-man hunting party that managed to get separated and shoot each other in the woods despite perfect weather conditions and broad daylight. The father who beat his son within inches of his life for changing the channel on the satellite television, the one real amenity in their double-wide trailers.

Sheriff Laskey dealt with them all. In his mind, they were all the same. He knew the law and he loved the Bible, and somewhere between the two he found peace in his job.

And the peace was about to be ruined.

For the last half-century, Nelson County had been infamous for one thing. A small meteorological record that is unlikely to be broken unless God reneges on His word and sends Noah back down to work on a second rendition of the Ark.

In 1969, Hurricane Camille smashed into the Mississippi coast as a full-fledged Category 5 monster. The storm surge was estimated at twenty-five feet with wind gusts topping 200 mph. Entire blocks were wiped clean. Brick apartments were removed from their foundations and swallowed by the sea or blown inland bit by bit. One man purportedly escaped from the attic of his two-story home, barely squeezing out a small window before the house was engulfed by rising water. He lived over a mile from the coast. Still three days away, no one could have guessed the wraith Camille was going to let loose on a small county in central Virginia.

When the first raindrops started to fall in Nelson County,

Sheriff Laskey, who had not yet been voted into his current title, was busy with the tractor in the old red barn behind the family house. As darkness fell, so did larger drops of rain. By the time the radio was crackling out warnings and the TV had issued an emergency broadcast, it was too late to run. Over the next twelve hours, thirty-six inches of rain fell onto Nelson County's mountains and rolling hills. There were stories of mothers who carried their babies face down so the children wouldn't drown. A man trapped outside claimed to have survived by burying his mouth in the hollow of a tree to breathe as the storm reached its crescendo. Rain came down in sheets, no longer drops. Laskey gathered his wife and daughter in the hall on the first floor of the farmhouse to pray by candlelight. The shingles on the roof were no match for the relentless downpour and between Psalms and Proverbs, Laskey and his wife hopped from room to room on the second floor, catching drips from the ceiling in pots, pans, and buckets. The rain made noises Laskey had never heard, noises he had never knew were possible. It was as if the house was sitting directly under a waterfall, the long unbroken flow of water relentless.

Sometime before dawn, as Laskey emptied another bucket into the bathtub on the second floor, he heard the rumble. His wife sat up in bed and called his name as the rumble turned into a crash. Laskey ran downstairs, flung open the door, and looked out over the old porch into the night. He saw nothing beyond the flooded yard, a river where the driveway had once been.

The crash had lasted thirty seconds before it slowly disappeared into thunder and rain. There was nothing to do but wait.

Dawn brought little reprieve from the deluge, but by afternoon the word of tragedy had spread to every home with a working phone. The mountains in western Nelson County, drowning in flood waters the country had never seen, had crumbled like mashed potatoes being washed off a dirty plate after supper. Twenty feet of top soil, and everything living on it, had crashed down on the county, swallowing two hundred residents as they slept. Their houses were never found and the official death toll was merely a best guess by emergency workers a week later.

Now, forty some years later, Nelson County was about to gain notoriety for something non-weather related.

The phone on Sheriff Laskey's desk rang, and the sheriff arranged the hat on his head before he leaned forward in his squeaky chair to answer it.

"Laskey, Nelson County Sheriff's office,"

"Sheriff. This is detective Earl Wallace of the D.C. Metropolitan Police."

Laskey rocked back in his chair to another squeak. "D.C. police you say?"

"Yes, sir."

"We don't get many calls from D.C. down here."

Detective Wallace thought about the statement for a second and continued. "I guess not."

"What can I help y'all with?"

Detective Wallace noticed the contraction "y'all," and wondered just where the geographical line was when the population dropped "you" in favor of the southern extension. "Well, I have a dead body here in D.C. that we pulled out of the river. We ran the prints and found that they belonged to James Beach, a former convict in Petersburg, Virginia."

"Petersburg is on the other side of the state," Sheriff Laskey stated plainly.

"Yes, sheriff, I know. I already spoke with the assistant warden at Petersburg. I'm interested in locating one of his cellmates at Petersburg. Are you familiar with a Nelson County resident named Jackson Price?"

Sheriff Laskey nodded to himself as he spoke. "Yeah. I know Jackson Price, all right. Also known as J.P. around here, among other things."

"Class citizen?"

"He's been on the Nelson County catch and release program for years."

"What do you know about him?"

"What don't I know about him might be a shorter conversation."

Detective Wallace laughed. "I'll take the short version."

"Jackson Price came from a fairly wealthy family in Nelson County. His father ran a couple of car dealerships. One in Staunton. One in Charlottesville. One in Lynchburg. He was a good man. Raised two sons by himself after his wife ran off with a doctor from Richmond."

"Was a good man?"

"God rest his soul. Mr. Price passed away, oh, must be eight, ten years ago. Cancer."

"Sorry to hear that."

"Yeah, well, his sons were nothing but trouble before he passed and their behavior didn't get any better with their father in the cemetery. The older brother disappeared a few years ago with a couple of warrants on his head, but the Price family still has a home here. Over a hundred acres in southern Nelson County. A nice piece of land. Rolling hills and pastures. They grew apples for a while, until Mr. Price passed and Jackson decided to grow another more profitable crop."

"Marijuana."

"You got it. Got sent to the big house for cultivation and possession with the intent to distribute."

"Have you seen him around?"

"I've seen him a few times since he got out last year. Seems to be staying out of trouble, I guess. No one has called me about anything, if that's any indication."

"Would you mind seeing if you can track him down for me?"

"You expect he had something to do with the floater?"

"He may, may not. Just trying to figure out how an ex-con ended up in the Potomac."

"J.P. may be a stoner and a rebel, but I doubt he killed anyone. He just doesn't have it in him. His older brother, well, now, he's a different story."

Detective Wallace jotted in his ever-present notebook. "Just the same, I would be grateful if you paid Jackson a visit, or see if you can locate his whereabouts. You know how ex-cons are."

"Thick as thieves."

"It's like a brotherhood."

"Let me get your number, and I'll take a spin by the Price farm later this afternoon."

"Much obliged, Sheriff," Detective Wallace said with his best cowboy western impersonation.

Sheriff Laskey shut the door on the brown cruiser with his title emblazoned down the side in bold silver letters. He pulled out onto Route 29 south, and drove past the barbecue pit restaurant on the edge of Lovingston proper before turning on Route 808 for the winding two lane road that ran past the Price farm. True to the words of every county resident, he pulled up to the open gate exactly twenty minutes later.

His cruiser kicked up dust as it rolled down the gravel and dirt drive that meandered through a short grove of mature trees. At the end of the trees the road cut right and traversed an open field that led to a picturesque two-story farmhouse.

The sheriff's car came to rest on the left side of the house. The sheriff pulled his lanky frame from the vehicle and took a deep breath of the afternoon air before walking towards the front door. The sun was at its winter apex in the sky. He stepped on the front porch and premonition tied a knot in his stomach. There were no outwards signs that anything was amiss. There were no newspapers piled on the porch, not that the Price brothers would have bothered to read them if they had been delivered. There was nothing in the outward appearance to tell Sheriff Laskey that something was wrong. Nothing except the dull warning in his stomach, a feeling that had proven time and time again to be more accurate than real evidence.

He knocked on the door, waited, and knocked again. He found himself checking his weapon with his right hand and unsnapping the small leather strap that kept the gun in his holster. *It's just a hunch*, he said to himself. *Nothing but a hunch.*

He tried the door knob with no luck and stepped off the wooden porch with his hand still on his holstered weapon. He peered into a sitting room through a side window on the house and carefully walked to the back of the property, his eyes darting with alertness. He moved around a small plastic table and chairs resting on a patch of stone slabs that had been arranged to form a make-shift patio. He pressed his nose to the window on the back door and twisted the locked knob.

His nose against the glass, his warm breath fogging up the window, Laskey jumped as the sound of crashing wood rushed him from behind. His gun was in hand with the safety off before he turned around. Senses jumped to high alert. Laskey stepped from the porch, his weapon by his side. A few seconds passed and another collision echoed across the backyard. The sheriff stared out towards the large gray barn behind the house. He gingerly moved across the yard, less anxious than he had been a moment earlier. To him, old barns were something he had grown up with. Even angry old barns that were barking out warnings. Shadows from the sun through the naked tree branches covered the ground as he approached the edge of the barn. Laskey peeked his head around the corner, momentarily looking down the sights of his pistol before dropping it into a two handed waist high position.

"Nelson County Sheriff's Office," he announced to the empty stalls, the hayloft, and the work area in the back left corner.

Silence.

He walked through the barn, his boots landing on remnants of old hay and dirt. At the far end of the barn he stopped at the workbench and took inventory of the tools that hung on the wall. A large wood saw hung by its handle. An oversized wrench dangled from a hook. An assortment of hammers, files, and vises filled the area in no particular order. A basket of old horse bridles rested on the floor near the rear entrance of the barn.

The large door in the opposite corner of the barn slammed shut with surprising authority, the metal plate near the lock smacking hard against the door frame. Laskey whirled towards the noise. The sheriff, sweat beading beneath his gray hairline, pushed open the rear door and stuck a nearby pitchfork into the ground to stop the door from slamming in the wind. Silence restored, he stared out at the rolling acres that made up the Price family farm. He looked towards a large pile of weeds near a neglected fence line and scanned the horizon for anything suspicious. In the distance he could see the ski runs on Wintergreen and the snow covered tree-line that ran along the Blue Ridge Parkway at four thousand feet.

He brought his focus from the mountains in the distance and zoomed in on the Price farm. His eyes narrowed, the wrinkles in his forehead gathering near those between his eyebrows and the top of his nose.

Sheriff Laskey walked to the edge of the field and stomped over the dead grass to a row of withered plants, some half-heartedly standing, leaning in the winter wind, waiting for the arrival of a spring they wouldn't live to see. He reached down and picked a plant off the ground. The core stem was firm, hardy. He grabbed the stalk and held it next to his body to estimate the height. The plant towered his six-two frame. "Just what in the hell have we been growing here?" he asked.

The sheriff reached into his pocket and pulled out a bag of Red Man chewing tobacco. Brain food. He pushed his thumb and the first two fingers of his hand into the corner of the foil-lined bag and pulled out a wad of dark brown, intertwined tobacco leaves. He shoved them into the right side of his cheek and bit down several times to release the juice. He spit once, and moved the wad into the pocket of his gum-line.

"Now let's see what we have going on," he said to himself in almost a whisper.

With a hundred acres of land, the sheriff had no intention of walking the entire farm. When he finished his chew, he would be finished with his walk. For ten minutes he walked across the Price farm among the never-ending sea of dead plants, stopping occasionally to examine their remains, to pick at their seeds, the hopeful offspring for a future generation. When he reached the start of the old apple orchard, a faint smell in the air brought him back to reality.

He saw the boots first, the dangling toes of the shoes protruding from the side of an apple tree in the distance. As he approached, the large brass belt buckle in the shape of the initials J.P. stared back at him at eye-level. Jackson Price, or what was left of him, was three feet off the ground, his neck snapped, an old rope holding his weight from a branch above. His hands tied behind his back. "Godammit," the Sheriff said. He dislodged the chew from his cheek and spit it on the ground.

He picked up his radio and called his deputy sheriff. He checked for dirt on the bottom of Jackson's boots and then took a look at the man's face and tried to remember what he looked like before death had come calling. A stiff breeze kicked up and Sheriff Laskey made his way back to the house. He stood on the front porch and waited for the Cavalry. A cooler wind and the sirens in the distance were the only reply.

The Pig and Whistle was crowded, by Nelson County standards. Two men in camouflage, obviously on the return leg from stalking one of God's creatures that may or may not have been in season, stood in line at the small counter that served made-to-order sandwiches. The larger and dirtier of the two men asked old Mrs. Dalton what the sandwich-of-the-day was. Mrs. Dalton, hair tied back in a white hairnet with a matching white apron, gave her standard response. "Country ham on country wheat." It was an answer she had given everyday for thirty years and one that most of the population of southern Nelson County knew before it was given.

A teenage girl with an oversized jacket that made her look like a red Michelin man stood at the single soda cooler, trying to decide between three varieties of Coke. *The Pig and Whistle* had long since excluded itself from the Pepsi versus Coke battle played out in commercials and advertisements. The eight hundred square foot store didn't have room for variety. And there was no competition within ten miles to force them to do anything they weren't good and ready to do. At seventy-five, Mr. and Mrs. Dalton were past the time in their lives when they saw change as a good thing.

When Sheriff Laskey walked into the store, Mr. Dalton was hunched over the counter reading an old issue of the *Nelson County Times*. His white hair was combed over and the sheriff got a bird's eye view of Mr. Dalton's effort to conceal the effects of the recessive maternal gene. "Good afternoon, Sheriff."

"Good afternoon."

"What can we do ya' for?"

The two men in camouflage grabbed their sandwiches from Mrs. Dalton and squeezed past the sheriff to the register. Mrs. Dalton tracked the men from behind the counter and rang them up. Sheriff Laskey watched them as they left the store and headed for the mud-covered pick-up on the far side of the parking lot.

"You seen anything strange around here?"

"This gotta do with the body up at Price's farm?"

Sheriff Laskey's eyebrows jumped slightly. "News travels fast. Particularly to someone who is reading last week's paper."

"Small county. Don't need a paper for most of the happenings round here. Which one of them boys did you find up there?"

"Jackson."

"Figured as much. I was betting it was J.P."

"Betting with whom?" Mrs. Dalton chimed in.

"You seen him around?" the sheriff asked.

"Time to time. Haven't seen him for a few weeks. Haven't seen his brother in over a year."

"You ever see him with another guy? Someone who wasn't local?"

"Sure." Mr. Dalton paused to look at his wife who was listening intently. He looked out across the store at the Michelin girl who was still contemplating the soda cooler. Then he continued. "There was another guy who came in here with him a few times. Blond guy. Looked kind of like a surfer, though I can't say that I've ever seen one in real life."

"Anything else?"

Mr. Dalton looked over his shoulder at his wife for confirmation. Mrs. Dalton nodded her head slightly. "No. The guy was blond and had a few tattoos. But heck, everyone has a tattoo these days, so I don't reckon that narrows down your options much."

"Not much."

The girl in the thick red jacket at the back of the store walked forward and put her Coke Classic on the counter.

"You Ted Sherman's kid?"

"Yes, sir," she said from the depths of the coat with its huge rolls of contained goose down.

"You seen anything strange around here recently? People you don't know?"

"No, sir. No stranger than the usual."

Sheriff Laskey smiled.

Mrs. Dalton spoke. "There was a young man in here about an hour ago. Grabbed a sandwich, got gas, and asked for directions to Charlottesville."

"Charlottesville?"

"Seemed lost."

"You get many people in here asking for directions?"

"Sure, we get plenty. But most of them are looking for a fishing hole or a hiking trail or the ski runs. City folk and people from Charlottesville mostly. But we don't get many down here looking *for* Charlottesville. Not many people are traveling from the South. I got the impression he was from the city."

"What was he driving?"

"A little blue import. Toyota or Honda. I don't know much about cars. I think it had a Virginia Tech sticker in the window, but my eyesight is failing me. But it was a sticker with Virginia Tech colors anyway."

Mr. Dalton looked over his shoulder at his wife, surprised at the sudden sharing of observation skills he didn't know she possessed. "Probably nothing. A rich kid down at Wintergreen for the weekend who took a wrong turn."

"Probably."

"So, Sheriff, how did he die?"

"It looks like he hung himself. Tied off to one of the old trees in the apple orchard." Laskey looked down at the counter and away from Mr. Dalton. "The critters got at him a bit. Wasn't real nice."

"Jesus. Good thing his parents weren't around to see that."

"God rest all their souls."

Officer Wallace fumbled for the cell phone in the passenger seat of his unmarked D.C. police cruiser. He was in the middle of DuPont Circle, heading towards Georgetown, and he answered on the second ring.

"Detective Wallace."

"Good evening, Detective. This is Sheriff Laskey of the Nelson County Sheriff's office."

"Good evening, Sheriff."

"I have some good news and some bad news on the person you asked me to find."

Detective Wallace knew what those words meant. But if the good sheriff was willing to pitch a slow ball right across the plate, it would have been unprofessional not to at least take a swing at it. "Let me guess. The good news is that you found him. The bad news is that he's dead."

"Hung himself in an old apple orchard."

"Well, I certainly couldn't have guessed that ending. How long has he been dead?"

"A while."

"You sure it's him?"

"I don't have DNA proof, if that is what you mean. Won't have that for a while. But I know it was him. Had on a big J.P. belt buckle. Known that kid his whole life. It was him."

"Let me know when you have confirmation, if you don't mind. Not that I don't believe you."

"Sure thing, Detective. There was something else. Two things actually. First, it seems as if the deceased had been growing something on his farm."

"Sounds like his hobby. That's what sent him to Petersburg."

"It wasn't marijuana this time. I'm not sure what it is exactly. Big tall plants that look like weeds. But they were grown in rows, real orderly. Most of them are dead of course, being that it's winter. There were some seeds on the ground that I'm going to have someone take a look at. See if they can tell me what they are."

"What was the second thing?"

"There was an open Koran on the dining room table of the house."

"A Koran?"

"Yep. Don't think I have ever seen one before. Fancy book. Gold writing on the cover. Arabic on one side of the page and an English translation on the other. At least I think it was Arabic."

"You have a Muslim community there in Nelson?"

"Detective, this is King James Bible country. But I don't think Jackson Price had been going to church."

"Sounds like he was praying for something."

Laskey was leaning over his desk looking at a stack of notes when Debbie Ingle entered and added another to the pile. Debbie, the sheriff office's lone secretary and unarmed employee, exited the room quietly. The sheriff was thinking and she knew that meant to leave him alone. Debbie was in her forties but looked younger with her blonde hair in a short earlobe-length cut. She was married to a local math teacher who was a sort of a renaissance man among Nelson County circles. He taught math, but was also known for his poetry and plumbing prowess.

Debbie sat behind her large wood desk, dressed in her usual work attire—black slacks and a white button up blouse. She occasionally mixed in a skirt when she was feeling sexy, but the color scheme never changed. It was like working with a waitress. But what she lacked in fashion sense, she made up for in organization. She took phone calls, kept records, and made copies of everything that passed through her hands. Her husband had taught her how to use a computer and half of the office's files were now scanned and saved electronically.

"Did they get J.P.'s body to the medical examiner's yet?" Laskey asked from the next room in a loud but professional voice.

"I haven't heard anything, but I will make a call and check," Debbie answered as the sheriff came from his office in the back room.

"I need to check on something. I'll be back in an hour or so. Going over to the Seed and Feed."

"You walking?" Debbie asked as the sheriff headed towards the front door, the opposite direction from his car parked in the lot behind the building.

"Yep. Let's call it a foot patrol," the sheriff said pulling open the door.

"Ok, Sheriff. I'll radio you if I hear anything."

"And see if anyone knows where we can reach Jackson's two-bit brother. I need to notify next of kin, if I can find him."

Lovington Seed and Feed was a half-mile from the sheriff's office, past the gas station and just beyond a large field that had once been a horse stable but was now overrun with waist-high weeds. The field offered a nice backdrop for the Seed and Feed, the large red barn and slightly leaning silo providing a picturesque scene for any artist who was able to envision the field of weeds as a swath of winter wheat.

The sheriff threw in another chew of Red Man and stood

on the sidewalk for a minute, staring up and down the "main drag," a street that was less of the first and more of the latter.

Kenny Buckner, dressed in jeans, work boots, and a green flannel shirt, grabbed the last bale of hay and threw it in the back of the red Ford 150 pickup. He tossed the rope from one side of the truck bed to the other and proceeded to hogtie the half-dozen blocks of hay.

"Good morning, Kenny."

"Good morning, Sheriff."

"How's business?"

"Still afloat. Been a cold winter, which hurts us a bit, but we'll make it."

"Sometimes making it is enough."

Kenny finished tying the load in the truck and tugged at the taut ropes one last time.

"Can I get you a cup of coffee, Sheriff?"

"As long as it's inside."

Kenny Buckner put two Styrofoam cups of coffee on the table in the small Seed and Feed office. Sheriff Laskey reached into the pocket of his jacket and removed an evidence bag. "Ever seen these before?" he asked, putting the bag on the table.

"Is that evidence? Isn't it against protocol to walk around with evidence?"

"What have you been watching, CSI?"

"Yeah. The wife loves it. Thought she was a forensic specialist after the first season."

Sheriff nodded towards the bag. "Got those off the Price's farm. Seems they were growing them. But I'm not sure what they are."

"Sorry to hear about J.P. He and my son were friends until J.P got the devil in him. They say he killed himself."

"That's what it looks like. The body is on the way over to the medical examiner's for confirmation. Been a long day."

Kenny Buckner took a sip of coffee and opened the bag. He reached in and held one of the seeds to the light. "Looks a bit like a coffee bean."

"Thought the same thing myself."

Kenny rolled the bean in his finger and then pulled out his buck knife from the sheath on his waist. "Do you mind?"

"Go ahead."

Kenny pushed down hard on the seed and it cracked under the pressure of the sharp blade. Kenny wiped the small residue of oil off the blade onto his dirty jeans. Each man picked up half of the seed.

"Looks like a seed to me. Nothing strange."

"I agree. Except for the fact that Jackson Price was growing them on the family farm. And there ain't been nothing legal growing on that farm since the death of J.P.'s father."

Chapter 37

Clark had stopped to look at his discovery twenty minutes north of Charlottesville. The multi-colored gravel he had found all over the yard he had now re-classified as a seed or a bean. His precious cargo in need of an explanation was currently riding shotgun in the cup holder of his Honda Civic. The drive back to D.C. took just over three hours, half as long as it took him to find the Price family farm on his journey down the Blue Ridge Mountains.

His jaunt to Nelson County generated more questions. Who the hell was calling both his neighbor and a farm in Virginia? Why? Right now the only clues he had were the three large beans vibrating in the cup holder near the parking brake. The objects made him nervous, curious. As the lines in the road zoomed passed, Clark imagined himself getting in an accident, losing his beans in a sea of broken glass and twisted metal, mumbling to ambulance personal to locate his magic beans because he had questions he wanted answers to.

As his mind raced, he did his best to keep his foot light. He felt relief at the first sign for the Beltway. There was something about coming home, even when home was measured at five miles per hour, bumper-to-bumper.

The small print on the sign outside the Merrifield Garden

Center on Lee Highway read, "If you can't find it here, we'll get it for you. If we can't get it for you, it can't be found."

Clark pulled in at the far end of the parking lot near the edge of the white one-story building. Three large greenhouses in the back of the lot stared down at the shorter white building. Beyond the greenhouses, acres of bushes, plants, trees, and sod stretched in three directions.

The Merrifield Garden Center was holding onto some of the most prime real estate in the region. A quarter mile from the Dunn Loring Metro station, development surrounded the nursery on three sides. But Merrifield Garden Center wasn't in the selling-out business. They were in the growing business. And with most of the other garden centers and nurseries pushed into the far limits of the suburbs, Merrifield Garden Center had, through attrition, become a monopoly of sorts.

The automatic doors in the front of the store opened and Clark smiled at the middle-aged woman working as the greeter and director of traffic. "Can I help you find something today?"

"Yes, I'm looking for your seed section."

"Seeds are in the far back right of the store, just before the door to the fertilizers."

"So just follow my nose?"

"I guess you could," the woman answered with a smile.

Clark meandered through the store, checking out the selection of potted flowers with his mother in mind. Then his mind moved on to Lisa and he knew he would end up with two different arrangements. He passed a small display of garden pools, complete with fish, and turned left at the large palm tree which was as out of place in the D.C. winter as he was with a handful of beans.

The wall of seeds stretched forty feet and Clark whistled quietly as he took in the view. There were hundreds of bags hanging on shiny silver metal hooks. Clark walked down the wall, looking over the heads and shoulders of other patrons who were more certain about their horticultural needs. The seeds were listed in alphabetical order which did Clark no good as he had no idea what he had. A handwritten sign hung on the hook where marigolds were previously sold. The sign read "Due to a recent surge in the purposeful ingestion of marigold seeds for recreational use, we will no longer be carrying them."

Clark spent twenty minutes pulling bags from the display on the wall and comparing them to the bean in his hand. After reaching the midway point in the wall, he gave up and looked for help. In the hanging plant section he found the same middle-aged woman who had greeted him at the front door and cornered her as she finished doling out advice to a yuppie with a cartful of his wife's marching orders.

"Did you find the seeds you were looking for?" she asked.

"No, I sure didn't. Maybe you would know what kind of seed this is," Clark said as he pulled one from his pocket.

The woman picked up the almost dime-sized seed and held it towards the light. She ran her fingers across the unusually textured skin and she admired the chocolate swirl appearance. "I don't know what this is. But it sure looks more like a bean than a seed."

"Maybe it is a bean. I'm not even sure what the difference is, really. I don't know much about gardening."

"I know someone who does. Follow me," she said. She marched through a set of double doors and past a long stretch of cacti that lined a single shelf on the wall. Head up, apron flapping, she continued walking, her eyes focused forward on the bean firmly pinched between her forefinger and thumb.

Without stopping she turned the corner through an "Employees Only" doorway and Clark followed closely behind. She passed through a sparsely decorated break-room with a round white table and a vending machine, and headed straight towards an office on the other side of the room. She stopped at the doorway and rapped slightly on the frame.

"Jerry, there is someone here who has a question maybe you can answer for him."

"Send him in."

"You're in good hands now. Jerry will take care of you." The woman pressed the bean into Clark's hand. Her job finished, she disappeared.

Clark stepped into the office and found himself staring at the top of Jerry's head as the man looked through a magnifying glass. Jerry paused and looked up at Clark, whose head snapped back a little in reaction to the thickest set of eyeglasses he had ever seen. Jerry had a chiseled face and dirty muscular hands. The kind of hands you would expect from a man who spent a lifetime in a garden center. His well-kept black curly hair wrapped around the top of his ears. The man needed a new pair of glasses.

"Hi, Jerry. Nice to meet you. I'm Clark."

"Clark, grab a seat," Jerry said, now looking back through the magnifying glass. "I will be with you in just one second."

"What are you looking at?" Clark asked after a minute of silence.

"Not exactly sure yet. I'm trying to figure out what kind of herbivorous insect has been nibbling on my ferns like a salad. Never seen this character before."

"Are you a bug specialist?"

Jerry smiled. "Nope, not a bug specialist. I own this place. And as its owner I am trying to determine just what's eating my inventory."

Clark smiled back and Jerry pushed the magnifying glass to the corner of his cluttered desk. Jerry looked up again and Clark fought the urge to tell him his glasses made him look like the bug he was trying to identify. Clark took in the room. A bookcase on the wall sagged under the weight of a hodgepodge of topics from lumberjacking to flowering perennials to insecticides.

"What can I help you with Clark?"

"I was wondering if you knew what kind of bean or seed this is?"

Clark put the seed on the table and Jerry picked it up with his thick fingers. Dirt was encrusted under the edge of his nails, the skin on his hands was rough and cracked. "Where did you get this?"

"Found it on a farm in Virginia."

"And you have no idea what it is?"

"None."

Jerry got up from his seat and headed for the bookcase. He ran his fingers along the spine of his books as he read, whispering to himself as he went along. *Not this one. Not that one. There might be something in here.*

He grabbed a black covered book from the middle of the shelf and placed it on a pile of papers on his desk. He turned the pages deliberately, scanning every picture. "If that is what I think it is, you may want to keep it quiet."

"Why's that?" Clark asked.

Before he could answer, Jerry poked his finger down on one of the pages. "Right here. I think this is what we're talking about."

Clark read the description and plowed roughshod over the Latin pronunciation of the word. Jerry watched as Clark continued to read and when Clark's eyes opened a little, Jerry knew he had reached the good part.

"Holy shit."

"That pretty much sums it up."

"How much of this did you find?"

Clark reached into his pocket and pulled out two more beans. "There were a few, hundreds maybe, scattered on the ground. I took three of them."

"Where in Virginia?"

"Nelson County. South of Charlottesville."

"That's odd."

"Why do you say that?"

"Well, Ricinus Communis likes slightly warmer climates as a rule, but it could grow quite well there."

"Grapes like warmer climates and there are a lot of vineyards in central Virginia," Clark added.

"Yes there are a few vineyards. And you're right, the growing conditions for grapes and our friend here are not that dissimilar. But I don't think these were grown in the winter. It's just too cold."

"Ricin," Clark said aloud, as if his mind was on delay.

"The name Ricinus, and hence ricin, comes from the Latin word for 'tick,' which obviously someone thought these seeds resembled. Our friend here is more commonly known as the castor bean, though it is technically a seed."

"If they were grown during the summer, could they be stored?"

"Sure, sure. Hell, these plants grow wild in some states here in the U.S. They are classified as a weed in Florida, if I remember correctly."

"Classified as a weed? You mean it isn't illegal to grow?"

"Not at all. Illegal to process, not illegal to grow."

Clark read the passage in the book again. "Well, that doesn't sound like a good idea, just allowing anyone to grow them."

"The castor plant has been around for hundred of years. Maybe thousands. They use it in paints and varnishes. It's water resistant and is used as a coating for insulation and guns. And it's used as a medicine. Also as a motor oil."

"Medicine?

"Castor oil. What did you think that was?"

"I never thought about it."

"I remember reading there are over 200 metric tons of semi-processed ricin produced every year. If someone with ill intentions really wanted to get their hands on a lot of ricin, all they would have to do is park outside a castor production plant."

"Where is the nearest castor production facility?" Clark asked.

"India, probably."

"Maybe it would just be easier to grow it."

"Maybe. Either way, stolen or grown, gram for gram, it is a hundred times more deadly than most conventional poisons, man-made or natural."

"Pretty nasty stuff."

"The meanest bean on the planet. You say you only found a few hundred?"

"It was hard to say. They were on the ground, in the grass,

on the driveway. I didn't find a mountain of them if that is what you are getting at."

"Well that's good news. In order to get ricin from the bean it needs to be processed, and you would need more than a hundred to make it worth your while."

"Worth your while?"

"Yeah, economically it would be cheaper to get a gun than to get the machinery necessary to process a handful of castor beans."

Clark laughed nervously. "You know what they say—it's not guns that kill people. It's the people pulling the trigger on the guns who kill people."

"Have you ever been shot?" Jerry asked.

"Not yet," Clark answered.

"Well, I haven't either, but I don't think a person with a bullet in their ass really cares if it was the gun or the person behind the gun."

"Probably not."

Jerry looked at one of the beans under the magnifying glass for another minute. "You know, you should probably call the authorities."

"It was on my mind."

"After 9/11 the florist industry received communication from the FBI warning us to keep an eye out for large orders of potentially hazardous plants."

"Like what?"

"There are more than you can imagine. Hemlock, a Shakespeare assassin, looks like a big carrot and is quite deadly. Mistletoe berries will drop you like a ton of bricks. Yew, jasmine berries, the leaves from rhubarb. God didn't skimp when it came to giving plants and animals the ability to evolve with a little kick-ass of their own."

"Don't worry about contacting the authorities. As it happens, I'm on a first name basis with an FBI agent. We had lunch last week."

"Give him a call, just to be safe."

"I will. Thanks for letting me pick your brain."

"No problem," Jerry answered. Before Clark reached the door, Jerry offered parting advice. "Do us all a favor and throw those away, just to be on the safe side. We don't need someone trying to grow them around here. You would feel awful if someone ended up digesting the by-product from those."

Chapter 38

The windowless side-room stretched the width of the garage, fifteen feet wide and sixty feet deep. The lone working entrance, a set of double doors, was near the back of the warehouse, two steps from the unused one stall bathroom with a sink and shower, and ten paces from the door to the small office in the main warehouse floor.

Each of the three machines resided in a third of the room. The roller was at the far end, the farthest from the double-doors that led to the warehouse. The crusher was next, taking up the middle position on the side-room floor. The pulverizer was nearest the exit.

Each machine weighed over a ton, heavy enough to crack most floors but not nearly heavy enough to cause the thick concrete beneath the warehouse to protest. The warehouse had originally been designed to withstand a couple of cars, the odd truck, and the four-ton wrecker that brought the injured autos to the shop.

Ariana opened the double doors and her three-man team eagerly stepped forward. When you are stuck in a warehouse, and a portion of it is off-limits, natural curiosity reaches unnatural proportions. Just ask James Beach.

Ariana spoke. "It's time to get to work."

"What are they?" Syed asked, stepping past Ariana from

the rear. Karim followed Syed and moved for a better view.

"This room is our processing facility. We'll have to do some modification to the environment, but it should work."

"What are we processing?"

"Ricin," Ariana said. "From the seeds of the castor plant."

"Is that what's in the truck?" Syed asked.

"Yes."

"How deadly is it?" Abu asked. "James said he had enough material in his truck to kill ten thousand men."

"It's possible. Ricin is five thousand times more poisonous than cyanide and ten thousand times more deadly than cobra venom. It only takes a very small amount to kill an average size man. But, I won't know the final potential until the seeds are processed. Ricin is only part of the plant. We are not extracting it from the seeds. Meaning once we process the seeds, a percentage of the final product will be ricin. Maybe five percent by weight."

"How do we process it?" Abu asked, looking at the control panel on the crusher.

"I'm going to show you. And, if you follow the rules I set up, only one of us will be in real danger."

"Only *one* of us?" Abu asked. "We are down to three."

Ariana ignored the second half of Abu's statement. "Yes. Only one."

"Let me guess. It won't be you," Syed said.

Ariana smiled and then pursed her lips. "No, it won't be me."

"Was there ever a moment of doubt?" Abu added.

Ariana moved on. "We have three machines. Production will begin at the far end of the room and will work its way towards this door. The first machine is a high-impact roller made by John Deere for the farming industry."

Ariana walked the men towards the red machine at the end. It was squat, four feet high and six feet square. A wide conveyor belt fed into a narrow opening on the machine. "It looks like a pizza oven," Syed said. "One of those that run a conveyor belt through it."

"The roller is pretty basic. It crushes the seeds and removes the oil. The oil is harmless and will pool in a reservoir on the bottom that will need to be changed as it becomes full. We will store the oil in the metal barrels along the far wall. At this point in the process the crushed seeds will be relatively benign. As long as no one decides to eat one."

"I don't think you have to worry about that," Syed said.

"We may need to let the crushed seeds dry for a day or two. I will decide that once I see the output from the roller. I have manually processed a small number of seeds and I don't think the oil will present us with any problems. It dries quickly with the proper treatment, and according to my calculations, based on the roller's specs, ninety-eight percent of the oil will be removed."

"You have not tried these machines?" Karim asked.

"I tested them to make sure they work." Ariana paused. "And that will have to be enough experience."

Karim shrugged his shoulders in unenthusiastic support.

"The next machine is a little more complicated." Ariana stepped towards the oversized light blue piece of machinery. "This one is the JEX Paw Crusher. It can process ten pounds of material per minute. It weighs a little over three tons. The crushed seeds from the roller will go into the chute on the far side of the machine and will come out the vertical tube on the side. The output tube connects directly into the large bin on the floor next to the machine. This is where the hazard begins.

"Once the seeds have entered the crusher, there is the potential for lethal dust in the air. But this crusher is top-of-the-line. It is designed so that dust is self-contained. It is gasket-sealed on all seams, and has a multiple chamber design with inward facing air vents. There should be very little collateral exposure. Unless there is a malfunction, or the machines need to be cleaned. I think we can avoid the latter. We only need to use these machines once."

The three men looked at the large semi-translucent bin at the end of the crusher. "How do we transfer the seeds from the crusher to this last machine?"

"Well, the last machine, the pulverizer, will extract what is left of the seeds directly from the bin. The machines are designed to be used in tandem. But there still may be some collateral dust."

"How large will the seeds be when they exit the crusher?" Syed asked.

"They won't resemble seeds at all. At its maximum setting, the output should be approximately 150 mesh."

"How big is a mesh?" Syed asked.

"It's not measured that way. There is no such thing as 'a mesh.' A mesh is a unit of measure based upon material passing through a one-by-one inch square. 150 mesh means that there are 150 holes per square inch. The output should be small enough to fit through one square inch with 150 holes."

"That's pretty small," Karim said, now looking at the conveyor belt that fed the first machine.

"By most human standards of measurement 150 mesh is very small. About 100 microns."

"Which is how big?" Syed asked.

"Think along the lines of fine sand." Ariana thought for a moment. "Or on the order of flour."

"I assume at 150 mesh the seeds would be dangerous," Abu asked.

Ariana looked at each man, each face waiting for a response to the question.

"Yes. At 150 mesh, the seeds will be a very fine powder. They will be at least five percent ricin by weight. They will be very dangerous."

"How do we protect ourselves?"

"I'll get to that in a minute," Ariana answered.

The men exchanged glances and the cool dampness of the room felt as if it dropped several degrees.

Ariana continued. "The output bin to the crusher will hold about five hundred pounds of powder. The bin is built on a steel platform frame and it has wheels. As you can see, it can be rolled to the pulverizer."

"The pulverizer? I like the name," Abu added unprovoked.

Ariana rolled her eyes slightly and stepped towards the odd looking machine. She highlighted the bells and whistles on the pulverizer like a model at a car show. "On the far end is the intake tube and on this end we have an elephant trunk-like output tube."

"This is an ultra-fine pulverizer and is designed to take anything from a small grain to a powder and pulverize it. The intake tube on the front will go into the bin of ricin powder, the output from the crusher. There will likely be some leakage, though it should be minimal. The pulverizer has an output between 500 and 700 mesh."

"Which is…?" Karim asked.

"Something a little smaller than an individual spore of plant pollen. A single red blood cell is about 1200 mesh. For those thinking in terms other than mesh, we are talking about thirty microns. The lower limit of visibility for the naked eye is in the neighborhood of forty microns."

"So it will be invisible?" Syed asked.

"Yes, theoretically, a singular piece of processed seed will be invisible to the human eye. But, obviously, as a powder you would be looking at large quantities and it would be identifiable as a very fine powder. Probably more fine than anything any of us have ever touched or seen. Needless to say, when the final product comes out of the ultra-fine pulverizer, the powder will be the most deadly substance for a thousand miles in any direction."

"Fort Detrick is only fifty miles and that houses ebola, among others," Karim added referring to the military installation that studies deadly virus and biological agents.

"I know," Ariana said. "And my statement stands."

A moment of silence, mixed with excitement, filled the air.

"How long will it take to process the ricin in the truck?" Abu asked.

"Twenty four-hours. Maybe forty-eight."

Abu went back to the key point of the conversation. "If

this powder is so fine, how do we prevent from inhaling it? I assume there will be powder everywhere."

"If these machines operate as they should, and believe me they should for the price tag that came with them, then there most certainly will not be powder everywhere. But, in the interest of being thorough, I have a half-dozen gas masks that are military grade. Tough to come by."

"How did you get your hands on those?" Abu asked.

"I don't want to know," Karim answered.

Ariana was in the mood to talk. "All of us will wear gas masks for the duration of the process, but only one of us is in real danger. Timing will be important. If there is an accident, well, then, we will spend our last days taking out as many people as we can."

"Only one person will be in here?" Abu asked, looking around the room.

"Yes. And that person will be fitted with a chemical suit."

"Where did you get a chemical suit?"

"Fire department surplus."

"Why only one?"

"They only had one," Ariana said. "Under the chemical suit, the machine operator will wear a CamelBak."

"What's a CamelBak?" Syed asked.

"It's a backpack filled with water. It has a tube that delivers the liquid to the wearer's mouth. It's popular among bikers and mountain climbers and for people who need their hands during physical exertion."

"I know what they are; I didn't know they were called CamelBaks."

"Now you do. The person in charge of manufacturing will not be able to eat and will not be able to remove the chemical suit for the duration of the process. I have adult undergarments as well."

"That's one way to make them work fast," Karim said a matter-of-factly.

Abu and Syed nodded in agreement.

"The three of us not doing the processing will be in the sleeping quarters on the far side of the warehouse. We will have gas masks on. The door will be sealed from the outside with towels and tape, by the machine operator, before he begins work.

"The machine operator will be in the facility for the duration of the task. It will be him, the seeds, the machines, his suit, his CamelBak, and a garden hose attached to the bathroom sink. Primitive, but that is what we have to work with.

"When the processor is finished, and the ricin is in the delivery mechanisms that I provide, the processor will hose down the room. There is a drain on the floor near the crusher. Just as there is on the floor of the main warehouse. When the person is finished, he will hose the room down again. Top to bottom. And then he will hose it down a third time. He will repeat this until he feels comfortable enough to take his chemical suit off."

"A good way to make sure the job is done right," Syed noted.

"Yes it is," Ariana said. "But keep in mind, this room should not be dusty. There may be some collateral dust between the crusher and the pulverizer, and there may be some between pulverizer and the containers I will provide, but these machines have been chosen for their ability to process without contaminating their environment. The water is merely a way to prevent unintended contamination.

"Once the ricin has been placed in delivery mechanisms, and the room has been hosed to satisfaction, the processor will cover the machines with plastic drop clothes which will be in the shower stall. Then he will shower with the chemical suit on. Using the body wash that is also in the stall.

"The truck will be backed up to the double doors. The containers will be transferred into the truck. After the chemicals have been transferred, he will then shower again, take the chemical suit off, and put on a gas mask. Then the doors to the production room will be shut. At that point we are on the clock."

"How long before we start?" Syed asked.

"I will know in a couple of days. I have to prepare the dispersion containers. And pray for good weather."

Karim spoke. "Then there is only one question left. Who is the lucky person?"

Everyone looked at each other.

"I'll do it," Abu said. "I do not fear death."

Chapter 39

The writing down the side of the car and Laskey's official uniform, both financed by the fine taxpayers of Nelson County, allowed him to pass through the first barricade near D.C. Police Headquarters on Indiana Ave. Tire-shredders guarded the inner sanctum of the parking lot and without a pass code Laskey made the easy decision to follow the small access road around to the back of the building. He pulled his car in behind a set of Jersey walls and grabbed the plastic evidence bag off the front seat. He got out of the car and stared at the sea of security that engulfed the nation's capital from Capitol Hill to Union Station. He was suddenly thankful for the relative peace of Nelson County.

The guard behind the bulletproof glass spoke as Laskey approached the one-man booth. "How can I help you today?"

"My name is Mike Laskey and I'm the sheriff of Nelson County, Virginia. I'm here to see Detective Earl Wallace."

"What's in the bag?"

"Evidence."

"Anything potentially hazardous?"

Laskey knew the truth was only going to be the beginning of trouble. "No, they are seeds."

"Sign in on the bottom line, Sheriff."

Laskey pulled the clipboard through the security crack

at the bottom of the window and signed in with the pen that dangled on a small chain.

"Up the stairs to the second floor. Detective Wallace is on the north side of the building."

Laskey looked up at the sun to determine which direction was north.

"There are signs in the building that will tell you where to go," the officer added. "Turn left at the top of the stairs. Or take the elevator and go right."

"Do I look that I old?"

"Just trying to be helpful. I give the same response to everyone."

Laskey climbed the concrete stairs to the second floor and turned left. An officer in a crisp suit shoved a hand-cuffed perp in gang-banger clothes head first through a pair of swinging doors. Laskey followed in the wake of vulgarities that the suspect unleashed on the officer. The gang-banger continued to yell about human rights abuse as he was thrown into an empty wooden chair.

The female officer behind a desk on the second floor looked at Sheriff Laskey in his best outfit. His brown uniform was ironed. His shield gleamed. His gray hair was combed to perfection.

"I'm looking for Detective Wallace."

"Does he know you're coming?"

"I called him this morning."

The woman behind the desk stood and looked out across the room. The floor buzzed with activity. Desks filled the center of the room and a dozen officers in street clothes typed on their computers and talked on their phones.

"He's in the corner on the far left," the female officer said pointing in the direction of a large man in rumpled clothes.

"The guy with the red tie?"

"That's him."

"Thanks."

Detective Wallace, a twenty-four year veteran with the rank of Sergeant, sensed Sheriff Laskey approaching and ended the phone conversation he was having.

"You must be Sheriff Laskey."

"And you must be Sergeant Wallace."

The two law enforcement officers with fifty-plus years of experience exchanged handshakes.

"Have a seat."

"I would prefer to stand. Been sitting for three hours."

"Fair enough. You want something? Coffee, tea?"

"No thanks. Got somewhere we can talk?"

Detective Wallace looked around at the offices that lined the north end of the floor. "Follow me."

Wallace shut the door as Laskey walked into the office with a glass interior wall. Laskey set the evidence bag on the table and Wallace looked down.

"So these are the little things that have been keeping you up all night?"

"Yes they are."

"What are they?"

"That's just it; I have no idea."

"But they kept you up all night?" Detective Wallace asked in his on-the-job tone usually reserved for guilty faces on the street.

"I have good instincts. Hunches really. Not to mention there was a dead body on the farm where I got these. And there were a lot of them."

"Ah, yes. The dead body. Got one of them myself here to deal with. Though I may be making progress. You said you found a Koran at the house of your deceased."

"That's right. Fancy looking book."

"Well, I got in touch with my dead guy's p.o. and he told me, off the record, that my dead guy had converted to Islam in prison. They've got an imam behind bars in Petersburg and he has quite the following, evidently."

"Was your dead guy a blond, California surfer type?"

"He has brown hair now. Dyed. And he certainly doesn't look like a healthy golden boy anymore. But with blond hair, I guess he could be mistaken for a surfer. Why do you ask?"

"I poked around a little and some people in town saw

my dead guy with someone who looked like a surfer."

"Probably the same."

Both men nodded and their eyes dropped to the bag of seeds on the table.

Wallace grabbed the bag and held it to the light in his thick black hands. "Let me make a few calls."

Jerry was chasing an odd-colored ladybug around his desk when Detective Wallace and Sheriff Laskey entered the office to the Merrifield Gardening Center.

Handshakes and credential flashing ensued before Detective Wallace pulled the bag of beans from his pocket.

Jerry glanced at the beans in the bag through the magnification of his thick glasses. "You are the second person to bring those in this week."

"So you know what they are?"

"You ever heard of ricin?

Wallace dropped the bag on the table.

"Well, not exactly ricin, but the raw material for it. Those are castor beans. Which is really a misnomer. They are actually seeds."

"Castor beans?"

"Same bean that makes castor oil. It's used in a million different applications. Body lotion. Lubrication."

"My mother use to give my brother and me castor oil for upset stomachs when we were kids," Sheriff Laskey added.

"I thought ricin would kill you?" Detective Wallace asked.

"Parts of the beans will kill you deader than a door nail," Jerry answered. "The oil won't."

"I don't follow."

"Well, if you process castor beans properly and extract the oil, the leftover mash can be processed into a poison. Ricin. Deadly stuff."

"How much does it take to kill a person?"

Jerry recalled what he read in the book days earlier. "Less than five microns."

The plant and insect expert could see by his guests' reactions that they had no idea what a micron was.

"Five microns would be a fraction of the size of a grain of salt. Something along the lines of a small piece of dust."

"You've never seen the dust in my house," Detective Wallace said.

"No, and I think I'm thankful for that."

Sheriff Laskey tried to put things into perspective. "How many people do you reckon we could take out with this small bag here?"

"I don't know. Dozens I guess, once it gets processed. But you would need a whole lot more to make a weapon of mass destruction, or at least a weapon of mass hysteria."

Wallace felt the hair on his neck stand-up, like an animal's reaction to an impending earthquake. He knew what was coming.

"How much more?"

"Thousands of plants."

Sheriff Laskey added his own hysteria to the equation. "How about a field of plants. Twenty or thirty acres. A plant every few feet."

Jerry's head drooped a little in fear. His mind tried to calculate a reasonable number. "That could be millions of beans. But the scary part is this. Those beans remain deadly for years. If someone were growing them, say on a farm as you suggest, they could reap more than one harvest."

Wallace turned white, for a black guy, and Laskey nodded his head slowly in a moment of shared understanding.

"Tell me you got the name of the person who came in earlier in the week?"

"His name was Clark. He had three beans with him. Said he got them on a farm in central Virginia. Also said he was friends with an FBI agent and that he would take it up with him or her."

"You didn't bother getting a last name?"

"Not really. This kid was white suburbia."

"Terrorists are recruiting all nationalities and ethnicities these days."

Jerry looked at Detective Wallace. "If you were a terrorist

and you had deadly material on your hands, would you take it to someone and ask them to identify it? Wouldn't you think he would know what he had? Why raise suspicion?"

"You got me there."

Sheriff Laskey got the investigation back on track. "Do you have security cameras in the parking lot? Maybe we can go through the tapes and you could identify the person who paid you a visit earlier. This Clark character."

"We have surveillance cameras, but I'm not sure they will help. We keep them on a twenty-four hour loop. Had a problem with some vandals a few years back, and a couple of Japanese Red Maples went missing around the same time. Those Red Maples can be expensive."

"I'm sure they are," Detective Wallace said.

"If the tapes are on a twenty-four hour feed, our kid is probably not going to be making an appearance," Laskey said. "So all we have to go on is that this kid's name is Clark."

"Sorry. That's all I can tell you, other than that he is harmless."

"Just the same."

"And if he were up to no good, he probably wouldn't be using his real name."

"Thanks for the deductive reasoning."

"Let me know if I can help."

"Will do."

In the parking lot Detective Wallace looked over the top of his car at Sheriff Laskey before entering the vehicle.

"How many seeds did you find out there on the farm?"

"The ground was littered with them. There were hundreds. Thousands. I don't know. But most of the plants I saw were stripped bare. No telling how many were there before the plants were stripped."

"I think we need some answers and we need them yesterday."

"I was hoping between the dead guy you pulled out of the

river, and the dead guy I pulled out of the tree, we would be able to figure it out."

"Maybe, but before the end of the day I'm going to need to run this one up the flag pole. The FBI is going to get involved, Homeland Security, you name it."

"Sounds like a recipe for disaster. Get a bunch of people pissing on each other, overstepping boundaries, drawing lines in the sand. A thousand chefs with a thousand hands staring down at a single pot."

"How do you know so much about bureaucracy?"

"We got politics in small towns. And besides, this Administration has been parading their incompetence for the world to see for a few years now. I may live in the country, but I'm not stupid or isolated … unless I want to be."

"You have any ideas on how to find this kid?"

"Just one. There's a chance he may have stopped at a gas station in Nelson, filled up, and asked for directions. If he paid with a debit or credit card, I can get the name with a single call."

"Then make the call. If we can find this kid, maybe we can drag him to a meeting with the Feds."

Debbie Ingel answered the phone at her desk in the Nelson County sheriff's office.

Sheriff Laskey didn't let her get through her standard greeting. "Deb, this is Mike."

"Yes, Sheriff."

"I need you to call down to *The Pig and Whistle*. Talk to the Daltons. Tell them I need the credit card and debit card receipts from everyone who bought gas or a donut for the last two weeks. Start yesterday and work backwards. The first name on the receipt should be Clark. That should help narrow it down."

"It may take a while."

"I don't have a while. I need it within the hour. Tell Mrs.

Dalton to skip making sandwiches today. The world will survive without her ham on wheat."

"Will do."

Sheriff Nelson looked over at Detective Wallace who had pulled the bag from his pocket again and placed them on the roof of the car.

"What ya' thinkin' about?"

"How something so small and so innocent looking could kill a man."

"One bean doesn't worry me."

Debbie Ingel called back twenty minutes later.

"You might want to apologize to the Daltons. Apparently our request screwed up their lunchtime business."

"They'll get over it. I'll look the other way the next time they are caught sellin' beer to underage kids."

"You still need the information?"

"Sure do."

"Well, you hit the nail on the head. There was a Clark Hayden who purchased gas with a Bank of America debit card at *The Pig and Whistle*. Purchased it yesterday morning, right before you went out to the Price farm. You couldn't have missed him by much more than an hour or two."

"I need you to run him through DMV."

"Already did. His current address is listed as 202 Dorchester Lane in Arlington, Virginia."

"Let me get a pen."

Laskey searched his pockets with his free hand. Wallace threw his detective notebook, pencil stuffed into the wire binding, onto Laskey's lap. The sheriff scribbled on the first open page he could find and showed it to Detective Wallace.

The detective nodded as he hit the gas pedal.

Chapter 40

Are you Clark Hayden?" Detective Wallace asked through the closed storm door.

"Who's asking?" Clark replied. He was wearing jeans that were tattered on the fringe of the legs, wool socks, and a striped sweater that made him look like Charlie Brown. His mother was at his aunt's and he wasn't due to pick her up until the next morning. He had the house to himself for the day, and in the evening was planning on Lisa coming over for sex, under the auspice of watching a DVD.

"D.C. Police," Wallace answered, flashing his badge. The heat from the house created condensation on the glass in the storm window and Clark squinted to see the details of the badge. He sighed heavily and opened the door. "Come in."

Wallace extended his hand, and Sheriff Laskey removed his hat.

"Detective Earl Wallace. D.C. Metropolitan Police. This is Sheriff Laskey, Nelson County, Virginia."

Clark shook hands and looked each officer in the eye as his pucker meter inched up. "Have a seat," Clark offered, gesturing towards the sofa with large cushions. He pulled the old wicker rocking chair to face the sofa, the well-worn coffee table between him and his guests.

"You know why we are here?"

"I could guess, but I'd just rather you tell me. I have been doing a lot of speculating recently. I'm all guessed out."

Detective Wallace looked at the young man in front of him. Twenty-five years old. Six foot. One hundred and eighty pounds. Solid build. Looks athletic, except for the overly geeky glasses with the black frames. "Rumor has it that you have some beans in your possession that could kill a few people."

Clark swallowed hard. "That wasn't the question I was expecting. You working with the FBI?"

"No," Detective Wallace said. He looked at Sheriff Laskey and the men nodded to each other. The sheriff pulled the bag of ricin seeds from the pocket of his winter jacket. "Jerry at Merrifield Garden Center told us you came in with a few of these."

"I did. But I didn't tell him my last name, so how did you find me? It was only yesterday."

"You trying to hide something?"

"Not at all. But people usually don't go around dropping their last name. Unless it's Trump or Hilton and you're going to get a reservation at a restaurant. Unfortunately 'Hayden' doesn't come with any perks."

Sheriff Laskey smiled. "No, I guess not."

"So … how did you find me? Not that I'm entirely sad to see you."

"Investigative techniques," Wallace added. "Believe it or not the badge is real and I'm an actual detective."

"Fair enough." Clark was silent for a moment and his armpits started to perspire. The black detective was sitting directly across from Clark, piercing eyes measuring his every movement. Every twitch. The white sheriff was doing the country version of the same. Clark stared back for a few seconds, his eyes bouncing from one guest to the other. "I found the beans on a farm in Nelson County. But given that the sheriff here is the law in Nelson County, I figure you already know that."

"You pay attention," Sheriff Laskey said. "But we don't call the sheriff 'the law' anymore. Except on *Western Movie Day*."

Wallace laughed out loud and Clark relaxed a little. If these guys were ball-busters they were waiting to bring out the testicle hammer. Clark got the feeling that the men were like him, just looking for answers. Besides, from what he knew, most cops handcuffed first and asked questions later.

"Did you grow them?" the sheriff asked.

"The seeds?"

"Are we talking about anything else that grows?" Wallace added.

"Hell, no. I didn't even know what they were until Jerry the-plant-guy told me."

Laskey looked at Wallace. Chalk one up to old Jerry's intuition.

"What brought you to the farm?" Wallace asked.

Clark squirmed and the proverbial cat reached out and grabbed his tongue. And it was a full-grown tiger that hadn't eaten in a month.

"That's not so easy to explain."

"Give it your best shot."

"Ok. But I'm warning you up front it may sound a little kooky."

"We have been warned," Wallace answered.

Clark delved into the story of his mother calling the CIA, the visit from the FBI about terrorists across the street, his Pakistani neighbors disappearing, the explosion at his neighbor's house, his dead neighbor, the calls from a stolen phone in Pakistan owned by a low-level diplomat.

"So I called the guy in Pakistan and asked him if any other calls were made from his phone. He told me yes and gave me the number. From there it was easy."

"And you had never been to the farm before?"

"No."

"And you wouldn't know anything about a dead guy hanging from a tree in the back field?"

Clark's heart kicked up a notch. "Uh, no. I didn't see any dead guys. Hell, I've only seen two dead bodies in my life: my father's and my grandfather's. I went to the farm and walked around the house once. It was kind of spooky. Desolate. You could just tell no one had been there. I headed back to my car and dropped my keys. I saw these seeds on the ground and picked up a few. Then I heard a door or something banging in the distance and decided to leave."

"That's it?"

"That's it. Like I said, it was spooky. I mean, I grew up in Northern Virginia. I haven't spent much time on farms. But one of my roommates in college used to love to tell the story of how he was trouncing through a farm near some family land in Bath County and got shot by a neighbor with rock salt. For some reason, standing out there on that farm, that story came back to me."

Laskey smiled again. "Hardly anyone uses rock salt anymore. Nowadays they shoot you with real bullets. Though I did get a little rock salt in the ass when I was younger. In hindsight, I probably deserved it."

Detective Wallace chimed in. "OK. So we've established that neither of you deal with urban crime much. I've been a cop for thirty years and have never even seen rock salt … So what happened next?"

"Came back here."

"Here being D.C.?"

"Here being Northern Virginia."

"When did you go to the Merrifield Garden Center?"

"On my way home."

"And after you found out you were carrying ricin, you didn't feel compelled to call the authorities?"

"I did. I called the FBI agent who came to the house a few weeks ago and left him a message. It was at 8:07 last night. He didn't call me back and I called him again at 9:21 this morning and left another message. You can check my cell phone's outgoing calls."

"I believe you. Did you mention ricin in your phone call?"

"No. But I told him that I had some very interesting information on my neighbors."

Wallace's face wrinkled as he digested deep thoughts that came to mind.

Laskey asked a question. "Exactly, how many seeds did you bring back?"

"Three."

"Why three?"

"No reason. Like I said, the whole situation was a little nerve-wracking. Poking around, uninvited, on someone's farm, looking for people who can answer a question about a phone call from Pakistan, made on a stolen cell phone. If my hands weren't cold and I hadn't dropped my keys, we wouldn't be having this conversation. Besides, all the seeds looked the same. There was no reason to bring back a ton of them."

All three men stared down at the bag on the table. "Yes, they do look the same," the sheriff concurred.

"Where are the ones you brought back with you?"

"Downstairs. In my dresser. In my underwear drawer."

"Would you mind getting them?"

"Not at all. Give me a sec."

When Clark returned he put the beans, which where now safely stored in an empty prescription medicine bottle, on the table.

"You never told me how you found me."

"Gas station receipt."

"*The Pig and Whistle.*"

Sheriff Laskey nodded. "Nice deduction."

"Good ham and wheat sandwiches."

"The best in Virginia."

Clark took a page from his mother's book of hosting guests and asked if anyone wanted coffee. Laskey and Wallace shook their heads.

"If I may ask, what brought *you* to the farm?"

"I think that conversation needs to be answered downtown. Let's find your FBI buddy."

Agent Rosson chose the same windowless room where his boss, the Director of the Joint Terrorism Task Force, laid down the law for all investigations leading to Dorchester Lane.

Detective Wallace had his notebook on the table and a plain manila folder in front of him. "This feels like an interrogation room."

"It was. In a previous life. Most of the interrogation rooms were relocated to the first level of the basement. Or to another offsite location," Agent Rosson answered. "Now we use this room primarily for private conversations. The type of conversations that shouldn't leave the premises."

"Understood. At police headquarters we use the john," Wallace said.

"We are a little more civilized here at the Bureau." There was a pecking order in law enforcement and Agent Rosson was making sure that everyone in the room knew their position.

"I think we both got our suits at *Men's Warehouse*," Wallace responded. "Two for $149 during the spring sale last year."

Clark watched the banter and tried not to laugh. Grown men in the professional sandbox.

Agent Rosson deflected the attempt to be lumped into the same group. "What are we here to discuss?"

"Ricin," Detective Wallace answered. Everyone in the room, even Clark, could tell the answer caught the agent off guard.

"Ricin?"

"Didn't Clark here tell you? I understand he left several urgent messages for you to call him back."

"There was no mention of ricin in his calls," Rosson answered.

"Well, if you returned his call, maybe you wouldn't look like you were just taken from behind. At any rate, we're here now."

"Please go ahead."

Detective Wallace nodded towards Clark. Clark cleared his throat. "There have been several developments with regard to my neighbors across the street."

"203 Dorchester Lane, Arlington, Virginia."

"That's correct."

Agent Rosson motioned with his hand for Clark to continue. Clark started with his neighbors supposedly leaving the country and finished with Detective Wallace and Sheriff Laskey at his front door.

"Are you sure it's ricin?" Agent Rosson asked.

Sheriff Laskey pulled out his evidence bag and Clark's prescription bottle of seeds. "We're sure. You want to try one?"

"Tell me, just how did you get involved?" Rosson asked the sheriff.

"I got a call from D.C. asking me to check on a residence in my jurisdiction."

"And your jurisdiction is…" Agent Rosson asked as he squinted at the badge on the sleeve of the sheriff's jacket.

"Nelson County."

"Home of Wintergreen."

"Yes, indeed. Home of Wintergreen, and as of yesterday, home of a ricin plantation."

In his best condescending tone Rosson kept his hand on the conversation throttle. "We'll get there in a minute. You were talking about a call from D.C."

"I got a call yesterday morning from Detective Wallace, asking me to check on the whereabouts of a Nelson County resident."

Rosson turned towards Wallace. "And you were interested in this person, why?"

"He was the cellmate of a body I pulled from the Potomac earlier this week. A dead guy named James Beach. Former guest who spent a couple of years choking down three squares a day on taxpayer money at the Petersburg Correctional Facility in Virginia."

"Anything unusual about the body?"

"Nothing really. Still waiting on the toxicology report, but initial indications are that he drowned."

"And the call to Nelson County?"

"Trying to notify next of kin. Wanted to ask a few questions to someone who might have known him."

"Procedural duties."

"If that's what you call them here at the Bureau," Wallace answered.

There was a brief pause and the door to the room swung open. Eric Nerf, the Director of the Joint Terrorism Task Force walked in the room.

"That *is* what we call them at the Bureau. In fact, consider your entire visit here a procedural duty."

"Thin doors for an interrogation room," Wallace said, standing from his seat. "We haven't met." Wallace's large frame shadowed the table and his mitt-like hand engulfed the well-dressed director's.

"Eric Nerf, Director of the Joint-Terrorism Task Force for the Federal Bureau of Investigation," he announced to the room.

"Is that your full title?"

"Yes it is."

After shaking hands, Wallace took his seat again, this time further from the table, one ankle resting on his other knee.

"And you are Detective Earl Wallace of the Washington D.C. Metropolitan Police Force. Rank of Sergeant. Robbery and Homicide division. Lead detective on the Senator Day case, but I don't think we need to go into the details of that here."

"Well, if you're chasing the terrorists with the same energy that you're doing your homework on other law enforcement officers, I think we can all sleep easy tonight."

Agent Rosson got his boss up to speed on the conversation with only a minor air of superiority. Clark sat back in his chair, taking in the room and the conversation. He told himself to be stoic but his stomach was bubbling beneath his Charlie Brown sweater.

The director took his favorite position, sitting on the corner of the table. There was something about putting your ass at table-level that created resentment among those seated at the table. It was an insult he had perfected over the years. Wallace, Laskey and Clark all took silent offense.

"Well, I'm fascinated by this conversation. I truly am. But what I'm about to tell you is highly confidential. Consider it top secret. And the only reason I'm telling you is out of professional courtesy and, of course, because I don't want anyone in this room stumbling over something they shouldn't."

"The CIA has informed the Joint Terrorism Task Force, in other words, me, that they have an operative on the case. This operative has worked for years in pursuit of a high-profile target. This agent's contact with the CIA clandestine office is on an "as-capable basis," meaning that there are long periods of time when the operative is dark. Completely off the grid. There are thousands of man-hours at stake in this intelligence effort, not to mention national security. With all due respect to everyone in the room, there is to be no further investigation of anyone involved. Right now 203 Dorchester Lane doesn't exist. Leave it alone."

"Is that an order?" Wallace asked.

"That's a professional request. But if you call your captain, he will convey it as an order, if that would make you feel better."

The room fell into an uneasy silence. Wallace brooded. Laskey fumed; his first foray into the politics of big-time law enforcement was even uglier than he imagined. Clark sat at the table, his mind running through the details, the analysis of the situation in full-steam-ahead mode. His mouth opened before his brain could backtrack.

"What about the ricin?"

"We'll take care of it," the Director said.

Wallace looked at Clark and Laskey. Clark started to speak and Wallace cut him off. "They said they'll take care of it."

Clark missed the hint. "You know, there's no one at 203 Dorchester Lane. The house is empty and has been for several weeks. Not to mention it suffered a severe fire."

"Then it should be easy to let go," Rosson added.

Wallace clapped his hands together. "Well, then, I guess our job here is done."

Clark and Sheriff Laskey followed Detective Wallace's lead and got out of their seats.

"Agent Rosson has some NSAs for you to sign before you leave," the director said, turning his back on Detective Wallace's extended hand.

"One more thing," Wallace said, moving the hand into the manila folder he brought with him. "Pass these prints along to the CIA. They are from the body I fished out of the Potomac. If they match their internal CIA files, tell them their agent is dead."

Agent Rosson was in the director's office, stealing glances out the window at the cabs and black "for-hire" sedans on Pennsylvania Avenue two blocks down from the White House. "What do you think?"

"The case is closed."

"And the ricin? I don't remember that being mentioned."

"I'll take care of the seeds. As far as you are concerned, you never saw them. I have only one concern. That the report in the database for that address remains closed. Just as it was the day you amended it. The CIA wants jurisdiction, the CIA can have jurisdiction."

"Are you going to give them the prints?"

"Of course. But I don't expect them to get back to us one way or the other."

"So, we just wash our hands of it?"

"The way I see it, that report was officially closed before the CIA contacted us. Technically, our hands were never dirty."

Chapter 41

If that is Washington D.C. hospitality, you can keep it." Sheriff Laskey said, getting into the passenger side of Wallace's car.

"I hate to say it, but that's Washington politics."

"Kind of like grabbing your ankles to me. Y'all have a funny way of catching criminals. I mean, we have the occasional turf war with the state police, but we try not to lose sight of the goal. Putting bad guys behind bars. The way I see it, the three of us in this car just went to the FBI with a bag full of material that could be turned into a weapon of mass destruction and they told us to go home."

"So now what?" Clark asked from the back of the unmarked D.C. police cruiser.

"I thought the director made it pretty clear," Wallace said, testing the air.

Clark spoke. "He told us not to investigate 203 Dorchester Lane. I'm talking about locating a missing neighbor. There is no harm in that."

"You trying to convince us, or yourself?"

"Both..." Clark said.

"What was the reference to Senator Day all about?" Laskey asked.

Wallace let out a grunt-like hum. "You all know what happened to the senator?"

"Sure. Who doesn't."

"Well, I was involved in the case, only I didn't know exactly what the case was until it was too late. I caught a lot of heat for the way things turned out, through no fault of my own. Senators and congressmen have the ability to squeeze just about anyone they want to here in D.C."

"You mean you're on thin ice."

"Let me just say I am still on a lot of people's radar screens. But I try not to let that stop me."

"Here is my thought. What if the director is wrong?" Clark asked.

"You're a young man. The question you should be asking is what if you are wrong?"

"What's the worst that can happen?"

"Non-enemy combatant status. Labeled a traitor. Maybe a vacation in Gitmo. End up in a brig on some military base without ever being officially charged with any crime. I can think of a list of things, and they all start at bad and head downhill to worse."

"I think you two have more to lose than I do. I have the responsibility to locate my neighbor, if for no other reason than to let her know her house is gone."

"You gotta love the youth of today," Wallace said, ignoring Clark in the backseat.

"What about you, Sheriff?" Clark asked.

"To tell you the truth, I got a bad feeling about all of this."

"I think that's a healthy response," Clark said.

"The first thing I'm gonna do is go back to Nelson County and burn what's left of that field where we found the seeds. It might take me a few weeks to torch that many acres without causing a forest fire, but I know just the boys to call in. No fuss, no muss. No one is going to question the sheriff burning a field on a convicted drug dealer's farm. As you said, 'I am the law.' I'm also going to dig around a little and see who knew what about those plants. Check out what kind of equipment they have on the farm. I'm sure they didn't plant or harvest those plants by hand. Probably needed some farming equipment."

"Farming equipment?" Clark asked.

"That's right."

"Large scale farming equipment?"

"Something bigger than a tractor and a back hoe. And they probably needed some fertilizer. I have a few things I can check out without causing too many waves in the pool. Put it down to investigating a murder, which I'm still legally obligated to do."

The collective wheels of the three men were spinning silently as Wallace ran through a red light.

Sheriff Laskey continued. "But I imagine the dead guy from the river killed the dead guy in the tree because someone was going to open their mouth."

"You think the dead guy from the river is a CIA agent?"

"The likelihood occurred to me about mid-way through the conversation with the director, if you can call that ass-chewing a conversation," Wallace said.

"It is if you can consider a proctologist just a doctor," Clark answered.

No one laughed and Clark continued. "Follow my logic for a moment. Let's assume this dead guy is the CIA agent."

"Ok," Wallace answered.

"Then the agent is dead, the CIA doesn't know, and the FBI is off the case. The only thing left is us."

Laskey spoke. "We also have to assume that this CIA guy was in so deep he was willing to kill another American citizen. Jackson Price, the dead guy from the tree, was a troubled soul. No question about it. But he was still an American."

"I have no doubt that a CIA agent would kill another American. For ego, national security, career advancement, money. All that jazz," Clark said plainly.

"Well, if you believe it, then it's got to be true," Wallace jibed.

"Have you watched the news at all in the last few years?" Clark asked.

"The boy's right about that."

Wallace took his turn at verbally working the case. "So, if we follow Clark's logic, there is a sleeper cell running around out there who just jettisoned their CIA agent into the Potomac."

Clark added the obvious. "And they have a shit-load of ricin."

"And we were just told by the FBI, and the CIA indirectly, to butt out," Wallace added.

"I'm not saying that we *do* anything. Just poke around for some information."

Wallace felt the pinch of his career and the pain of doing the right thing closing in on his heart from both sides. He tried to take a deep breath and failed. "Get my cigarettes and lighter out of the glove box, would you?"

"You a smoker?" the sheriff asked, fumbling with the latch.

"Only when absolutely necessary."

Wallace lit his cigarette and cracked the window on his side. The nicotine rushed his system and he felt relief as he exhaled. He looked in the rear-view mirror at Clark, who was perched forward in the back seat. "What do you know about this neighbor?"

"Nothing that has proven to be true. She was married to a man named Nazim Shinwari. They have a daughter named Liana. That is what I know for certain. The husband is purported to be dead. Everything else is either a lie, or so close to bullshit that I can't tell the difference. But hell, I'm not sure what to think. A month ago I was a student trying to take care of my mother. In the last few weeks I have met the IRS, the FBI, the D.C. Police and a sheriff from Nelson County. I have had a neighbor die, though I am not sure about the connection there, my missing neighbor's house exploded and almost got me in the process, and I have stumbled upon ricin. That's too many strange occurrences for me for one month."

"All right. All right," Wallace said. "Take it easy. Take it one step at a time. Breathe."

Clark tried to collect himself by looking out the window at the snow which had just started to fall. His eyes moved from the snow outside to the inside of the unmarked police cruiser. The computer attached to the dash caught his eye.

"What does that computer on the dash access?" Clark asked.

Wallace's eyes met Clarks in the rear-view mirror. "Does your neighbor drive?"

"Sure."

Detective Wallace pulled over into the International House of Pancakes parking lot in Ballston, next to the Metro Station. "Let's run her through the system. Just an ordinary traffic stop violation." The detective punched in the address and name into the Virginia DMV system. A few seconds later the image of a driver's license flashed onto the screen. The information on the license was replicated in fields on the screen below the image of the photograph.

"That's the information, but that's not her," Clark said leaning forward.

"Right address?"

"That's the right address. Right name. The picture is different."

"She's wearing one of those veils," Laskey added.

"It's a hijab. And my neighbor always wore one. Never seen her without it. But the face is different. Similar, but different."

"With that hibachi it's no wonder."

"*Hijab. Hibachi* is a Japanese grill."

Wallace interrupted. "I'm not surprised. After 9/11 and the investigations that followed, the Feds busted three DMVs for gross violations of procedures in issuing licenses to undocumented individuals. Two of those three DMVs are within four miles of where we sit. One of them was in Georgetown, the other in the Tysons Corner, Virginia. If she wanted a license, she came to the right place to get an illegal one. Heck, the DMV will still allow people to get a driver's license based on the name and address on a phone bill."

"No offense to you two guys, but the government is fucked up. How hard is it to hire people who speak English and have common sense?"

Wallace shook his head. "You have no idea. You want to talk scary, listen to this. For years the INS issued citizenship papers on naturalization certificates with photographs that were attached with glue. No security features. Which means that Joe Alvarez could go through the process of getting citizenship, get sworn in by the government, and walk out onto the street with a certificate granting citizenship to anyone who wanted to put their photo on it. That person could take that certificate and get a passport, a driver's license, whatever. Keys to the kingdom."

"I'm sure they've fixed that process."

"A little too late. It's not like these certificates were recalled … And in case you didn't know, you can get your passport through the Postal Service. A Postal Service employee swears the customer to honesty, and then ships the paperwork to the Department of State. Now, how secure do you think that process is?"

"What are you saying?"

"What I'm saying is that if your neighbor wanted to live her life under an assumed name, she only needed a reasonable I.Q. and some perseverance."

"Well, I'm damn sure she wasn't an average housewife."

Wallace took another drag from his cigarette. "I'll tell you what. You dig around a little and see what you can find out. See if you can locate your neighbor. But if you see anything out of the ordinary, see anyone following you, you mind your business. The sheriff and I will try to solve our murders, which we are obligated to do. Maybe something will come from connecting those dots. In the meantime, if you need help, or hit on anything certain, you let me know."

The interior of the car grew quiet, before Wallace added, "But do me a favor, call me from a pay phone to the main work number at the precinct, and then get transferred to me. Don't be leaving any long messages about terrorists or Dorchester Lane. If anyone asks, I want to be able to say I don't know what the hell you are doing."

Clark smirked. "Of course."

Chapter 42

After memories of the first dates have faded, after the flowers have drooped and the chocolate has settled into cellulite, the first fight in a relationship is when fluid-exchanging partners really get to know each other. The good façade can only be maintained for so long.

When it comes to the female half of the equation, no man really knows what he has until that façade is temporarily tossed aside. Unfortunately, peeking at the undercurrent of true emotions is much like testing a bulletproof vest with a real person and live ammunition. Some women cry, some women hit, some women sulk, some women brood, some women scream. Clark was about to find out which camp Lisa fell into. He was hoping that Lisa didn't come from the Lorena Bobbit school of anger management.

"How the fuck could you do that? I could lose my job."

"I know, I know. It was stupid. It was irresponsible."

Lisa interrupted his self-reprimand. "It was dishonest."

"I know. But…"

"There is no 'but,' Clark. I should turn you in. You deceiving shit."

Not bad for a geeky looking C.P.A., Clark thought. "You don't want to turn me in. You could get in trouble. Doesn't the Treasury Department teach you to keep your computer secure? Not keep your password written down where just anyone could find it?"

"Fuck you, Clark. It was in my apartment. The doors were locked. It wasn't stolen by some unknown entity. How about some respect for other's property?"

Clark got down from his verbal podium. "It was a mistake. I'm sorry."

Lisa flopped onto the sofa and stared at the laptop on the small coffee table. "What exactly did you do?"

"I poked around a little."

"Exactly what did you poke around and see?"

"I went into the IRS database."

"The MFDA?"

"It's pretty impressive really."

"Clark. You're an asshole."

"I put in my mother's address just to see what would come up."

"I thought you were checking out your neighbors…"

"I was, but not at first … or I guess I was, but I wanted to see some information that I thought I knew was correct before I started poking around."

Lisa shook her head. "And…"

"Well I saw the information for my parents, their address, names, tax history. Place and dates of birth. Real estate transactions. Pensions. Their account was flagged with a message indicating that they were being audited."

"Did you share this information with your mother?"

"No, not at all."

"Did you print anything out?"

"No, I didn't have time."

Clark winced at his poor choice of words and then shoved his foot deeper into his mouth.

"And you came out of the bedroom and dragged me back to bed."

"You betrayed me and then minutes later had sex with me?"

Clark knew better than to answer that question. He dropped his head in mock shame.

"Go on," Lisa prodded.

"Well, I changed the address to Ariana and Nazim's across the street. It was the same type of information. Did you know that Muslim women typically keep their maiden names?"

"Probably because the men are allowed to keep four wives and it gets confusing if all of them are called Mrs. So-and-so," Lisa retorted, still angry with Clark, and by virtue of that, still angry with all men.

"Yeah, maybe. Hadn't thought of that. Anyway, as I said, Ariana called me from Pakistan and asked me to keep an eye on her house."

"You mentioned that."

"Well, she said that her father was ill and that she was in the hospital. But her files listed her parents as deceased."

"Maybe it was Nazim's father she was referring to. A lot of people refer to their fathers-in-law as 'fathers.'"

"Could have been, but Nazim's father, said father-in-law, was also listed in the no-longer-living section. And then I called Nazim's employer."

"And…"

"The guy said he also received a call from Ariana in Pakistan. He said that Ariana said Nazim had been killed in a car accident after they arrived."

Lisa looked uncomfortable. "Did you tell the FBI guy all of this."

"What do you think? I told everybody but the trashman what is going on."

"And the FBI told you, and the two cops, that the CIA was on the case?"

"Yes. But there are still a lot of answered questions."

"Clark, have you thought for a moment that the FBI and CIA can handle it? That you are getting in over your head?"

"I *hope* they're right. I hope they do have it covered."

"Then why are we having this conversation?"

Clark stumbled a little. "I just need to check on something. Something the detective said to me. And I could use your help."

"With what? Your idea that your neighbor is suspicious and has been lying to you? No, that's not in my jurisdiction."

"Don't have to be so testy."

"I'm still working through the feeling of betrayal. I can be testy if I want."

"I just thought maybe an IRS criminal investigator might have some criminal investigative powers."

"I do. And we do have some jurisdiction with terrorism. For one, we were trained to identify potential parties in the Hawala system. And of course, we have the ability to search bank records and look for potential money-laundering and terrorist support channels. But for the most part, the execution of that arm is done by FinCen, the Financial Crimes Enforcement Network. It's a group based out of the Tysons area, under the Department of Treasury."

"What is the Hawala system?

"It's an informal system of money transfers used in the Middle East, and other places."

"How does it work?"

"Let's say that you are in New York and you want to transfer money to Saudi Arabia without going through normal channels. The Hawala system allows you to make the transfer through informal channels. All you need is to know a Hawala broker. You bring your money to a Hawala broker in, let's say, Brooklyn, and they will arrange to have the money transferred to a Hawala broker in Saudi Arabia. But the key is that the money is never actually transferred. The whole system works on honesty. One broker agrees to pay the other at a later date, usually through a transfer of funds going in the opposite direction. Both sides keep a running total of what is owed to whom and eventually, with the participation of other brokers, the debts get settled. Imagine a big system of I.O.U.s. The Hawala brokers make money off of small commissions and generally avoid foreign exchanges, thus offering their services at a lower price than above-the-board remittance alternatives. Obviously, the system also lends itself to tax evasion. One could work in the U.S. for cash, send that money overseas without a transaction trail, and the taxman would be cut out of the equation."

"A system like that would never work in the U.S. There just isn't that much honesty."

"I wouldn't be so sure. The mafia has had similar systems. At any rate, the Department of Treasury received training on the financial systems of various regions in the world, all under the auspices of identifying unfriendly foreign elements and catching tax avoiders. The Hawala system was just one of these."

"You ever caught a Hawala broker?"

"I was an auditor until last month and have only been a criminal investigator for a few weeks, so the answer is 'no.'"

"Thank you for the explanation of terrorist financing."

"Why are you such a jerk? You were the one asking."

"You're right. I am just a little wound up, I guess. But there is something else that has been bothering me."

"Do tell."

"We had another neighbor die over the weekend. A new guy in the neighborhood. He died of reported organ failure."

"Where did he live?"

"A few houses up. Away from Ariana and Nazim's. The guy was only forty-three. A carpenter. No history of illnesses."

"Who told you about this?"

"Where do I get all of my information?"

"Mr. Stanley."

"Bingo. But with two neighbors passing away recently, well, it got me thinking about my father. He died from a never completely diagnosed illness that set-in rapidly."

"What a minute. Now, you think Ariana killed your father?"

Clark saw a chink in Lisa's armor. "All I'm saying is that my father has some longevity in his genes. He doesn't have siblings, but most of his relatives make it to their nineties."

"I just don't know, Clark. I just don't know."

"I'll tell you what I told the cops. We don't have to actually *do* anything. I just want to poke around a little."

Lisa looked straight ahead in a near trance.

"Let me ask you one question, Lisa. Wouldn't you hate to be wrong on this one?"

After a minute of silence, Lisa rolled her eyes and sighed. "Ok, Clark. Let's assume that everything you have found out, and a few things that you are speculating on, are true. Then what do you do?"

"Find out who she is."

"That simple? Find her and then what?"

"I'll know when I find her."

"And how do you propose to do this?"

"I have an idea. But you're not going to like it."

"If it involves me, you're probably right."

Chapter 43

Paul Cannon was on his sixth cup of coffee, three doses over his usual daily allowance. The stubble on his cleft chin was thick, his breath terrible, his hemorrhoids screaming. And he had never been happier, with the exception of the Red Sox ending their eighty-six year World Series drought. He had certainly never been more satisfied. Only a handful of people in the world had the experience he now had. He had just placed a working man-made craft on another planet in the solar system. The moon was for underachievers, he thought, as he walked out of work and drove past the huge gates with armed guards.

NASA didn't hire losers, and Paul Cannon was the upper echelon of an elite core. He had aced every standardized test he had taken since the sixth grade and his I.Q. was at a level where the best estimate was a mere guess. Only poor vision had kept him from his childhood dream of going into space. When he learned his degenerative eye disorder wasn't repairable, he did the next best thing to becoming an astronaut. He set his sights on becoming a NASA scientist. Even though thick glasses meant he would be collecting accolades for deeds done on Earth, his mind was rarely on the planet he called home.

Without sleep for three days, he hadn't seen his wife and son in a week. None of which prevented him from spending most of the past weekend with the true love of his life. The focus of his adoration stood two feet high, five feet long, nose to tail, and was currently scurrying around the surface of the fourth rock from the sun. The largest Mars exploration robot ever built by man was powered by an engine designed by Paul Cannon. He nurtured it to existence and made it work in reality. Nothing a genius I.Q. and a lifetime obsession bordering on a compulsive disorder couldn't do.

Long since trading in his tinker toy set and science project kits, his new BMW 5-series was Paul Cannon's lone adult toy. And the toy was pissing him off. The stuttering had started a week ago and had gradually progressed into a form of automotive break-dancing. As Paul turned onto the highway near Greenbelt, Maryland, the car beeped yet again and he glanced down at the dashboard. Next to the red check engine light, the yellow oil pressure light illuminated the back of the steering wheel.

"Fabulous," Paul said aloud over the NPR commentator speaking from the radio. He looked at the red digital clock in the dash and wondered if he would make it to his son's eighth birthday party, scheduled to begin in ninety minutes with the grand entrance of a two-hundred-dollar-an-hour clown. A quick stop to grab a birthday present, and hopefully outdo the clown, was the only thing on his mind. Other than why he hadn't listened to his wife and bought the Lexus.

Big Al's Hobby Shop, on the border of D.C. and the Maryland state line near Takoma Park, was three blocks west of the metro station, nuzzled into a strip of otherwise sketchy establishments that included a martial arts dojo that taught a Brazilian form of self-defense known as capoeira. The shady neighborhood did little to deter customers from Big Al's, which had the largest selection and cheapest prices of anyone on the East Coast. The store had once been the corner drug store, replete with a real soda fountain, before it became the prime location of failed drug store chains from *Dart Drug* to *Drug Fair* to *Peoples*.

Most of Big Al's customers were self-admitted geeks. The patrons were mostly men who spent more time on their hobbies than they did on their wives, kids, or full-time jobs, if they were lucky enough to have any of them. But if you needed a new rotor on a remote control helicopter or an artist easel or the latest philatelic collection book, Big Al's was the place, and Big Al himself was the man.

The king of pricing and selection, Big Al was the pauper of organization. Products lined his store in haphazard fashion, the shelves burgeoning, towering to a full height of ten feet. Big Al, a name that was anything but a misnomer, had long taken to hiring local teenagers who were both spry and coordinated enough to scurry up the ladders he kept in the store to pull items off the acrophobia-inducing shelves. And while the owner may have been too large and too old to climb the ladders himself, he knew where virtually every item in the store was located. The secret was easy. Everyday before he left for home, Big Al pushed his considerable waistline through the aisles and read the contents of every shelf to himself out loud. It was inventory by rote, and that suited Big Al just fine. It was as precise as his accounting method which had generated two decades of favorable tax returns.

Paul Cannon parked his car at a meter, half a block from Big Al's. He glanced around the street and back at his car as he fed a quarter into the meter, and then walked briskly towards the direction of the hobby shop. He had ten minutes to decide what to get, and his mind was already racing through the hodgepodge layout of his favorite store. Paul Cannon, the brilliant NASA mind, knew the contents of Big Al's hobby shop almost as well as its owner. And he knew that the metric conversion calculator in the glass counter in the back of the store was a must have. A gift any eight-year-old, son of a NASA scientist, would appreciate.

Big Al was half-perched on a stool behind the register counter when Paul Cannon threw open the door.

"Good afternoon, Paul," Al said. His closely cropped white beard was trimmed to perfection. His face was red, the capillaries bringing blood to the surface of the skin as it tended to do for those who favored their after-work sauce. "Can I help you find something?"

"No thanks, Al. I only have a few minutes. Got the kid's birthday in less than an hour and don't even have a card."

"Saw your robot on the news today. Pretty cool stuff."

Paul paused long enough to smile. "Thanks. We're all pretty excited."

"What's on the boy's wish list?"

"According to his mother, he wanted a clown."

"I'm all out of clowns this week."

"Then I guess I'll have to look around," Paul retorted, turning the corner of the far aisle that led to the do-it-yourself chemistry kits aimed at high school students but suitable for the son of a genius. Paul, his khaki pants and blue oxford wrinkled from three consecutive days of wear, pulled several kits from the shelf. He barely noticed the other customer slide past him in the aisle. It was the wake of her perfume that caught his attention. Box in hand, Paul Cannon turned as the woman stopped to gaze at various batteries locked in a standing glass case.

Paul Cannon stole a glance at the woman's recently curled and highlighted hair and admired her well-figured profile. As his eyes went from her hair to her waist to her stockings and back up, Ariana's face turned towards her stalker.

Paul Cannon's eye's jumped before gradually turning into an inquisitive squint. "Don't I know you?"

Ariana didn't flinch. She slowly turned back towards the glass case of expensive batteries, her attention still focused on the man next to her, his reflection in the glass case more than clear enough for her to identify him.

"Are you sure I don't know you?"

"No," Ariana said tersely, almost in a whisper.

Paul Cannon would not relent. Being right was hardwired into his ego, particularly his ego with regard to memory. And his ego wouldn't let it go.

"Wait … I got it! I may not remember your name, but I definitely remember you from…"

"Not another word," Ariana hissed. Her dark eyes were soulless, her voice on the verge of evil. "I don't know you. You don't know me." Ariana, turned her back and continued down the aisle in the direction of the door.

By the time Paul Cannon regained his composure, Ariana had exited the store and was on the way to her car.

Ten minutes later, Paul Cannon left the store with his metric calculator and chemistry kit encased in generic floral wrapping paper. He made his way to his BMW, threw his presents in the trunk, and got behind the wheel of the vehicle that had been nothing but trouble.

Across the street and down the block, Ariana watched from behind her oversized sunglasses as Paul Cannon drove down the street in the direction of home. With twenty minutes until clown-time he never once looked in the rear-view mirror.

Chapter 44

The three hearses were parked in the back of the Money & Ceasar Funeral Home as Clark pulled into the otherwise empty lot. He straightened his tie in the rear-view mirror, a fashion offering to the deceased in case he had the misfortune of running into one on their home turf.

An old black man washing the cars dipped a brush into a bucket of sudsy water and nodded to Clark as he passed.

"How often do you wash those?" Clark stopped and asked out of curiosity.

"Every other day if the weather is nice and they've been in service. If they haven't been out from under the carport, I don't clean em.'"

"You wash them by hand in the winter?"

"I take 'em to the car wash when it gets *really* cold, but I try to wash 'em by hand most of the time."

"This isn't *really* cold?"

"Really cold is anything below freezing. Can't wash a car with ice. We are near forty-five today. Gives me something to do."

"I guess everyone's last ride should be in a clean car," Clark joked.

"You got that right. Can't be driving the dead around in dirty cars. Bad for business. Bad for karma."

"Washing them every other day is bad for the finish."

"No worrying there. The owner buys a new one every few years."

"Which owner, Money or Ceasar?"

The man looked up at the sign on the back of the building. "Hell, old man Ceasar died forty years ago. The only one left is Money." The man in the black overalls lured Clark closer with a flick of his head.

"You here for a service? Did someone pass?"

"No, I'm here for some information."

The old man looked around as if he were about to spill a state secret on embalming. "You know what the family calls these vehicles when they think nobody can hear them?"

"No idea."

"Money wagons."

"Jesus," Clark said, catching himself in mid-blasphemy.

The old man laughed in a deep baritone. "Money likes his money. Hell, I don't even think Money was his birth name. Probably just liked the sound of it. But I tell you this, you'll hear all kinds of things whispered at Money family gatherings. Things that will make your skin crawl, make you lose your dinner, and get you thinkin' about cremation." He finished with another laugh and Clark wasn't sure whether to believe the man or not.

Clark knew the funeral parlor business had a bad reputation. Over the years, news reports on the expose beat had included the funeral parlor business with increasing regularity. At the top of the sin list was price fixing on coffins and screwing over the elderly with exorbitant service add-ons that were free to those with tighter reigns on their faculties. Death was good business, unless you had a funeral parlor in a "regentrified" area of town. Yuppies just weren't prone to kicking the bucket fast enough to break-even.

"How many funerals do you have a week?" Clark asked.

"Depends on how many people have been dying. You get a bad year with the flu and we have a lot of elderly pass. Two services a day is not unusual in the winter."

"You drive the cars?"

"Wash them and drive them."

"You ever get used to it?"

"What's that?"

Clark paused as an image of his father flashed through his mind. "Death. Dealing with dead bodies."

"I guess it takes some gettin' used to. It's not for everybody, that's for sure. Had a young man a couple years back who only made it through one day of work. He had a problem locking the legs on the casket carrier and when he went to pull the casket from the car, bam! The casket popped open and out fell a body about the same age as the employee. The deceased had been in a car accident and gone through the windshield. Shook the boy up pretty good."

"Poor guy."

The old man nodded in silent agreement and then added, "But he should have locked the wheels, like I told him to."

"That thought will haunt me all day."

"You know, the problem people have with death is that they don't think it is going to happen to them. Funeral services, funeral homes, cemeteries … they are places people try to avoid. Trying to avoid thinkin' about the unavoidable. I try to remind my kids that there isn't one person left on Earth who was here one hundred and twenty-five years ago."

"I see your point."

"Just food for thought."

The old man dipped the brush back into the water and gave his full attention to the back wheel. Clark took the change in focus as a hint and headed up the sidewalk towards the back door.

The door opened silently on well-greased hinges and Clark stepped into the main hall and proceeded slowly across the burgundy carpet. A large chandelier hung overhead, the sparkling crystals compensating for a room with a permanently somber mood.

There were four viewing rooms off the main hall. All of

them held caskets. Clark wondered if they were full or if the funeral parlor used them as showrooms to drum up business in an industry where demand is determined by God and not the consumer opening their wallet.

There was a grand staircase to the far end of the main hall, and Clark walked forward slowly as if trying not to disturb the air.

"Good afternoon. May I help you?" a voice echoed through the hall.

Clark visibly jumped.

"My apologies. I didn't mean to startle you." Phil Money, a week past his fiftieth birthday bash, stepped from the small office near the front door and walked towards Clark, hand extended. He was wearing a dark suit, not quite black, but in the neighborhood of the darkest charcoal. The suit was accentuated with a subdued blue tie, knotted in a double Windsor. Clark saw a thick gold watch dangling from the cuff of his wrist and he thought about the old man washing the cars outside in the middle of winter. Money likes his money.

"My name is Clark Hayden. I wanted to have a word with you, if I could?"

"You are the young man who called this morning."

"Yes, I am."

"Please. If you would step into my office," Phil Money said, gesturing with an open hand.

Clark walked into the office and found a seat on one of the two sofas near the bay window looking out the front of the building.

"May I interest you in some tea or coffee?"

"Tea would be fine."

Money opened a cabinet on the far wall and removed two cups and saucers. He opened the cabinet next to the cups and the shelves burgeoned with tea alternatives. "We have Earl Gray, Darjeeling, green tea, caffeinated and decaffeinated, ginseng, chamomile, and oolong..."

"I'll have Earl Gray," Clark answered, unsure he would recognize any further choices.

"Fine selection. I will have one myself." Money flipped the switch on a modern white Braun water heater that fit the décor of the room. "It will only be a moment."

"Thank you," Clark answered, trying to remain as polite as his host. It was a tough act to follow. Money's delivery was polished, his manners impeccable, his grooming exemplary, his selection of tea unmatched. What looked like an office could have passed as a Far East tea den.

"What may I help you with this morning, Mr. Hayden?"

"I'm looking for a contact name and number for a neighbor who recently passed away. I was told that you don't give out information over the phone on former customers, and I didn't have a fax machine to put the request in writing."

"Yes, I do apologize for our policy here at Money & Ceasar. We try to avoid getting involved in the circumstances of our customers, as you put it. Society is so litigious these days. Money & Ceasar tries to avoid being used as a pawn in the affairs of the deceased. Gold diggers and money grubbers come out of the woodwork when there has been a death in a family, particularly when there is an inheritance to squabble over. As a rule, we avoid giving out personal information."

Clark tried to diffuse the suspicion. "The deceased was a neighbor. His name was Allan Coleman. I was unfortunately out of the country when he passed, and have been unable to locate his family." Clark had a momentary feeling of guilt for lying about the timing of the death and his trip overseas, but forged ahead. "I wanted to pass along my condolences to his family."

"I see," Money said without moving. "You were close to this neighbor?"

"Not super close, but he was a neighbor. He lived on the next street over."

"And none of the other neighbors have forwarding information?"

"I asked, but it seems that Mr. Coleman was a bit of a recluse."

Money gave Clark the once-over and decided that the young man was trustworthy. "You are looking for next-of-kin?"

"I'm looking for someone to whom I can send a condolence card."

The hot water heater beeped once and Money stopped what he was doing to pour the water and steep the tea. He placed a cup on the table in front of Clark and excused himself to the inconspicuous laptop that was on the corner of his desk. He typed in Allan Coleman and a one page file filled the screen. He took a sip of his tea and said, "His brother's name is Greg Coleman, and he lives in Warrenton, Virginia. Shall I write down the address?"

"Please," Clark said. "That would be super."

Money wrote on a memo pad with the company letterhead, the gold pen tracing out the address in perfect cursive letters.

"There you are," Money said, handing the paper to Clark as he rejoined his guest on the opposite sofa.

Clark folded the paper and put it in his front pocket.

Money took another sip of his tea and cleared his throat slightly. "So Mr. Hayden, have you considered purchasing a plot or making other post-life decisions? You're never too young to consider your post-life future."

Clark swallowed hard to refrain from spitting his tea on the table.

Greg Coleman answered the phone groggily even though it was three in the afternoon.

"Mr. Coleman?"

"Speaking," the gruff voice said on the other end of the phone.

"Mr. Coleman, my name is Clark Hayden and I was a neighbor of your brother, Allan."

Silence filled the line for a moment before Greg Coleman spoke. "Yes."

"I wanted to extend my condolences to you and your family for your loss. Your brother was a good neighbor."

"Clark was it?"

"Yes."

"I appreciate your call, Clark, but I know the neighborhood didn't think highly of my brother. It took him two years and three trips to the Town Council before he could get a permit to build that monstrous addition on his house."

"I don't know anything about it. Your brother lived on the next street over from my parents', well, my mother's house. I grew up there, but I have been living at school until recently."

"Thank you, then. I appreciate the phone call."

"Before you hang up, I wanted to ask another question," he blurted.

Greg Coleman was thinking about his brother, the wounds still fresh. He didn't want to have a conversation on the topic. He certainly wasn't ready for what Clark was about to say.

"What's your question?"

"Did your brother have an autopsy done before he was buried?"

Greg Coleman's hand gripped the phone and the blood coursed through the tightening veins in his neck. "What the hell is this, a prank call?"

"No, sir. Not at all. I wish it were. I lost my father last year and I wouldn't jerk you around on the death of your brother."

"Then why the questions? Nothing is going to bring my brother back. Let him and our family rest in peace."

"Please, Mr. Coleman. It's important. I wouldn't ask if it weren't."

Greg Coleman grunted a little. "No, we didn't have an autopsy performed. My mother was against it. As you probably know, my brother wasn't in the best of health. The police found him dead on the floor with his heart medication spilled on the desk. It didn't take Einstein to figure out what happened. He was two-hundred pounds overweight, didn't exercise, smoked, and had a plethora of medical ailments that were trying to kill him. He died because he didn't take care of himself."

"I understand," Clark said, feeling the sorrow over the phone. "But I think there is a chance your brother didn't die of natural causes."

Chapter 45

The two-woman flight attendant team marched down the aisle in their light blue uniforms giving orders like a female Gestapo unit. Tray backs were pushed forward and seats snapped into their upright position. A high-school student watching a DVD on his laptop grudgingly shut it off after his third warning, the last of which implied the use of an in-flight emergency exit for non-compliance.

Clark stared out the window as the plane banked towards his side of the aircraft. He looked down at the city below, the high-rise buildings in the business district stretching upward, the tallest structures for hundreds of miles. Beyond the center of town, the city expanded in nearly symmetrical blocks—a river, train tracks, and the occasional highway dissecting the geometric perfection. The flight attendants found their seats as the captain made an announcement for final approach, "We will be touching down in Kansas City in approximately ten minutes and should have you at the gate five minutes ahead of schedule." Clark looked at Lisa who was asleep, and had been since before the plane left the Reagan Airport runway.

The National Record Center for Immigration and Customs Enforcement resided in Lee's Summit, a quiet suburb just outside Kansas City. The interior of the building shined with state-of-the-art architectural features designed to wow the politicians who continued to fund the project. Carpeted floors, glass walls, and exposed ducts splashed in funky colors made the N.R.C. at Lee's Summit one of the most progressive buildings in the government. The exterior was harder to appreciate. The N.R.C. was 200,000 square feet of office space constructed into the opening of an existing cave. Thirty million files wedged into the earth in the middle of the country's heartland. The government knew no boundaries when it came to spending money.

"I can't believe I let you talk me into this," Lisa said, pulling her jacket closed.

"It's information that we could have obtained through a Freedom of Information Act request, if we could wait three months. Besides, I told you we may well come out of this looking like heroes," Clark responded.

"Or felons," Lisa answered.

Lisa walked through the automatic doors as Clark stared at the entrance to the building from the outside. "Let's go, Clark," Lisa said, not agitated, but sounding like she was. Criminal Investigator Lisa Prescott pulled her badge and showed it through the thick glass to the Immigration and Customs Enforcement employee. The elderly pale white woman with a terrific set of dentures leaned far enough forward to see the picture on the badge and then moved back into her seat.

"I'm here to see Don Christie."

"Who are you with?" the woman asked. Clark looked at Lisa, wondering exactly what the lady's position was. Obviously, it wasn't checking identities.

"The FBI," Lisa responded in jest.

"And him?" she asked with a flick of the thumb in Clark's direction.

"He is my witness. I need him to identify the person in question."

The old woman pushed a clipboard through the counter level hole in the glass. "Please sign in and have a seat. Someone will be with you in a moment."

Lisa and Clark signed in and the door opened with a buzz long before they made a move for the chairs.

"You the IRS agent?"

"That's me," Lisa answered. "Call me Lisa."

Clark's mind flashed back to their first meeting and Lisa's call-me-Agent-Prescott mandate.

"And him?" Don Christie asked.

Clark took a crack at introducing himself. "Clark Hayden. Here to provide insight into the investigation as a material witness."

Don Christie shook Clark's hand with a knuckle grinding grip and nodded to the woman behind the glass who pushed through two visitor's badges.

"These must be worn at all times."

Don Christie waddled as he walked. It wasn't a strut or a show of force. It was the way the bones of his skeleton interacted with one another. Clark walked next to Lisa and considered that their escort, from the backside, could almost pass as a silverback in a suit.

Don spoke over his shoulder as he walked, his voice bellowing. "Welcome to the National Records Center, or what we call the N.R.C. We used to call it INS NRC, but technically the INS doesn't exist anymore. It's all rolled under the Department of Homeland Security and Immigration and Customs Enforcement. In reality, we haven't quite gotten over the hump with the new name. INS still rolls off the tongue."

"Yes it does," Clark said.

"Besides, most of the documents we use still have INS designated on them. We have over thirty million files under our supervision, with millions more arriving every year. We have been consolidating records from regional INS offices for years, and the boxes keep pouring in. We have storage on site and in two locations around the city. We are also in the process of formatting all the files for electronic storage and applying barcode technology for faster retrieval."

"In the process, you said?" Clark asked.

"Well, as you can imagine, it takes a while to scan thirty million folders, some of them an inch thick."

"How many have been converted electronically?"

"I'm afraid it's not that simple. Each region had its own filing system. Some filed according the INS file number. Some filed them alphabetically. Some filed them by year and month."

"I don't think I like where this is going," Lisa said, unbuttoning the top button on her blouse.

"Probably not," Don answered. He pushed a glass door open into a large work area. As he walked around the edge of workspace, Don continued the tour.

"Most of the people here are working on the classification of documents and electronic formatting. Unfortunately it is a manual process. We have to take every folder out, undo the center clips and then run them through scanners and put the folders back together. Then there is data entry for each folder so that we can retrieve the information from the database."

Clark rolled his eyes imperceptibly. "So how many folders have been entered into the database?"

"About two million. What name are you looking for again?"

"Ariana Amin."

"The beginning of the alphabet."

"Is that good or bad?" Clark asked.

"Bad, I guess. We started our electronic conversion at Z."

"But, of course," Lisa added.

Don raised an eyebrow and continued. "Well, the folders with the last name of Z were the smallest in number. We started there for a sense of accomplishment. That, and we were mandated to have certain percentages of the alphabet finished by certain intervals. So Z is completely in the database. Easy to search."

"And the 'A' section?" Clark asked.

"We've started, but haven't finished. So you may get lucky, and you may not." Don led the pair around the corner to a set of stainless steel elevator doors. "We're going down two stories to the main storage facility."

"Any chance this place was originally built to withstand a nuclear war?" Clark asked.

"Not that I know of. If there were a nuclear war, I hope the country would have higher priorities than keeping these folders safe." The elevator opened with a small ding. "After you," Don said, ushering his guests into the elevator. The silver doors opened on sub-floor two into a hall that stood behind a glass wall. The glass overlooked a huge floor of metal bookcases full of boxes and folders.

Clark spoke first. "Holy shit. That is a lot of files."

"That's generally the reaction we get down here in Sub-Two from our visitors. Most people have never seen anything like it."

Clark and Agent Prescott pressed up against the glass and gawked at the hangar-sized room large enough to park a pair of 747's end-to-end and wing-to-wing.

Lisa muttered in disbelief. "This could take all year."

"I hope not," Don answered. "I get off at six and I'm the only one here today with authorization to bring visitors to Sub-Two."

"Then take us to the 'A' section."

Don Christie turned down the third aisle from the end and ran his finger along several boxes reading the names and numbers on the outside.

"I think this is the area to start. This row runs from 'AG' to 'AS.' All of what you see is not in the database yet. These are the original hard copies.

Clark looked down the aisle and up at the top of the seven-foot shelves. "Are they in order?"

"In places they might be, in some places, probably not. Remember, these files came from different regions, so if the folders are still in the box, there is no telling what system they used. It all depends."

Don looked at Lisa. "Let me know if you need anything, I will be around. Just ask for me."

"Can we get any help?" Clark asked.

"I'll see if I can't have someone come down after the staff meeting."

"Thanks."

"Good luck."

• • •

"So, what do you think?" Clark asked.

Lisa answered. "There were nine Ariana Amins in the computer system." She pulled out the list of names and addresses. "All we have to do is locate the correct box and file for each of the nine people on the list. Then we will know where they got citizenship."

Clark ran his fingers along the outside of the box and squinted at the scribbling on some of the labels.

"It may not be that easy. Let's say that Ariana Amin, from Virginia in the IRS system, got citizenship in Miami before she had tax information and then moved to Washington D.C. In the IRS system, it would show her current address, but not necessarily her address when she applied to the INS."

"So, if she hasn't moved, the location would be the same," Lisa paused. "Which percentage of the population moves in a year?"

"That's not the question. The question is, which percentage of terrorists would move after gaining citizenship or legal residency?"

Lisa looked at Clark and answered. "All of them."

"Yeah."

"What do you suggest?"

"Intuition," Clark answered. He shut his eyes and took five steps down the aisle towards the center. Eyes still shut, he stuck out his right hand and tapped a box. "I'll start here."

Lisa looked at Clark as if he were crazy before shutting her eyes, spinning around once, and grabbing the first box in front of her as she completed the turn.

It took two hours to go through a dozen boxes. File by file. Page by page. Photo by photo. At their current rate, Criminal Investigator Prescott would reach mandatory retirement before they made it half-way down the aisle. Empty Styrofoam cups that once held coffee were stacked behind Agent Prescott in a poor attempt at a pyramid. Pouring through the boxes, each person checked the photo on the file and then the name. Clark stood from his crossed-legs position on the floor. "This could take a lifetime. And my butt is already numb from this floor."

"We don't have a lifetime and don't blame the floor. It's kind of nice to be in another city and feel that D.C. isn't the only place with a chill."

"I don't know if I would call it nice."

"Yeah, that's true. Snow just isn't as much fun as it is when you are younger. The only thing I know enjoying this winter is my neighbor's new puppy. He loves the snow. I watch him play from the window sometimes. Watching him brings out the pure joy of snow."

Clark paused for a moment at the thought of Lisa's neighbor's dog frolicking in the snow. Something clicked. He picked up the files on the floor and put them back in the box that was in front of him. He paused again, cocking his head to the side as if a voice was calling out to him from the edge of his hearing. Clark looked down the aisle at the insurmountable task and walked past Lisa who was flipping through folders at a feverish pace.

Clark scanned the handwriting on the outside of several boxes and moved farther down the aisle. He read, paused, and then read again before stopping in front of six boxes, the same words written on each in red permanent marker. INS. Boston District Office, JFK Federal Building. 1996-2001. There were six more boxes dated 2002-2007. Beneath the title of each box was a designation for a part of the alphabet. Clark's eyes moved to the second box in the first set of dates. "AG" through "AP."

In the back of his mind, Lisa's words tumbled. *A new puppy playing in the snow.*

"Lisa, when was the first time you saw snow?"

"I don't remember. My parents used to take me to Maine in the winter to visit my uncle. I guess I was playing in the stuff since I was little. Why?"

Clark pulled a box off the shelf. The white cardboard bottom made a thud as it hit the cool tile floor. "You just said something that reminded me of a story Ariana told my mother and me," Clark started. He sat down again on the floor, the nerves in his butt giving notice that they were sore in addition to cold. "It was a random story, but something I guess I never forgot. She said that a friend of hers, who had never seen snow, ran outside one morning to play in a foot of fresh powder. Ariana took the time to put on boots and gloves and headed for the door when her friend came running back into the house. Ariana asked her friend where she was going and her friend said 'back inside.' When Ariana asked why, her friend answered plainly. 'I didn't realize snow would be so cold.'"

"What's your point?"

Clark dug through the file with verve and a certain amount of anticipation. He passed a folder with the name "Amen, Jesus," written on the outside, and stopped to look at the picture, out of curiosity. Who wouldn't?

"Well, I guess the reason the story stuck with me is simple. If you have never seen snow, never been exposed to snow, didn't come from a climate where they had snow, I guess you wouldn't necessarily realize that snow is cold."

"I guess it's possible. Now, what's your point?"

Clark raised his pointer finger and then dove back into the files. Ten seconds later he found his first "Amin." His heart rate picked up. Abdul Amin, born in Egypt. Al-Mohamed Amin, from Saudi Arabia. Assad Amin, Jordan. Ariana Amin, Pakistan.

"My point is that when Ariana told the story about the first time her friend saw snow, she said she was in Boston," Clark said tapping the side of the folder with a smile.

"Is it her?"

Clark opened the folder and read frantically. "The name is the same. Same nationality."

Agent Prescott pulled her stiff frame off the floor with the help of the nearest bookcase.

Clark fished for the photos which had become detached from the top page but were still in the crack of the folder which he held between his hands. He turned the picture upright and looked at it, moving it directly under a light that was fifteen feet above. "It's not her."

"Are you sure?"

"Pretty sure. She is not wearing a hijab, which Ariana always wore, but the nose is a little different. They are similar, but it isn't her."

"Let me see that file."

"Don't trust me?"

"I don't trust anyone."

"You need therapy."

"I've been. It didn't help."

"What did you go for?"

"Shooting my partner."

"I'm not your partner."

"Lucky you."

"What do we do?"

"You think it is her? There are eight others on the list."

"Well, I remember Ariana telling me that she had been in the States about ten years. But that was a few years ago. The IRS file shows the first date for her as a taxpayer as 1997. So her age is pretty close."

Lisa spoke. "Let me make a call and see if I can't get more details on Boston Ariana here." Lisa opened her cell phone and the screen told her what she already knew. Caves were not a good place to get a signal.

"What should I do in the meantime?"

"Keep reading."

When Lisa returned, Don Christie was by her side. Lisa reached for the folder and handed it to Don Christie. "We would like a copy of this folder. Every page."

"Did you find something?"

"Just an address."

"Are we done here?"

"We can either check out this lead, or spend the rest of the week in this aisle."

"Just say the word."

"We're booked on a plane for Boston that leaves in two hours. It gets in after midnight."

Chapter 46

Imam Alamoudi entered the inner sanctum of the mosque and headed for the living quarters. A Persian rug worth twenty grand spread from the doorway to the window, wall-to-wall. A large cushioned sofa was placed under a set of windows, seats reserved for the elderly. Pillows balanced precariously on the end of the sofa. Generous portions of larger multi-colored pillows littered the floor in neat piles on the hand-woven rug. The pillows were for the imam and his guests. At over 300 pounds, the imam's favorite activity was lying on the floor, his belly hugging the tightly knitted Persian rug, his eyes fixated on the satellite feed of Al Jazeera that was pumped in from the six foot satellite dish on the roof.

Imam Alamoudi pressed the intercom on the wall and ordered lunch in his native Urdu. He shut the door behind him and loosened the belt on his salwar, his pants. He didn't see Ariana until her hands were on his shoulder. Imam Alamoudi's naturally-stressed heartbeat quickened.

"Long time no see?"

"You should know better than to bring trouble here."

"I didn't bring trouble here."

"Your neighbor was here."

"When?"

"Last week."

"He came on his own. I never even mentioned where I pray. And if not for my husband, I would have never come to this mosque. Prayer is between woman and Allah. The mosque is only a building."

"You're incorrect. Prayer is between *man* and Allah."

Ariana repeated herself and then added. "What did the boy want?"

"He wanted to know how to reach you. He said that you asked him to watch your house. Now he wants to know how to contact you. He said there was a fire in your home."

"Nosey fucking American."

The imam looked at Ariana, judging her vernacular and delivering a stern warning with his eyes.

"I know, I know. I have been living with a group of men."

The imam headed for the sofa and motioned for Ariana to join him.

"What brings you here?"

"Money."

The imam walked across the room and his weight sunk into the cushions on the sofa.

"And men."

"Why not blood too?"

"Don't tempt me."

"How much do you need?"

"Fifty thousand."

"That is not a trivial amount."

"But can you get it?"

"Of course."

The imam slung his weight back into a standing position and walked across the room to a small table in the corner. He opened the drawer and removed a cash box the size of a large dictionary. With his back to Ariana he punched in the combination and opened the top.

Ariana's hand reached the cash before the imam's. The imam grabbed for Ariana's wrist and found himself with his arm pinned behind his back, hand empty.

"I have never seen your trained side. Very impressive."

"You have no idea," Ariana replied.

"Take what you need."

Ariana smiled as she took the box back to her seat on the sofa. She counted out fifty thousand in neatly stacked hundred dollar bills wrapped in thick rubber bands. Then she threw two additional stacks on the pile. "Just in case," she added as she put the box on the cushion next to her.

"You know, when I first heard about you, I doubted whether it was true. You play a housewife and mother very well."

"Not everything is as it seems."

"This is very true. In your case, anyway. I assume by the presence of your neighbor that a plan is underway."

"Yes. We are past the point of no return."

"Have you covered your tracks?"

"I have been preparing for years. The most recent developments are just icing on the cake."

"How many men do you need?"

"Six if I can have them. Less if there are less available. I need young men with unshakable faith."

"I have several in training. A few even speak your native tongue."

"I need native faith."

"I will give you the best I can find."

"How much time do you need?"

"I need them by next Tuesday."

"Then you shall have them by next Tuesday."

"Where?"

The imam thought for a moment. "There should be a pencil and paper in the cash box."

Ariana handed them to him and the imam scribbled an address. He handed the note to Ariana, who read it. "Are you serious?"

"The owner is one of the faithful."

Ariana stood expressionless until the imam spoke again. "I assume this is the last time we shall meet."

"This will be the last time. If we see each other again, the outcome will not be good for you."

"Then I wish you well."

Chapter 47

Wellesley, twenty minutes outside Boston when the traffic moves, was still ten minutes away after an hour of bumper-to-bumper. Between Natick and Newton, the quaint town of Wellesley was home to the eponymous all-women's college catering to elite intellectuals and average intellectuals with elite family pocketbooks. At over forty grand a year, Wellesley was one of the most expensive schools in the country.

And while downtown Wellesley had remained a bastion of wealth, an idyllic slice of New England Americana, the surrounding area had spent the last two decades being consumed by the ugly dragon of urban sprawl. Wellesley, a sanctuary of knowledge and wealth, now rested firmly in the beast's stomach. The town square was still picturesque, but two miles down the road, across from the rival cross-town high school, the new Super Wal-Mart had tarnished the remnants of the small town atmosphere. Only the college's three billion dollar endowment was keeping the city planners at bay, the threat of more strip malls at a distance.

Lisa read the map on her lap as Clark weaved among some of the most hostile drivers on the planet. By all accounts, New York drivers were tame in comparison to their northeast corridor neighbors who took delight in tailgating, cut-offs, and middle-finger salutes. New York drivers were tough, but Boston drivers relished in rudeness. Rush hour in Bean Town was not for the faint of heart. Clark swerved away from a monster pothole and into the next lane of traffic. Eyes wide, Lisa glanced out the driver's window for a close-up view of a delivery truck covered in road salt and winter grime, the metal side of the vehicle close enough to wipe clean with her sleeve.

She scooted over in the direction of the driver's seat as Clark found his lane again. Ten minutes later they pulled in front of a two-story, white frame house with no garage. A chain-link fence enclosed the treeless front yard. The white siding was in need of a fresh coat of paint and the gutters sagged from the edge of the roof.

"Number 812. That's us," Clark said to his girlfriend, zipping his jacket before opening the door and exiting into a balmy single-digit wind-chill.

A student in a Boston College sweatshirt opened the door after three knocks. "Yo," the student said, his voice trailing off as he realized his visitors were strangers.

"Good morning," Clark said. The young man in the BC sweatshirt with screaming red hair looked through bloodshot eyes at Clark with suspicion. His eyes then turned to Lisa and his face perked up.

"Who are you?"

"My name is Clark Hayden and I'm looking for someone who used to live at this address. I wanted to ask you a few questions."

The student looked at Clark suspiciously. "Who's your partner?"

Lisa stepped forward and pulled out her IRS badge. "IRS criminal investigator, Lisa Prescott."

Clark longed for a badge to flash.

Lisa's badge had its intended affect and the sleepy young man on the other side of the doorway took a huge step towards coherence. Police at the door tended to scare most people. The IRS at the door made people tighten their sphincters.

With the resident's full attention, Clark plowed forward.

"I'm a graduate student at Virginia Tech. You can Google me if you want. I'm on the robotics team; there should be a picture of me out there."

The student looked behind himself into the house and around the room.

"Can we come in for a minute? It's freezing out here," Clark added.

The redheaded BC student just stood there, his toes peaking out from the shredded fringe of his jeans.

Lisa added her soft touch. "Relax, we are not interested in you, your taxes, or whatever weed you may have stuck between the couch cushions."

The BC student stepped back from the door and Clark and Lisa walked into the room, hurriedly shutting the door behind them. Beer cans were scattered on the small dining room table in the corner. Pieces of newspapers littered the sofa. A small lamp with a crooked shade stood precariously next to the sofa. There wasn't a text book in sight.

"You live here, I take it…"

"I hope so. Otherwise I would have some explaining to do."

"You rent this place?"

"Lease with an option to buy."

Clark ignored the smartass statement. "Who's the owner?"

"The old woman next door. Mrs. Crowley."

"Is she around?"

"She is, like, ninety. She's usually home. She takes a walk in the afternoon. But I don't see her outside much when it's this cold."

"How are Mrs. Crowley's faculties? Is she lucid? Forgetful?"

"Well, she doesn't forget when the rent check is due, if that tells you anything."

Lisa laughed a little.

"Do you get along with her?"

"She's a little hard of hearing, which makes her a pretty good neighbor. She doesn't complain about noise at night. Why, did something happen next door?"

"No. Well, not that I am aware of anyway. I'm looking for information on a neighbor of mine in D.C. She disappeared and I'm trying to dig through her past a little to see if I can locate her."

The young man's eyes darted between Lisa's and Clark's.

Lisa asked another soft question. It was something she had learned in her IRS interrogation course. When you run into resistance, ask a simple question. Soften them up a little.

"How long have you been living here?"

"This is my second year, so about three semesters."

Clark pulled out a sketch of Ariana that Mr. Stanley had drawn with the same easel he had drawn a portrait of his wife. "I know this is a long shot, but have you ever seen this woman around?"

The redheaded student grabbed the picture between his freckle-laden hands and quickly handed it back to Clark. "Never seen her before."

"You sure?"

"Yeah, I would remember if I had seen a woman in a hijab around here. There might be a few at Wellesley, but I don't spend much time there, obviously. You have to have a female escort just to get in the gate."

"I'd think it would be a good place to meet women," Clark said.

"Wellesley girls don't date BC guys. They go for Harvard all the way. Everyone knows it. Until a few semesters ago, both Harvard and MIT used to send buses to Wellesley to pick up girls for the weekend. These buses would come right to the main gate on Friday night and drive the women across town. On Saturday and Sunday another bus would come and drop the girls back off. I imagine some of them got shagged all weekend."

Clark had a lot to say but bit his tongue. Girlfriends tended to suck the testosterone out of most male conversations. On the surface, at least.

"You see any other Muslim women around?"

"There are a few Muslims at BC, but they are nice people. Quiet. Only one or two wear a hijab. And the woman in your picture there isn't one of them."

Clark pressed. "She would have been younger than she is in the picture."

"Dude, I haven't seen her."

Lisa knew it was time to cut their losses with BC's finest. "Which side is Mrs. Crowley on?"

"The ugly green house to the right. You can't miss it."

"Thanks for your time."

A minute later, Mrs. Crowley opened the door and looked up at her visitors from her hunched position. She had a small cane in her left hand, the decorative end of the walking stick wrapped in a ball of old fingers and wrinkled skin.

"Good afternoon, Mrs. Crowley. My name is Clark Hayden, and this is my girlfriend, Lisa. We are looking for a tenant of yours who used to live next door."

"You with the police?"

"No, we live in Washington D.C. and we're trying to locate a neighbor of mine who has gone missing."

"You should call the FBI. They handle missing people."

"I have, but there are national security issues at stake which prohibit the authorities from assisting with this particular investigation."

"The FBI won't help?"

"Pretty much."

"Then just say so. No reason to get all fancy pants on me with your national security issues and authorities crap," Mrs. Crowley said, barking the last part of the sentence out in a reasonable impersonation of a TV detective.

Lisa laughed.

"Well, come on in, I'm not trying to heat the rest of the neighborhood."

Clark and Lisa stepped up the single stair and wiped their feet before entering the warm house.

Mrs. Crowley moved across her small living room with

ease. Clark wondered if the cane was for show, or for smacking people upside the head.

"Please have a seat."

Mrs. Crowley liked flowers. More specifically, she liked roses. On the wall over the rose-patterned sofa was an oil painting of a large bouquet of the same. The throw pillows on the rocking chair were knitted with another bouquet of a slightly different color. The upright piano on the far side of the room was covered with rose-patterned doilies, on which a small vase of glass roses gathered dust.

Clark took a seat on the roses on the sofa. Mrs. Crowley put her weight into motion in the rocking chair. The room was hot but Mrs. Crowley had on a sweater and a shawl, the latter of which was a light blue, nearly the same hue as her hair.

"Can I get you some coffee?" she said with a pronounced Boston accent. "Some tea?"

"Whichever is easier for you," Clark answered.

"What kind of answer is that? Boiling water is boiling water."

"Coffee would be great. Thank you."

"See? How hard was that?"

Clark now suppressed a laugh. The charming coffin-dodger was definitely using her cane to crack skulls.

"And for you?" Mrs. Crowley asked Lisa.

"Coffee, black. Please."

Mrs. Crowley walked to the kitchen and returned a moment later. "So, how can I help you this morning?"

"I'm looking for information on someone who was a tenant of yours next door."

"I've had a lot of tenants. Some of them good, some of them bad. Which one are you looking for?"

"Ariana Amin."

"Ariana?"

"You recognize the name?"

"Of course," Mrs. Crowley said, wringing her hands together. Clark pulled a photograph from the manila folder and handed it to Mrs. Crowley. "Is this picture Ariana Amin?"

"Yes, that's her."

"She listed your house next door as her address in her INS documentation."

"Did she?"

"Yes."

"What can you tell me about her?"

"Well, for starters, she's dead."

Clark tried to not look startled. Lisa took over the questioning after a brief pause. "What do you remember about her?"

"She was quiet. Kept to herself, mostly. She had two roommates, but I am not sure how friendly they were. She hung out with other young women from time to time. Used to see them stop by and pick her up."

"Wellesley students?"

"Hard to say. There are so many colleges and universities in the Boston area. Harvard, UMass., MIT, Boston University."

Lisa nodded and Clark pulled out the hand drawn sketch of his former neighbor. "Was this girl one of her roommates, or maybe a friend?"

Mrs. Crowley looked at the picture through her bifocals. "No. I don't recall having ever seen her before. Who is she?"

"We aren't exactly sure. Her name, as far as we can tell, is also Ariana Amin."

"What did she do?"

"We don't know exactly."

"Then why are you looking for her?"

Clark looked at Lisa, who nodded. "I think she killed my neighbors and then vanished."

Lisa spoke with officialdom. "We call her an 'unsub,' or Unidentified Subject."

"Thank you for the bullshit explanation," Mrs. Crowley said.

"What can you tell me about Ariana's death?"

"Well, she disappeared. They found her abandoned car burned out in a remote area near Marlborough. They never did find her body."

"Did anyone come to claim her belongings?"

"Someone did, yes. I can't remember if it was a brother or a cousin, but it was someone around the same age, maybe a little older. It wasn't her father, I don't think. That, I would have remembered."

Ms. Crowley paused.

"The police figured she was kidnapped and murdered. Buried in the woods. There are a lot of trees in western Massachusetts, a lot of places to dispose of a body."

"Is that what the police said?"

"That is what I said. The story was all over the news for weeks. The car was burned to a skeleton and there wasn't much left to investigate. The police came to interview me and they interviewed some friends of hers, but it was routine."

"When was this?"

"Oh, let me see. It was in April 1998. I don't remember the date. Sometime around Easter."

The boiling teapot brought Ms. Crowley to her feet. She went to the kitchen and Lisa and Clark could hear the rattling of china, the refrigerator closing, the soft clanking of silverware.

"April 1998."

"I heard," Clark said.

Lisa looked at the file from the INS. "The last document in the folder is her naturalization certificate. It was awarded April 17th, 1998."

"So she stole her identity?"

"That would be my guess."

"So who is she?"

"I have no idea."

Chapter 48

Clark sprawled on the queen bed in the Holiday Inn near Newton, Massachusetts waiting for Lisa to finish blow-drying her hair in the bathroom. He turned off the TV and checked the weather on the back page of the local section of the Boston Globe. Old man winter was still feeling ornery, and the forecast for the rest of the week was calling for more arctic air.

He glanced at the weather map of the U.S. and allowed himself to wonder what it would be like on a beach in Hawaii. After a month of ice and snow, Waikiki would be perfect. Clark flipped back to the second page and perused the small hodgepodge of one paragraph articles. The first story was about a sixth grader who came to school with a loaded .44 magnum. *Dirty Harry goes to Show-and-Tell* was the title of the news snippet. The second article caught Clark's attention and his stomach sank as he sped through the opening sentences. The burned out remains of missing NASA scientist Paul Cannon's BMW had been found in a remote suburb of Northern Virginia. The scientist, a Boston native and MIT graduate, had been employed by NASA in Greenbelt for seven years and was considered a pioneer in new energy propulsion systems. The missing man had also once held the record for reciting Pi to the 10,000th decimal place. *That's where I recognize the name,* Clark thought.

Clark reminisced about his attempt to recite Pi and then his mind jumped back to the opening sentences. *A missing man with a burned out car found in a remote area.*

Clark felt cold sweat bead up on his neck. "No fucking way."

Chapter 49

Sealed in the sleeping quarters, Ariana, Syed, and Karim waited. Per protocol, each person wore a military-grade Hycar gas mask with a polyurethane shield lens. Each mask had a nosecup to prevent fogging and a standard mechanical speaking diaphragm which allowed the wearer to speak clearly without undo effort. The head harness was adjustable without the need to deal with unwieldy rubber straps. When it came to warfare, Uncle Sam had the best gadgets.

Syed spoke through the mask, his words intermittent with the muffled wheezing of air through the mask. "Those machines. Do you think Abu can operate them properly?"

Ariana nodded. They had been in the room for over nine hours and Ariana struggled with boredom. Syed and Karim had grown accustomed to the room, the silence, the downtime. Ariana was still on the steep section of the learning curve. "We did a trial run with coffee beans. The output was good. The machines themselves aren't difficult to operate. I set the machines to the required specs, which should remove further variables in the equation. All Abu has to do is run the machines. Whether or not he follows the procedures, well, that's a different story."

"What are his chances?"

Ariana tilted her head slightly to the side.

"Fifty-fifty."

"You said the risk was low."

"If he follows instructions, he may make it."

Silence, and breathing, followed.

"You should have told him," Syed said.

"He knows what he signed up for. We all do," Karim answered, joining the conversation.

"Let's say you inhaled a lethal dose of the processed powder. How long would you have to live?" Syed asked.

Ariana answered, speaking slower than usual though her words were completely audible. "An educated guess is forty-eight hours. There really isn't much research on the subject, for obvious reasons. I think most of the knowledge we have comes from testing animals."

"How does it kill?"

"At the cellular level. Ricin acts as a ribosome-inactivating protein."

"Which means?"

"It breaks down the ribosomes in proteins, until protein synthesis ceases."

"Is there a less technical explanation?"

"Ricin poisoning is very complicated. It prevents the cells in the body from making proteins, and that will kill the cell and eventually the person. It causes clumping and breakdown of the red blood cells, hemorrhaging in the digestive tract, damage to vital organs. Within eight hours of inhalation, symptoms would start to appear. The symptoms would be different, depending on the method of ingestion, but for inhalation it would start with respiratory distress, coughing, tightness in the chest. Nausea, sweating, and fever would follow. Seizures and hallucinations might occur. Within two or three days the kidneys, liver, and spleen would stop working."

"And there's no treatment?"

"There is treatment, but no cure. Medicine can treat the symptoms, and ricin is not one hundred percent fatal. A person can recover on their own. Ricin in various forms is actually used medicinally. In particular, it is used in treating some forms of cancers and in bone marrow transplants."

"So it may not be lethal?"

"A few people may get lucky."

Syed considered the thought. "I guess that's the difference between a mass killing and an assassination. I'm trained to kill, and given the right weapon no one is getting lucky."

Ariana looked at the soldier sitting on an army cot. "Don't worry; there will be enough for you to kill as many as you want."

No one spoke for a minute and then Syed began anew. "I don't understand why we are using ricin. There will be no violent images, no destruction. We need a spectacle of violence to attract the next generation of fighters. To show the world that we are serious."

"Ricin is what we have."

"But a nuclear bomb is what we need."

"It is planned," Karim said. "But highly enriched uranium is hard to come by. We are relying on a small supply stream from southern Russia, passed through north Ossetia and Georgia. The Russian nuclear stockpile is for sale ... if you have enough money and ask for small quantities. Large requests make everyone a little nervous. Too nervous. You may remember last year a Georgian man walked into a restaurant with three ounces of HEU in a plastic bag. Unfortunately, he sold it to an agent of the CIA."

"How can you carry it in a plastic bag?" Syed asked.

Ariana answered. "You can touch highly enriched uranium without protection. Unlike plutonium which is very deadly."

"How much uranium is needed for a bomb?"

"It takes over a hundred pounds of HEU to produce a bomb equivalent to the one dropped on Hiroshima. Ounce by ounce we will make it. We almost had six pounds of HEU in one transaction, but it was intercepted by Czech security," Karim said.

"It would be nice to have it now."

"Yes, it would," Karim answered.

Another moment of silence passed before the loquaciousness reappeared.

Karim started. "We have other efforts underway. We have men scouring the caves on the border between Kenya and Uganda. The Kitum cave on Mount Elgon is particularly hopeful. Wild elephants have been known to frequent the Kitum cave to lick its walls, which are laden with salt. It is also one of the known locations for the Ebola and Marburg virus. On two separate occasions the virus has been traced to this single cave."

"How do you capture the virus? You would need specialized equipment. Specialized medicine. Doctors."

"We are not trying to *capture* the virus. We are trying to *contract* the virus. We have a network of men who are prepared to contract the virus, travel to another location, and then spread the virus to the next person in the chain. We could have infected men in London, New York, Washington, and Paris in less than a week."

"That still lacks a certain mass appeal. The faithful are not as moved by sick bodies in bed as they are by body pieces in the street."

"Consider yourself a pioneer," Karim said.

A long silence followed and Ariana spoke. "There is something else to consider about our plan."

"What is that?" Karim asked.

"We need more men."

Chapter 50

The quad in the middle of campus was quiet. The benches along the crisscrossing sidewalks were empty, the graffiti of white Greek letters standing out against the dark wood of the seatbacks. The guerilla advertising on unofficially designated benches was overlooked by university police. Limited "sanctioned vandalism" it was called. To give the campus some character.

Washington D.C. may have been suffering through a cold spell, but Boston was in the freezer next to the gamey meat. The local news was having fun with rumors of polar bear sightings in Boston Commons, America's oldest public park. The frozen Charles River acted as a wind tunnel to the campus of MIT, pushing gusts from the hills in the distance into downtown Cambridge. Unassailable, the winds tore through the largest conglomeration of scholastic intelligence in the free world before continuing on to pelt urban Bean Town.

Old universities ooze knowledge. They perspire with culture. They drip history. They breathe civility. Walk the halls of Princeton or Yale or Harvard or Oxford, and the average person feels smarter. Knowledge hangs in the air, hundreds of years of education forming some unidentifiable aura of cerebral worthiness.

The 430,000 square foot Stata Center on Vassar Street on the MIT campus was different. Stainless steel walls, interspersed with modern brown brick siding, jutted from the building at odd angles giving the feeling that the building was growing from the Earth haphazardly, like unkempt grass. Ninety degree angles were rare in the behemoth building whose construction was partially funded by Bill Gates. The only central recurring theme in the architecture was the lack of one. The madness of the first several floors of the building housed everything from artificial intelligence to linguistics. The towers on either side stretched upwards in swooping curves. Classrooms with inward sloping walls gave some students vertigo. George Jetson would have been right at home.

Clark and Lisa walked the hallway and stopped near the elevators to Tower D, the bulletin boards still covered with colorful fall semester notices and advertisements pinned to the corkboard. Cars for sale. Houses for rent. Roommates wanted. Guitar lessons available. Happy Hour with a band called Randy Dick, in honor of the singer and drummer.

Clark looked around at the glass interior walls and the team of intellects that worked like bees in a translucent hive. "It's not what I expected," Clark said to Lisa as they waited for the elevator.

"What did you expect?"

"History. Oil paintings on the wall. Wooden staircases. This place lacks a certain je ne sais quoi, which I believe is French for 'really old stuff.'"

"For someone so smart, you say some pretty stupid things."

"Just going for the laugh."

"I'm not sure we have time to be laughing."

The elevator opened in the basement of Tower D and the architectural feeling Clark had been searching for became an even more distant hope. He looked at the signage on the wall and followed the arrow towards *Robotics Research*.

"No wonder we lost the robotics competition. Virginia Tech is practicing robotics in stone buildings with walls that perspire and these guys are developing robots in Buck Rogers' apartment."

Clark knocked on the open doorframe under the Robotics Research sign. A girl in jeans and an MIT sweatshirt turned towards the door.

"Hi. I'm Clark Hayden and I'm looking for Mayank Malhotra."

"Mayank?"

"Yes. I called ahead; he should be expecting me."

The girl got up from her seat and shook hands with Clark and Lisa. "I'm Tara Patel. Mayank's this way."

The girl went through a pair of swinging doors, the type hospital staffers open with the end of a gurney, and led Clark and Lisa down a hall lined with shelves of electronic equipment and boxes. She turned left at the end of the hall, went through another set of doors, and the eight-foot ceiling of the passageway opened to thirty feet. A miniature car with a blinking light on top zoomed by on the floor in front of Tara's feet.

"Welcome to the most expensive playroom on the East Coast. Wait here and I'll find Mayank."

A remote control helicopter came into view and hovered in the air a few yards in front of Clark. A small flash of light emitted from the helicopter before it disappeared into the far corner of the room.

Tara returned and passed Clark and Lisa on her way to the door. "He's on his way," she said, smiling as she walked through the double swinging doors.

As promised, Mayank arrived a moment later with a remote control device in his hand, the antenna extended.

"Clark, good to see you again."

"Thanks for seeing me."

"I'm wondering if I should pat you down or blindfold you. For all I know you are here on a university robotics intelligence mission."

"I wish I were."

Clark introduced Mayank to Lisa.

"Did Clark tell you we met in Tokyo? We competed with each other in the World Robotics Championship."

"Yes, he mentioned it. It's some place you have here."

A yellow flag at the end of the antenna on the remote control had a number written on it. Lisa asked "What's the number for?"

"Frequency," Clark answered. "You can't have different toys running on the same frequency. It makes control a little difficult."

"Bad things happen," Mayank said, elaborating with his free hand slamming into the side of the controller to indicate a crash. He put the remote control on a chest-high table near the door. "Let's go somewhere we can talk."

Clark and Lisa followed Mayank back to an office with three glass walls and no windows.

"It is quite a building," Lisa added.

"We are part of CSAIL, the Computer Science and Artificial Intelligence Laboratory. We have a bit to work with."

"That would be an understatement."

"So, Clark, what's going on? You said on the phone you were in Boston and it was important."

Clark gave the Reader's Digest condensed version of the story. He started with the missing family who claimed to have returned home suddenly, touched on two dead neighbors in the last several weeks, a house fire, a car mechanic in search of a new employee to replace his dead one, a visit from the FBI after his mom called the CIA, and the beans of death he pulled off a farm in Virginia.

Mayank Malhotra looked at Clark with a little concern. "And the IRS is involved, how?" he asked, looking at Lisa. Lisa smiled and Mayank felt a little blood flow south.

"She's investigating my parents for tax evasion."

"*Was* investigating," Lisa clarified.

"Right, *was* investigating."

"Now we are seeing each other."

"Given those two alternatives, I would say you have chosen wisely," Mayank answered.

"She's helping me poke around a little," Clark added, trying to ignore the joke he left hanging out there, over the plate like a slow pitch softball.

"And you think your neighbor is an MIT graduate, why?"

"Paul Cannon," Clark answered.

"The NASA scientist?"

"The same."

"I don't see the connection."

"Neither would have I," Clark started. "But we think this woman, my neighbor, stole the identity of a Wellesley student in 1998. The student went missing out near the University of Massachusetts. Her car was found burned out. Her body was never found."

"Just like Paul Cannon."

"Exactly."

"Sounds like a hunch."

"It's more than a hunch, it's the culmination of a series of hunches. A cacophony of hunches, bells, whistles, and sirens that have been going off in my head for the last month. All I need is to confirm something."

"The girl's identity," Lisa chimed in.

"And then what?"

"Then I'll find her."

"How are you going to do that?"

"I don't know just yet."

"Maybe I've seen too many movies, but if you have two dead neighbors, maybe you won't need to find her. Maybe she will find you."

"Let's see what we've got," Mayank said, turning towards his computer. "We have any guesses on the girl's name?"

"No."

"Then how do we know we are looking for the right person?"

"We don't know her name, but we believe she is Pakistani. We think she graduated sometime between 1996 and 2000."

"That's not much to go on."

"How about Paul Cannon? Can you tell us when he graduated?"

"You really think they're connected?"

"It's my theory."

"I hope you're wrong. MIT is a small community. And one that is very well-connected through research, alumni, internships, email, websites, blogs, etc. I hope it's nothing insidious between our MIT brethren."

"I read that Paul Cannon graduated from MIT in 1998. Maybe we can start with that year." Clark pulled out the hand-drawn picture of Ariana Amin done by Mr. Stanley. "And this is a rough picture of what she looks like."

"Did you do that?"

"No, why?"

"Looks more like a portrait than a police sketch."

"I'll let the artist know."

Mayank turned his attention back to the computer. "This database has every graduate from the university since its inception," Mayank explained as he typed, an action he augmented with the occasional click of the mouse.

"Of course the data from the old days is just a list of vitals: name, permanent address, grades. It wasn't until 1996 that we really started doing cool things with the student data."

"The advent of the Internet," Clark said.

"That's right. 1996 was the advent of the Web browser anyway. Of course, MIT had the internet from before Al Gore. But with the internet, came a formal university intranet, or rather an institutional wide interest in its intranet. And with that, the underground programmers came to the surface and everyone's job got a little easier around here."

Mayank continued to explain. "We can search by name, social security number, student ID number, year of graduation, field of study."

"Can you search by sex?"

"You know … I don't know." Mayank pecked around for a minute. "Not a searchable criterion. But women make up less than ten percent of the student body. In 1998, the number was even smaller. It shouldn't take long."

"It has taken forever to get this far," Clark said under his breath. Mayank Malhotra typed into the keyboard and then clicked with his mouse. "Here we are. Paul Cannon, graduated in 1998 with a Ph.D. in alternate energy propulsion."

"Can we search for students in that program and related programs?"

"Let's start with related programs. That sounds like a specialty Ph.D., even by MIT standards." Mayank clicked a few more boxes and a list of names appeared on the screen in blue.

"Do any of them look familiar?"

All three looked down the list. Names from every corner of the globe, and a few from off the radar, populated the screen. Taiwan, Bangladesh, Moldova, Australia, Uruguay, Germany. It was the cream of the crop, the topping on the best intellectual sundae the world had to offer. A global alliance of brainpower.

"Try the third one from the bottom," Clark said.

"Not sure if that is a man or a woman," Mayank said. "Could be either." He clicked on the link and a picture popped into the upper left hand corner of the screen. The man with the turban and moustache was neither the right sex nor the right religion.

Two more clicks, two more misses. Mayank scrolled down and read the next name on the list.

"Safia Hafeez. Definitely a woman's name."

Mayank clicked the link and a picture appeared on the screen. No one spoke. Clark and Lisa leaned over Mayank's shoulder, getting closer to the screen.

"Is that her?" Lisa asked.

All three looked at the picture on the screen and the hand drawing on the desk.

Clark leaned toward the monitor. "Hello, Safia."

"Are you sure?" Lisa asked.

"Yeah, that's her. I've never seen her without a Hijab. She looks good."

Mayank read the bio on the bottom of the screen. "Fulbright Scholar. Studied applied liquid propulsion. A second Ph.D. in Chemical Engineering. Master's in Electrical Engineering."

"Fuck. Nice combination," Clark said to himself out loud, his voice trailing off. Mayank looked up as if that word had not been spoken in the hallow halls of MIT since the sixties and the peace generation.

"Let me translate for my partner here," Lisa said calmly. "Any chance we can talk to one of her professors?"

"I can call around and ask. Class is still out of session, but there are a few professors around. Particularly in the science department. They have experiments and studies that go pretty much year-round. We have a dedicated staff and dedicated students who support that staff."

Clark suddenly felt like he was being recruited. "Can we try to reach one of the dedicated? We need to find this Safia Hafeez."

"Let me get my coat and we can walk over to the main chemistry building."

Professor Mike Ching was in his office with his soft-sided leather briefcase on his shoulder and his office keys in his hand when Mayank knocked on the door.

"Professor Ching?"

"Yes."

"Do you have a minute?"

"I was on my way out the door."

Lisa Prescott pulled out her badge and showed it to the professor. "It's important."

"That's an IRS badge."

"And I said it was important."

"I paid my taxes."

It was apparent that Professor Ching abided to the common misconception that the person asking the question was somehow inferior to the person being asked the question. Lisa was about to change that.

"Well, if you don't want to be audited for the next twenty years, give us a minute of your time."

Mayank fidgeted. Grilling a professor wasn't on his list of semester projects.

The professor put his briefcase on his desk. "Please sit down."

The office was decorated à la Fred Sanford meets Marie Curie. Papers and books filled every corner of the room. A mobile hung from the ceiling in the corner, protons, neutrons and electrons in some configuration that would baffle the average Joe, but was covered in MIT freshman chemistry. A 3-D periodical chart with all the elements was attached to the wall in the corner.

"What can I help you with?" Dr. Michael Ching asked in perfect English. Clark plopped his butt in an old wooden chair. He looked up at Mayank who was eavesdropping, still standing at the door.

Lisa took control of the conversation. She turned towards Mayank.

"Mayank, thanks for your help. If we could excuse ourselves for the moment, we would like to keep this conversation close to our vest, if you don't mind the gambler's parlance."

"Oh, sure. I understand. Let me know if there is anything else you need."

Clark tried to soften the blow. "Yes, there's something you could do. Could we get any addresses she listed, as well as a list of classes, the professors, and whoever you can identify as classmates?"

"I'll have it by the time you're done. But I want half of any reward."

"Deal," Clark answered, before turning towards Professor Ching.

"What can you tell us about Safia Hafeez?"

"Safia Hafeez. That's a name I haven't heard in a while. Why are you interested in her?"

"We're interested in her as a material witness. We think she's been living under an assumed identity for several years. We'd like to know whatever you can tell us."

Dr. Ching sighed and ran both hands through his hair, one on each side of his head. His eyes settled on Clark.

Clark preempted the question he saw coming. "I'm just here for identification purposes. As a material witness, if you will."

"A material witness for a material witness," Dr. Ching said curiously. His black hair had streaks of gray, but his face was youthful. His eyes were penetrating. He paused briefly as if considering speaking, and then moved his bag to the side of his desk and leaned back slightly in his chair.

"Safia Hafeez was a gifted student."

"Aren't most of the MIT students gifted?"

"Sure. But I'm speaking in relative terms. From a natural perspective, Safia Hafeez had a gift. There are all kinds of protégés in this world. Mathematical, musical, artistic. Things that cannot be explained by anything other than Godly intervention. Or, if you are atheist, we can call it dumb luck. There is nothing that can explain a seven-year-old boy who walks by a piano for the first time, sits down, and plays a perfect stanza to Beethoven's fifth symphony. It just doesn't happen. And when it does, everyone tries to capture the magic in a bottle, as if it is something we can keep, analyze, harness, replicate."

"And Safia Hafeez was like this? She was a protégé?"

"She was unlike anyone I have taught at this university. She had an electrical engineering background. I got the impression she had been around engineers growing up. She had an understanding of electricity, mechanics, and chemicals that was unmatched. And it was seemingly untaught, or maybe self-taught. When I lecture, most students try to keep up. They take what I tell them, digest it, and try to apply things I teach in the classroom to experiments in the lab. Not Safia. When I lectured, she took random notes, and the rest she committed to memory. She drew her own conclusions about compounds and what would work best under circumstances of pressure, friction, heat. On the surface, it may sound very easy. When you talk about combining this knowledge to send a man to the moon, it becomes a little more complicated. Safia could talk about chemistry, biochemistry, physics, electrical engineering, as easily as you and I would talk about the weather. And that was *before* she got into the program."

"What exactly did she work on?"

"Chemical engineering and propulsion systems."

Clark shook his head slowly, unconscious he was doing it. "What's the problem?"

"We think Safia may have nefarious intentions against the general public," Lisa said.

Professor Ching's face turned pasty. "That's not good news."

"Why do you say that?" Clark asked.

"Because if this woman wanted to start trouble, she has the expertise to take out a thousand people with the household chemicals in the average broom closet."

Clark and Lisa left the professor at his desk with a business card in his fingers. Dr. Ching looked out the window, staring at the heavier flakes of snow that had started according to the weatherman's forecast. *Safia Hafeez*, he whispered to himself. *God I hope they are wrong.*

Clark and Lisa walked briskly down the hallway, as if distancing themselves from where they were would bring them closer to where they needed to be. Neither knew where that was.

Clark spoke as they hit the stairs. "Looks like we have one potentially dangerous bitch loose on the streets."

"You know what scares me?"

"What?"

"She has a twelve-year head start," Lisa said. "We may never catch up. We may never see her again."

"I hope you're right. I hope we never see her."

Chapter 51

Most major cities have a street named International Drive or Road or Court, but there are few that live up to their billing like the one in D.C. Wedged into a horseshoe-shaped strip of pavement in northwest Washington, beyond the glamour of the major embassies, International Drive housed embassies from Israel to Bahrain to Ghana to Ethiopia. They weren't the most distinguished embassies in the capital city's repertoire, that title long since claimed by the G-8 member nations and their prime real estate on what was affectionately known as Embassy Row. But where Embassy Row was sprinkled with old-money residences, International Drive was an embassy monopoly. It was void of local riff-raff, even those in Bentleys.

With over a dozen embassies packed into a quarter-mile of looped blacktop, the embassy protection detail on International Drive was a walk in the park for the myriad diplomatic security personnel. With the exception of the Israel Embassy, which tended to focus on its Mossad contingency on anything that moved with intelligence value, the other embassies on International Drive had a certain level of shared security. Given the close proximity of so many embassies, a bomb for one was a bomb for all.

"It's quiet in here," Clark said.

Mr. Khan, Counselor of Community Affairs for the Pakistan Embassy, let the silence shower the room for a moment, as if Clark had laid a new thought out for inspection. "Yes, it is rather quiet. But then again, embassies are not what you see in the movies. Most of them are quiet, serious places. We try to represent the best of our respective countries. Yelling, screaming, fighting … well, these things are not useful in situations requiring diplomatic solutions."

"True. True. I guess the movies do give embassies a bit more flare than they really have."

"Hollywood is not in the honesty business."

Clark feigned a look of concern. "I'm not sure who is in the honesty business these days. In fact, I'm not sure there's an honesty business at all."

The counselor looked at Clark suspiciously. "So, Mr. Hayden. I understand that you have a few questions about the Fulbright scholarship."

"Yes, sort of. I had several questions I was hoping you could answer for me. The Fulbright scholarship is just one aspect."

"I think perhaps your own government may be in a better position to answer your question."

"My question was more geared to Fulbright scholars from Pakistan."

The counselor sighed. "I see, well, as you may or may not know, Fulbright scholarships are awarded to the brightest and the best of the academic world. Fulbright scholars are students who we believe will lead a generation of leaders in the area of law, medicine, academia."

Clark noticed that Counselor Khan's words were crisp, clean, exact … and with a hint of a British accent.

"Your English is impeccable. If I may say so without sounding condescending."

"I was educated in Britain."

"That would explain it," Clark added. He was running out of things to compliment the counselor on. He had started with the picture on the wall when they entered the room, had moved to office furniture, and was now on the counselor's language skills. The local curry shop in Shirlington was next on the list. He dug for something better. "And the Fulbright scholarship is sponsored through the U.S. Department of State…"

"Correct. In the case of Pakistan there is additional funding through the U.S. Agency for International Development and Pakistan's Higher Education Commission."

"How many scholarships are awarded to Pakistanis every year?"

"The number is fluid, dependent upon funding approved by the presidential approval board."

"The U.S. President."

"Correct. The President of the United States."

"So Fulbright scholars are funded by the U.S. Government and the selection of the scholars is done by a President-appointed board?"

"Correct. And to answer your previous question, Pakistan had over 150 Fulbright scholars last year. One-third of those were Ph.D. students."

Wow, only 150 potential U.S. government-funded terrorists in training, Clark thought. *Beautiful.*

"And what are the requirements of the Fulbright scholar? What's the overall purpose of the program? What does the U.S. get out of it?"

"It can be argued that the main goal of the Fulbright program is to influence the future leaders of foreign nations. Once a student has lived in the U.S., and tasted the democracy of the U.S., they are far more likely to be U.S. sympathizers. They will never look at their home country in the same way as before. At the very least, they will have a more global view of the world."

"Perhaps," Clark said. He thought his neighbor might not be on board with that assessment.

"Another stipulation of the Fulbright program is that

each scholar must promise to return to their home country for a given period of two to three years, depending on the scholarship they receive. They are not permitted to work in the U.S. until this home country requirement has been fulfilled. This is necessary to ensure that the home country receives some benefit from the program as well. Otherwise, in many instances, the brain drain would be instantaneous. Under the current guidelines, the home country gets at least two years of service from the scholar."

"And what if they don't go home?"

"They have to re-pay their education expenses."

"How many choose this route?"

Counselor Khan laughed. "Not many. The average salary in Pakistan is under three thousand dollars per year. Very few could afford to pay the cost of tuition, particularly at a private U.S. school. Pakistan is still a very poor country. We have a less than a fifty percent literacy rate."

"Interesting," Clark responded before dropping his bomb. "I'm here on a strange request, or quest, as it has turned out. One of my neighbors is an American citizen, or possesses dual citizenship. I'm interested in a 'Welfare and Whereabouts' request."

"A 'Welfare and Whereabouts request?'"

"Yes. I have an acquaintance in the consular services world and he told me that would be the appropriate wording. My neighbor, and her family, recently returned to Pakistan to tend to family affairs. I received a phone call from them asking if I would look after their home, water their plants. The usual. Their house was recently heavily damaged by fire, and I have no way to reach them. I was wondering if the Pakistan Embassy could help in my search."

The counselor looked thoughtfully at Clark. "If they are American citizens in Pakistan, it may be better to go through the U.S. Embassy in Islamabad."

"I'm afraid I don't have much to go on, in this case. There is no record of the neighbor having any residence or relatives in Pakistan. I only have a name."

"Which is?"

Clark watched carefully for any recognition in the counselor's face. "Her name is Ariana Amin." If the counselor recognized the name he had missed his calling on the World Poker Tour. There was not a flinch. Not a twitch. Not a momentary flash of recognition. Clark dealt the river card. "But I believe her real name is Safia Hafeez. She was a Fulbright scholar, sponsored by the Pakistani government, and she studied at MIT."

The counselor's expression did not change. "I'm afraid the name doesn't ring a bell."

Clark sat there for moment. "Would it be possible to search your records and see if you can locate a last known address or contact for my neighbor? I would think that she would want to know that everything she owns in this country has been either charred beyond recognition or soaked in 20,000 gallons of water."

The counselor pulled out a piece of paper and scribbled some notes. "I will see what I can do," he said, pausing in between sentences as he wrote. "But there are no guarantees that I will be able to find anything."

"All I can ask is that you take a look."

"That is a fair request."

As Clark exited the Embassy, the large black metal gate to the adjacent parking lot was slowly shutting behind an equally black Lexus sedan. The car gently pulled into the spot closest to the building's employee entrance, just beyond a sidewalk and behind an eight-foot security fence. A guard decked out with the latest military hardware eyed Clark as he made his way from the visitor's entrance to the main gate booth armed with two identical soldiers. Clark took in his surroundings as he mulled over the conversation he just had inside the Embassy. *Maybe I was wrong,* he thought. *Maybe, I am just jumping to conclusions.*

Clark nodded as he walked the sidewalk towards the main guard booth and the property's exit. As he turned towards the direction of the main street, the back door on the black Lexus opened. Clark was less than ten yards away when the precocious two-year-old exited from the back of the car, waved her lollipop, and smiled.

Clark stopped.

"Hi," Liana said, clearly, her hand gripping her red candy-on-a-stick.

The woman exiting the back of the car panicked, exchanging concerned glances between Clark and Liana.

"Wait!" Clark yelled as the woman quickly scooped up Liana and disappeared into a pair of plain white double doors. Clark, heart racing, took one step off the designated sidewalk in the direction of the security fence and was immediately reprimanded by the guard who was now on full alert. The AK-47 was still on his shoulder, but the eyes and body language told Clark all he needed to know.

"Not one more step," the guard said clearly, pointing down at the sidewalk, the official line of demarcation.

"But, I know that girl," Clark blurted.

"Step back," the guard repeated, one hand now on the grip of his holstered firearm.

Clark took a large step back. The guard put his finger to his ear, listened for directions via the wireless security device, and then looked back at Clark. "It is time for you to leave," the guard said, unequivocally.

"But, I need to speak with Counselor Khan."

"No sir, you do not. You are to leave the premises immediately."

Clark drove home, hands shaking. He was scared. The kind of scared that kept therapists in business. There was only one possible explanation for seeing Liana at the Pakistan Embassy. His instincts had been correct. Counselor Khan, with his perfected poker face, was lying through his teeth. There was an undeniable connection between Ariana and the Embassy. Clark wondered how deep it went.

His stomach knotted and a wave of nausea washed over him. There was only one thing he could think of. Finding a safe location for his mother ... if such as thing as a safe location existed anymore. When you consider state-sponsored terrorism, hiding places become scarce.

It took a majority of the afternoon to convince his mother it was in her best interest to go to her brother's house in Annapolis. The conversation was like rationalizing with a toddler who was in the "why?" phase of childhood. And unfortunately for Clark, Maria Hayden was past the point where she could simply be lifted off her feet and strapped into a car seat.

Clark pressed down on the suitcase until the latches were aligned. With a final grunt and additional ass weight, the old American Tourister finally complied.

"Did you get my medicine?" Maria asked for the fifth time.

"I have all your medication, Mom. It is in the backpack. I have your shampoo, your make-up and your hair dryer. I packed five pairs of shoes and enough clothes for a month-long trip around the world. We are good to go."

"And why am I going to Annapolis again?"

Clark had given the truthful answer multiple times, but his mother, on this day at least, was not absorbing the facts. Clark finally succumbed to a brief explanation. "Because there are some things I need to do, Mom."

"But I've been living alone for the last year. I don't need you to take care of me."

"You're going to have to trust me on this."

"I trust you. I trust you," Maria Hayden said as Clark dragged the third suitcase towards the door.

"I have another question," Maria said, sitting down on the sofa as if she were unaware of the impending departure.

"What, Mom?"

"Why am I going to Annapolis and did you pack my medicine?"

Chapter 52

Saturday night brought in half of the Kabob Keeper's weekly business, but Tuesday night brought in the weekly quota of weirdoes from the local design school. Nestled between the backside of the *Crystal City Restaurant*, a strip joint with a family-friendly name, and a 7-11 that hadn't shut its doors since 1969, the *Kabob Keeper* took up residence among a set of shops that had once been under the single roof of a carpet store. The parking lot was tight, the spaces full, and the smell of puke and urine from the back door of take-it-off central tended to waft over during the summer.

Ariana parked her blue Toyota at a space with a broken meter on 23rd street, a few hundred yards from the Kabob Keeper, and walked once around the block. The pulsating rhythm of pole-dancing tunes could be heard in the parking lot, an old chair with a sordid history left to prop open the back fire door. The 7-11 parking lot had surveillance cameras, and although she could never avoid all the cameras in a city with eyes on every corner, she wasn't above avoiding the ones she knew about. But time was short. And, if things went well it wouldn't matter how many cameras had captured her image. Dressed as an Americanized woman, complete with Levis and a sweater, Ariana felt like a foreigner as she entered the restaurant. She knew every food by sight, could taste the dishes with her eyes, knew the ingredients by the smell. Her mind drifted back to her youth: carrying bowls of sevian, nehari, mango, and milk tea to her grandparents across the street in her native homeland.

A dropped dish brought her back to the restaurant. She felt a tension that heightened her awareness. The Kebob Keeper may have been named to appeal to the masses — the office workers, young professionals, and college kids who wolfed down the curries and kebobs, but the eyes of the workers told Ariana something else.

Ariana nodded as she approached the counter and the elderly man in a sweaty white t-shirt nodded in return before turning his back and retrieving a loaf of nan from the inside of the cylindrical clay oven.

"Excuse me," Ariana said over the din of orders being relayed. "I'm looking for Khalid." She pulled out the handwritten note she had received from the imam and moved it gently between her thumb and forefinger.

The man put the nan bread on a tray with the long thin metal rod that he wielded effortlessly. He looked at the group of design students, all with different color hair, waiting at the far end of the counter for their food. His focus on the waiting customers drew Ariana's attention to the other end of the counter, and the man grabbed the note from Ariana's hand. It was a professional move, Ariana noted, and one she shouldn't have fallen for.

The old man unfolded the note as he turned to face the soda dispensers. He finished reading and looked over his shoulder at the clock on the wall. "You are right on time," he said in Urdu.

With the nod of his head he motioned her behind the counter.

"The imam only sent three," the old man in the t-shirt said in a whisper as they approached the office in the back of the store. The heat from the kitchen, initially a welcome from the cold, became more oppressive near the rear of the restaurant.

Ariana understood why the old man's shirt was clinging to his body. The four-man kitchen staff moved swiftly through the heat, perspiration on their faces. The clank of metal pans was interrupted by a ringing bell indicating that an order was ready.

Through the stainless steel shelves, Ariana felt eyes watching her every move.

The old man pushed the office door open and the three volunteers sat up in their chairs. They were seated at a round table. Used Styrofoam plates balanced in a stack in the small wastecan near the desk. The smell of lamb filled the room, hanging thick in the air. Ariana was suddenly hungry. Freeze-dried meals had made great improvements over the years but they couldn't compete with handcooked meals. Even those made in quantity.

Ariana nodded to her host and the old man shut the door as he left. Three young faces looked up at her. They all had similar features. Pointed noses, narrow chins.

"Brothers?" Ariana asked after a moment of silence.

"Yes," the oldest of the three answered. "My name is Farooq. We have met."

Ariana recognized the young man's wispy sideburns and peach fuzz, intermingled with the random long whiskers. "You are the imam's understudy."

"Yes," Farooq answered.

"How old are you?"

"Twenty-one. My brothers are eighteen. They are twins."

"Fraternal…"

"Yes, fraternal."

The pudgier of the two brothers dipped his head and spoke. "My name is Jameel." He was wearing a tattered New York Giants jacket and a pair of sneakers that he tapped on the floor in a smooth steady beat.

The slender twin looked up with naturally wide brown eyes. "My name is Omar."

Ariana nodded. "You know why you are here?"

"Yes," Farooq answered.

"I need an answer from all of you."

The twins both raised their voices and replied, "Yes."

"Farooq, Jameel, and Omar," Ariana said rhetorically, as if measuring their names and the suitability to the task. The brothers looked at each other and smiled as if they had been recognized for greatness.

"So everyone knows why they are here. If anyone has cold feet, they need to leave now."

Ariana waited for a response. No one moved.

"I'm glad you have chosen to stay the course. I would not have enjoyed killing all of you in this room. Three brothers would have been messy."

Fear joined the smell of lamb in the air.

"Here's the deal. It's very simple. I will pay each of you $10,000 dollars to help me for the next forty-eight hours. If you agree, however, you will do exactly as I say, exactly when I say it. There will be no negotiations. No complaining. No questions. Unless the questions are operational in nature."

Jameel looked at his older brothers before speaking. "How do we know you have the money? Or that we would live to see it?"

From her purse Ariana pulled a ten thousand dollar stack she had received from the imam. She put the money on the table and the eyes of the younger brothers stared, their eyelids refusing to blink. "I have the money. Living to see it, well, I have no guarantees. That is in Allah's hands. Tell me who should receive it in the case of your death, and I will see to it that they do."

Farooq looked at his twin brothers and shook his head towards them. "We are here for our father and Allah, not for the money."

Jameel and Omar nodded in agreement.

"Very well then," Ariana said. "You have passed the second test. I am looking for men of conviction, not greed."

The young men stared ahead stoically until Ariana asked, "Where is your father?"

"Dead," Omar answered from beneath his wide eyes.

Ariana paced back and forth slowly, her eyes moving deliberately from one recruit to the other. "This is your last chance to run," she added, moving her body to mockingly create an opening towards the door.

She was the only one smiling.

Forty-eight hours. The countdown was on.

Chapter 53

Clark went through the daily delivery from Mel, stacking and sorting bills and junk mail into separate piles. The thought of sitting down and writing checks, stuffing them into envelopes, getting stamps, and having the postman pick them up was almost comical. He hadn't written a check in over a year. The younger generation had found the Internet and electronic bill payment. And they were not coming back to the "write it, stuff it, lick it, and send it" world.

Clark got to the last letter and his heart sank a little. Neatly printed on the business envelope was the name of his father's company, Hayden Ltd. He ran his finger down the side of the envelope and began reading at the top of the sheet near the word "invoice." There were half a dozen line-items, three with prices in the BMW, low-end Mercedes neighborhood. Clark scanned the dates, looked up at the name on the invoice again, and reached for the phone.

He spent five minutes navigating the hide-the-real-person voice commands of the company's main customer service number. His seventh correct selection came with a reward. "Hunter Scientific," the female voice on the other end of the phone answered with uncommon morning pleasantness.

"Good morning. My name is Clark Hayden, and I need to speak with someone in the billing department."

"This is the billing department."

"Thank God."

"I get that response a lot," the voice said. "How can I help you?"

"I'm looking at an invoice for my father's company and I think there's a mistake."

"There could be. Let me pull it up for you. What's the account number?"

Clark found the account number at the top of the invoice and read it slowly to the woman. As they waited for the information to pull it, the woman gave Clark her speech for the week.

"We have had an unusual number of billing errors this month. One of the ice storms last month took down some trees nearby which hit a transformer. We got a surge of electricity to our computer system here. Caused us to lose more than a few records. It has been a big mess. We have been going through files manually. A lot of end of the year documents are going out. The early bird taxpayers are calling us non-stop for documents."

A one syllable chuckle escaped Clark's mouth. "You think you've had a bad month, let me tell you about mine. I have had run-ins with the IRS, the FBI, and the police. Two of my neighbors have died and another's house burned down." Clark stopped himself before he labeled his missing neighbor a terrorist with connections to the Pakistani government.

"You win," the woman said. There was a pause and the woman segued into a work conversation. "My computer is back up … Now what exactly were you looking for?"

"I'm looking at what I assume is the latest invoice for my father's company. My question is how could my father's company receive an invoice for machines that were delivered a few weeks ago if my father has been dead for over a year and his company only had one employee—my father?"

There was a long silence on the phone. Clark tried to resuscitate the conversation. "Helloooo…"

"That *is* a good question, indeed," the woman answered. Through the phone Clark could hear the keystrokes being pounded frantically.

"And when was this account closed?"

"I don't know exactly. The summer before last. Eighteen months ago maybe."

"That is interesting," the woman answered, sounding concerned. "My system shows that your father's account was never closed. In fact, it has remained active for the past year and a half with ongoing activity."

The bile in Clark's stomach churned and almost made an unexpected appearance. "Exactly what was ordered?"

The woman read from the list on the screen. "Multiple orders of aluminum, magnesium, titanium. Cylinders. Sheets. Blocks. Total weight over two hundred pounds. There was a separate order for bolts, servos, connectors, sixty feet of wire. Twenty feet of yellow, red, blue. I have a record of seven shipments over the last eighteen months."

"Shipped to this address?"

"Which address is that?"

"The one where I received the invoice. 203 Dorchester Lane, Arlington, Virginia."

"No. That's listed as the previous address of Hayden Ltd. That invoice was probably processed manually and they used the old address. These seven orders were shipped to 9345 Georgia Avenue, Northwest. Warehouse C, Washington, D.C."

"Wait, wait," Clark said, frazzled. "Let me get a pencil."

"I'll hold," the woman in billing said as if she were doing Clark a favor.

Clark ran, his wool socks slipping on the floor as he turned the corner in the kitchen. He stuck his hand into the junk drawer and pulled out a pen. He swiped the Post-it notes off the counter, his mother's guide to her daily routine, and sat down at the table. His hand shook as he fumbled with the top of the pen.

"Go ahead."

Clark scribbled the address on the paper. "Could you fax me the list of shipments? I don't have a fax, but I can give you a number where I can pick it up."

"Not a problem. But you know, the invoices have all been paid in full. There's nothing to worry about."

"I wouldn't count on it."

Lisa knocked on the door once, then entered the house panting. Her face was flush from the cold and the sudden burst of exercise.

Clark got up from the round dining room table which was littered with papers and files. His hair was unkempt, but the bounce in his step had returned. Lisa was glad to see that the energetic guy she had first met had reappeared, evicting the slow moving replica that had taken over her boyfriend with increasing frequency.

"You look alive."

"Amazing, because I haven't slept in a week," Clark said.

Lisa placed some folders on the coffee table. She unzipped her coat and put it over the arm of the sofa. She reached out and gave him a hug. Clark buried his nose in her neck for a moment and then put a kiss where his nose had been. He inhaled her perfume, a vast improvement over his non-showered body.

"I brought my video camera and the fax. Though I have no idea what you are up to. I also found some information that may be helpful," she said, patting the seat next to her on the couch.

"Helpful is something that has been lacking until this morning. Or maybe luck would be a better word."

"What's with the fax?"

"It looks like my helpful neighbor has been helping herself to my father's company, using it as a means to order whatever it is that she was after. I've been contacting different companies for the past hour and she has been busy."

"Why would she do that? If she had connections at the embassy, she could get anything she wanted."

"Maybe she was working on something unsanctioned."

"Maybe. But I'm not so sure terrorism is that discerning. I did a little poking around after you mentioned seeing Liana at the embassy. I ran a check on Ariana's and Nazim's credit cards."

"Smart girl. Still within the domain of the IRS."

"Except that I'm not investigating your neighbors."

"So you fat-fingered a key and got the wrong address. The same thing happened to me."

"And then I continued my way through the wrong file?"

"It happens," Clark said sarcastically.

Lisa shook her head and tried not to smile. "Anyhow, there's no record of Ariana purchasing a plane ticket on any of her credit cards. In fact, there are no charges at all on any of her cards since the first week of January. No withdrawals from the bank either."

"Meaning she had cash, which comes as no surprise." Clark thought about his next statement. "You know, there is a possibility that my parents' problems with the IRS may have been orchestrated by Ariana. The timeline fits."

Lisa put on her auditor's cap. "I'm not sure what the motive would be, but nothing would be a surprise at this point."

"That's good, because I'm all out of my befuddled look." Clark examined the papers on the table. "Anyway, I have been going through my father's files. All the blueprints he has. All the material he ever ordered. I took inventory of the material in the garage. Whatever Ariana was after, she hid her tracks. But the address I was given may have the answers."

"I think the combination of materials and machines being ordered, and the fact that there is ricin involved, maybe you should just eat some crow and call the FBI back. Just to be sure."

"I will, but first I need to borrow your video camera."

Chapter 54

Abu sat slumped in the desk chair in the office. Ariana watched him from her seat across the room. A small metal green wastebasket was between his legs on the floor. His breathing was labored. He hunched over, coughed, spit blood into the trashcan, and then tried to straighten himself, pushing on the arms of the chair.

Karim motioned Ariana to the door of the office. As she reached the doorway, Karim whispered, "You think he will make it?"

"No. I would guess he has less than twenty-four hours."

"Maybe we should keep him in here. The new recruits don't need to see what is waiting for them. They are young; they may not have the needed conviction once they see the outcome."

"I can solve that."

"I trust that you can," Karim said.

"Get the troops ready. I'll be a moment."

"What are you doing?"

Ariana raised her voice. "You want to sit in?" she asked Abu.

"I did all the work," Abu said in a surprisingly strong voice. Ariana nodded.

Across the warehouse floor, Karim poked his head in the crowded sleeping quarters. "Make room. Feet off the floor."

The three new recruits and Syed positioned themselves on the four cots in the sleeping quarters. Ariana pushed Abu, seated in the wheeled office chair, to the doorway of the sleeping quarters. She slid past the chair in the doorway, sat on the cot next to Karim, and unfurled the map on the floor.

The brothers glanced at Abu, who smiled weakly.

"I assume everyone here, with the exception of Syed, is familiar with the D.C. Metro?"

The younger brothers, Jameel and Omar nodded. Farooq grunted as if the question were preposterous.

Ariana paused and singled out Syed. "You are the only one who has not ridden the Metro before, so try not to get on the wrong train. You will all be given Metro cards with sufficient funds on them. You will not need to use the vending machines. Simply run the cards through the slot in the turnstile, arrow end first, face up."

Ariana pointed towards the floor. "This is the map of the Metro system."

"There are five lines. Green, Yellow, Blue, Red, and Orange." She paused. "Is anyone here color blind?"

"Color blind?" Farooq asked.

"Yes, color blind. It affects nearly one percent of the population. Problems distinguishing between red and green run at a higher rate. Males are more commonly affected than females."

Heads moved back and forth.

"Good. Then I won't have to worry about anyone getting lost for that reason. There are around eighty stations in the entire system. Over half a million riders per day."

"We will be focused on the Red, Blue, and Orange lines only. The Yellow line is a non-central line and the Green line runs through some of the rougher areas of town, which presents several potential problems."

"Such as?" Syed asked.

"One, a well-dressed Middle Eastern man with a suitcase is likely to either stand out, or get mugged. Neither of which would be good."

"I think I can handle a mugger," Syed responded, running a finger across his throat.

"Yes, perhaps you could." She looked at the younger brothers, two eighteen year olds with more faith and conviction in their eyes than muscle on their bones. "But not all of us are trained."

"Let her speak," Karim said.

"As I said, we are focusing on three lines. The Red, Blue, and Orange. There is only one spot where these three lines intersect: Metro Center. The name should be easy to remember. We will have three teams: Team Red, Team Blue, and Team Orange. I assume everyone can figure out the naming scheme."

Omar, the brother with oversized eyes, chuckled.

"The Blue and Orange lines share the same track and the same platform at Metro Center. The platform between the two lower tracks is where a majority of the targets will be hit. Team Orange team will be arriving from one end of the station and Team Blue will be arriving on the same tracks from the opposite direction.

"The Red line intersects the Orange and Blue lines on tracks above the lower platform. This should make for good fall-out and maximize our kill potential. Syed, the D.C. subway is not like New York. The stations are cavernous, the platforms intersect on bridges. There are minimal tunnels. All things that work in our favor.

"There will be five of you. Each of you will be carrying two bags apiece. Three of you will be carrying suitcases, dressed like businessmen, with tickets to the airport or train station. The other two, Jameel and Omar, will be dressed like students. Duffle bags and backpacks. For those keeping up, we have two profiles: the students and the businessmen. We also have three teams: Red, Blue, and Orange. Does everyone understand?"

All heads nodded.

"I want the twin brothers on the Orange line. Team Orange. Students. Both of you will be going west. One of you will be dressed as a University of Maryland student. The other will be a student at American University. I want one of you on the second car from the front. The other will board the train on the second car from the rear. The appropriate clothes will be provided. You will look like students. Well-groomed, clean-cut students. Karim has all the pocket litter for you as well."

"Pocket litter?" the thinner twin, Omar, asked. In the light from the lone bulb in the sleeping quarters his face seemed oddly elongated, like a stretched balloon, almost caricaturized.

"Pocket litter is papers and I.D. that makes you look legitimate. For this operation they are probably unnecessary, but we will consider it a precaution."

Ariana pointed at Syed. "You are on the Blue line. Businessman. Team Blue. You will be going in the direction of Reagan Airport. I want you to ride in the middle car. It will likely be crowded, so force your way in if you have to. Between you and the twins, you will cover a majority of the lower platform.

"Karim, you and Farooq are on the Red line. Also businessmen. Team Red. Karim, you will be arriving from the south or east, depending on how you look at the map. Farooq, you will be arriving from the north. Both of you aim for the center car. When you exit the train, you will be on opposite sides of the tracks, with the Orange and Blue line platforms beneath you." Karim looked at the eldest brother and their eyes locked in anticipation. Then they both smiled.

Ariana pointed at Farooq. "When was the last time you wore a tie?"

"It's been a while."

"Well, you will have a suit and tie provided to you shortly. Try not to fuss with the tie too much. It gives you away as someone who usually doesn't wear one."

Ariana looked around the room at her soldiers, making deliberate eye contact with Karim and Farooq. "I want you clean-shaven. I have put hair clippers and scissors in the bathroom. Either you do it yourselves, or I will help you.

"This is how it's going to work. The routine will be the

same for everyone. Everyone will be dropped off at a pre-selected location, in this case a designated Starbucks that is either across, next to, or otherwise in close proximity to the station I have selected."

"Why Starbucks?" Syed asked.

"Because I don't want anyone having to remember their location ... Everyone will buy something to drink and a *Washington Post*. Don't look around, it makes you suspicious. If you need to look at something, look at your watches. This is D.C.; people like to act as if they are busy. I want everyone to arrive at Metro Center on their designated train at 8:30 am. Do not panic if you are late by a minute or two. I will be tracking each of you. Oh, and don't bring your coffee into the train stations. It's one thing that will most definitely attract police attention.

"I will drop each person off from a minivan I have at my disposal. It will take between sixty and ninety minutes to get to all the locations and drop everyone off, which means your potential wait time is ninety minutes, so plan accordingly. Fill in the crossword puzzle. Do sudoku.

"The twins will be first. They will be dropped off in Rosslyn at the Starbucks across from the station. For the twins, it is a seven-minute ride from Rosslyn to Metro Center. At 8:15, Team Orange needs to be heading into the station. The Rosslyn escalator is long and takes an extra minute or two just to reach the trains."

"Why 8:30?" Syed asked.

"Most of D.C. is government employees. We are fortunate that everyone arrives and leaves work at relatively the same time. 8:30 is near peak. 8:40 is probably the busiest time, but for simplicity sake, we are shooting for 8:30. Any questions, Team Orange?"

The fraternal twins shook their heads and answered, "No," in near unison.

"Syed, you are Team Blue. You will be dropped off at Capitol South. There is a Starbucks next to the entrance to the station. You will be eight minutes out from Metro Center. You need to be in the station by 8:20."

"Team Red," Ariana said, pointing towards Farooq. "You will get on at Cleveland Park. There is a Starbucks just past the CVS. You are also eight minutes out. Be on the train by 8:20 as well."

Ariana looked at Karim. "You are also Team Red. You will be dropped off last, in Chinatown. There is a Starbucks with the name written in both English and Chinese. You will be one stop away from Metro Center. One minute of transit time. Be on the platform by 8:25.

"Our main concern is the timing of the trains. Metro does not have a schedule. There is a published timetable but I have yet to see any train run in accordance with it. Trains are habitually late. They stop in the tunnels as a matter of course, a phenomenon that is unique to Metro. In virtually all trains systems in the world the only time trains stop in the tunnels is when there is an emergency. But here, well, it is a variable we will have to contend with.

"What I have tried to do is have everyone six to eight minutes away, and assume a three-minute wait time. Teams Orange and Red—if you get to the station before 8:30, I want you to get off the train, look a little lost, and hold your position at the end of the platform, as if you got off at the wrong station.

"For Team Blue, Syed, mill about as if you are waiting for someone, but stay in the middle portion of the platform. You will be key to the operation and the most centrally located. Regardless of anyone's timing, do not panic. Keep in mind that Metro Center is crowded in the morning. No one should notice you whether you're standing or walking. Metro employees are of no concern whatsoever. They have scraped the bottom of the employment barrel for these men and women."

"Unless you are eating or drinking," Karim added.

"Right."

"I've seen dog patrols before," Jameel added, shedding his New York Giants jacket. The room was getting warm, a combination of the six bodies shoulder-to-shoulder and the topic at hand.

"There's nothing I can do about the dogs. I don't know what substances they have been trained to detect and react to. If you see a K-9 unit coming your way, try to mix with the crowd. Don't run. If the dog reacts to your bag, comply with the officer and give them your cover story. We are running on a pretty tight timeline, so the chance of being questioned in the small window of operation time should be very slim. If you are questioned, be polite, answer the officer, and be prepared."

"What kind of explosives?" Syed asked.

"TATP. Made by yours truly. Also known as the 'Mother of Satan.' Sensitive to heat, friction, and shock." Ariana looked around at her team and then added. "So be careful handling your bags."

"How do we set them off?" Farooq asked.

"I will control the charge remotely. All of the bags are being tracked via a GPS system and my laptop. Once you all arrive at Metro Center, I will detonate the devices. The bags are loaded with directional explosive charges large enough to send their contents half the length of a six-car Metro train. The charges in the backpacks are set to blow out the sides, in both directions, not backwards. The charges in the suitcases will blow outward, towards the front of the suitcase and away from the suitcase wheels and the carrier if he is following usual luggage carrying convention."

"How large will the explosion be?" Syed asked.

"The explosions will be large, but perhaps not lethal, unless you are standing in the way of the suitcase when it blows. The force will turn the top of the suitcase into a dangerous projectile. My goal is to spread the contents of the bags. This is best done through a directional discharge."

"What about the contents?" Farooq asked.

"A powdery substance. That is all you need to know."

"What is the estimated death toll?" Syed asked.

"Four trains, eight cars apiece, and three crowded platforms. Maybe an exposure of two thousand with the initial blast. But the beauty of this is the collateral damage. Once these bags detonate and people realize they haven't been killed by the explosion or shrapnel, there will be mass hysteria. The rush for the exits will be fierce. Every person who has powder on their jacket, their bags, in their hair—everyone will become a human transfer agent. A delivery mechanism. So if two thousand people are impacted at Metro Center, it will be four thousand by the time they hit the street and come into contact with other people. Multiplying the effect of transfer agents, the number could be as high as sixteen thousand exposures by the time the original targets clean themselves off. By the time the bio-hazard teams arrive and figure out what they are dealing with, thirty-two thousand people could be exposed. Health workers. Colleagues. Good Samaritans. All on the way to their deathbeds with nothing but twenty-four to seventy-two hours of despair in front of them."

"Brilliant," Syed said.

Looks of fear crept across the twin brothers' faces. Ariana tried to appease their concerns. "Don't worry. I have an oral vaccine for you. A simple pill. Some of us have already been inoculated." Ariana motioned her hand towards Abu. "This is what happens to someone who refuses. The choice is yours."

Karim looked at Ariana. Her words from an earlier conversation rang in his ears. Indeed, she was no longer the girl he once knew.

"If there are no more questions, I will leave you all to pray and prepare. I will bring everyone their clothes, some money, their Metro cards, and pocket litter."

"When do we go?" Syed asked.

Ariana checked her watch. "We have thirteen hours before detonation."

Karim followed Ariana out of the room, past the slumping Abu who was still breathing, his eyes open and fixated on the three brothers in the sleeping quarters. Syed whispered to them about the importance of being calm under pressure. Not panicking.

Karim pulled Ariana to the side, out of earshot. "That was unnecessary."

"What?"

"Giving those boys hope. Martyrdom is without fear."

"Perhaps. But I cannot have them second-guessing things at the last minute."

Karim thought and rubbed his beard. "Shave it off?"

"Yes," Ariana answered. "I don't want the others to think you are not following protocol. But you won't be going into the Metro tomorrow. You will be with me. We have something else to do."

She reached into the pocket of her oversized sweater and handed him a cell phone.

"This is what I need..." she started, leaning in close.

Chapter 55

The address is 9345, right?" Clark asked.

"I thought you were a number Jedi," Lisa answered from the passenger seat.

"Just tell me if I am right."

"9345 Georgia Avenue. Warehouse C," she replied.

"We just went straight from the eight hundred block to the eleven hundred block."

"And the neighborhood didn't improve at all."

"Well, we're not stopping to ask for directions."

"Usually I would call you a typical male for that comment." Lisa looked out the window at the brick corner market with its riot doors pulled down to the sidewalk. The bars on the windows protected the store's thick Plexiglass from projectiles and prying neighbors. A homeless man slept under a pile of fabric at the foot of a newspaper machine, the door to the machine long since ripped off. Garbage overflowed from the large trashcan at the corner of the store's property. "But in this case, I'm with you. There's no need to stop, much less ask for directions."

"Let's turn around and give it another look. It has to be here somewhere."

Clark slowed down as the traffic light turned from yellow to red.

"I think you should come back in the daytime. I don't even like stopping at the traffic lights."

"That's why I brought you. You have a gun, Criminal Investigator Prescott."

"I have a gun, but it's at home. Besides, I don't think there is much tax evasion in this zip code."

"Unless you count drug dealers. Like that guy there," Clark said, pointing with his nose.

Lisa glanced in the same direction Clark indicated. A large figure dressed in a black leather coat lurked in the shadows of a doorway to an old hardware store. "How do you know he's a drug dealer?"

"Because it's twenty degrees outside and he's just standing there." A moment later a car pulled up to the stoplight, flashed its high beams, and rolled down its passenger window. The man stepped from the safety of the shadows, exchanged his goods for money, and returned to his covert position.

"Did he just do what I think he did? Right here in front of us?"

"I don't think he was out shaking hands. Doesn't look like a politician running for office to me."

"Jesus."

"Has nothing to do with it."

The light turned green and Clark drove down the block before doing a three-point turn in the middle of the street. "One more pass and I'm calling it quits for tonight."

"You don't have to try to convince me."

Clark slowed down at the end of the old hardware store. A small alley ran between the hardware store and the boarded up building to its left. On the brick wall was a small sign that read 9345, with an arrow pointing ominously into the darkness.

Clark made the turn and Lisa squirmed in her seat. "This does not look good."

"The sign said 9345."

"The sign should have said 'call 911.'"

"Let's just see where it goes."

The Honda crept forward and Clark put on his bright lights. At the end of the building he was forced to turn left by the intimidating fence directly in front and to his right. The car dipped through a rut and the headlights bounced, beaming into the fenced lot ahead.

"Junkyards," Lisa said.

"I see them."

"Look for a place to turn around."

"I'm looking."

Clark followed the small road to the left and the narrow strip of pavement and dirt opened into a larger lot of the same making. Clark's high beams cut across the darkness.

"God, it's dark."

"Like every source of light in the vicinity stopped working with Marion Barry."

Clark turned the wheel to the right and then navigated a large swooping, looping left-hand turn. As he completed the turn his lights flashed against the front of several buildings.

Lisa squinted through the windshield. "I think we found the address."

"Which one?"

"The far right."

"It looks like a garage."

"And it doesn't look like anyone is home."

"I can't imagine why. The neighborhood is fabulous."

On cue, a dog went berserk somewhere in the darkness, followed by a slamming door and human screams. The incident ended with several canine yelps and another slamming door.

"I'll come back in the morning when it's light."

"And you'll come back without me."

"Oh, I don't plan on coming back alone. I have two friends who are coming with me."

Chapter 56

Clark pulled into the parking lot of the 7-11, past the group of Latino day-workers who swarmed a white van as it approached the edge of the convenience store's property. Clark got out of his car, walked across the gum-spattered sidewalk, and reached for the phone. The dirty, blue and silver communications dinosaur was posted on a pole beneath a 'no loitering' sign written in both English and Spanish.

"I need to speak with Detective Wallace," Clark said to the police operator.

"May I ask who's calling?"

"The same guy who called three times yesterday. I'm providing an anonymous tip on a case he is working on."

"Just a minute."

A full minute passed as Clark blew hot air into his cupped hands, the phone wedged between his ear and his shoulder.

"Detective Wallace."

"Detective. This is Clark Hayden. I have been trying to reach you since yesterday afternoon."

Detective Wallace was standing next to his desk and he looked around the room as he spoke. "I was in Baltimore yesterday. Out of pocket. You didn't leave a message."

"You told me not to."

"You calling from a pay phone?"

"Do you have any idea how hard it is to find a pay phone these days? Much less one that is working?"

"Is that a yes?"

"Yes." Clark watched as six of the day-laborers climbed in the white van. "I have some information I would like to share with you."

"I was wondering if you were going to call. Half of me was hoping you would. The other half was really hoping you wouldn't."

"Any progress on the guy pulled from the Potomac?"

"We are still trying to locate next of kin. Cause of death was officially reported as drowning."

"Did anyone check this guy for ricin poisoning?"

"Yeah. As I said, the *official* cause of death was drowning. I heard that a couple of suits paid a visit to the medical examiner. We may never get a straight answer on that one. How about you? How did your search go?"

"Well, I think I found the woman I was looking for."

There was a long silence on the phone. "Then I guess that presents me with a dilemma."

"I figured it might. So here's what I was thinking. What if you happen to stumble upon her while in the midst of solving another crime?"

There was a long silence followed by, "Then that would be just dumb luck."

Clark laughed. "I'm not sure if you meant that intentionally or not, but it could be a little of both. A little dumb and a little luck."

"I guess it could."

"I'll be in touch."

Clark called Detective Wallace back an hour later, this time from his cell phone.

"As dumb luck would have it, I made a trip into D.C. and someone broke into my car. Smashed the window."

Detective Wallace sighed and smiled to himself. "What's your location?"

"9345 Georgia Ave, near Tenth and Aspen. Warehouse C, around the back. A left turn behind an old hardware store that looks like it is out of hammers and very soon out of business. It is a good place to get crack at night, though."

"I know the area. I'll be there in twenty minutes. Don't go walking around the neighborhood."

Clark looked around his surroundings. "I wouldn't dream of it." Clark checked his watch, turned up the heat in the car, and made sure the doors were locked.

Eighteen minutes later Clark got out of the car and scoured the lot between the warehouse and the junk car piles next door. Large swathes of blacktop were missing, leaving exposed ground, puddles, rocks. Clark walked to the edge of the lot, expecting a rabid dog to appear on the other side of the fence, ready to mark his territory with whatever piece of Clark's body he could get through the chain links. Clark bent over and picked up a stone the size of a softball. He tossed it in his hand to check the weight and smiled. He took two steps towards his car, wound up, and threw the stone through his passenger side window. *Just covering everyone's ass*, he said to himself.

Five minutes later, Clark was sitting on the hood of his car when Detective Wallace pulled around the corner.

The detective parked his car near Clark's and pulled himself from the passenger seat by the doorframe. He was dressed in black slacks and a black sweater. His badge was hanging from his belt, a spot of gleaming gold in a black sea of an outfit. There was an obvious bulge on his right hip.

Detective Wallace looked at the broken window on Clark's car. "A smash and grab?"

"I guess," Clark said, sliding off the hood. His butt was slightly warm from the heat dissipating off the engine from the morning's drive.

"You expect me to believe that?"

"That's my story."

"Did they take anything?"

"An old *Poison* CD is missing. It's a classic."

"*Poison*? You trying to be funny?"

"Maybe."

Detective Wallace looked around. The junkyard was behind him, crushed cars stacked five high. A vacant lot was to the left, the fenced area littered with miscellaneous garbage ranging from tires to old refrigerators to hypodermic needles.

Detective Wallace finished his 360-degree surveillance scan and his eyes stopped where they began, on the closest pile of crushed cars. "I think that's a 72 Cadillac there on the bottom."

"You know your cars. Looks like a 72 accordion to me."

"I had one before I was married."

"A bachelor boat?"

"The women liked it."

"Back in the day," Clark added.

Detective Wallace flashed the look he gave his grandchildren when they did something wrong, but hilarious. "So, what are we doing here?"

Clark pointed to the far warehouse, over fifty yards away. "Warehouse C."

"What's in warehouse C?"

"My missing neighbor."

"How did you find her?"

"I didn't. An ice storm did. It's a long story. My neighbor's real name is Safia Hafeez. But I imagine she stopped calling herself that so long ago she wouldn't even answer to it now. She stole the identity from another girl when they were both students in Boston. The other girl went missing and her body was never found."

Detective Wallace nodded. "Smart girl. You use a missing person, not a dead one. A lot of jurisdictions have started matching death certificates with other systems, like Social Security. But if the person were only missing, and the family never filed a death certificate..."

"It didn't look like the girl had much family."

"Probably chosen for that reason. What else did you find out?"

"She's an MIT graduate. A doctorate in bad news stuff like chemical engineering and propulsion systems. Fulbright scholar. Pakistani national. Wife and mother of one. Has diplomatic contacts at the Pakistan Embassy. She has been living in the U.S. for over the last ten years under the name Ariana Amin. She has also been using my father's company to buy material and equipment."

"For what?"

"I have an idea but no evidence. I spent all yesterday afternoon and last night going through blueprints, invoices, orders." Clark paused. "You ever heard of a hail cannon?"

"No, what is it?"

"These farmers, and now some car dealers, take this big, long vertically standing tube, called a hail cannon, and shoot pressure waves into the air."

"Pressure waves?"

"Yeah, the cannon and its waves are supposed to disrupt the formation of hail in the atmosphere. Great for farmers with sensitive crops and car dealers who lose money on hail damage. Nissan opened a car plant in Mississippi and they even bought one. I guess if you think about it, all those cars have to sit outside until they get shipped to wherever they are going."

"Guess so. And..."

"Anyhow, when I started poking around for info on my neighbor a few weeks ago, I talked to my mailman trying to get an inside scoop. He told me that my neighbor had received some large-scale farming equipment catalogs. It didn't mean anything to me until I got the invoice from the company in Maryland for the machines shipped to this warehouse."

"And..."

"Then I started asking around at different places. Made calls to a few farming equipment companies. Ariana, through Hayden Ltd., had requested info on the hail cannon."

"They told you this?"

"I gave my name as Clark Hayden, and I had all the

company information. I played dumb and said we were still interested in purchasing one."

"That would work."

"Except they cost over a million dollars. Anyway, how Ariana used this information, I don't know. Maybe she didn't use it at all. But there are a million companies out there selling a million different things that someone with her background could use. There was no way for me to contact all of them. One thing I do know for certain is that she isn't a farmer."

Detective Wallace nodded his head and looked over at the warehouse. "How do you want to do this?"

"You're the police…"

"Seeing that I'm responding to a smash and grab robbery of one classic *Poison* CD, I think we go with that."

"Meaning?"

"Didn't you say that you think you saw the person who broke into your car enter the far warehouse?"

"I believe I did."

"Then let's go have a look. See if there were any witnesses … But first, I need to send out a safety line." Detective Wallace pulled his cell phone from his pocket. He called his part-time partner and left a cryptic voicemail on Detective Nguyen's phone giving him the address and circumstances. Wallace finished with a not-so-cryptic, "So if you don't hear from me in an hour, send in a rescue team, bio-hazard, the works." When he hung up, he looked at Clark. "At least one person will know where to look for us."

"Make that one million. My girlfriend has a similar video message from me ready to be posted on YouTube. It will also be sent to the local media and the Institute for Justice, a non-profit law firm in D.C. that specializes in constitutional rights. If something happens to me today there are going to be a shitload of people who know my name, your name, Agent Rosson. Everything."

"Pretty ballsy."

"Yeah, well. I kind of figured 'fuck it.'"

Detective Wallace lifted his sweater on the side and exposed his police issue Glock. "I hope I don't have to shoot anyone today."

"Me, too."

"If things get dicey, you get the hell away from me."

"Don't worry, if you start shooting, you'll need to send out a search team to find me."

Detective Wallace pointed to the building on the far left. "We start on the left and work our way down from there. Walking across that open lot is not a safe approach."

Clark followed behind Detective Wallace, who walked nonchalantly as if he were making a business call. As they passed the middle warehouse and reached the edge of warehouse C, Clark tapped the detective on the arm. "Look at the ground. Fresh tracks."

"I see those, Kimo Sabe. More than one vehicle."

"And one was a truck."

"You sure about this address?"

Clark nodded. "One hundred percent."

Wallace approached the solid metal door with his hand on his weapon.

He pounded hard with his free hand and identified himself as a D.C. police officer. Clark was stooped over at the waist, prepared to run, though he had no idea in what direction or what would trigger his mad dash. Detective Wallace slammed the edge of his closed fist on the door again, waited, and repeated the procedure. After thirty seconds of banging, he turned to Clark. "Looks like Plan B."

Chapter 57

Ariana pulled the white minivan up to the curb in a no-parking lane in front of the Starbucks, across from the Capital South Metro. Karim was sitting on the floor, the seats long since removed. He sat with his back to the side wall of the minivan, behind the driver's seat, avoiding the exposed metal in the middle of the minivan floor. It was Syed's turn in the front passenger seat, the last stop before martyrdom. As she had done for each departing passenger, Ariana said a prayer.

Then she thrust her hand behind her and Karim placed a gun in it. Smiling, she pulled the handgun forward and passed it to Syed, handle first.

Karim watched from the back of the vehicle as Syed's face lit up with joy.

"The safety is on and it's loaded," Karim said.

Syed gave an instant assessment. "A Beretta Px4 Storm. Nine millimeter. Magazine capacity of seventeen. Nice gun."

"Now put it away," Ariana said, checking the van's mirrors.

"What's it for?"

"It's for the twins, Jameel and Omar."

"Why?"

"If you get a sense they're going to run, or back out, kill them. They are on the same platform as you. If they follow instructions and ride the second cars from the front and the back, then they will be less than thirty yards from your location. Can you hit them from that distance?"

"With that piece of hardware, I can hit them from eighty. But I could just as easily use my hands."

"Whichever. The only reason they were brought in was to carry the bags. I couldn't have one person carrying six bags and have them dispersed over the necessary area. So if you have to kill them, keep the location of their bags in mind. Do not let them out of your sight."

"They are boys, but they will not run."

"Just in case," Ariana said, dipping her head in the direction of the gun.

"Thank you."

"Have a safe journey, my brother," Karim said from the floor of the backseat.

"You have twenty-five minutes. Grab a coffee. Be on time," Ariana added.

Syed opened the passenger door and moved to the sliding side door. He pushed the door open just enough to grab his luggage as Karim pushed the heavy cases from his position inside the minivan. With the luggage on the street, the two men locked eyes through the closing side door.

"Allah Akbar."

"Allah Akbar."

Chapter 58

Detective Wallace opened the trunk and looked down at the black, three-foot battering ram riddled with scars and scrapes. The paint was chipped, the blunt end slightly rusted.

"Christ, you carry that with you wherever you go?" Clark asked, looking at the thick metal cylinder. He was speaking quickly, almost in a whisper.

"I don't want to hear anything from a guy who carries a robot in his trunk," Detective Wallace said, motioning towards the electronic contraption on the ground next to the car.

"The robot is homework."

"Well, consider this *my* homework."

"What else do you have in there?"

"Shotgun, vest. Extendable baton, though it's not entirely police issue. Tear gas mask," Wallace said. He pointed at this favorite toy in the trunk. "But this baby right here is known as Betty."

"My aunt's name is Betty."

Detective Wallace gave Clark his police-issue interrogation face.

"Ol' Betty, here," Detective Wallace said, joining Clark in half-whisper mode, gesturing with his head towards the battering ram, "has opened more than a thousand doors in her life. She weighs only forty pounds but when swung properly generates forty *thousand* pounds of force. Unless we are dealing with a blast door or a bank vault, she always gets invited in."

"You need help with that?" Clark asked.

Detective Wallace shook his head. "Stand back, young man. Let me show you what Betty is all about."

Detective Wallace's large frame hunched over the open trunk and he stretched for the battering ram's handles. One hand grip was near the rear end of the device and was used for generating most of the power. The second handle was on the top of the device, near the midway point, its strategic location providing both power and the mild ability to steer the force of the blow towards the intended target.

"Looks heavier than forty pounds," Clark added, ribbing Wallace.

"Are you and your toy ready?"

Clark turned on the remote control in his hand and pushed the paddle forward with his right thumb. The two-foot high robot lurched from its parked position. Clark put the headset to the radio remote control over his ears and nodded. "Let's do this thing."

Detective Wallace approached the front door and tested the weight of the battering ram. He took one practice swing several feet in front of the door, and let out a grunt like a gladiator about to make an entrance into the Coliseum. With the conclusion of his warm-up, Detective Wallace set the battering ram in motion, the arc of the cylinder swinging back and upward.

"Wait," Clark yelled, his ears still covered with his headset.

Detective Wallace tried to reign in the weight of the ram as it surged forward. He stepped back as the battering ram continued forward, scraping the metal door but leaving it intact. Wallace grimaced, his lower back unappreciative of the sudden change in inertia.

"What?" Wallace asked, bouncing the battering ram in his powerful hands, the weight of the tool comfortable on his massive shoulders.

"What if it's booby-trapped?" Clark asked.

Detective Wallace looked at his partner for the day, speechless.

Clark continued. "All I'm saying is that I think this woman has quite a few dead bodies under her belt, and a booby-trap would fit her hobbies perfectly. Who know what she has on the other side of this door. Not to mention the missing ricin."

After a long thoughtful pause, Detective Wallace responded. "Good call." The detective eyed the warehouse exterior. He sized up the building and looked at the large steel roll-up doors on the front of the warehouse. He peeked his head around the corner. "Follow me."

"Where are we going?"

"Let's check out the back."

Detective Wallace took a swing at a small padlock and the door on the chain-link fence near the back of the warehouse swung open. He looked down the back wall.

"No back door," Clark said, stepping to the detective's side.

"Then we go through the wall. It's made of cinderblock."

"How long will it take?"

"Longer than the hinged door, that's for damn sure. But we only need a few feet of space. The rest is up to you and your robot."

"You make it sound like it's a pet."

"I call them like I see them."

"I'll have you know this robot here is a technical marvel. And this is an old model."

"A gamer's wet dream."

"Start pounding, John Henry."

"Is that a racist joke?"

"Heck, no. Was John Henry black?"

Detective Wallace shook his head in disbelief. "Youth."

"What do you know about gaming, anyway?"

"Had a double homicide once over a gaming tournament. Punk kids who couldn't remember the last time they went to school. Sitting around playing each other in video games. Violent games, too. It was a thousand bucks to enter the tournament, financed by drugs, and it went on for three days. The first man out of the tournament shot the host and then strangled the friend he lost to. Strangled him with the cord to his control pad. Learned more about gaming than I ever wanted to know."

Clark examined the wall. The cinderblock was in need of paint and mortar. It wasn't likely to get either.

"I don't need much room for the robot. Aim for the crack that's already there. It should be a weak point."

"Are you a mason?"

"No."

"Good. Just so we got that straight."

Detective Wallace swung the battering ram backwards and as the heavy cylinder reached the apex, Detective Wallace added his own 240 pounds to the physics equation. 40,000 pounds of force sent the head of the battering ram halfway through the wall. Three strikes later the hole was large enough for a basketball.

"Just a little more," Clark said. I can almost put the robot through if I lie him down horizontally."

Detective Wallace grunted as the battering ram lunged forward. "What makes a robot a 'him?'"

"I don't know."

"Sounds queer to me."

"Can we make the hole bigger?"

Detective Wallace took two more John Henry swings and looked at his handiwork. "Big enough?"

"It'll do," Clark answered.

Clark took the robot—an eight-wheeled, two-foot high, self-correcting vehicle with a video panel—and pushed it through the hole.

"What if it lands upside down?" Detective Wallace asked.

"It doesn't matter. It has wheels on all sides. It also has a roll-over feature, so if it gets stuck on something, an arm will extend and push the robot over in the other direction. We designed it so it won't get stuck. Well, at least not easily."

"And you can see what the robot sees?"

"Once I connect the monitor to the remote control and raise the camera on the robot." Clark took a second and plugged a blue cord into the side of his remote controller. He handed the video monitor to Detective Wallace. "Now let's see what we have."

The monitor gave Wallace and Clark a dog-level view of the room on the other side of the wall. Clark adjusted the sight on the robot with a thumb stick on the controller and the view on the monitor focused upwards.

"Looks like an office."

"Yes it does. It's a little dark."

"I can fix that," Clark said. A second later a light illuminated from the robot.

"Neat toy."

"A multi-thousand dollar toy. Years of research. And like I said, this is an old model. The new ones can operate in total darkness, go through water, up stairs."

Clark maneuvered the robot through the office, skillfully avoiding the legs of the table and desk. At the wall, the robot took a right and followed the light into the main room of the warehouse.

"It is a little lighter in here," Wallace said, flashing the video screen towards Clark.

Clark focused the robot's eyes upwards.

Wallace gave his play-by-play, standing next to Clark, sharing the monitor. "Windows." The detective looked up at the back of the building and pointed. "Twenty feet in the air."

Clark nodded and gave the throttle a little juice. The robot zigged and zagged around the warehouse floor as it made a cursory lap through its new environment.

"It's a big open floor," Detective Wallace said looking down into the monitor.

Before Detective Wallace could get the words out, Clark's thumbs jumped from the dual pad controller.

"Looks like we got a body," Wallace said, squinting at the monitor as the shoeless feet came into focus. Clark moved the robot slowly forward and its light shone on the body.

Clark moved until a face entered the screen. Blood trickled from the body's mouth. Clark became ashen. Detective Wallace steadied him by the shoulder. "You all right?"

"Yeah. I'm all right. Didn't expect to see that."

"You get used to it."

"I hope not," Clark said, taking a deep breath of cold air. "Let's go in for a closer view."

Clark maneuvered the robot past the feet and toggled back and forth so that they could get a view of the whole corpse.

"I would say our body looks like a male, in his thirties. Middle-Eastern descent. Bad scarring on his cheek. Can you pan up?"

Clark did as he was asked.

"Looks like he is handcuffed to one of the main support beams. Not very nice."

Clark kept the robot moving, slowly casing the body in an investigative circle. He steered the robot around the pole, ventured in for a close-up of the cuffed hands, and stopped near the head. Eyes glued to the monitor, his ears focused on the silence coming through his earphones, Clark jumped when the face on the screen turned towards the robot. Clark's response startled the detective, who also jumped, in turn causing Clark to let out a "whaaaaaaa" like Shaggy from Scooby Doo.

"Looks like our dead guy isn't dead," Detective Wallace updated.

Clark pushed the robot to full power and its wheels screeched, running into Abu's side and then backing away.

"Easy. Easy. Don't kill the guy."

Clark settled down and a voice came through on his headphones. "Yeah, don't kill the guy."

Clark looked at the monitor. "We have audio." He pressed a button on the remote control and a small screen flipped up, rising from the main body of the robot in front of Abu's eyes. He pressed another small button and the camera feed on the remote controller indicated it was on with the illumination of a small red light.

"Now he can see us, too" Clark said. "In addition to audio."

"You have an extra earpiece?"

"No," Clark answered. "If you want to hear, lean close. He should be able to hear us speak normally."

Abu cleared his throat and attempted to say something before his voice choked out like an engine on a small plane in a freefall.

Abu swallowed hard. "Neat toy," he said in a raspy voice, looking directly into the screen in the middle section of the robot. He could see both Clark and the detective's faces wedged into the field of view.

Clark introduced himself and then tilted the remote control entirely at Detective Wallace. "And this is Detective Wallace of the Washington Metropolitan Police Department."

"Glad to see you," Abu said, groggily. "Listen carefully. My name is Adahi Uhad, but for the last seven years I have been known as Abu Safi. I'm a clandestine operative working for the Central Intelligence Agency. US-born American citizen."

Gone was the brutish, hot-headed veneer that he had maintained for the last seven years. Back was a well-educated, calculating CIA operative who was trying to give his assessment of the situation as the only witness.

"Is the door booby-trapped? Can we come in?" Wallace asked, looking into the small camera lens on the remote control for the robot.

"The door isn't booby-trapped, but this whole warehouse needs to be treated as a high level bio-hazard site. I wouldn't suggest entering the premises without protective equipment. Level Four protective equipment."

Clark and Wallace looked at the hole in the wall, and then took several large steps back into the open lot.

"Ricin?" Clark asked.

Abu's head nodded slowly.

"You were poisoned?"

"Accidental ingestion. It was a calculated risk. I volunteered to process the ricin with the machines in the side room. I changed the settings and proceeded as slowly as I could. I was hoping to buy time. I processed the ricin, and the output was a fine powder, though not as fine as they think. I put the powder into cylindrical plastic containers that were sealed and then washed. After that, Ariana further configured the containers with explosives and put them in suitcases and backpacks."

"Do you have I.D.?" Wallace asked.

"No, and if I did, it wouldn't be real." The rest of Abu's story came between labored breaths and bloody coughs. "I'm a graduate of the University of California, Berkeley. Born a Muslim, raised an American by Pakistani parents. I have a wife and two kids. I've been undercover for over seven years. I've been out of contact with the agency for over a month. I left for the U.S. from Pakistan in December. All this can be verified. Prior to December, I spent four years in training with Al-Qaeda. Learning explosives. Or enhancing my CIA training, as it turns out. I was injured in a blast two years ago by a fellow bomb-making student who was careless. I was originally inserted into Guantanamo Bay in 2004, completely undercover. Few people at the CIA knew of the mission. I was working a target in the Pakistani government named Karim Al-Housad. He has high-level connections. Diplomatic connections."

Clark looked at Detective Wallace and then back down at the monitor.

"A man?"

Abu nodded. "Yes, a man"

"I think you may have been after the wrong person."

"The thought occurred to me."

"Should we contact someone?" Clark asked into the mouthpiece on his headset.

"I need you to call a number and enter a passcode. Leave a message and give them this address, wherever I am. Nothing can be done for me, except maybe morphine for the pain. Also, tell the CIA that the tracking chip in my left forearm has been disabled."

"Tracking chip?" Clark asked.

"Yes," Abu answered weakly. The pace of his speech

increased and decreased with each wave of pain. "The chip was disabled by 80,000 volts of electricity delivered through a stun gun. Very clever, really. Totally unforeseen on my part."

Clark spoke. "You aren't the only one the woman we're looking for has fooled. Her husband, two governments, a university, INS, DMV, a neighborhood."

"You need medical attention," Wallace said.

"If you want to call, you call after I convey what I know. You will need a bio-hazard team, not just an ambulance."

Abu swallowed again then continued. His lucidity was fading and he repeated parts of the story. "My name is Adahi Uhad. The woman you are looking for has approximately six hundred pounds of processed ricin she plans on using. I spent two days processing it. I tried to lessen the lethality by processing it to a larger size than specified, but it is still very deadly and very fine. Deadly enough to have killed me, and I was dressed for the occasion."

Abu coughed. His head rose off the floor and then dropped back down onto the concrete.

"She has lost two members of her team, but she may have more people at her disposal." Abu grit his teeth and inhaled deeply. He continued slowly. "She is going to use the Metro and aim for Metro Center. Explosives will deliver the ricin and will be detonated via cell phone signal to homemade triggers. Black suitcases. Large, blue backpacks. Three men dressed as businessmen. Two younger men dressed as students. At least five terrorists in total. Spread out along the length of both platforms. One of the terrorists is taller than average. A tall Middle-Eastern man, about 6 foot 3 inches, approximately thirty years old, pulling a black suitcase with wheels, in Metro Center. There can't be many targets meeting that description."

"When?"

"Today, 8:30. There was a truck and a car parked here inside the warehouse. There was also something in the far room that I never saw. Maybe a van. I think I heard a sliding door shut."

"What does the truck look like?" Wallace asked.

"A fifteen, seventeen footer. It had Piedmont Delivery on the side, but that was painted over with white spray paint. An amateur job."

Abu's eyes rolled into his head as he kept talking. "Call this number." As Abu recited, Clark nodded into the remote control screen. "Do you need me to repeat it?"

"No, I'm good with numbers."

"Call the number. Tell them my name and location. Tell them about the chip. Someone will come. Tell them it is a bio-hazard site."

Abu's breathing started to labor anew. "Tell my family that I miss them. Tell them that I love them. Tell them I made the sacrifice for them and for Islam. To show them there are people who will die for their Islamic beliefs ... when they are righteous ones."

Abu mumbled the word "another," and then coughed. Blood rolled from the corner of his mouth.

"There is something else," Abu rasped. He slowly curled himself upward into a ball, his body wrapped around the support beam he was handcuffed around. His breathing disintegrated into a choke. Ten seconds passed as Detective Wallace and Clark watched the man struggle. Slowly, Abu uncurled. "Check my hand ... I found this on the floor of the office."

Clark moved the robot to Abu's hands and focused the camera as close as its magnification would allow. The bright red ribbon with the number on it gave Clark the chills followed by a loosening of his bowels. Clark looked at detective Wallace. "That's not good."

"What is it?"

"I'll explain in the car."

Chapter 59

Detective Wallace checked his watch and yelled into the dash mounted radio in his car. "No, no, no. I need the wireless communication link to Metro disengaged, and I need all traffic coming into Metro Center held at their location."

"You are not authorized to give that command," the voice said on the other end of the radio. "You will need to have your captain notify the chief of police with that request or supply the appropriate emergency code."

"I'll give you the appropriate code. Disable the fucking link to underground Metro wireless communications and get that station evacuated or you will kill a thousand people."

"Hold just a moment," the radio dispatcher responded.

Detective Wallace kept the radio in his hand as he hit the breaks to avoid a taxi.

Clark opened his flip phone and his thumbs danced through the Central Intelligence Agency number that Abu gave him. The other end of the phone rang once. A recorded, computerized voice greeted Clark with a three-word sentence. "Enter your passcode."

Clark punched the numbers into his phone and a series of high-pitched computerized beeps followed. When the beeps stopped Clark left a rambling message, repeating the name and location of the ill agent. He ended with a designation of the location as a bio-hazardous site and hung up.

"You forgot to mention the tracking chip," Wallace said between orders, barking police codes into the dash-mounted radio. The police cruiser was up to sixty miles an hour and traffic was forcing the detective into NASCAR maneuvers, one hand on the radio handset, one hand on the wheel.

Clark tugged on his seatbelt to make sure there was tension. "If a call to a CIA number with a secret passcode and a CIA agent's name and location doesn't get a reaction, nothing will."

"I would expect a call back."

Clark didn't answer. "You think we should have left him?"

"I don't think we had a choice."

The car bounced and Clark's head ricocheted off his headrest. He glanced at the speedometer and the needle was rising through the seventies as they headed south on Georgia Avenue. A group of homeless wandering across the street scattered as the police cruiser roared past the District's largest shelter.

"You should have said ten thousand deaths. Maybe that would have gotten the dispatcher's attention," Clark added.

"Maybe. You better hang on. I have an idea."

Syed, the soldier-businessman, stepped off the Blue line train. He tugged the large wheeled suitcase over the crack between the train and the platform, holding the second bag, a sizeable carry-on, in his left hand. His new present, the Beretta Px4 Storm, was safely shoved into the back waist of his pants and covered by his suit jacket.

The platform teamed with bodies, six deep. Lobbyists hurriedly elbowed consultants who cut off tourists. Government employees pressed slowly in every direction: on and off the train, up the escalators, down the platform. Syed pulled his bags through a throng of business suits and a retirement group from Oklahoma with matching t-shirts. He found his way to the large concrete bench in the middle of the platform and stood his bags on the tile ground. He recalled what Ariana had said about the direction of the blast, and he adjusted his suitcases for maximum damage, placing them front-to-front.

An Orange line train pulled into the station and Syed pretended to read his paper, looking past the headlines of the business section. He peered over the heads of most of the commuters, thankful for his advantage in height. Passengers on the Orange line train were shoulder-to-shoulder, standing room only. Faces pressed against the glass as the train left the platform and Syed casually looked in each direction for Jameel and Omar. Then he waited for the next train.

Above him, a Red line train pulled into the station and another rush of people pushed down the escalator to the lower platform. Farooq, now cleanly shaven, stepped from the middle car and walked to the wall of the upper platform. He positioned his bags according to Ariana's direction, as Syed had done twenty yards below.

A young couple stood from their seats and Syed sat down on the end of the large slab concrete bench next to his bags. He turned the page in his newspaper and checked his watch. It was 8:27 as the next Orange line train pulled into the station. Syed looked over his shoulder as the train arrived on the platform, brakes squealing slightly. With another surge of bodies, Jameel stepped from the train, the straps from the backpack over his shoulders, a duffle bag in his hands. Syed couldn't see Omar, but knew where there was one brother, there was another. He stood from his seat and peered up at the upper platform. He could see Farooq from the shoulders up.

There was nothing to do but smile at the upcoming carnage, and wait. Three minutes.

Karim drove and Ariana opened her laptop with her Verizon wireless network card and checked the progress of her soldiers.

Four blips appeared on the screen, all of them transposed over a Google Map image of the Metro Center area. She could see the office buildings and the roads, as well as an outline of the underground passages and tracks of Metro Center.

"Syed and Farooq are positioned and the Orange Team is just arriving." She checked her watch. "Right on schedule." She reached for the cell phone and turned it on. "Keep driving. South on the GW Parkway."

Chapter 60

Detective Wallace took a hard right onto Constitution Avenue and gunned it. The big eight cylinder growled as the pistons were fed a heavy dose of gas. Clark was pushed back in his seat and grabbed for the handle over the door as Detective Wallace swerved into oncoming traffic. The car zoomed past the Department of Commerce and the White House, the morning traffic blasting their horns as Wallace weaved his car through the automobile slalom.

At the E street ramp the car rolled hard and the tires screeched. Near the stoplight at the mouth of the Rock Creek Parkway Detective Wallace pushed on the brakes.

"Last chance to get out."

Clark tightened his seatbelt. Wallace nodded.

"This is the unofficial way to get things done."

Detective Wallace hit the gas and the black unmarked patrol car jumped the curb and headed across the grass between Rock Creek Parkway and the Four Seasons hotel. Wallace fought to steer the car as it bounced in the uneven field, the engine roaring, the Thompson Boat Center passing by in a blur on the left. Clark braced himself as the car raced towards a chain-link fence in the distance.

"Slow down, slow down, slow down," Clark said

frantically, followed by "too fast, too fast, too fast."

Detective Wallace took his foot off the accelerator and yelled "hang on," as Clark chimed in with "Ohhhh shit."

The car cut through the chain link fence, dug through a patch of gravel, and smashed into the large green electronic box with a shower of sparks. The airbags in the car exploded from their designated locations and Detective Wallace and Clark slammed into the impact-reducing devices. The four foot high electronic box tipped to forty-five degrees but didn't fall.

Detective Wallace took inventory of himself and muttered through the aftermath of the collision. "You all right?"

"Jesus," Clark said, the deflating air bag gathering in his lap. He rubbed his nose and shook his head to clear the cobwebs.

"Are you ok?" Detective Wallace repeated.

"I think so."

"Good." Detective Wallace threw the car into reverse. Gravel and dirt flying beneath the tires, he backed the car up fifty yards, flattened a piece of fence that had been dislodged by the original impact, and hit the gas again. With the second impact the green box fell, wires torn from their moorings.

Wallace backed the car up again and cut the ignition. Clark stumbled out of the cruiser first.

Detective Wallace exited the car and stepped towards his handiwork to admire the destruction. "Mobile phone exchange," Detective Wallace said aloud. "Originally only Verizon had service to the Metro underground. Now, all the major carriers are routed through this transfer terminal."

"Well, I think that took care of it," Clark said. "How did you know where this was?"

"Had a homicide near this spot two summers ago. Rich woman from the Watergate across the way. Never solved that one. The location stuck in my memory, as most things do when you are a detective."

"Does the car still drive?"

Detective Wallace turned, looked at the car, and kicked at the grill. The front bumper dropped to the ground. He peered under the engine block. Multiple streams of liquid sizzled as they dripped down through the heated engine.

"I need to get back to my house," Clark said.

"Why your house?"

"I need to get something."

"Taxi," Wallace said as he started jogging towards the intersection of K Street and Rock Creek Parkway, over the tire tracks he just left.

Clark followed Wallace up the hill, the police cruiser now smoking behind them. The detective, oversized waist bouncing and arthritic knees creaking, pulled out his phone and called his part-time partner with an update. Nguyen answered the phone on the first ring.

"I got your message. You're still alive, I take it."

"Barely. You may hear about this on the news."

"Sounds familiar. Try to keep my name out of it this time."

"I need you to call Metro and have the system emptied. All trains going through Metro Center. We have five terrorists in or approaching Metro Center with explosives and ricin. Middle-Eastern men. Three are dressed as business men with suitcases. Two are students with large backpacks. One of the suspects is six foot three. Thirty years old. Dressed in a suit. Pulling a suitcase on wheels. Shoot first, ask questions later. Hunt down the captain or we are going to have a fucking mess on our hands. Tell the captain if I am wrong, he can have my badge. Call Metro police, call the station directly. Whatever you have to do. I tried to take out cell service to the Metro tunnels, but there may be a back-up trigger."

"I also need a bio-hazard unit sent to the address I left on your phone earlier. 9345 Georgia Ave. Warehouse C. Tell them there is also ricin at that location and an injured intelligence agent. Use extreme caution."

Detective Wallace raised his free hand and a cab driver pulled over. He flashed his badge and the cabbie raised his hands as if he were being held-up.

"Put your hands down," Wallace said through the closed window.

The cabbie let out a sigh of relief and Wallace walked around to the driver's side of the car and opened the door. "Out. Your car is being commandeered."

The cabbie started to protest and Wallace gave him the official don't-fuck-with-the-police expression. The cabbie got out of the car. Detective Wallace looked at the cab number on the roof and then back at the driver.

"You can pick it up later at police headquarters."

Clark apologized and jumped in the passenger seat.

Nguyen was listening to the proceedings over the still-connected phone and repeated Wallace's name several times before the detective answered.

"Where are you going?" Nguyen asked.

"Arlington."

"You don't have jurisdiction in Arlington."

"I do today."

"Get on the phone and tell D.C. and Arlington County that there is a cab being driven by an officer on a police emergency. Don't approach. Make it a BOLO with a request for assistance."

"Cab number?" Nguyen asked.

"4631."

Clark corrected him. "4361."

"Correction, cab number 4361."

"Got it."

"Reach me on my cell. My cruiser is parked near Rock Creek and K Street. No radio."

"Roger that."

"Now Nguyen. Now."

Ariana smiled as she closed her cell phone. "It is done."

Karim muttered a prayer under his breath.

"Get into the right lane," Ariana said. "The exit is up ahead."

Chapter 61

Farooq tried not to stare at the slow moving pair of Metro police officers entering Metro Center near the main security booth. He had ridden the Metro enough to know the routines; to see what was routine. His professional assessment was exactly that—a routine patrol. The officers, well-carved individuals with former military written all over their demeanors, took in the environment as they walked. Their heads swiveled slowly from left to right, eyeing the tracks, the waiting passengers, the group of youths who should have been in school. As the officers passed Farooq on the upper platform, Farooq smiled and nodded. The officer closest to him flashed a brief professional grin and returned his focus forward. It wasn't until one of the police officer's radio crackled that Farooq's eyes dropped back down to his newspaper. He checked his watch and started to sweat.

On the intersecting platform below, Syed pulled the sleeve on his suit and also checked the time. They had been waiting for five minutes, far too long in his military opinion. Operations were precise. Or at least they started precisely and then quickly disintegrated into mayhem. The platform was crowded. Jameel was thirty yards away, his back facing Syed, his backpack on, his duffle bag in his hand. Syed strained to spot Omar whose backpack poked in and out of sight through the moving commuters.

The sudden wail of an alarm sent people scrambling to cover their ears. Syed's eyes darted up, then left to right as blue and orange trains arrived from opposite directions. People rushed for the exits as panic echoed off the walls. Syed looked up at the platform above and saw a half dozen officers reporting to the scene with their guns pulled. A moment later, the two officers who had just passed Farooq had returned, their guns drawn on the young man with the backpack. Farooq's hands went up a second before his legs were kicked out beneath him and the bottom of a boot landed on his neck, pressing him to the floor.

The alarm wailed, a strong blast followed by a lull and then another wave. "Shit," Syed said aloud. In a well-trained motion, Syed pulled his Beretta from the small of his back. He stepped behind the concrete platform bench, aimed at the larger of his two suitcases, and pulled the trigger.

The explosion ripped through the suitcase and the six people rushing past it. Dust thrust out in all directions, a wave of death canvassing the middle portion of the cavernous tube-like structure of the Metro station, engulfing the upper platform as it made its way outwards.

Syed coughed and tried to catch his breath. He squinted through the aftermath and the temporary silence. Syed's ears trickled blood. His head rang. His hair, face, and suit were covered in a fine white powder. The bench he had taken cover behind was painted with bits of clothes and flesh. Syed shook his head and checked his weapon, balancing himself as he stood amidst the hysteria. He pushed his way through the stunned crowd, the alarm a memory those near the explosion were no longer able to hear. Police officers from the platform above fought their way down the escalators, guns drawn, their commands mixing with the alarm and the unintelligible Metro emergency message. From twenty yards, his aim above the crowd, Syed dropped the first two officers as their torsos appeared, feet first, on the downward escalator. Syed staggered down the platform and spotted the outline of Jameel with his backpack and duffel bag. The young man was frozen, his body rigid, his eyes shut as he waited for his bag to explode. Syed raised his gun, exhaled, and pulled the trigger. Jameel fell to the platform, his duffle bag rolling over the edge onto the tracks. His backpack was still intact, facing away from Syed. The former soldier scanned the madness and continued down the platform, his mind blocking out the rush of bodies that surrounded him. He stepped to the other side of Jameel's twitching body and started to unload his magazine into the large backpack from point blank range.

He didn't hear the warning before the shot from the police issue handgun tore through his skull.

Chapter 62

So what was the red ribbon the CIA guy had?"

"It's the flag off a radio remote control. One that my father used to fly when I was a kid. It had the same frequency number written on it. I would recognize it anywhere. The flag's color alone actually tells you the frequency range for that device, but my father was very particular. Overly cautious in some regards."

"Why does this woman need a radio control? What about Metro Center and using a cell phone signal as a detonator?"

"Maybe that was plan A. Or maybe that was plan B. But the more I think about it, she may have finally slipped up."

"What do you mean?"

"Well, she may know a lot about explosives and poison and rockets and propulsion systems. But my guess is she doesn't know shit about model airplanes. Or at least that's what I'm hoping for."

Wallace's phone rang. "Wallace here."

"This is Nguyen. An explosion has been reported in Metro Center."

"Fuck," Wallace yelled.

"What?" Clark asked.

"An explosion."

"Shit."

"Keep me updated," Wallace yelled into the phone. His request was met with silence. He looked at the phone and the *Call Failed* message appeared on the screen.

A prolonged moment of silence engulfed the car.

"Get me home," Clark said.

Clark dug through two standing metal cabinets and ran his eyes along the shelf on the far wall of the hobby room in the basement. He breathed heavily as his hands quickly felt up the nooks and crannies of the room. In a space beneath the stairs Clark's fingers danced over a dust-covered shoebox. He pulled the box through a cobweb and opened the top. "Fucking A," he said to himself in a whisper.

Organized neatly in the box were ten stacks of cash, each wrapped with a thin rubber band. Clark plucked the stack off the top and ran his thumb across the edge of the money, listening to each bill snap as it flipped by. He repeated the action, this time looking at the corner of the bills in motion. Fifties and hundreds. *Enough for a year at school*, he thought. Maybe even two with room and board. He put the money back, shut the lid, and replaced the shoebox on the shelf. *One problem at a time.*

Clark yanked his head from beneath the stairs and continued his frantic search. He tore open three cardboard boxes stored near the hot water heater, then spotted the large clear plastic container in the corner. *Oh Dad, let this be the one*, he said to himself as he grabbed the black controller from the plastic box. He snagged a 9.6-volt battery pack off a stack on the shelf in the corner and ran upstairs.

Clark came out of the house and jogged across the front yard to the cab. He flopped into the passenger seat.

"You got what you need?"

"Right here."

"Where to?" Wallace asked.

Clark paused to think. "Reagan National."

"Why?"

"Common sense … and a few other things."

"You want to share?"

"Start driving."

The taxi laid a thick trail of rubber on the street as Detective Wallace pushed the accelerator to the floor.

"Here's what I'm thinking. One, Ariana's daughter told me she liked to watch airplanes. Strange for the daughter of a housewife who never traveled. Two, if Ariana already attacked Metro and is looking for another target, a plane is the easiest. Three, it's what I would do."

Wallace opened his cell phone and tried to dial the precinct with one hand. The call froze in silent limbo. He tried again, this time with 9-1-1. Another call failed message.

The detective turned towards Clark. "Can you get through to 9-1-1 on your phone? I got nothing here."

Clark pulled his phone from his pocket and tried 9-1-1. "Nothing. The call was dropped."

"You know what that means."

"The news is out on the explosion in the Metro and now everyone in DC is trying to use the phone."

"Exactly."

"You don't have a radio?" Clark asked.

"Yeah, it's attached to the dash in the cruiser."

"A lot of good that does us."

"You know what else this means?" Wallace asked.

"It's up to you and me"

"Until further notice."

"Well then I hope I am right." Clark took the small rectangular box with thumb controls and raised the antenna.

"So what do you do with that remote control?"

"This is an old Proline 1100."

"I'll take your word for it."

"The name and model number is written on it. Anyhow, this particular controller in my hands had a long life in the world of model airplanes. But there is something special about this one that Ariana probably doesn't know."

"It tracks terrorists?"

"No. It's part of a buddy system. This is the master control. The one Ariana has, the one with the matching red ribbon in the warehouse, is a slave control."

"Meaning?"

"If we get close enough, I can switch off her transmitter and she will never know. I would be in control of her device, whatever that device is."

"Why would she need a remote control?"

"The better question is why would she have that ribbon if she wasn't going to use a remote control?"

"D.C. is a big city. Lots of high profile targets. Your guess is a shot in the dark."

"Maybe, but so far the CIA, the FBI, and the cops have all been playing catch-up. If I were a betting man, and had money, I would bet on myself this hand."

Clark tried 9-1-1 again and then gave directions. "Take the next right."

"We're still north of the airport."

"She's not going to the terminals."

Chapter 63

The long black car was parked, rear-end first, in the row of spaces nearest the park entrance. Across the parking lot, the Potomac River, in mid-winter murkiness, chugged downstream towards the Chesapeake. The large brown sign near the riverside park entrance posted the name, Gravelly Point, and the hours of operation.

The white minivan Ariana had driven into the gravel lot minutes earlier was parked over a hundred yards away, in a direct line between the river and her location in the black car. The alignment of the vehicles was perfect, the result of myriad trial runs and hours of trigonometry and calculus.

The gravel lot with the paved entrance held over two hundred cars when it was full, but on a chilly February morning two dozen vehicles sprinkled the lot. Every car had a row of spaces to themselves, each vehicle isolated by choice, like men in a public bathroom with a wall of urinals to choose from. Body heat steamed up the windows on a small import parked at the far end of the lot, the car rocking intermittently.

"What's the target?" Karim asked from the driver's seat of the long black car.

"Flight 1956. Delta Shuttle from LaGuardia. Arrives at 8:53. Passengers include thirty members of the United Nations

Terrorism Security Council and a team from Interpol. Some of the best and brightest anti-terrorist minds on the planet."

"Where did you get your intelligence?" Karim asked.

"The price of intelligence isn't what it once was. I obtained the information through more traditional channels—CNN. The summer before last there was a disturbance on a flight from New York to Washington. Some young men who had been up all night partying in New York continued right through to the morning, with Bloody Marys, on the plane. They got a little raucous, grabbed a flight attendant inappropriately, and verbally assaulted the crew. The news reported the incident and also divulged that the passenger list included the UN Security Council on Terrorism."

"You based this plan on one incident on one aircraft?"

"The original idea. But the United Nations website lists ongoing Security Council initiatives. One of those initiatives is a monthly meeting here in Washington. The second Wednesday of the month at 10:00 am."

"They don't fly on a UN-sponsored private plane?"

"Not since the UN adopted an environmentally-friendly protocol requiring members to fly on commercial flights when possible. They are trying to set an example by reducing pollution from private aircraft. I have followed their routine a dozen times over the last year. Right now there are at least eight UN limousines waiting at the terminal's ground transportation exit."

"And that is why today was chosen?"

"I've been planning for a while. Your arrival, and the ricin, was a last minute complication to my plan. Not the other way around. This is my original plan. This is what I have been working on."

Ariana picked up her binoculars and looked through the thick bullet-proof glass of the vehicle. A plane was approaching down the designated flight path over the Potomac between the high rises of Rosslyn and the flight-restricted skies over D.C.

"I was concerned that the Metro incident might cancel flights into the airport. So far, so good. According to plan."

"There has been nothing on the news yet," Karim said, gesturing towards the radio.

"Not yet, but any moment. Security has probably already been notified and will increase patrols. I expect the police to check this area as well. Protocol is predictable. First they will secure the terminal and increase security at check-in. We are 16 minutes after detonation at Metro Center. For now, we can count on bureaucracy to give us another 30 minutes. And that assumes they make a connection between Metro and the airport. There is no one on Earth who can draw that conclusion. That will provide additional time."

"And after this??"

Ariana spoke without taking her eyes off the sky. "Then I want to go home. I want to see my father again. I want to bring my daughter home. I want my daughter to meet her grandfather. I want my father to know that his daughter did not let him down. That his faith from those years ago paid off."

Karim looked out at the minivan in the parking lot. Joggers with winter gear appeared sporadically, popping out from the running paths near the river's edge and disappearing again near the large fence that ran between the lot and the airport terminal in the distance.

"Where did you get the van?"

"Bought it used in Baltimore. Paid cash."

"It seems rather obvious. A white minivan."

"It seems obvious now, sitting there in the parking lot. But you may recall there was a sniper in the D.C. area a few years ago. The news media latched on to the initial report that the first victim was killed from a shot fired out the back of a white truck or van. For weeks the entire region was on high alert … on the lookout for a white vehicle. As it turns out, white is a very popular color for trucks and vans. Drive through south Arlington alone and you will see hundreds of white vans. They line the residential streets between Shirlington, Bailey's Crossroads, and Seven Corners."

Ariana watched as a Southwest plane touched down safely

on the runway. Karim picked up the red remote control off the seat. "How does it work?"

"The van is parked directly beneath the flight path. The Delta Shuttle uses only MD-88s."

"McDonnell Douglas?"

"Yes. The MD-88 is forty-five meters from nose to tail with a thirty-two meter wingspan. Its approach speed is 130 knots or 150 mph. The vehicle is parked four hundred feet from the end of the main runway, runway 19. At that distance, the plane's altitude will be less than one hundred and fifty feet when it passes over."

"Amazing."

"What?"

"That they allow the public here."

"It's Washington. Allowing the public to move freely is a show of strength. In any other city this airport would have been closed after 9/11. But not in Washington. Reagan National is only ten minutes from the Capitol, and Congress is not about to drive forty minutes out to Dulles to catch a plane."

Ariana once again looked through her binoculars at the next plane on approach. The aircraft was still a dot in the distance, even through the 8x32 magnification of the Pentax binoculars.

"Tell me about the projectile system," Karim said.

"It is a borrowed design, of sorts, with some homemade modifications. The firing mechanism is compressed acetylene gas. The same component used in welding torches. Highly volatile. Very forceful. Not the optimal substance ... but it is easy to obtain, and purchasing it doesn't arouse suspicion. Especially when it's purchased by a legitimate business with a legitimate machine shop."

"The acetylene is compressed in a combustion chamber which is attached through a steel plate to the van by eight bolts. The gas in the combustion chamber is ignited via a remote control trigger—a modified servo—compliments of a deceased neighbor."

"You have a few of them."

"This neighbor was the first," Ariana answered before continuing. "Five vertical barrels are attached to the combustion chamber. Each barrel is four inches in diameter and holds a homemade titanium shell consisting of four smaller individual rounds. Each round is composed of a quarter pound of Tannerite."

"Tannerite?"

"A binary explosive that detonates on impact. Tannerite consists of two components. Individually, each component is non-lethal and perfectly legal to purchase. Together, the components will rip through most metals on impact. The aluminum skin of the airplane will offer little resistance."

"So, you have five tubes, four rounds per tube..."

Ariana finished the math with her eyes behind the binoculars. "At less than one hundred fifty feet, with twenty shots traveling over a thousand feet per second, I estimate more than a fifty percent hit rate. As high as perhaps eighty percent. The time between detonation and impact will be less than a third of a second. I only need one round to hit any number of vital targets. The wings, the ailerons, the elevators, and, obviously, the fuel tanks. Planes on approach are vulnerable."

"You seem sure."

"At this distance and altitude, with this explosive, it's like shooting a paper airplane with a shotgun. Ideally, I'm going for an explosion, but in reality I only need to create a roll of a few degrees. Gravity and the hard surface of the runway will handle the rest."

Ariana peered through her binoculars. She read the words *Delta Connection* written along the side of the plane and announced. "The plane is approaching."

"Do we know it's the right one?"

"Yes. It took off from New York fifty-two minutes ago. The next one is not due for an hour."

She grabbed the remote control from her lap and moved the control stick on the right-hand side. The sunroof on the van rose by an inch, and then slid back.

"Nice," Karim said.

"Original equipment modified to open remotely." Ariana positioned her thumbs on the controls. "Less than a minute to impact."

From the opposite direction, Detective Wallace steered the yellow cab across two lanes of traffic, narrowly missing an oncoming bus. The cab accelerated down the service road and then slid hard onto the gravel lot as it screamed past the entrance into the park.

"What's the maximum distance on that thing?" Detective Wallace asked.

"Two miles. Maybe farther. The limit, as a practical matter, is your vision. You can technically control a model airplane long after you can no longer see it."

"And you're not going to accidentally bring down a real plane with that controller? You know, they don't allow cell phones on airplanes for a reason."

"Impossible," Clark answered as the car came to a halt in the middle of the parking lot. "Different frequency."

Clark fully extended the antenna on his remote control. The approaching plane banked one final time as the pilot leveled the wings towards a direct descent to the runway. Clark flipped the bright red button on the master control as his father had done a hundred times.

And then he froze.

"What's the problem?" Detective Wallace asked.

"I can't move."

"What?"

"Well, the usual convention of the buddy system remote control is that the master controller takes over *control* for the slave controller. Usually to avoid a crash."

"And...?"

"In this case, I don't want to *do* anything. I want control so Ariana can't do anything. Which means I can't move. Any movement of these controls could be the wrong one."

"Then don't move," Detective Wallace said matter-of-factly. "I'm going to check on these vehicles."

Clark nodded as he stared at the black controller in his hands. "According to the CIA guy, we should start with those that have sliding doors."

"Heads up," Karim said. "We have a police officer getting out of a cab at three o'clock."

Ariana reaffixed the binoculars to her eyes. She focused on the badge attached to the detective's waist and then back to his face.

"And there's a second person in the car."

Ariana moved her eyes again and a close-up profile view of Clark filled her vision. "Impossible," she hissed.

"Who is it?"

"My neighbor."

"How…?"

"It doesn't matter. He's too late."

Karim nodded towards a short line of police cars heading towards the park entrance. "So much for your response time estimate. I think it is time to go."

"A few more seconds," Ariana said, her thumbs on the control pad as she slipped into her operational zone. The approaching MD-88's landing gear was fully down, its wing flaps extended to increase the drag on the aircraft, slowing its speed.

Ariana's lips moved as she watched the plane continue to descend. She started her countdown from ten as the plane passed the far end of the rugby field. Her lips still silently counting, she smiled as the plane passed over the line of Don's Johns at the near-end of the park. With one swift motion, she pushed both thumbs up on the control pads as the plane passed directly over the van. She repeated the movement, jamming her thumbs forward with more force each time, as the plane roared past on approach,

"Now," Karim yelled. "Now!"

She replied with a tirade in Urdu.

Ariana and Karim, curses flowing, watched helplessly as the target landed safely, the tires touching down on the runway in a small cloud of burned rubber. Ariana let out a guttural animal scream and threw the remote control into the dashboard of the car, breaking off the antenna. She grabbed the binoculars from the seat and looked back at Clark, still in the taxi cab. Then she noticed the metal of the antenna pointing upwards toward the windshield.

The two police cars at the end of the police convoy blocked the entrance to Gravelly Point as the leading cars ripped into the lot. Karim took a deep breath as he drove the long black car slowly forward, approaching the impromptu barricade. "Relax," he said. "And put that controller out of site."

Ariana pushed the remote controller under the seat with the heel of her shoe and threw the binoculars on the backseat. The black car approached and an airport police officer stepped from his car, the lights on the vehicle still flashing in intermittent red, white, and blue.

Karim held the button on the armrest of the driver's side and the thick glass retracted halfway down.

"Identification, please," the officer said, his reddish hair appearing at the doorframe of the black car.

Karim reached into the breast pocket of his suit jacket and removed two diplomatic passports. Smiling broadly, he handed the official documents to the officer. "As you can see, we're diplomats with the Pakistani Embassy. My name is Nazim Shinwari and this is my wife Safia Hafeez."

The officer opened the pages of each passport and examined the photographs on the inside cover. "Enjoying your morning?"

"We were just taking in the sights. Unfortunately, we were called back to the embassy as part of a security alert. Embassy protocol demands that we return immediately. Our progress cannot be impeded."

"Just a moment," the officer said, keeping the passports in his hand as he walked to the front of the car and noted the diplomat license plates. He walked back to the open window and handed the passports back to Karim. "Have a good day."

"Thank you," Karim said.

Ariana leaned across the front seat towards the open window. "Officer, it may be none of my business, but there is a young man in the passenger seat of that parked cab. He is acting suspiciously. I think he has a gun."

The officer looked over at the car as Ariana pointed for guidance. "We'll take care of it. For safety's sake you may want to get moving." As Karim raised the window on the car, the officer reached for his radio.

Clark watched as a second plane passed over, the corners of the remote controller firmly in his hands. Across the parking lot Detective Wallace placed his nose to the window of an empty SUV before moving in the direction of the white minivan.

Concentrating on the remote control in his hands, Clark shook as the yell reached his ears. "Let me see your hands. Hands up. Hands up! Do not fucking move!" Clark followed the last command and looked into the side-view mirror of the cab to locate the voice. Above the warning that *Objects in the Mirror are Closer than they Appear*, Clark saw the business end of a police-issued nine millimeter pointed at the rear flank of his head.

Karim drove slowly down the service road to the entrance of the GW Parkway. Ariana stared out the window as the police surrounded the yellow cab and Detective Wallace raced across the parking lot to intervene. The detective, badge in his raised hand, arrived on the scene and slowly the officers surrounding the cab lowered their weapons. *"Nine lives,"* she muttered under her breath.

Karim turned on the radio and the report of an explosion in Metro Center was followed by several beeps and an emergency broadcast message. "The day was not in vain," he said proudly, looking over at Ariana.

Ariana sneered. "Easy to say when you did not waste years of planning. Living as a housewife to a man you despised. Being submissive. Hiding your intelligence."

"It is over now. And your mission was a success."

The long black car merged into traffic heading towards the Memorial Bridge. Ariana coughed and looked up at the next plane on approach to Reagan. She gazed skyward and then followed the plane as it flew over the field in the distance, over the swarm of police now in the parking lot of Gravelly Point. She started to speak, coughed again, and cleared her throat. She noticed the taste of iron thick in her mouth and swallowed hard. She pulled down the sun visor on the passenger side of the front seat and looked into the mirror as the heavy flow of blood from her nose ran over her lips.

Chapter 64

Clark sat down at the small kitchen table and Mr. Stanley delivered a cup of coffee, no cream, no sugar.

"You read the paper today?" Clark asked.

"No, I just moved it around on the table."

Clark smiled. "And...?"

"Not watching the news?"

"Haven't turned on the TV in days."

"I'll save you some time. The paper is saying the same thing it's been saying every day since the incident. Finger pointing over the incident at Metro Center. Twenty-six people dead, another hundred in local hospitals in various conditions, ranging from critical to simply "quarantined." Mr. Stanley paused. "You want to fill in the blanks?"

"May get you in trouble. Classified material."

"I'll take my chances."

Clark shrugged his shoulders. "Ariana was dropped off on the doorstep of Georgetown University Hospital in the throes of death. She lived just long enough to tell the authorities absolutely nothing. They believe she accidentally ingested ricin. Her chief accomplice is a Pakistani national with diplomatic immunity. But you aren't going to hear that in the news."

"I suppose not. There's no way the American government is going to blame the Pakistani Embassy in Washington, D.C. of coordinating or supporting a terrorist attack on our home soil."

"More than likely our government will use it as a stick to persuade Pakistan in other matters."

"Now you're thinking like a politician."

"That's an insult."

"I'm glad you think so." Mr. Stanley took a sip of his coffee and put the cup back on its saucer.

"Anyhow, looks like they are hanging the whole incident on this dead Syed character. The CIA is portraying him as the mastermind behind the attack and that faulty homemade triggers on the bombs prevented further disaster."

"No shock there. The CIA is in the business of *misinformation* as much as they are in the business of collecting information."

"Even so, I'm not sure how they managed to keep a lid on the minivan loaded with explosives at Reagan National. By the time we were removed from Gravelly Point, there were a lot of eyes on the scene: Airport police, D.C. police, tourists."

"I guess I shouldn't expect to see an article on a young man and police officer who prevented a thousand casualties..."

"Saving a thousand lives but losing a hundred is not much of a consolation prize."

"No, I guess it's not. But so far, only 26 are dead."

"Many of those exposed won't make it."

The appropriate level of silence fell on the conversation with the mention of mass causalities. "Are the CIA and FBI done with you yet?" Mr. Stanley asked.

"They didn't demand that I come downtown today."

Mr. Stanley steered the conversation away from Clark. "Did you see they came back to clean out Coleman's Castle?"

"I thought the house was already empty."

"Empty is a relative term. *Now, it's empty.* After they discovered the firewood laced with cyanide and realized that Allan didn't die from lack of vegetables or exercise in his diet, I guess things changed. Last night they sterilized the place.

Big trucks with no markings. Movers with masks. They took everything. I saw them wheeling out the refrigerator, the stove, the water heater. Even insulation. They took the whole shed from the backyard, uprooted from its foundation."

"Probably the same team that went through the charred remains at Ariana's."

"Probably."

"You know, at this point, I really just don't want to know any more. I'm sure there are a few bodies out there we'll never know about. Nazim was never found, for one, but you know he didn't make it far. Detective Wallace told me they are investigating the disappearance of a delivery guy from the company that sold Ariana the machines used to process the ricin. He also mentioned that they're looking into the suspicious death of a sales guy at an outdoor adventure store in Bailey's Crossroads. They traced some of the material found in the warehouse back to the store and have the dead employee on surveillance tapes selling camping equipment to Ariana."

Mr. Stanley paused. He wiped a crumb from his morning toast off his burgundy pajama top and took a sip of coffee.

"You still interested in finding out whether Ariana had anything to do with your father?"

Clark looked out the window at a fresh blanket of snow on the tree limbs. "My father lived a long life. Nothing will bring him back. Besides, my mother would never allow for his body to be exhumed. She still has the last tube of toothpaste he used, for crying out loud."

"How about your police officer friend? How did he fair with all this?"

"We all got the same deal. The detective, Lisa, the sheriff, myself. *Keep our mouths shut and all will be forgiven.*"

"Not much of a deal for heroes."

"Not much of a choice either."

"And the IRS?"

"I am still working through that one."

"Well, just remember what Ben Franklin said."

"What's that?"

"Death and taxes, son. Death and taxes. The two are inevitable."

Chapter 65

Clark approached Lisa at a secluded table at the back of Jammin' Java. A band was setting up for the evening's early performance, a trolley full of equipment parked next to the stage. The long haired guitarist was perched on a stool on the far side of the stage, strumming an acoustic guitar and staring out the window at the alley behind the building. A heavy-set man in need of a belt stooped and re-stooped to pluck equipment from the trolley. The rest of the band entourage moved around the stage at a slow steady pace. Mics, speakers, wires, and instruments all carefully found their way to the appropriate locations.

Clark feigned left and then went right, kissing Lisa on the ear as he sat. He placed his backpack conspicuously in the middle of the table.

"How are you holding up?" Lisa asked.

"Good. Today was quiet. Hopefully it is the beginning of a trend. And you?"

"I filed an official report on my involvement in the case directly with the Commissioner of the IRS. I will have an official warning placed in my permanent file, but the warning will be without explanation. If I keep my nose clean, the warning will be removed in two years. A slap on the wrist, essentially."

"But without saying why."

"Exactly."

"Our government ... I swear."

"Well, I think both you and I would be in more serious trouble if not for the fact that you saved a few lives and the fact that the CIA and FBI don't want any of this to go public. A grad student, an IRS agent, a police officer, and a sheriff were all one step ahead of the FBI. Technically, the CIA was one step ahead of all of us. I mean, their agent was implanted in a terrorist cell on U.S. soil. That is some modicum of success."

"True enough."

Clark started to speak again, mumbled something unintelligible and then paused.

Lisa rescued him. "What's in the bag?"

"Why do you ask?"

"You put it on the table. You must want to show me something; otherwise you would have put it on the floor."

Clark looked at the bag sheepishly. "Well, you know how I was adamant about my father being on the up and up with regard to paying taxes?"

"Yes, I remember very clearly."

"Well, there is a teeny tiny possibility that I may have been wrong." Clark unzipped the backpack and removed the old shoebox he had found in the basement. He pulled the lid and put it on the table next to the backpack and the shoebox.

"Holy crap," Lisa replied, looking at the contents.

"Yeah."

"How much is in there?"

"Well, I didn't take it out of the rubber bands, but I flipped through the upper corner of the bills. Somewhere just over $67,000."

"Where did you find it?"

"In the basement. But I have been carrying it around in this bag for the last couple of days. I was kind of hoping I would be mugged so I wouldn't have to make a decision on it."

"Why didn't you tell me sooner?"

"I was going to."

"But you were thinking about keeping it? Please tell me that is not the case."

"I would be lying if I said 'no.'"

Lisa sighed and rubbed her temples with both hands. "Well, I will handle it."

"Sorry," Clark said. "There was a lot of temptation there."

"I am going to chalk it up to stress. Who knows, maybe this will count in my favor. I mean, technically, if you did just find this in your house, then I don't see how either of us could end up in any more trouble. But you should have called me sooner."

"I thought about bringing it over to your apartment the other night, but I didn't want to send the wrong message. Some girls would take issue with a man sleeping over and leaving a pile of cash on the bedside table on their way out."

"Some. But this is not a few hundred dollars. Some girls may actually be flattered by this much cash. It could do wonders for a girl's ego."

"How about just a cup of coffee from a broke grad student who happens to also be a super hero in disguise?"

"I guess it will have to do," Lisa replied in feigned disappointment. "For starters."

About the Author

Mark Gilleo holds a graduate degree in international business from the University of South Carolina and an undergraduate degree in business from George Mason University. He enjoys traveling, has lived and worked in Asia, and speaks fluent Japanese. A fourth-generation Washingtonian, he currently resides in the D.C. area. His two most recent novels were recognized as finalist and semifinalist, respectively, in the William Faulkner-Wisdom Creative writing competition. The Story Plant will publish his next novel, *Sweat*, in 2012.